Ryan

The anger behind Seth's eyes got worse. The blood vessels around his forehead looked freakishly ready to explode. "Some girl named Fred Oday got my spot."

"A *girl?*" I was speechless. My eyes narrowed.

"Here's the best part," Seth continued, his voice growing raspier. "Coach isn't even making her try out." He chuckled darkly. "He handed my spot right to her." His glassy eyes stared back at me. "Sweet deal, huh?"

I shook my head. Hardly.

I didn't even know this girl, but I already hated her.

Fred

I'd been in Ryan Berenger's classes since freshman year, and he picked today to finally acknowledge my existence.

I'd seen him tons of times at the Ahwatukee Golf Club over the summer, too. He and his short stocky blond friend were always speeding by the driving range in a golf cart. Lucky them, they didn't have to wait till after five o'clock for the chance to play for free like I did. Ryan could play whenever he wanted.

And now we were teammates. As my brother would say, that was irony.

That would also explain why he'd glared at me in English class and gripped my book as if he wanted to shred it to pieces. Apparently he'd gotten the news that I was on the team, too. What else would make him so angry?

It's game-on for Fred and Ryan!

HOOKED

LIZ FICHERA

H HARLEQUIN® TEEN

Recycling programs
for this product may
not exist in your area.

ISBN-13: 978-0-373-21072-5

HOOKED

Printed in U.S.A.

For the memory of my mother and father,
Mildred and Joseph F. Fichera

When you were born, you cried and the world rejoiced. Live your life so that when you die, the world cries and you rejoice.

—Chief White Elk (Oto Nation)

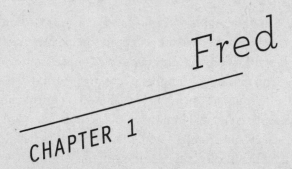

Fred

CHAPTER 1

I BELIEVED THAT MY ANCESTORS lived among the stars. Whenever I struck a golf ball, sometimes the ball soared so high that I thought they could touch it.

Crazy weird, I know.

But who else could have had a hand in this?

Coach Larry Lannon towered over Dad and me, his shoulders shielding us from the afternoon sun. "So, what's it gonna be?" he said, his head tilted to one side with hair so blond that clear should be a color. "Are you in?" He paused and then lowered his chin. "Or out?"

I drew in a breath. Even though Coach Lannon had said that I could smack a ball straighter than any of his varsity players at Lone Butte High School, his confidence still rocked me off my feet sometimes. He wanted me on the team. Bad.

"Chances like this don't happen every day," he added, and I ached to tell him that they never happened, not to my family. Not in generations.

See, here's the thing about Coach Lannon. I met him by accident at the end of the summer as I waited for Dad at the Ahwatukee Golf Club driving range. At first I thought he was some kind of golf-course stalker or something. He kept gawking at me as I hit practice balls. It was kind of creepy. I figured he'd never seen an Indian with a golf club.

Anyway, I pretended not to notice and concentrated on my swing. I smacked two buckets of golf balls beside him with my mismatched clubs as if breathing depended on it. After my last ball, Coach Lannon walked straight up into my face and declared that I had the most natural swing he'd ever seen. The compliment shocked me. And when I told him that I was going to be a junior at Lone Butte, one of only a handful from the Gila River Indian Reservation, the man practically leaped into a full-blown Grass Dance.[1] He'd been stalking me at the driving range ever since.

Now that school had started, he was making his final pitch to get me to join his team.

"Will you at least come to practice on Monday and give the team a try? Please? If you don't like it, you're perfectly free to quit. No questions asked." Coach Lannon's lips pressed together as he waited for my answer, although the question was directed mostly at Dad.

From the knot in Dad's forehead, I could tell he was unconvinced. And the coach didn't bother hiding his urgency, especially after telling us that he was tired of coaching the worst 5A golf team in Maricopa County. Another losing year and Principal Graser would send him back to teaching high school history fulltime, something he didn't relish. I'd never had a teacher confide something so personal to me like that, not even at the Rez[2] school.

Dad pulled his hand over the stubble on his chin, studying Coach Lannon. Deep red-and-black dirt outlined each of his fingernails and filled the crevices across his knuckles, one of the consequences of being the golf club's groundskeeper. "I don't know," Dad said in his lightly accented tones.

---

1 A Native American ceremonial dance expressing harmony with the Universe.

2 *Rez* is short for *Reservation*. It's what all the cool Indian kids say. I try to be cool when I can.

Coach Lannon leaned down to hear him.

"Is it expensive?" Dad asked.

"Won't cost you a thing," the coach said quickly.

"But how will she get to the tournaments? We only have one car."

"A bus takes the team. There and back. I can drive her home, if it's a problem."

"Are the tournaments local?"

"All except one, but don't worry about that. I'll have her back the same day."

Dad exhaled long enough for Coach Lannon's eyes to widen with fresh anxiety.

"I'd look after Fred like she was my own daughter," the coach blurted out. "I've got three of my own, so I know how you feel."

I sucked in another breath as I waited for Dad's answer. I knew that he wasn't fond of me traveling off the Rez. The daily trip to the high school was far enough, and not just in miles. He'd agreed to Lone Butte only because our tribe didn't have a local high school.

After another excruciatingly long pause, Dad said, "I guess when it comes right down to it, the decision isn't mine. It belongs to her." He turned to me and placed a steadying hand on my shoulder.

I exhaled.

Dad's forehead lowered, and he looked at me squarely with eyes that were almond-shaped echoes of mine. "It's time you made up your mind, Fredricka. Is this what you want?"

I cringed at my old-lady name, but as quickly as it took me to blink, I answered Dad with the lift of my chin. Coach Lannon had said that there'd be a chance I could get a college scholarship if I played well for the team. He said college recruiters from some of the biggest universities attended high school golf tournaments flashing full tuition rides for the best players. No one in my family had ever gone to college. No one even uttered the word. How could I refuse? I only hoped Coach Lannon understood the power of his promises. I wanted college as badly as he wanted me on his team, probably more.

Only a few silent seconds hung between us, but it seemed another eternity. This was the moment I'd been waiting for these past few weeks—my whole life, really. I'd been hoping for something different to happen, something special.

There was only one answer.

"I'll be there on Monday. I'll join your team."

Coach Lannon's shoulders caved forward, and for a moment I thought he'd collapse into Dad's arms. He'd probably wondered whether I had the courage to join an all-boys' team, and why shouldn't he? It wouldn't be easy for anybody, least of all a Native American girl from the other side of Pecos Road and the first girl to join the Lone Butte High School golf team.

Before I could change my mind, Coach Lannon extended his beefy hand.

I placed mine in his and watched my fingers disappear.

"We'll all look forward to seeing you on Monday after school, Fred. Don't forget your clubs." Coach Lannon turned to Dad. "Hank?" He extended his hand, along with a relieved grin. "You've got quite a daughter. She's got one heck of a golf swing. She'll make you proud." He smiled at me, and my eyes lowered at another compliment.

Dad nodded, but his smile was cautious. He was still uncomfortable with me competing with boys, especially a bunch of white boys, the kind who grew up in big fancy houses with parents who belonged to country clubs. That was why it had taken me two weeks to mention it to him.

But Coach Lannon had explained that there wasn't enough interest in a girls' golf team. "Maybe there'll be a girls' team next year," he'd said. "Or the next." Except by that time I'd be long gone. It was the boys' team for me or nothing.

And Dad knew me better than anyone. When I'd finally told

him, I hadn't been able to hide my excitement. It would have been easier to hide the moon. Truth be told, it had surprised him. He'd never dreamed that I'd love golf like breathing; he'd never dreamed I'd become so good.

Neither had I.

Fortunately, Dad never had the heart to say no to his only daughter.

"Happy?" he said after the coach disappeared down the cart path, leaving the air a little easier to breathe.

I nodded, my eyes still soaking in the attention. I was beginning to kind of like Coach Lannon. He was okay, for a teacher.

"Good," he said. "Then I'm happy, too. For you."

Still dizzy from my decision, I nodded.

Dad sighed at me and smiled. Then he picked up my golf bag, one of his many garage-sale purchases last summer, along with my clubs. The red plaid fabric was torn around the pockets and the rubber bottom was scuffed, but it held all fourteen of my irons and drivers with room to spare. Dad had told me yesterday that he'd try to buy me a new one, but between his job and Mom's waitressing, there wasn't a lot of money for extras. And the plaid bag worked just fine.

"Come on, Fred," Dad said, threading the bag over his shoulder. "Let's go home and tell your mother. We're late. She'll be worried."

"Uh-huh," I replied absently as I smashed one last golf ball across the range with my driver. The ball cracked against the club's face and made the perfect *ping*. It rose above us like a comet before it sailed high into the clouds.

Thank you, I said silently to the sky, shielding my eyes from the setting sun with my left hand. I waited for the sky to release the ball. *One one-thousand, two one-thousand, three one-thousand,* I chanted to myself like a kid gauging a thunderstorm. The ball hung in the air an extra second before it dropped into the grass and rolled over a ridge.

And that's when I knew.

My ancestors heard me. I imagined that they asked the wind to whisper, *You are most welcome, Daughter of the River People*. I was as certain of their loving hands on my destiny as I was of my own name.

We drove south on the I-10 freeway to the Gila River Indian Reservation in our gray van that was still a deep green in a few spots on the hood. Despite the peeling paint, it ran most of the time. Somehow Dad always found a way to make sure it got us to school and work and then back home.

Home was Pee-Posh, at the foot of the Estrella Mountains where the earth was as dark as my skin. That's where we lived; that's where my grandparents had lived and my great-grandparents before them. To reach it, we had to drive for miles along narrow roads with no stoplights, over bumpy desert washes dotted with towering saguaros and tumbleweeds that scattered across the road whenever it got windy. Most days, I wished Dad would keep driving, especially on the days when Mom started drinking.

"Maybe we shouldn't tell her that I joined the team. Not yet anyway," I said to Dad without turning. My bare arm folded across the open window as the air tickled my face. I closed my eyes and pretended that the wind was a boy kissing my cheeks. When Dad didn't answer, I opened my eyes and sighed. "Let's wait a while. A week, maybe." Good news only stoked Mom's bitterness, especially after a few beers.

"You sure?" A frown fell over his voice.

"Positive. Please don't say anything."

He smacked his lips, considering this. "If that's what you want," he said with a shrug. "Maybe waiting a week is wise. By then we'll see if you still like being on the team. You could always change your mind—"

"I won't," I interrupted him, turning. How could he even suggest it? "Why? You think I'll fail?"

"Hardly." Dad turned his head a fraction. "That's not what I said."

"You don't think I'm good enough?"

He chuckled. "Now you're being foolish. Of course I think you're good enough. I just don't want..." His lips pressed together, holding in his words.

"Don't want *what?*"

He inhaled. "I don't want you to get your hopes up and then be disappointed. That's all. You've never played on a team before. And that coach, the boys you'll play with—well, their ways are different than ours."

I frowned at him. *Of course I know that,* I wanted to tell him. But I hated when Dad talked about the old ways. They sounded primitive. And hadn't I already survived two years of high school?

"Don't doubt me, Fred. You'll learn soon enough."

I turned back to the open window and lowered my chin so that it rested on my arm, considering this. It was true. He had a point. Sort of. I'd never played team sports. I'd never played much of anything; that was part of my problem. "Let's just not tell Mom, yet. Okay?" I said without turning.

Dad sighed, just as tiredly. "Okay, my daughter. We'll do as you wish."

My brow softened with an unspoken apology for being curt, but there was no need. With Dad, forgiveness began the moment the wrong words left my lips. So I smiled at him. But my happiness faded as soon as we drove up the two narrow dirt grooves that led to the front of our double-wide trailer.

Our nearest neighbor lived a half mile away, which is to say that most days it felt like we were the only ones on the planet.

Two black Labs circled the van and started barking as Dad parked under a blue tarp alongside the house. The engine sputtered for a few seconds after the ignition turned off, and then the desert was quiet again except for the doves in the paloverde tree next to the trailer. They cooed like chickens.

Mom sat outside in the front yard on a white plastic chair. Her legs were crossed, and her right leg pumped up and down like it was keeping time. She had a silver beer can in one hand and another crushed next to her chair. "Where've you two been?" she yelled. Her words slurred, but there was still enough of a smile in her voice for my shoulders to relax a fraction.

Mom was still in the happy stage of her inebriation. But the happy stage usually morphed into the overly talkative stage, which then blended into the argumentative stage where she brought up a laundry list of regrets, like having gotten pregnant so young or earning a living waiting on stingy rich white people at the Wild Horse Restaurant at the Rez casino. "You'd think a five-star restaurant would attract a better class of people," she'd complained a thousand times. And that's exactly when I'd wish that I could disappear into the sky like one of my golf balls. I'd fly high into the clouds and never come back.

"Had to work late," Dad said. His tone was cautious, like slow fingers checking the wires of a time bomb. "I brought dinner, though." He raised a box of fried chicken in the air.

"Good." Mom grinned. "After the day I had, I don't feel like cooking." She lifted her hands, spilling some of her beer, revealing splotchy fingers that had spent most of the day juggling hot plates.

Dad bent over to kiss her cheek before turning for the front door, and for a moment the corners of Mom's eyes softened. "Just need to take a quick shower." He reached for the torn screen door. It creaked whenever it opened. "I feel like I'm covered in golf course."

Mom laughed and my throat tightened. Mom used to laugh a lot more. Everybody did.

Then Mom took a long swig from her shiny beer can before resting her narrowed eyes on me. Her head began to bob. "So, Freddy, tell me something that happened today. One happy thing." She framed it like a challenge, as if answering was statistically impossible. A second beer can crunched underneath her sandal while she waited for my answer.

My mind raced. I sat in the plastic chair across from her and wondered how long it would be before I could retreat to the safety of my bedroom, if you could call it that. My room barely fit a twin bed and nightstand, but at least I didn't have to sleep on the pull-out sofa in the living room like my older brother, Trevor. "Well," I said, dragging my tongue across my lips to stall for time. There was no easy way to answer her question. I'd lose no matter what. "I got an A on a social-studies pop quiz today," I said finally.

"Social studies?" Mom's wet lips pulled back. She stared at me like I'd grown a third eye. Then she reached inside her blue cooler for another beer. "Who needs social studies? What exactly is that anyway? *Social studies?*" Her words ran into each other. "How's that going to help you pay for your own trailer?"

My jaw clenched as I coaxed my breathing to slow. I knew this was only Mom's warm-up, and I wouldn't be dragged into it, not today. It wasn't every day a high school coach begged you to join his team. I only hoped that Mom would drink the rest of her six-pack and pass out like she always did. Then I could practice next to the house where Dad had built me a putting green with carpet samples from the dump.

"I'm not real sure," I said. "Anyway, it's not that important." I certainly wouldn't share that I'd earned the highest score. That would only make the night more painful, especially for Dad, and I often wondered how much more he could take. He'd left us once, two years ago, and that had been the worst three months of my life.

Mom jabbed her third beer can at me, and a few foamy drops trickled down her fingers. "Don't lie to me, girl." Her face tightened into the mother I didn't recognize. "I can always tell when you're lying." Her dark eyes narrowed to tiny slits as she peered at me over her beer can.

"I'm not. Really." I rose from my chair, my toes pointed toward the trailer, anxious to be inside. "You want me to get you anything?" My voice turned higher. "I'll heat up the chicken."

Mom sighed heavily, slurped from her can and let her head drop back. She stared up at a purplish-blue sky where stars had begun to poke out like lost diamonds. The beer can crinkled in her hand. "No," she said. "Just leave me alone. Everybody, just leave me the hell alone."

I climbed the two concrete steps to the front door, biting my lower lip to keep from screaming. Even though we were surrounded by endless acres of open desert, sometimes it seemed like I lived in a soap bubble that was always ready to pop.

"Hey, Fred," Mom said, stopping me.

I gripped the silver handle on the screen door and turned sideways to look at her.

"They're short a couple of bussers at the restaurant. Wanna work tomorrow night?"

My jaw softened. "Sure. I need the money." I'd been saving up for a new pair of golf shoes. A little more tip money and I'd have enough. And, thanks to Coach Lannon, I now had a reason to own a real pair.

Mom smiled and nodded her head back like she was trying to keep herself from falling asleep in her chair. "Good girl," she slurred. "You'll want to make sure the chef likes you so you'll have a job there when you graduate."

I bit the inside of my lip again till it stung. Then I quickly opened the door wider and darted inside. The screen door snapped shut behind me.

A crescent moon hung in the sky by the time Trevor coasted his motorcycle down our dirt driveway. Low and deep like a coyote's growl, the engine blended with the desert. I knew it was Trevor because he always shut off the front headlights the closer he got to the trailer. Less chance of waking anyone, even the dogs.

I waited for him on the putting green. With my rusty putter, I sank golf balls into the plastic cups that Dad had wedged into the carpet samples. Dad had even nailed skinny, foot-high red flags into each of the ten cups to make it look authentic. The homemade putting green wasn't exactly regulation, but it was better than nothing, and he had been so excited to surprise me with it for my birthday last year. The moon, along with the kitchen light over the sink from inside the house, provided just enough of a glow over six of the twelve holes.

"Hey, Freddy," Trevor said after parking his bike next to the van. The Labs trailed on either side of him, panting excitedly.

"Hey, yourself," I said after sinking another putt, this time into a hole near the edge that I couldn't see. I liked the hollow sound the ball made every time it found the edges of the cup. It was strangely comforting. And predictable. The ball swirled against the plastic like it was trapped before resting at the bottom with a satisfied *clunk*. "How was work?"

"Oh, you know, same shit, different day." Trevor's usual reply.

I smirked at his answer. I should be used to it by now, but a small part of me wished that once, just once, he'd surprise me with something different. Something better. Something that could take my breath away.

Trevor worked at a gas station in Casa Grande off the Interstate doing minor car repairs like fixing tires and replacing batteries when he wasn't making change for the never-ending cigarette and liquor purchases. His long fingers ran through the sides of his thick black hair as he waited for me to pull back my club for the next putt. His hair hung past his shoulders, all knotty and wild from his ride. If he wasn't my brother, I'd have to say that he looked like one scary Indian.

"When are you going to quit that job?" I looked up at him.

"And do what?" He chuckled but not in a sarcastic way.

"I don't know," I said, purposely casual. I struck the ball and looked at him. "Go back to school, maybe?" I walked over to the cup and reached inside for the ball. "You always said you wanted to open up a repair shop one day."

"Don't need school for that, Fred." He sat on the edge of the carpet, stretching out his legs and crossing them at the ankles.

"Wouldn't hurt."

"Yeah, well, when I win the lottery, I'll let you know." He looked up at the kitchen window and lowered his voice. "Don't worry, you'll find out soon enough."

I swallowed. I worked hard not to picture the future at all. I couldn't imagine working at the gas station, the restaurant or even the Indian casino for the rest of my life. Whenever I did, it felt like someone pressing on my chest with both hands.

"Mom?" Trevor said.

"Asleep. Finally." I laid down my putter and sat next to him, pulling my bare knees into my chest. "So's Dad. I think."

"Bad night?"

My shoulders shrugged. "Same shit, different day," I said, regretting it instantly. I hated swearing. My chin dropped to my knees.

"You don't mean that, Fred." Trevor placed his arm across my shoulder and pulled me closer. "You really don't want to let yourself get angry. Because once you start, it's hard to stop." His voice turned softer. "Look what it's done to Mom."

My eyes closed as I sank deeper into the corner of his arm. His shirt smelled like grease and cigarette smoke, but I didn't care.

"And just remember," Trevor said, "it hasn't always been like this."

"It's getting harder to remember when it wasn't."

He pulled me closer, and together we stared up at the stars. There were so many filling the sky that there didn't seem to be enough room for the moon.

"Are you staying home tonight?" I lowered my chin to my knees again. Somewhere in the distance, a coyote howled, and both Labs lifted their snouts from their paws long enough to grumble.

"Nope." He stroked the smooth coat of the black Lab next to him. "Just gonna go inside for a quick shower and change."

"Where to tonight?"

"Not sure. There's a party in the Estrellas—"

"Take me?" I interrupted, sucking in a breath.

"No way. You're too young." His stock answer. In Trevor's mind, I was perpetually ten years old.

"Am not." I frowned. "I'm sixteen."

"Forget it, Fred. You can't come. This crowd isn't for you."

"What crowd is?"

"Not this one."

"Killjoy." I lightly punched my fist against his chest. I never went to parties. I never got invited to any either. It was depressing, really. "Will you come home after that?" My tone remained hopeful.

"I'll probably head over to Ruth's. Haven't seen her in a couple of days." Ruth was Trevor's girlfriend. They'd been dating for almost a year, but Ruth lived on the other side of the Rez near Coolidge. Between Trevor's job and Ruth's night shifts at the Walmart, they didn't see each other very often.

"How about tomorrow?" My eyebrows pulled together as I felt the weekend sinking away. I was probably the only teenager in all of Phoenix who counted down the hours till Monday mornings.

Trevor's eyes squinted into the darkness. "Not sure."

"Oh." I swallowed back more disappointment. Home was always way more fun when Trevor was around. The air inside the trailer felt lighter. Mom didn't snap at everyone as much, probably because Trevor was always making her laugh, knowing exactly when to lift her spirits right before they threatened to nosedive.

"Don't worry, Freddy. I'll be back Sunday. Monday at the latest." With a heavy sigh, I lifted off his shoulder and padded across the carpet to where I'd left my putter and golf ball. I placed the ball about six feet away from the nearest cup. I could barely see the hole, but I gripped the club handle, right hand over left, and pulled back the club just enough before hearing the satisfying *plunk* inside the cup. I smiled when it hit bottom.

"Good shot," Trevor said, standing. "Hey. How'd it go today with Lannon?" Trevor was the first person I'd told about the coach's offer to join the team, even before Dad. But I hadn't told Trevor the whole story.

"He asked me to be on the team," I said with mock disinterest. "And I accepted."

"No kidding?" His teeth glistened in the moonlight. "That's great. Congrats."

"There's just one catch," I said as I sank another putt.

"What?" He laughed. "He didn't dig your groovilicious golf bag or something?"

I ignored his jab. "I'm on the team." I paused, making him wait. "It's just that I'm officially on the boys' varsity team."

Silence.

Trevor's neck pulled back. In the soft glow, I watched the whites of his eyes grow dangerously wide. If he hadn't been certifiably scary-Indian-looking before, he was now.

I lowered my gaze, focusing on the ball.

"Um, Freddy, did you say the boys' team?"

"Yep," I said, popping the *p*. "Lone Butte doesn't have a girls' team."

He scratched the side of his head, considering this. "I don't know, Fredders. A boys' team? A bunch of spoiled, rich white boys? That doesn't sound..."

"What?" I prodded.

"Normal," he blurted finally.

My voice got louder. "Why not?"

His voice got louder. "Because the boys there ain't gonna like it."

"And why not?"

He stepped closer, his hands jammed in his front jean pockets. "Because that means you're taking someone's spot, someone who'll think he deserves it more than you."

Air sputtered through my lips. "Well, that's just stupid," I said. "What'll it matter, if we win tournaments? The coach told me I was probably the best player on his team."

Trevor chuckled as his chin pulled closer to his neck. "Oh, great. He told you that, too? Believe me, Freddy. It'll matter. It'll matter to someone."

I swallowed hard but said nothing. Till now, I'd never thought that I'd be taking someone else's spot. I'd thought Coach Lannon had merely created a new one. He was the coach, after all. Couldn't he do such things?

"You're being paranoid," I said finally.

"Am I?" His doubtful tone caused a line of goose bumps to fly up my neck. "Just be careful," he said before turning toward the front door. "You're gonna need to watch your back. Stick close to the other kids from the Rez when you're at school, at least at first."

"That might be kind of hard. Not to mention freaky." There were only seven Rez kids in my entire school, four boys and three girls, including me. Kelly Oliver and Yolanda Studi were both seniors. Kelly was the only other person I'd ever heard utter the word *college,* mostly because she wanted to become a nurse. Yolanda was her cousin and best friend, and I was pretty sure Kelly was the only reason she hadn't dropped out. Yolanda had a mouth and attitude worse than my mother. Then there were Sam Tracy, Peter Begay, Martin Ellis and Vernon Parker. Vernon was a freshman, skinny and quiet as a saguaro; Martin was a sophomore; and Sam and Peter were my age. Sam was big enough to play football, but he had no desire to be on the Lone Butte team. Like most of my people, there were trust issues with anyone off the Rez that ran so deep I couldn't begin to understand where the puzzle pieces started and where they ended.

I'd known these Rez kids my whole life; they were like family, even if we rarely hung out. They all lived miles away from our trailer. But just like family, whenever we bumped into each other, like in the school hallways or sometimes in the cafeteria, our conversations pretty much continued where we'd left off, whether it had been a day, a month or even six months.

"Just promise me you'll stick close to them. Will you do that, Fred?" Trevor said again.

I nodded reluctantly, not because I didn't love my friends, but because I certainly didn't need any babysitters. "Turn the light out for me? In the kitchen?"

"Why?" he said, opening the screen door.

"I want to make sure I can sink putts with my eyes closed."

"You're possessed." He chuckled again.

"Maybe," I murmured but not loud enough for him to hear.

I swung my club back just below my waist and waited for the whirling noise of the ball against the plastic rim. It spun around and around before it finally settled in the bottom of the cup.

I could sink putts all night.

RYAN

CHAPTER 2

"DUDE, WHERE THE HELL HAVE you been?"

I ran to Seth's silver pickup and threw open the passenger door before the truck had a chance to stop.

Seth slammed the brake, and the truck lurched forward. Under the dim glow of the dome light, his grayish-blue eyes narrowed as he glared at me. "What are you, my mother?"

Friday night was definitely off to a bad start.

I was already fighting with my best friend, and I hadn't even jumped in his truck yet.

I shook my head and climbed in anyway, slamming the door. My heart was racing a million miles a minute. "Just blow," I told Seth, sinking lower into my seat and not bothering with the seat belt.

"Okay, man. Whatever." Seth shifted the gear. "We're outta here."

Just hearing those words lightened my shoulders.

The tires screeched across our circular driveway and then straightened toward Pecos Road. The front end almost took out a saguaro near the mailbox next to the street, but Seth didn't lift his foot from the accelerator for a second. He always drove crazy that way. Crazy Seth. Even crazier than me.

Seth didn't bother asking me what was wrong either. He already knew. "Where to?"

"Anywhere." I pulled my baseball cap lower on my head.

"Fisher is having a ripper. His parents are in Hawaii." Seth's eyebrows wiggled.

The night was improving exponentially.

"Some of the girls from pom team were invited, too." He shot me a sideways glance. "Maybe even Gwyneth..." His voice trailed off in a grin.

The corner of my mouth turned up in a careful smile.

Gwyneth Riordan had been hot for me since the eighth grade. Don't ask me why, but I'd have had to have been blind not to notice and crazy not to want her. I was a little of both. We usually hooked up on the weekends and had become a couple by default.

"Beer?" I breathed easier the farther we got from my street.

"Some." Seth's head tilted toward the backseat. I turned and spied a brown bag. He could always swipe a six-pack from his stepdad's stash unnoticed. "Where's yours?"

"My dad was home," I grumbled, remembering that my original plans for tomorrow night were now officially deep-sixed. "I couldn't chance it. But I need something stronger."

Seth pulled a hand over his chin, considering. "Like what?" he said carefully.

"Anything."

"You got cheddar?" It really wasn't a question.

I tapped the pocket to my jean jacket that held the four fifties from Dad. He expected me to buy a birthday present for Mom's party tomorrow night. "Plenty," I said, staring into the darkness. All I could see was my angry reflection in the passenger window. It glowed an eerie green from the dashboard lights. I opened the window and leaned my arm along the frame, inhaling a gush of fresh air. Warm wind billowed into the front seat, almost knocking off my cap. Black as oil, the Gila River Indian Reservation stretched across the right side of the four-lane road, with Pecos Road the clear dividing line. Even when I squinted, I couldn't see a single spec of light anywhere—not a porch light, headlight, even a firefly. It was like squinting at the edge of the world. When I was a kid, I'd wondered if anyone lived beyond Pecos Road. Sometimes I still did.

I'd been on the reservation twice in my entire life. One time with Seth to buy beer and cigarettes with our fake IDs at a gas station near Casa Grande, the other time on a school field trip in the fourth grade to spend the day with reservation kids. It had felt like the bus had driven us into the middle of the desert. Tumbleweeds had bounced across the road like lost brown beach balls. *Where are all the houses?* I remembered wondering. *The parks? The malls? The people?* When we'd finally arrived at their school, which was one big musty-smelling room with desks pushed to the edges, we'd sat on the floor in a circle, our legs crossed, and listened to an old man. He must have been at least one thousand years old, with braids that stretched down to his knees and skin with more wrinkles and folds than I could count. He'd talked as softly as a whisper, telling us crazy stories about coyotes and stars. I'd sort of half listened, peering around the room at the reservation kids, who'd numbered half as many as the ones in my class. With jet-black hair and eyes to match, they'd all looked alike and fidgeted just as uncomfortably as we had—all except one girl with ponytails high above her ears. She'd sat across from me. When our gazes had met, her eyes had sparkled like marbles. She'd smiled at me, revealing a gap between her two front teeth, but the grin had lasted only an instant. The girl with the shiny ponytails had never given me a chance to smile back.

"Let's make a stop in Chandler. I hear Grady's selling," Seth said.

I blinked. "Cool." Then I closed my eyes and filled my lungs with more desert air as Seth cranked the stereo to something with plenty of electric guitar. We flew all the way to the Interstate with the reservation right beside us, still and endless. It felt like driving straight into the sky.

When we reached the light before the freeway on-ramp, Seth pulled up alongside a big dude on a motorcycle. The guy was dressed all in black like he was freaking Zorro or something. We were the only vehicles waiting for the green. This light always took forever to change.

"Let's have some fun," Seth said, turning down the stereo.

"Don't—" I said, but I was too late.

With one arm draped over the steering wheel, Seth lowered his head to peer out the passenger window and yelled, "Nice leather!"

The guy turned, the whites of his eyes widening with surprise. Black hair blended with his jacket and hung down to the middle of his back. First he looked at Seth. But then, with his nostrils flaring, he glared at me.

My heart began to hammer against my chest. I spoke through clenched teeth, "Don't do anything, Seth."

Seth revved the truck engine anyway.

Biker Guy shook his head like we were both idiots. After a few agonizing seconds, he pulled back on the throttle. The motorcycle roared one hundred times louder than Seth's engine.

There was only one thing left to do.

The light turned green and Seth and Biker Guy jumped on their accelerators, tires squealing, racing toward the freeway.

Seth let out his maniacal laugh, the one that meant we were headed for nothing but crazy trouble and I would end up regretting it the most.

I braced my arm against the door as the truck picked up speed. "Don't!" I yelled into the wind. "Don't race this guy!" The last time we'd road-raced a guy from school, Seth had almost flipped the truck.

Still laughing, Seth replied by cranking the stereo. The bass competed with my pounding temples.

As the lanes merged from two into one, Seth ground the accelerator to the floor. Blue-and-white smoke billowed around our windows in angry circles.

The front of the truck stayed even with the motorcycle. One heartbeat later, Seth flew the truck past Biker Guy, pinching him off. On purpose. Biker Guy had to swerve into the emergency lane to avoid getting clipped, but not before glaring one last time at our truck, his gaze settling squarely on me.

"Dumb Indian!" Seth yelled, even though the wind and the stereo drowned out his voice. "Nothing can beat my truck!" He slapped the steering wheel with both hands.

I turned to Seth, breathing like I'd just run a marathon, and shook my head.

He mouthed, *What?*

"You're freakin' crazy!"

He kept grinning, the green lights from the dashboard glinting in his eyes. "I told you we were gonna rock tonight!" He offered me a fist bump.

I ignored it. But then a smile slowly built across my face when I looked in the rearview mirror and saw Biker Guy stopped on the side of the road, the front tire of his motorcycle still spewing gray smoke. He was giving us the finger. For some reason, I thrust my hand out the window and returned the gesture, maybe because I was mad at him for challenging Seth, mad at the whole world for simply existing or just relieved that we'd never see Biker Guy again.

Mostly I was glad no one had wound up in the hospital.

My head was spinning and my lips were feeling rubbery when someone at Zack Fisher's party mentioned something about Coach Lannon.

My ears began to function, even though Gwyneth Riordan was sitting in my lap, grinding against my crotch. She had been saying something about renting a houseboat at Lake Havasu for spring break. "We just need your parents' credit card for the deposit," she said after getting me so hot that I would have gladly stolen all of Dad's credit cards and given them to her.

Three of my teammates from the Lone Butte High School golf team and their girlfriends were crashed around a glass table in Zack's backyard next to the swimming pool. Music blared from hidden speakers in the corners of the patio, and the pool lights cast a wavy glow across everyone's faces. I had to blink a few times to focus.

"Coach said he was going to make a big change to the team on Monday," Zack yelled over the music as he chugged from his beer can. The table was littered with gold-and-silver cans and empty bags of potato chips. Zack crushed his can underneath his foot and tossed it with the empties. "Didn't say what, though. But that's what I heard."

Zack was an okay dude, but he was always hearing things; most of the time he got it wrong.

"Who said that? Who said he was making a change?" I leaned forward, pushing Gwyneth's legs to one side, struggling to stop seeing double. Gwyneth pouted, but golf was one of the few things at school that mattered to me. The team had struggled last year, and this year we expected to do better. We had to. Every varsity team at Lone Butte except ours had won a state championship—football, basketball, wrestling, even fencing. Who fences?! Anyway, we wanted our trophy in the glass case at the front of the school with all the others. And Principal Graser wasn't exactly shy about pointing out its absence at assemblies.

"Walesa said so. He overheard Coach talking to another teacher during gym class."

"When?" Seth asked, sitting straighter.

"Friday morning," Zack said.

"When will he tell us?" My lips sputtered as I tried to release a strand of Gwyneth's blond hair from the side of my mouth.

"Monday after school, I think," Zack said. "Maybe he's made

some changes to the schedule. Maybe we're in more tournaments this year or something." His shoulders shrugged like it was probably nothing major.

I leaned back against my chair. I turned to Seth, who also gave me a shoulder shrug as if to say, *Hey, it's no big deal.* And then he smirked and nodded toward Zack. *Consider the source,* he mouthed.

Gwyneth turned herself around in my lap, eager for more attention. She wrapped her arms around my neck and pressed her glossy lips against mine. She tasted like candy. Her hair cascaded over my shoulder, invading my nostrils with strawberry.

My nose wrinkled. It felt as if I could suffocate from the sweetness in her hair, but I pulled her closer, searching for her tongue with mine. She wanted me, and I guessed I wanted her, too.

Tomorrow I wouldn't remember a single thing anyway.

Saturday night, all available bussers and waitresses at the Wild Horse Restaurant, along with a gray-haired guy on a sad-sounding wooden flute, sang a Native American birthday song to Mom for her fortieth birthday, even though she'd begged everybody not to. The song seemed better suited to a funeral than a birthday. No one in my family understood the lyrics either, the words sounding more like grunts and heavy exhales.

Dad grinned uncomfortably at the six-person wait team who'd tended our table all evening, clearing dozens of white porcelain plates and soup bowls, filling crystal water goblets whenever they drained only a fraction, scraping crumbs from the linen tablecloth with razor-blade knives. My younger sister, Riley, and I sank lower in our chairs while everyone else in the packed restaurant interrupted their five-course dinners of grilled venison and mackerel salads and turned to stare at our round table smack-dab in the middle of the floor. The only thing missing was a strobe light pulsating above us as we watched the presentation of a six-layer, custom-made mesquite-honey mousse cake. It was pure torture.

I tried to tune out the misery by picturing the cheeseburger and fries that Riley and I would scarf down as soon as we got home and ditched Mom and Dad for the nearest Burger King. The sooner this nightmare dinner was over, the better.

Mom beamed at her cake, pressed her hands against the base of her neck where her birthday present rested, mouthed *I love you* to Dad and then blew out the half-dozen candles in the middle of the cake. "Thank you for not ruining this gorgeous cake with forty candles," she told the waitress, a thin woman with black hair and matching eyes. Her twisted bun was pulled back so tightly that it raised her smooth cheekbones. Like the rest of the restaurant staff, she wore black pants and a long-sleeved white shirt. The only color she sported was a teal-blue silk sash threaded through her belt loops. *The real colors,* the menu boasted, *should unfold on your plates and through the restaurant windows where you can see uninterrupted desert all the way to the Estrella Mountains.*

Riley had laughed when I'd read it aloud to her with a haughty English accent, and Mom had frowned from across the table, but, you had to admit, it sounded cheesy.

The waitress cut the cake in four equally huge slices and placed each slice on a microscopically small plate even though the only one who'd eat it was Mom. As the waitress cut each piece, she handed the plate to a younger girl, the same one who'd kept dropping things all night—the rolls from the bread basket, the extra soup spoon Dad requested, ice cubes from the water pitcher that crashed down into our glasses whenever she poured. I wondered why our waitress didn't simply banish her someplace else. She was definitely not waitress material. Even I could see that, hungover or not.

The girl's eyes remained lowered as she used both hands to deliver a dessert plate to each of us. Everything proceeded smoothly until she delivered the last piece.

Mine.

Her eyes rose and flickered at me as she moved alongside my right elbow, brushing against it.

I was still majorly numb from Zack's party, so I barely noticed—until the piece of birthday cake that I didn't want, in a fancy restaurant with my parents where I didn't want to be, eating weird food that I hated, fell off the edge of my white plate like a brown avalanche and plopped straight into my lap.

"Oh, god!" the girl gasped. The plate dropped to the floor and shattered. Her hands flew to her mouth.

I leaped out of my chair, but it was too late. "Shit!" I said as the gooey mess rolled off me in a solid, heavy lump. In the confusion, my wooden chair crashed backward like a gunshot, reverberating inside my head.

A lady screamed behind me.

I glared down at the girl, angry and more than a little embarrassed. "What is your problem?"

The girl's black eyes widened. "I am so sorry." She reached for a linen napkin on the table and tried to blotch out the chocolate stain on my pant leg but succeeded only in spreading it. And making me a million times more uncomfortable as her hands reached dangerously close to my crotch.

My breathing quickened. I could hear it whizzing through my teeth as I continued to glare at the girl.

No doubt every head in the restaurant had turned to watch the entertainment as the room grew silent, except for harps and flutes, playing through hidden speakers, that sounded just like the mind-numbing music played in the girls' yoga classes at school.

"Settle down, Ryan," Mom said, her gaze sweeping about the room. "It was an accident, for god's sake." She grabbed my arm as

Dad watched from across the table with tightly pressed lips, his disappointment as obvious as the wet stain on my pants.

Not a huge surprise.

Riley, meanwhile, tried to stifle nervous laughter by biting down on her linen napkin.

All in all, epic! Why hadn't I stayed home? Pretended to have the flu or something?

"Can we get some towels over here?" Dad called to the waitress on the other side of the room, the one who seemed to be in charge of our table. He waved his hand over his head. The woman darted over to us.

"Certainly, sir." She began pointing to other bussers for water, napkins and possibly even another mesquite-honey mousse cake. "My apologies," she added. "We'll take care of it."

I would have told her not to bother, but I was too preoccupied with the wet stain on my pants and the girl who'd caused it. She kept trying to blotch it with a napkin.

My breathing was still pretty heavy. "Just...just leave it alone," I stammered, sitting back down in the chair, which someone had picked up for me. "You've done enough already," I said as she took a step back, the stained napkin still clutched in one hand, poised and ready.

"Fred?" the waitress called from behind the girl. "We need you in the kitchen. *Now.*"

I looked around, blinking, waiting for a quarterback with a wide neck to appear with an armful of heavy trays. Instead, I watched as the girl darted for the kitchen, her chin buried in her neck. I blinked again, my gaze finally clearing. The last thing I saw was her braid, swinging across her back like a windshield wiper. It almost reached the teal-blue sash wrapped twice around her waist.

Brighter than the sky, it was the only color I remembered all day.

"I'm disappointed in your behavior, son," Dad whispered behind his hand.

I swallowed, pulling my eyes away from the blue sash. "It wasn't my fault."

Mom's nostrils flared. "I'm going to make another appointment for you with Dr. Wagner." But she directed it to Dad, like I wasn't even there. Done deal.

My head dropped back, and I sighed. "I don't need to see Dr. Wagner." My temples began to pound louder. I'd vowed last time that I wasn't going back to our quack family therapist. It was a complete waste of time. All he did was talk in circles.

"I'll be the judge of that, Ryan," Mom said. Mom thought everything could be cured by doctor visits and enough medication.

"Are we done yet?" I snapped. My feet fidgeted like I was readying to run a marathon.

"Yes, we are." Dad's lips pressed together again. "And thank you for ruining your mother's birthday. I hope you're satisfied."

I stared back at him, speechless. My life totally sucked.

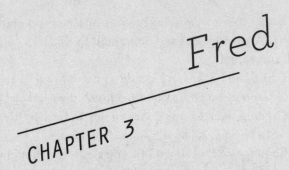

Fred

CHAPTER 3

"I TALKED TO A FALCON SITTING on top of a paloverde tree this morning."

"Where?" I asked while Dad tinkered underneath the van. I sat on a towel in the dirt beside him, handing him tools. It was Sunday, but that didn't mean Dad got a day off. The van leaked again, bluish-black oil as gooey as tree sap. That couldn't be good.

"The one out by the road. The same one you and Trevor used to climb when you were kids. Remember?" He paused to bang something against the van's metal frame. "Hand me the silver wrench, will you?"

"Yeah, I remember," I said, handing him a tool that held more rust than silver. I squinted against the morning sun toward the tree, which stood not far from the road that ran alongside our trailer. Trevor had carved our initials into one thick green branch, but the tree had grown so high that I could barely see the letters anymore. "How'd you know it was a falcon? Maybe it was just a crow," I said as if that would make the sighting less significant.

Dad chuckled. "I think I know a falcon when I see one, Fred. Aren't many out here, you know."

I lowered my chin to my knees, considering this. A falcon could mean something. A falcon could be another sign. My life was full of them lately. It was one thing to see a falcon; it was quite another to understand its meaning. "What'd it look like?" I asked, still a little doubtful. The Rez was covered with birds—mourning doves, quail, crows as chubby as cats, even hawks and the occasional horned owl. But falcons? I hadn't spotted too many, at least not around the trailer.

Dad yanked on the frame as he spoke, and it sounded like he was talking through gritted teeth. "Pretty thing. White breast, notched beak, gold-and-brown feathers that look like a checkerboard." He stopped to suck back a breath before giving the van another *whack*. "I haven't seen her in a while."

"How'd you know it was a she?"

He chuckled again. "Thought I heard some of her chicks chirping nearby."

"Well, what'd she tell you? Did she happen to mention when I'm going to get a new pair of golf shoes?" I said glumly. After last night's restaurant fiasco, I figured that I was permanently banned from any kitchen within a hundred miles. I wouldn't be asked back, not unless the chef got desperate. And that meant an end to my source of cash. The Rez wasn't exactly brimming with teen job opportunities.

It was just that I was nervous about Monday's practice, my very first with the team, especially after what Trevor had said about needing to watch my back. I'd never had that worry before. Usually it was the complete opposite. Was life easier when nobody noticed you?

Like an idiot, I'd dropped things all night—silverware, napkins, bread, rolls—and then finally the dessert right into the boy's lap. That had been the last straw, though it wasn't like he didn't deserve it. I'd recognized Ryan Berenger from English class at school, although I'd bet my parents' trailer that he hadn't recognized me, not that he would. Boys like Ryan and girls like me moved in different circles—well, I was pretty sure he had a circle; I simply moved.

I couldn't understand why he'd sat and glared at everybody all night, even his own family. He'd acted as though he would have preferred to jump through one of the restaurant windows than enjoy a dinner with them. And his parents seemed so lovely, so perfect. They'd looked like the perfect family, out enjoying a perfect dinner on a perfectly good Saturday night. How nice would it be to have your parents treat you to a fancy restaurant with a special birthday cake and everything? Where's the misery in that? Clearly Ryan Berenger was deranged.

Dad slid out from underneath the van on a piece of dusty cardboard. "No, the falcon didn't say anything about shoes." He sat up and brushed his hands together as if he was trying to wipe away my sarcasm. His hands were coated with dirt and grease that never seemed to wash away, no matter how much he scrubbed. "The falcon told me about something better than a pair of new golf shoes."

I could manage only a half grin. "Better?" Dad always told me old stories and Indian legends when he thought I needed a bit of cheering up. After last night, he'd be right.

But I needed more than cheering up—I needed a decent pair of leather golf shoes, with real cleats, that didn't pinch my toes when I walked. Was that asking the ancestors for too much?

"The falcon is a clear sign of new beginnings and adventure, but you already know that, don't you?"

I nodded, the smirk disappearing from my face.

"With a flutter from her wings on the tree's tallest branch, she asked me to remind you that yours is just getting started," he said without a trace of humor in his voice. "The falcon said, 'Tell the child born to the mother of Akimel O'odham and father of the Pee-Posh that her adventure has just begun. She should not fear the journey.'" He stood, dusted off the front of his overalls with a few pats and then walked to the driver's door of the van.

I watched him, saying nothing, because what could I say? I would never doubt my father or the wisdom of the animal spirits.

Dad had taught me all about them, from the mole to coyotes to bob-cats, just like his father and his grandfather before him. Animal spirits were as much a part of our lives as eating and breathing. Only a fool wouldn't listen. And a bigger fool would mock them.

I stood and brushed the dirt off my shorts while Dad pulled open the glove box in the van and rummaged inside. With his hand behind his back, he walked to where I stood in front of the van. Then he held out a thin package as long as an envelope wrapped in brown paper. "For you. From your mom and me."

"Mom?" My eyes widened.

"Well, yes. And no. She doesn't know I bought it, of course."

My smile returned. At first all I could do was stare blankly at the package, too startled to open it. It wasn't every day I got a present, especially when it wasn't my birthday.

"Open it, Fred. Go on, now. It's for you."

Finally, I accepted the gift from Dad. I took my time tearing off the wrapping paper and laid it on the hood. Openmouthed, I stared as a piece of leather as luscious as butter fell into my hand. The leather was white with pale pink accents around a mother-of-pearl button.

"It's not a pair of golf shoes, not yet. But you needed a new golf glove, too." Dad stuffed his hands in the front pockets of his overalls so that only his thumbs showed.

Speechless, I tried on my new glove. It slipped easily over my hand. I snapped the button at the wrist and then stretched my fingers and clenched my fist, testing the leather.

"Golf pro at the clubhouse said that one's the best. Size small, too, just what you needed. Now you'll be able to grip your clubs a whole lot better," he added when I didn't say anything. His eyes narrowed. "Do you like it?"

I swallowed back a lump growing in the back of my throat. "Like it? It's perfect," I whispered. Then I wrapped my arms around Dad, not saying another word. One more syllable and I would have started blubbering, and crying made Dad all fidgety, like he didn't know what to say.

Dad patted my back when I didn't release him right away. "Now, now, Fred. It's just a glove," he said in my ear.

Just a glove.

I sniffed back a tear and then pulled away reluctantly, still unable to speak.

"New beginnings, Fred. Greet them with your eyes wide open. Don't forget that. That's what that old mother falcon told me this morning." Dad's forefinger pointed to the cloudless sky, as if that golden-brown bird circled somewhere above us, eavesdropping.

"I won't," I said finally, unable to look away from my new glove. Suddenly a new pair of golf shoes seemed unimportant, at least for today.

Tomorrow I could think differently.

The next morning, Dad dropped me and my golf bag off in front of Lone Butte High School, along with Sam Tracy and Peter Begay, who'd ridden in the backseat. Pete's dad had overslept and couldn't get them to school in time, and they'd been thinking about ditching until we saw them hanging out at the gas station by the freeway. Dad had insisted they hop in.

"Thanks for the ride, Mr. Oday," Sam said, turning to me.

"Next time, call if you need one," Dad said. "It's no trouble."

Sam nodded. "Need help with your bag, Fred?"

"No. I can manage. Thanks anyway."

Sam hitched his backpack higher on his shoulder, looking doubtfully at my golf bag lying in the back of the van. "See you around."

"Later," I said as I walked around to the back door and retrieved it.

Dad pulled away, leaving me alone at the curb. And I felt alone. Really alone. Like only-person-in-the-universe alone. I realized, too late, that maybe I'd been too quick to refuse Sam's offer.

The air had grown so thick that I wondered if the sun had swallowed all of the oxygen. My plaid bag made being inconspicuous impossible. It might have been my anxious imagination, but I felt tracked by a thousand pairs of beady eyes in the front of the school. They peered at me from everywhere, even the windows.

Head lowered, I struggled to keep from hyperventilating as I carved a path through the crowd toward the rear gymnasium door. The back door was supposed to take me to the coaches' offices, exactly as Coach Lannon had instructed. But to get there, I had to trudge down a narrow sidewalk lined with students all vying for spots in the courtyard where the popular kids hung out. Up ahead, I saw Sam's and Pete's dark heads, but they were too far away for me to catch up—not unless I started running with my golf bag thumping against my back. Why not present me with the Biggest Dork Award and get it over with?

It felt like the first fifteen minutes of freshman year all over again, only worse. Despite my best efforts, I felt my cheeks burn all the way down to my neck.

"Plaid much?" someone murmured while another girl giggled beside her. With wide eyes, they looked me up and down like I was sale merchandise.

I didn't stop to argue. What was the point? The bag was hideous.

So instead I kept my head down, walked faster and focused on the bottom of my shoes as they slapped against the pavement.

One, two, three... I counted each step as I absently twisted my hair into a roll to give my free hand something useful to do, all the while ignoring more giggling and hushed voices. It seemed forever before I reached the end of the courtyard and another narrow sidewalk that took me to the rear gymnasium door.

The gray metal door had a sign that said No Admittance, but I pulled on the handle anyway.

It didn't budge.

I moaned. Then I tried again.

Locked.

I knocked hard till it made a hollow sound.

No answer.

My stomach sank. Maybe Trevor was right. Maybe this was a mistake.

But I'd just die if I had to walk all the way to the front of the school again, and what about my bag? It wouldn't fit inside my locker, and forget about calling Dad. He'd never leave work, not unless I was being rushed to the hospital or something.

I sucked back another breath, feeling stupid for banging on a locked door, but I knocked again anyway. This time with a balled fist.

Miraculously, the door opened and my breathing resumed.

"Fred." Coach Lannon smiled before opening the heavy door as wide as it would go. "So glad you didn't change your mind."

I nodded and tried to match his enthusiasm, but smiling only made my cheeks feel like they would crack. I slipped through the door and waited for Coach Lannon to lead the way down the bright hallway. I'd never seen this part of the school before. It was one colorless office door after another separated by gray-speckled linoleum tiles and pale yellow walls. The hallway smelled like the girls' locker room, musty and thick, almost as heavy as the air outside.

Coach Lannon stopped at the second door on the right side of a wide hallway. "You can leave your bag in my office during the week," he said. "Some of the other boys have already been by to drop off theirs."

My back stiffened.

Although I was anxious to get started, I wasn't ready to meet my new teammates. I'd already lost sleep imagining what they'd think about me, the lone girl on the team. Would it be too weird?

"And don't worry. Your bag is always safe in here."

An anxious chuckle rumbled inside my chest as the coach took my bag. *Someone steal my plaid bag and rusty clubs? Not likely.*

I quickly scanned his office. Besides his desk and the other golf bags stacked against the wall, there was barely any room to stand. His desk was littered with folders, but I did notice a framed photo— a woman and three teenage girls, all smiling, probably around my age. I smiled inside. At least Coach had been honest about having daughters.

"Practice starts at 3:30," he said as he led me outside his office. Like I could forget.

I nodded, tried to smile again and then lowered my head before walking down the long, musty hallway that I hoped would lead me to the classrooms and oxygen.

Coach Lannon called after me. "One more thing..."

I stopped and turned, my shoes squeaking on the linoleum. I'd almost made it to the end of the hallway.

A grin spread across his face. "Welcome to the team," he said, just as two boys, one tall and one short, with dark golf bags threaded over their shoulders, barreled down the hallway. Their bags brushed my shoulders as they passed. They exchanged confused looks.

Instinctively, my gaze returned to the dotted specs on the linoleum floor.

It was going to be a very long day.

RYAN

CHAPTER 4

WHAT'S UP WITH HER? I TRIED to mind-meld with Seth as we passed a girl with the ends of her black hair wrapped around her hand. She looked at the floor as soon as we spotted her, like we'd caught her snitching or something.

As Seth and I approached Coach Lannon's office, the coach filled his doorway, absently scratching the side of his head.

I'd seen that pinched look on his face before. He looked a little pissed, and I wondered if word had gotten back to him about Friday night's party. We'd been in trouble with the coach a couple of times last year for partying, but nothing major. He'd given us the "don't do drugs" speech and warned us about how alcohol burned brain cells, and we'd halfheartedly promised to stay out of trouble—or at least promised ourselves behind his back not to get caught. I'd heard that one of Zack's neighbors had called the police because of the music, but, really, I barely remembered any of it.

"Seth," the coach said, clearing his throat as we stopped at his door. "Got a sec?" The warning bell buzzed in the background, indicating a ten-minute window before Homeroom.

"Sure, Coach." Seth balanced his dark blue TaylorMade golf bag in front of him. He grabbed the sides with both hands and waited.

The coach's right eyebrow shot up. *"Alone,"* he said. "Sorry, Ryan."

"Oh, right," I said as I wedged myself and my bag between them. My best guess was that the coach was going to give Seth another warning about failing grades and ditching class, two things that Seth had done really well last year. Although I'd probably ditched as often, I'd maintained a decent grade-point average without trying too hard. Seth really needed to start taking the coach's rules seriously. One more warning and he'd probably be off the team. Before I could think it through, I said, "If it's about Friday night, I can explain—"

The coach cut me off with a wave of his hand. "What about Friday night?" But then he shook his head and sighed. "Forget it. It has nothing to do with that, Berenger." His jaw clenched, and I realized that I'd just made things worse.

Before I could make him angrier, I dumped my golf bag inside the office where six others already crowded one of the corners, including a busted-up plaid one that must have been someone's idea of a joke. Then I turned around for the hallway without stopping. "See you in class," I mumbled to Seth as I passed through the doorway.

Seth flashed me a grateful grin, but I could tell by the way his lip twitched that he was anxious.

Coach Lannon barely gave me a chance to leave before he closed the door.

That couldn't be good.

The next time I saw Seth, his nostrils were flaring.

He marched into Homeroom with his fists clenched. His eyes blazed and his chest heaved as if the coach had just forced him to do one hundred push-ups. The veins in his forehead looked ready to pop.

Seth scanned the room until he found me. I nodded at him

from the back row and lifted my backpack from the empty seat next to mine.

I wasn't the only one who noticed Seth. At least thirty other faces in Homeroom watched him storm his way to the back of the room. He dropped so heavily into his seat that his desk knocked into the guy seated in front of him, but the dude didn't turn around and bitch. Probably too scared.

I feared the worst. "What'd the coach say?" I whispered to Seth as he jammed his backpack underneath his seat. Fortunately the Homeroom teacher was too busy going through her attendance sheets to care.

Seth shook his head and stared into space, then garbled something unintelligible. Totally not like Seth to act so out-of-control crazed.

I leaned in and tried again. "Come on. Tell me. What happened?"

Seth's face darkened another shade, and all I could think was *He got expelled.* That had to be it. I wondered if I should get a hall pass to see Coach Lannon and try to explain a way out of this. I could promise that both of us would be on our best behavior all year. We had practiced so hard over the summer. The coach had seen us tons of times at my parents' country club. And if I had to, I'd even break down and beg Dad to reason with him. Dad was an expert at convincing people to do stuff they didn't want to do.

Finally, Seth spoke, but his teeth stayed clenched. "Dude, you are so not gonna believe this." He exhaled as the principal's voice filled the room over the loudspeakers with a list of upcoming SAT test dates.

I pulled closer, full-on curious.

"He. Kicked me. Off. The fucking. Team."

"Say what?" My shoulders caved forward. "That is so busted!"

Seth nodded, nostrils still flaring.

"Maybe if I talked to him. Maybe if my dad talked to him..."

A frenzied smile took over his face. He looked as whacked as I'd ever seen him. "Don't bother," he said, surprising me again.

"Don't bother?" My chin pulled back. Seth never gave up without a fight. "Why not? We could talk to him. We could talk him out of it—"

"Save it, Ryan," he said.

"Why?" I said. "Why not try?"

"Won't matter," he fumed.

"But the coach saw you at the club this summer, practicing your ass off." Seth might not have been the best player on the team but he had gotten a lot better. The coach had to have noticed.

Seth half laughed, half snorted. "Seems I got axed anyway."

"Did it have to do with the party? Did he hear about it?"

"Had nothing to do with the party."

"What, then? Why?"

Seth's tight-lipped smile faded, but the anger behind his eyes only got worse. The blood vessels around his forehead looked freakishly ready to explode. "Some girl named Fred Oday got my spot."

"A *girl*?" I was speechless. My eyes narrowed. There was that odd girl name again: Fred.

"Here's the best part," Seth continued, his voice growing raspier. "Coach isn't even making her try out." He chuckled darkly. "He handed my spot right to the bitch." His glassy eyes stared back at me. "Sweet deal, huh?"

I shook my head. *Hardly.*

I didn't even know this girl, but I already hated her.

Homeroom was only fifteen minutes, but it felt like fifteen hours.

Afterward, Seth stormed into the hallway. "I gotta ditch," Seth told me. "I need to chillax before my head explodes."

"I'll go with you."

Seth shook his head, surprising me again. "No, I just got to figure out how to explain this to my parents. They're going to go ape-shit." What Seth really meant was that his stepdad would freak. Getting cut from the golf team would give him one more reason to be disappointed in Seth. Unfortunately, Seth's stepdad had a habit of showing his disappointment with a few well-placed punches, most of which left a bruise or two.

There was no stopping Seth either. He darted toward the student parking lot to get his truck.

Students with backpacks as big as tortoises shuffled alongside me as we all carved our way down the narrow hallways before the next bell. Normally I hated the claustrophobic feeling of the hallways and all the pushing and shoving, but today I barely noticed. I was still trying to wrap my head around Seth's news: *Some girl named Fred Oday.*

Some girl? Had Seth heard that right?

She's already got a spot on the team.

How was that fair?

Coach isn't even making her try out.

Not even an informal tryout?

And her name is Fred Oday.

Fred? What kind of a girl's name was that?

My temples began to throb as I replayed the news in my head. None of it made any sense.

And where had I heard the name Fred? Where had I seen her? Surely she hadn't just dropped out of the freaking sky. She must be at least a junior. And why would Coach Lannon put a girl on an all-boys' varsity golf team? Was he high? Weren't there rules against stuff like that? Shouldn't there be? Our chances of winning the state championship had just crashed.

Still numb, I almost head-butted Zack Fisher on my way to English. I was going through the door as he was busting out.

"You hear?" Zack said to me, predictably. Of course Zack had heard. Thanks to him, probably everyone in the entire school already knew about Seth.

I stared back at him, still a little dazed.

"Well? Have you heard?" He grabbed my shoulder.

I shrugged Zack's hand off my shoulder. "Yeah. I heard. I sit right next to him in Homeroom. Remember?"

"Can you believe that?" Zack's head of tight brown curls shook indignantly, his eyes shiny and wide with the news. "And now we've got a girl on the team? Are you kidding me?" His voice got higher, louder. Angrier. "Why don't they just start a girls' team?" Several freshmen glanced curiously in our direction as they passed us in the hallway.

"I know," I said, unsure what more to say.

"You know her?"

I shook my head. "Never heard of her."

Zack chortled. "Well, she better be good. That's all I got to say." He said it as if he didn't think it was even remotely possible. I wanted him to be right.

"Yeah," I said. Especially since she just got my best friend kicked off the team.

The bell rang, and we both turned for the door. Mrs. Weisz, our English teacher, was already at the podium and shuffling papers. She peered at us over her wire-rimmed bifocals. A quick flicker of her eyelids reminded us about her views on tardiness. But then I realized, too late, that I'd rather be anywhere other than inside her stuffy classroom discussing lame hundred-year-old books that never made any sense. I should have ditched with Seth.

Too late now.

With my backpack slung over my right shoulder and my hands jammed in my front pockets to keep them from punching a hole in the door, I wove my way to my usual spot next to the window.

Every seat was taken, and the rows were so tight that there was barely any room to wedge between the desks. When I finally made it to the last row, I passed by a girl seated in the front desk and accidentally knocked over her book with my backpack.

"Sorry," I murmured, bending over to retrieve it. When I stood up, my eyes swept over her desk and then landed on her face. It was the same girl who'd walked out of Coach Lannon's office.

For a moment, we locked gazes, and I began to piece it together. But then before I blinked, the girl lowered her eyes and began fidgeting with a strand of her hair. It twirled around her finger like a shiny black ribbon as she stared down at a blank page in her notebook. Her eyes hid under feathery eyelashes.

And then, for some odd reason, I squinted at the cover of her book in my hand: *The Great Gatsby* by F. Scott Fitzgerald. In the right corner, written in perfect cursive letters in black ink, I saw another name: *Fred Oday.*

My jaw dropped. *Fred Oday?* That *Fred Oday?*

My temples started to pound again. My eyes traveled back down to the girl's forehead. Her brow was furrowed, and her eyes stayed lowered. She was sure as shit avoiding me.

You're Fred Oday? I wanted to shout.

I almost choked out my question until Mrs. Weisz said, "Mr. Berenger? Something wrong?"

I didn't answer her. My gaze refused to unlock from the top of the girl's head.

"Will you take your seat, Mr. Berenger?" Mrs. Weisz snapped.

I nodded numbly. And then I remembered.

All of the details came flooding back as clearly as the writing on her book. Everything.

She was the girl who'd dropped cake right into my crotch at Mom's birthday dinner, almost as if she'd done it on purpose. She was the girl who'd passed Seth and me outside Coach Lannon's office. And she was also the girl who'd robbed my best friend of his spot on the golf team.

I dropped the book onto Fred's desk. It landed with a *splat*.

Then I stormed down the row and dropped into the last empty seat.

Fred

CHAPTER 5

I WANTED TO HIDE IN COACH Lannon's office for the rest of the day.

The whispers and hushed voices started in earnest sometime after Homeroom on my way to English, even worse than when Dad had dropped me off at the curb. When I tilted my head and struggled to eavesdrop on hallway conversations between classes, voices faded. It was like trying to catch words in the wind.

But then in first-period English, for the very first time, *he* looked at me: Ryan Berenger. The pretentious, moody guy who couldn't be bothered to have dinner with his family, the one who always had his arm around the bleached-blonde girl from the pom squad who was always pictured in the school newspaper on top of parade floats and at dances that I wouldn't dream of attending. Usually. Anyway, they always sat together all cozylike at lunch. Ryan let Blonde Girl thread her thin, pale fingers through his hair like she owned him.

They deserved each other.

But I'd been in Ryan Berenger's classes since freshman year, and he picked today to finally acknowledge my existence.

I'd seen him tons of times at the Ahwatukee Golf Club over the summer, too. He and his short, stocky blond friend were always speeding by the driving range in a golf cart. Lucky them, they didn't have to wait till after five o'clock for the chance to play for free like I did. Ryan could play whenever he wanted.

And now we were teammates. As Trevor would say, that was irony.

That would also explain why he'd glared at me in English class and gripped my book like he wanted to shred it to pieces. What else would make him so angry? Apparently he'd gotten the news that I was on the team, too—or he was still pissed that I'd ruined his pants with a piece of mushy birthday cake.

"Don't fear the journey," I murmured as the day's last bell rang. At my locker, I closed my eyes and tried desperately to picture the falcon with the gold-and-brown feathers perched at the top of our mesquite tree at home. For a moment, my shoulders lightened, and I was able to drown out the negative thoughts invading my head. After a few calming breaths, my eyes opened slowly. My vision cleared. "Don't fear the journey," I exhaled one final time.

A girl with red spiky hair and a silver nose stud standing at the locker next to mine slammed her army-green locker shut.

I jumped when it closed and then turned to her.

The girl rolled her eyes like I was crazy.

She might be right.

"Okay, men—" Coach Lannon said but then stopped himself. He turned sideways, his thick arms folded across his chest. He cast an apologetic smile at me. "And lady," he added, as if he was doing me the world's biggest favor.

I groaned inwardly.

It'd be more comfortable standing beneath a spotlight surrounded by a marching band.

Leaning against my golf bag like it was a lifeboat, I stood with my seven teammates on the largest of the four grassy fields that surrounded Lone Butte High School. The open field was as large as a football field. My teammates stood beside me but not too close, each straddling their own golf bags that looked newer than mine by at least three decades. Coach Lannon stood across from us in the middle of our half-moon lineup, eager to start barking out orders by the way he kept fingering his whistle.

After spending several excruciatingly long seconds introducing me to the team, he mercifully reverted into his coach persona, the one I'd gotten to know at the country club, long enough for me to resume breathing again. Small miracle: at least he introduced me as Fred Oday and not Fredricka. That would have been beyond humiliating.

No one said hello, not that I expected or needed pleasantries. I simply wanted to play golf and lots of it. I hadn't joined the team to make friends. And their sideways glances when they thought I wasn't paying attention suggested that building friendships wouldn't be an option.

"We got a best-ball tournament with Hamilton High on Thursday, so we got our work cut out for us this week. I hope you boys have been practicing over the summer?" Coach Lannon's eyes scanned the boys standing to my right. A few fidgeted in place, especially the one with the brown curls named Zack. He bounced around like he had an army of red ants crawling up his leg. Coach Lannon didn't bother staring me down. He knew exactly where I'd spent most of the summer, and my eyes begged for his silence. Mentioning it would only elevate my status to something below Teacher's Pet.

"Bus will leave here at two o'clock," he continued, tapping his clipboard.

My chest caved forward, grateful. The coach must have sensed my unease.

"You're all excused from your last class," he continued. "I've already cleared it with your teachers. Bus will be back here by seven."

A few happy gasps filled the air at the thought of missing a couple hours of school.

"But be on the bus no later than two. Understood?" Coach Lannon's eyes widened, daring disobedience. "Any questions so far?" He said it in a way that indicated he didn't expect any. But someone got his brave on.

"What about Fred, Coach? Does she get to tee off from the women's tees at the tournament?"

A few of the guys snickered as the hairs prickled on the back of my neck.

Women's tees?

Carefully, I turned sideways till my eyes landed on Ryan Berenger. His eyes shifted back to the coach when I glared at him.

"Well, Ryan," Coach Lannon said, scratching the side of his head, as if he hadn't fully thought about it, and my jaw dropped. Certainly he'd spent at least one minute of his time pondering this. There was only one answer.

"No!" I blurted.

All seven of the boys, including Coach Lannon, turned to gape at me. Clearly no one had ever answered for the coach before. "I won't hit from the women's tees. I can hit from the men's tees. I do it all the time." My teeth ground together as my hands shook.

One of Coach Lannon's blond eyebrows rose with something resembling admiration as he slowly scanned the boys' faces, reading their reactions. Collectively, their lips pressed together. A few fidgeted with their bag tags, but no one uttered another word.

Then the coach smiled. "Well, I guess you heard her, men. And don't underestimate her," he added. "I'll wager she's got a straighter shot than anyone else on this team."

I groaned inwardly. Again. The coach wasn't making my life any easier.

The boys began to whisper among themselves, and I returned to studying my feet, coaxing myself not to hyperventilate.

"Well, okay, then," murmured the boy next to me. "Let's see her hit." He said it like a challenge.

"Yeah," piped in another low voice.

"Show us," taunted a third boy.

My throat had turned drier than dust. I clutched the drivers and irons that poked above the top of my bag. I reached the edges for support. It was probably the first time I'd ever been grateful that my bag was almost as tall as I was. My stomach churned, and I felt a little dizzy. The relentless afternoon sun and the cloudless sky didn't help.

"Okay." Coach Lannon exhaled loudly, the verbal equivalent of wiping his hands together. "Grab some balls and spread out!" he barked.

Each player slung his bag over his shoulder and walked to a ridge at the edge of the field that faced the rear of the school. I quickly claimed a spot on the end where the grass was matted and spotted from divots. I removed my driver and a couple of stubby white tees from the side pocket of my bag. I'd found the stubs on the Ahwatukee Golf Club driving range where other golfers had left them for trash. They were as good as new. I laid my golf bag on the ground because my bag didn't have one of those fancy built-in stands like the newer ones.

As I readied myself for my first swing, I felt every pair of eyes on me like a dozen clammy fingers. I knew that they were silently critiquing everything—the way I reached into my bag, my rusty clubs, the obvious lack of proper golf shoes. I walked over to one of the ball buckets, my chin high but my eyes lowered, and scooped out a handful as my forehead began to throb.

Returning to my corner spot, I teed up the first ball on a patch of matted-down grass and then stood behind it. Balancing my club against my hip, I removed my new golf glove from the back pocket of my khaki shorts where I'd kept it all day like some kind of lucky rabbit's foot, pulling it out every so often just to touch the soft leather. I carefully slipped it over my hand, snapping the mother-of-pearl button at my wrist. Then I clenched my hand a couple of times, mostly to stop my fingers from trembling. No one said a single word, not even the coach. Only the distant school bell rang on the half hour.

I began to concentrate on my breathing. Gaze still lowered, I took another deep breath and spread my legs shoulder-width apart a few feet from the ball. I took a practice swing, then another, letting the club swing backward and forward around my body till my arms and shoulders lost some of their tension. Then, very methodically, I approached the ball perched on its tee and swallowed back more dryness in my throat. I aimed the face of my club at the ball, pulled it back around my body and swung.

And muffed it.

Crap!

The ball dribbled off the tee and rolled pathetically no more than six feet, not even to the edge of the ridge.

Totally embarrassing.

Someone chuckled.

"Nice shot," another chided from somewhere up the line. It sounded like Zack Fisher, but I didn't look up. A few more dry laughs followed, the raspy kind that always sounded creepy.

My breathing quickened along with my heartbeat.

I bent down for another ball and placed it on the tee. I wiped a thin layer of sweat from my forehead with the back of my left hand. Then I closed my eyes, just for a second, and pictured myself striking the ball clear across the field in a perfect arc. When my eyes opened, I spotted a lone bird drifting overhead. I lifted my face to the bird, squinted into the sun and smiled, just a fraction. It could have been any type of bird—a crow, grackle, hawk, even a falcon—but I nodded at it anyway, once.

And then I gripped my club with both hands, right over left, approached the golf ball, bent my knees, lowered my forehead and smacked that friggin' white ball high into the sky and clear across the field. It pierced deep into the sky like a gunshot.

"Now, that's what I'm talking about!" Coach Lannon roared, walking toward me with quick steps, his eyes still tracking the ball. He even clapped a couple of times.

I ignored him. I ignored everybody. I didn't need their praise. Instead, I waited for the ball to drop from the sky, still holding on to my follow-through with the club arched over my right shoulder. Picture-perfect form.

"I don't think you'll find that ball! That one's a goner!" Coach Lannon grinned.

"Shit," someone muttered. "Where'd it go?"

"Dunno," said another disappointed voice.

I didn't turn to Coach Lannon and wait for any more of his compliments. Truth is, I hated compliments. I didn't boast either or flash my teammates an *I-told-you-so* smirk. Instead, I reached down for another ball with a trembling hand and teed up my next shot. Then another.

And another.

It was like my arms were on fire.

"The rest of you goofballs, quit your gawking and start swinging! Let me see what you got! We got a tournament in three days!"

I swung at another ball. Harder. The next one sailed farther than the last.

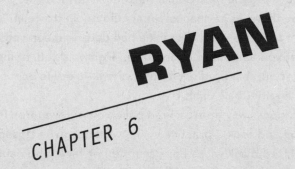

RYAN

CHAPTER 6

DECENT.

That's what I thought when I watched Fred's swing. Although she'd completely muffed her first tee shot, her form was tight: knees bent, chin lowered, hands gripping the club on the sweet spot. Her club swept back and then crushed against the ball as if swinging a club was the easiest thing in the world. Some golfers had it and others didn't. Fred Oday definitely had *it*.

I'd be lying if I said that I hoped she was good, because I wanted Fred to fail. I wanted an epic fail right in front of the coach, in front of everybody. And I wanted it bad.

"Jeez, the Fred freak sure can crank it," Henry Graser said. He swung next to me and sounded as disappointed as I probably looked.

"Yeah," I growled underneath my breath as I fiddled with a new box of tees stuffed in the front pocket of my golf bag.

"Well, we'll see." Henry stopped to lean against his Ping nine-iron. He wiped a thin layer of sweat from his pale forehead. "Coach always says practice is one thing, tournaments are another. Maybe she'll choke on Thursday." He tapped his iron against the heel of his golf shoe, releasing a clump of dirt.

Tournaments. My shoulders lightened. The coach was right.

Let's see how she does on Thursday. That ought to set everything straight again. Maybe then Coach will realize he made a big mistake. Maybe there was a chance Seth could rejoin the team....

"And just because you can crank a ball doesn't mean you can putt. Or get yourself out of a sand trap," Henry added, trying to convince us both that Fred's golf skills were a fluke. He bent over to balance another ball on his tee.

Three stations away from us, Fred pulled out a seven-iron from her golf bag and took a practice swing with her eyes closed. A light wind lifted black wispy hairs around her face. She paused to twirl the loose strands behind her ears when they drifted too close to her eyes.

I pretended not to notice that Fred was more than just a little pretty.

Hold up. What am I saying?!

I lowered my head over my ball and pulled my chin into my chest. I closed my eyes and took a steadying breath. Fred was starting to psyche me out, and I could kick my own ass for even thinking it.

Sucking in a gulp of warm air, I pulled back my driver and cracked the ball clear across the field, but the ball hooked left almost immediately. It didn't sail straight like Fred's. Not even close. Waiting for it to land, I whacked my club against the ground.

In my periphery, I caught Fred watching me, studying me. I swore under my breath. If only she'd seen my last shot. That one had been perfect.

What was wrong with me? Why should I care, and most of all, why *would* I care what she thought? I tapped the side of my head with my club.

"Not bad, Berenger. Not bad!" Coach Lannon yelled from the other end of the field. "Except you hooked it."

Gee, thanks, Coach. Tell me something I don't know.

"And check out that bag." Henry continued his ongoing commentary, lowering his voice. He chuckled. "Where'd she find that thing?"

I tried to ignore Henry but failed miserably. "Shut up, Graser," I snapped. "You're messing with my concentration."

Henry's neck pulled back, palms lifted. "My bad, Tiger Woods. Just having some fun."

I shook my head and then tried to concentrate on the next practice ball.

"It must be real busted, losing the team's top spot to a girl," Henry added.

"Yeah, real busted," I said, not bothering to hide my sarcasm.

It was all I could do not to wipe off Henry's grin with the end of my club. He was lucky his father was principal of the school, or I would have seriously considered it.

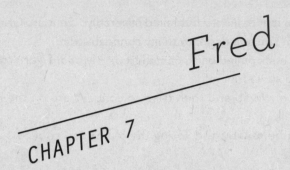

Fred

CHAPTER 7

I SAT ON THE CURB NEXT to the gym after practice, pretending to be engrossed in *The Great Gatsby* perched on my knees as I waited for Dad. Too bad F. Scott Fitzgerald never knew what it was like to be the lone girl on an all-boys' golf team.

My backpack was propped against the front of my bare legs. The sun began to set over the Estrella Mountains, painting orange-yellow streaks across the sky. The campus was almost peaceful.

Almost.

All of my new teammates raced out of the school parking lot like it was the last day before summer vacation. They peeled across the pavement in SUVs, convertibles, sedans, a pickup—one even drove a Hummer—each one newer and shinier than the next.

No one offered me a ride, not that I expected one, especially when they'd behaved like I had some kind of incurable skin disease. No matter. I'd be mortified if any of them drove me all the way home. Better to let them believe I lived in a tepee with no running water or television. That was probably what they thought. That was probably what they'd all like to think.

Ryan Berenger was the last one to leave. He made a show of racing through the parking lot in a shiny silver Jeep Cherokee. His tires never stopped screeching.

Someone sat in his passenger seat, but I couldn't see who it was. I kept my head lowered toward my book and watched Ryan through the safety of my eyelashes. The radio blared through his open windows, and yet he scowled through the windshield.

What a waste. Why would someone with his own car need to scowl? And why was he always staring at me when he thought I wasn't looking? He'd kept glancing over at me during practice. It was...unsettling.

After Ryan drove away, I exhaled and closed my book.

"Hey, Fred."

I turned, startled. It was Sam. "What are you doing here?"

Sam walked toward me, his backpack threaded over his shoulder. "Stayed late to work in the lab on a project. Mind if I catch a ride home with you?"

I smiled at him. "'Course not."

And that's when Dad drove through the front entrance. I heard the familiar chug of the van's engine a block away. Perfect timing.

I looked at him through his open window and smiled tiredly. Gratefully. It was so nice to see Dad's face.

"How's my daughter?" he said as he pulled the van alongside the curb.

"Fine, Dad," I said with a tinge of forced brightness.

"Hey, Sam."

"Hey, Mr. Oday." Sam grabbed my backpack from the sidewalk. This time he didn't ask, and I was too tired to protest.

Sam followed me as I opened the rear door. With one hand, he tossed my pack into the back of the van. I placed a purple Lone Butte High School golf shirt from Coach Lannon on top of it. It was a men's large, but it had been the only shirt left. I was supposed to wear it to all the tournaments. I'd have to hem the sleeves a couple inches before Thursday's tournament. Otherwise the shirt would hang past my elbows.

Dad's brow continued to furrow as he watched me over the front seat. "Really?" he said. His tone was doubtful. "Everything's really fine?"

I slammed the door, because that was the only way it closed. Then I climbed into the passenger seat, anxious for once to get home. Sam slipped into the seat behind mine. "Really," I said, still a bit forced.

"How was practice?"

"Fine."

He chortled. "That's it? That's all you got for me? *Fine?*"

I nodded and looked out the passenger window as he pressed the accelerator and proceeded to the exit.

"How'd you do?"

"I did okay."

"Just okay?" His eyes widened. "Look, are you going to tell me how practice went or not? I've been worried all day."

I dragged my tongue across my lips, then turned to him and smirked. "It was about what I expected."

"And what did you expect?"

I sank lower in my seat as we approached the stoplight, hiding the bottom half of my face below the dashboard. Ryan Berenger's silver Jeep sat at the red light only two cars ahead of us.

Dang it!

I swallowed again, not taking my gaze off the back of his vehicle. There was a gold Ahwatukee Golf Club Member sticker on his rear window.

"Well, Coach Lannon had us warm up on the school's driving range. Then we practiced our short game and putting." I shrugged my shoulders like practice was no big deal. "I did fine. I think."

Sam grunted behind me like he thought I was being too modest.

I'd done better than fine, even after my embarrassing first practice shot. I'd attacked the ball at every opportunity, because I didn't have a choice. The boys had expected me to fail—wanted me to fail. I'd sensed it. And I wasn't about to give any of them an ounce of satisfaction.

"And what about your teammates? What are they like?"

My lips sputtered while I crossed my arms over my chest. I really didn't want to say too much in front of Sam. It felt kind of weird. And embarrassing. "They're just..." I paused, looking ahead for Ryan's Jeep. "They're just a bunch of guys. You know..." My voice trailed off.

The light changed to green, and the cars began to cross the intersection. Dad stayed in the left lane to take the freeway home; Ryan turned right toward the Ahwatukee Golf Club and the sea of pink-tiled roofs.

And breathing became easier again. I rose a notch in my seat.

"How'd they feel about having you on the team?" Dad asked quietly.

My shoulders shrugged. "Okay, I guess. Coach Lannon didn't give them much of a choice. How could they feel?"

Dad didn't say anything. And neither did Sam.

Still, I could see both of their brains churning, even if they didn't utter a single word.

RYAN

CHAPTER 8

ZACK FISHER WOULDN'T STOP talking about Fred Oday. I cranked up the car stereo another notch.

Zack sat in my passenger seat. He'd needed a ride home, but I regretted my offer to drive him.

"Man, I hate to say it, but she's badass," Zack yelled over the music, reaching for his seat belt as I pressed my foot against the accelerator, hard. The Jeep lurched forward.

My hands gripped the steering wheel till all my knuckles turned white. First Henry Graser, and now I had to listen to Zack Fisher all the way home. All anyone could talk about was Fred Oday.

"Did you see her sand shot?" Zack shook his head like he still couldn't believe it.

Yeah, I saw it. My jaw clenched.

"I don't think she missed a single putt either." He whistled annoyingly through his teeth. "And I used to think you were the best putter on the team," he said even louder. "Not anymore, dude. Sorry." He chuckled darkly, slapping his hand against the door frame.

I raced to the stoplight just past the school exit. The light turned red, and my foot pressed the brake when it really wanted to stomp on the accelerator and fly down Pecos Road.

"You think with her on the team we might actually take State this year?" Zack turned to me.

My expression stayed frozen till my gaze traveled to the rear-view mirror. Then I shook my head and sighed.

"What?" Zack asked.

"Nothing." I frowned. I wasn't about to tell bigmouthed Zack that I was starting to see Fred Oday everywhere—at restaurants, in class, even in my rearview mirror. And she was in the passenger seat of a rusted-out van—at least, it looked like her. Dark hair, coppery skin, hair pulled back, forehead lowered. Always lowered. And for some reason, that ape of a guy Sam Tracy was in the van, seated behind her. It was kind of hard to miss him. His neck was as wide as a tree trunk.

"So, what do you think?" Zack prodded again.

"About what?" I mumbled as the light turned green. My fingers drummed against the steering wheel.

"About the team? About winning?"

I exhaled loudly. "I don't know what to think, so just shut up. I'm trying to drive. Do you want a ride or not?"

Zack's neck pulled back, and his eyes widened. "Sure. That's cool." His eye roll told me he would have preferred walking home. "You wanna hang at my house for a while?"

"No, I've gotta get home," I lied.

I'd promised to stop by Seth's house after practice. I didn't know which would be worse: avoiding Seth's questions about golf practice or listening to Zack's nonstop babble.

When the light finally changed, I made my turn and checked the rearview mirror. Fred was gone, and I could think clearly again.

Fred

CHAPTER 9

AFTER THE USUAL QUICKIE DINNER of hot dogs and canned corn, I begged Mom to drive with me back to Phoenix to shop for a new pair of shorts for school. That was the only way Dad would let me go, and, surprisingly, Mom agreed. I'd had my license for almost a year, but Dad had a thing about me driving long distances at night. And when you lived in the middle of nowhere, everything was long-distance.

Being September, it was still too warm for jeans, and my two pairs of shorts had become embarrassingly faded and frayed around the edges. My khaki pair I'd worn since the eighth grade.

I was certain my fashion faux pas hadn't gone unnoticed at school where most of the girls, especially the popular ones, rotated fashion as often as their boyfriends. I simply had to have something new to wear, at least an updated pair of shorts, maybe even a new tank, before the first golf tournament.

The closest mall to the Rez sat next to the freeway. It was halfway between our trailer and Lone Butte High School. The mall was completely enclosed and so enormous that it should have had its own zip code. There were three floors of continuous stores wrapped around a central courtyard with a fountain. A strong scent of melted cheese and warm pretzels permeated the air. Even though it was a

Monday, the stores buzzed with people and chatter like it was the last day of Christmas shopping.

I loved the mall. I could window-shop every day. Mom? Not so much.

"Just a couple of stores tonight, Freddy," Mom said, pulling closer to me as the other shoppers jostled around us with their elbows and strollers. "Let's not make it a marathon. The air in here always dries my eyes." Her nose wrinkled when someone's shopping bag brushed her arm.

"'Kay, Mom," I said. Mom had never been a fan of crowds, especially in places outside the Rez. She always said the mall made her nervous, but I suspected it was the people, especially the ones with designer purses and overflowing department-store bags from Nordstrom and Macy's. They probably reminded her too much of the people she had to serve at work.

Still, I always secretly wished that she was the type of mom who liked to shop and do all the fun things I imagined that normal girls did with their mothers, maybe even stop at a restaurant in the food court afterward to critique our purchases over a cheeseburger and soda. Wouldn't that be so cool? Except we never did stuff like that.

"Where to first?" Mom said.

I nodded to a Gap store next to my favorite golf-goods store. I'd been in the golf store a few times with Dad but never to buy anything, only to look. And dream.

Mom's eyes followed mine. She let out a long exhale. "You didn't drag me all the way out to this godforsaken place to look at golf clubs, did you? When I could be home with my feet propped up enjoying a cold beer?"

I cringed at her loud tone. "Already got clubs," I said softly. Nonchalantly, my eyes trailed across the display window. A silver ladder with women's golf shoes perched on each step filled the corner, and my eyes beaded on a white leather pair with soft pink piping around the laces. I sucked back a breath through my lips. Those shoes matched my golf glove. I just had to take a closer look.

"Freddy..." Mom's voice ratcheted up another notch. "A pair of shorts is why we're here, remember?"

"Yep, I know. But I just need to look at something for a second. Please? I'll be back outside before you know it. Promise."

Mom's lips sputtered. "Okay, okay. But only a minute. I'll be in here." She nodded toward the Gap. "I'll start looking for the clothes on sale, but if you're not inside this store in five minutes, we're leaving. Anyway, I think I'm getting a migraine." Her eyebrows pulled together.

I nodded. "I'll only be gone a minute." I glanced again at the golf shoes, half expecting giant hands to swoop them off the display before my very eyes.

"How much money you got?"

"Probably enough for two pairs of shorts," I said. "That's all I need."

"Good, because I sure as hell didn't bring any." Mom's shoulders shrugged, and then she turned for the other store. "At least it's less crowded in here," she muttered as she walked away. "And there's a chair!"

I spun on the balls of my feet and darted inside the golf store while Mom trotted off to nab the chair. I rushed to the shoe section to find the white pair with the pink piping. My eyes landed on the price tag: $110.

I sighed.

It might as well have said one million.

My fingers brushed the soft laces. I'd need a few more weekends at the Wild Horse Restaurant to afford them, if the chef allowed me back at all.

RYAN

CHAPTER 10

SETH AND I DROVE TO THE MALL off the I-10 freeway. I'd picked him up at his house after golf practice, and we'd gone to mine. But chilling at the mall was way better than hanging around the house and listening to Mom nag about homework that bored me and college entrance exams that I didn't want to take. Seth felt the same way. It was one of a million things we had in common.

I'd lied and told Mom that I already signed up for the SATs, just so that I could get out of the house. Fortunately, she'd bought it. I should feel guilty about lying to her all the time, but I didn't. Not really anyway. Maybe because the more I lied, the easier it got.

Seth only wanted to hang because he wanted to hear all about Fred. I was going to have to lie to him, too. The truth would only crank him.

"Movie?" Seth asked me as we passed through the food court.

"Maybe."

"What, then?" Seth stuffed his hands in his front pockets.

My shoulders shrugged. "I don't know yet. Let's just walk around."

We started on the first floor and walked to the south end of the mall.

"So Zack texted me after practice and said the Indian wasn't so bad."

I cringed a little when he said *Indian* and kind of looked around to see if anyone had overheard. Seth hated Native Americans, all of them, mostly because a drunk one had killed his real dad when he was driving home from work one night on the freeway. Hit him head-on. It had happened when Seth was a baby. He knew his real dad only from pictures.

I didn't answer him. But Seth wouldn't let it go. "Well, what do you think?" he said. "Is she as good as Coach thinks?"

I considered it as if I really hadn't given Fred much thought. "I don't know," I said finally. "She did okay, I guess."

"Okay?" Seth stopped abruptly and faced me, toe to toe. I had no choice but to stop. "She does *okay,* and she gets handed *my* spot on the team like I don't even matter?"

I searched his widened eyes but said nothing. I certainly wasn't going to rub it in that he was the worst player on our team apart from Henry Graser. But Henry was Principal Graser's son.

The problem with Seth was that he really didn't even like golf. He played to please his stepdad. Why, I would never understand. Seth's stepdad was the baddest guy I'd ever met.

"Coach Lannon told me to go out for wrestling," he snarled. "Said I was built for it."

"Well, why don't you?"

He shook his head. "I don't want to wrestle. I hate wrestling. No one cool is on the team anyway. And I didn't practice golf all summer long to go out for wrestling." Hands jammed in his front pockets, Seth began walking again. "I still can't believe it," he muttered. "It reeks. It's not fair. And then there's my stepdad..." His voice trailed off.

"Was he pretty mad?" I asked carefully.

"Way mad. The usual." Seth shrugged as though it was no big deal, but I knew better.

"What'd he say?"

Seth's tone was flat. "He called me worthless and stupid. Said I didn't practice hard enough. Blah, blah, blah. You know, his usual crank. And there's no way I was going to tell him that I got kicked off because of a girl. And a fucking Indian."

I winced. "Sorry, Seth."

"At least he didn't whack me," he added. Too casually. "He hasn't done that in a while."

I shook my head. I really wished Seth didn't have to live with his stepdad. But as mean as he was, his stepdad was the only father Seth had ever known. I wasn't sure if that was good or bad.

"Well, we've got to do something about Fred." He spoke as if the decision had been made.

That stopped me cold, and the shoppers behind us practically slammed Into our heels. "Like, what are you thinking?" I chuckled doubtfully. And what could we do? Coach Lannon's mind was made up. Fred was all that.

Seth continued walking, and I caught up with him as we reached the golf store where we'd bought our golf bags last year. We stopped in front of the display window. "I don't know yet." Seth sighed. "But this isn't over. I'll think of something."

"There's really nothing you can do." My eyes narrowed. I didn't want him to get madder than he already was. "Coach was pretty clear. He likes her. I don't think he'll change his mind, not this time."

"What if she chokes at the tournament?" Seth said. "What then?"

My head tilted, considering this. "Maybe," I said, but not too confidently. I honestly didn't expect Fred Oday to fail, not with her swing. Unless both of her arms were amputated by Thursday, she would probably do better than at least half the players on the team.

Seth's nostrils flared. And just as I was going to open my mouth to try to encourage Seth to go out for wrestling again, I glanced into the golf-store display window. My teeth clamped shut. Then I mumbled, "I don't believe this..."

Inside the store, Fred Oday picked up a white golf shoe and fingered its laces. A tiny smile brightened her face. Her smile faded into a sort of frown, a sad frown, when she turned the shoe over in her hands. Strangely, I wondered what crossed her mind. It was just a lame shoe—and a golf shoe. No big thing. But then she replaced the white shoe on the display, stood back to admire it with her hands clutched behind her back, only to pick it up a moment later like she was seeing it for the first time. Her hair fell over her bare shoulder as her head tilted sideways, covering half her face.

I gulped.

"Oh, no," Seth moaned. He drew back a breath through his teeth. "You saw her, too?"

I blinked and then turned to Seth. I nodded but then wished I hadn't. Now was not a good time to confront Fred Oday in the middle of the mall. She was the last person Seth needed to see.

"I didn't think you saw her," Seth said. "I saw them when we walked past the food court. I'm pretty sure they didn't see us."

My eyes narrowed. "Who are you talking about?"

"Your dad." Seth lowered his voice along with his chin, not that it was necessary. The mall noise muffled everything. "And that girl."

"*My* dad? Where?"

Seth's head tilted sideways toward the west end of the food court.

I followed the arc of Seth's head till my gaze landed on a round table next to the fountain. Through a fake potted fern, I watched as Dad chatted up a girl with spiky red hair. He was still wearing his shirt and purple tie from this morning except that his tie was loosened at the neck. The girl tossed her head back and laughed at something he said. She didn't look much older than my cousin Lauren. Except the girl seated across from Dad didn't look like she went to college. She wore a black smock with a white name tag, accentuating the paleness of her face. Her lips were bright red.

"I think that's the lady who cuts my dad's hair," I muttered. "She cuts mine, too. Sometimes."

Seth turned to me. "She's pretty hot."

"Shut up, Seth," I said.

"Well, she is," he replied, just as Dad placed his hand over hers in the middle of their tiny table.

My stomach did a somersault before my cheeks flushed hot. Dad looked as if he *liked* her. I found myself clenching my fists. "Let's get out of here."

"Sure. Where?" he said, but I'd already turned.

"Anywhere but here."

Seth jogged after me. "You gonna tell your mom about it?"

I snorted. "Don't have to."

"She already knows?"

"Why do you think she's always working?" Seth had to jog to keep up with me.

By the time we reached the parking lot, I was breathing so hard that my ribs hurt. I tried to stop thinking about Dad and his new girlfriend by thinking about Fred and her smile. But it didn't really work. I kept seeing my angry reflection staring back at me in store windows.

Seth knew me better than to ask what was wrong. "Why don't we head to the arcade and scare up some freshmen?"

"Nah." I shook my head.

"Come on," he said, reaching for the door handle to his pickup truck. "It'll be fun."

I climbed inside the truck, silent. I wasn't in the mood to terrorize the newest unsuspecting freshmen at Lone Butte High School who were dumbass enough to spend time at the arcade. Last time we did, Seth had had one redheaded dude practically in tears when he kept challenging him to a game of air hockey in front of his friends. The frosh had finally relented and bombed, although not after Seth had smacked the back of his head with his hand and told him to stop being such a tool.

"It'll be a good time," Seth said, not letting it go. "You know you want to." He wiggled his eyebrows.

I sighed. "Okay, okay. Let's go." It was better than going home. Anything was better than going home.

"Good answer," Seth said as the tires squealed across the parking lot toward the exit.

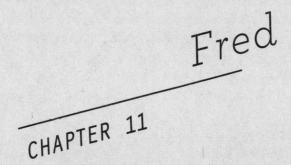

Fred

CHAPTER 11

THE NEXT FEW DAYS PROCEEDED almost exactly as the first.

Each morning before work, Dad dropped me off in front of the high school along with my backpack and sometimes my plaid golf bag, depending on whether I decided to take it home or leave it in the coach's office. I could leave my bag in his office every night if I wanted, but I preferred to bring my clubs home and practice my swing after I did my homework. Sometimes Sam and Pete would ride with Dad and me. On those days, I relented and let Sam drag my golf bag out of the van, if I had it. It was like Sam to be nice.

Then I tried to ignore all the stares and practically nailed my chin to my chest as I trudged through layers of high school kids to reach Coach Lannon's office. At least I had some new clothes to wear. I'll admit that it was better when Sam walked beside me, but it nagged me that he looked like some kind of an escort. It was stupid. And I had my suspicions that somehow my brother had put Sam up to Bodyguard Duty.

I attended all my classes and study halls but kept mostly to myself. At golf practice, I was mostly ignored, although Zack Fisher did ask me once which country club my parents belonged to. I almost choked on my answer.

After a sleepless Wednesday night, I walked straight to the No

Admittance metal door in the back of the gymnasium with my golf bag over my shoulder without stopping. I passed Ryan Berenger and his circle of friends in the courtyard. As I passed, their conversation stopped. Ryan pretended not to notice me and turned to his blonde girlfriend to hide his face. I figured he was probably rolling his eyes by the grin on his girlfriend's face. Her perfect pale cheeks filled with air like she was trying to swallow a laugh.

Nice.

I reached the rear door quickly, considering all of the weight hanging on my shoulder.

I knocked twice. Ten seconds later, Coach Lannon opened the heavy door and stood aside. "Morning, Fred," he said, yawning as he propped the door open with his back.

"Hi, Coach," I said as I walked through the opened door. It was familiar to me now and still barely wide enough for the both of us and my golf bag.

Coach Lannon smiled down at me as I passed. "Ready for the tournament today?"

"I think so," I said, too late, as we walked to his office.

I didn't have to look at his eyes to know they widened.

"I mean, yes," I clarified.

"Good." He was all toothy smile again. "'Cause I think we got a real chance at beating Hamilton this year." He rubbed his hands. "Glad to see you're wearing your golf shirt. Hope it wasn't too big on you."

For real? It's as big as a hogan.[3]

"It'll do," I said.

"The boys treating you okay?"

"Fine," I lied.

"Good," he said. "'Cause I expect you to tell me if they don't. Okay?"

I nodded without looking at him.

---

3 A traditional Navajo house.

When we reached his office, I scooted around the coach and dropped my bag in its usual spot while he plopped into the seat behind his desk. I stood back and frowned at it. My bag stood out like a laser light among all the stylish navy blue, black and gray bags with their trendy logos and shiny clubs that barely looked used. I tried to stuff my bag into the corner, but there was only so much you could do to make a thirty-year-old plaid golf bag look inconspicuous.

"Listen, Fred," Coach Lannon said as he opened a yellow folder on his desk. "There was something else I wanted to talk to you about. *Privately.* You want to have a seat for a minute?"

My stomach dropped.

He pointed to the chair in front of his desk. I sat down.

Had I done something wrong? Had he seen me muff the two short shots yesterday on the putting green? Was he angry already with my performance? Was he kicking me off the team?

My breathing quickened exponentially.

"I notice you wear tennis shoes instead of golf shoes." He made a tent with his fingers.

I sat higher in my chair. I wasn't expecting that. "Yes," I said with an equally careful tone. It was like tiptoeing around Mom.

"Well, I just wondered if your play wouldn't benefit from a pair of decent golf shoes—"

I interrupted him, surprising myself. "I haven't had a chance yet to buy a pair." I paused as my cheeks began to burn. "With school and practice and all. Maybe I'll get to the mall this weekend." Not a huge lie. It could happen.

Coach Lannon sat back in his chair. His eyes narrowed a fraction. "I see."

I inhaled once, deeply, through my nose. The office walls began to shrink.

His palms lifted. "If it's a question of money, let me help—"

"I don't need any help with the shoes, Coach, really, I don't. I just need time to get to the mall," I said quickly.

The coach lowered his voice. "Okay," he said, leaning forward again. "Didn't mean to upset you. But if you should change your mind—"

"Maybe this weekend," I said again, mentally calculating the tip money I'd already saved minus the money I'd just paid for two new pairs of shorts. And Mom had even promised to talk to the chef at the restaurant again. *I'll ask him when he's desperate for extra hands,* she'd promised the night before. *Then he'll have to take you back. Besides,* Mom had said, *you'll need the job when you graduate.* Her words had ingrained themselves in my brain like a bruise that wouldn't heal.

Coach Lannon lowered his chin. His tone was kind, and I felt a tiny lump grow in my throat. "You know, Fred, there's no harm in asking for help. When you need it."

I pulled away from his desk, swallowing back the lump. Then I popped up out of my chair like there was a spring in the cushion. Dad would be mortified if I ever accepted charity. "Thank you, Coach. I appreciate it, but I don't need any help."

"Would it help if I talked to your parents?"

I felt my face go ashen. *That would be a thousand times worse.* "No. Please, don't," I said. "They're busy enough as it is."

"You're sure?"

"Positive. Please, don't. Please, don't do anything." I wanted to tell him to just leave me alone and let me play golf. I'd never needed golf shoes before. I could survive without them for a little while longer.

The crease in the middle of the coach's forehead softened. I think he finally understood, but just as he was about to say something else, the first warning bell rang.

"I better get to class," I said, eager to be anywhere but trapped with Coach Lannon and more questions.

The coach sighed and followed me reluctantly to the door. He leaned against it. "One other thing, Oday," he said in his coach voice as I stepped into the hallway.

I was still breathing heavily through my nostrils, anxious to sprint. I turned.

"I'm pairing you with Berenger at the tournament today."

"Ryan?"

"Yeah." He squinted at me like he was surprised that I wouldn't know. "You two are our best players. You're in the top spot, and he's in the second."

"Oh." My voice squeaked. "Right." More unexpected news.

"Anyway, don't forget the bus leaves here at two sharp."

I nodded and then finally turned and charged down the long hallway. When I got to the end, I nearly knocked over Ryan and his stocky blond friend, another white boy at Lone Butte High School with a permanent snarl that contradicted his angelic face.

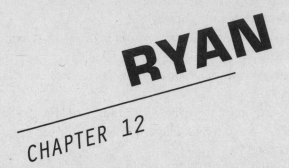

RYAN

CHAPTER 12

"IS IT JUST ME, OR IS that girl whacked?" Seth muttered after Fred passed between us in the hallway, forcing us to part abruptly. She barely glanced at us.

Seth glared over his shoulder. "Nice," he yelled after her. "Walk much?" he added.

"Seth..." I frowned at him. "Come on."

"What?"

"Let's just go," I said, tugging at the thick black strap digging into my right shoulder. "I gotta dump this." I was anxious to be rid of my golf bag, but what I really craved was more distance from Fred Oday. I didn't want to start the day arguing with Seth about her all over again. I'd had enough of it at the mall.

Outside Coach Lannon's office, I placed my hand on Seth's shoulder. I nodded at the coach's brass nameplate next to the door. I was pretty sure that next to Fred Oday, Coach Lannon was the last person Seth needed to be around.

But Seth strode inside the office anyway, chin up. "It's cool." A strange grin spread across his face when he saw the office was empty.

Quickly, I walked around him and headed straight for the corner, grateful to release the golf bag from my shoulder. I wedged it between a half-dozen other bags while Seth dropped his backpack to the ground, bent over and unzipped the top pocket.

"What are you doing?" I said to him.

Seth looked up at me, still grinning, before rummaging inside his open backpack. He pulled out three red bricks, each the size of a dictionary.

My eyes narrowed. "What's with the bricks?"

Seth held them up like each was a gold bar, two balanced in one hand, one in the other. His smile broadened. I hadn't seen that look since the time Seth had figured out how to hot-wire his mom's car before either of us had had a driver's license. He'd succeeded. And then received a month's grounding along with a purple welt on his arm, compliments of his stepdad.

"Dude, what are you doing?"

"Shut up. Watch the door for me," Seth whispered. "You'll see." He went to the wall of stacked golf bags and moved two to reach the bright red plaid one partially hidden behind them. It was impossible to miss.

He shook his head as he pushed the clubs inside the plaid bag to one side. He wrapped one hand around the irons. "Friggin' thing smells like mothballs," he muttered, head still shaking. The clubs clanged as they jostled together in his hand, and I instinctively turned toward the opened door, expecting Coach Lannon to bust us at any second.

We were so screwed.

"Um, Seth?" I said again, my eyes darting between Seth and the door. "What are you doing?" I repeated, my tone more anxious.

But Seth still didn't answer. He was too preoccupied with dumping the bricks to the bottom of the bag, one by one.

Thump.

Thump.

Thump.

"There." He wiped his hands against his thighs. "That should do it." Then he arranged the plaid bag behind the others and turned to me.

My eyes widened. "Do what?"

"Let's see how well Pocahontas does today carrying around a load of *that.*" His head tilted toward Fred's golf bag. His eyes dipped conspiratorially to the bottom. But then his grin faded as his expression darkened. "Serves the bitch right for stealing my spot."

I swallowed back a hollow feeling of nausea. "She didn't exactly steal it."

Seth glared at me.

"Well, not exactly," I added.

His glare lasted only an instant. Then he patted my shoulder. "But don't worry." He lowered his voice to a raspy whisper. "I was never here."

Without another word, we turned for the door and headed down the long hallway for Homeroom while I pictured three heavy bricks lying at the bottom of Fred's golf bag.

They might as well have been lining the bottom of my stomach.

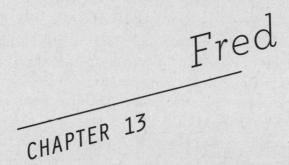

Fred

CHAPTER 13

I WAS THE FIRST PERSON TO board the bus before our first golf tournament. Not a huge surprise. I'd probably been stressing about it the most.

I slipped into the empty seat behind the bus driver at 1:55, relieved that Coach Lannon had already loaded all of the golf bags in the storage compartment below the back of the bus. "What are you carrying in your bag, Fred?" he teased when he climbed inside. He made a dramatic show of wiping his shiny forehead with the back of his hand. "You're only allowed fourteen clubs, you know." But then he winked at me, and I knew he was joking, his attempt to get me to relax.

Like that was possible.

Coach Lannon didn't need to remind me that my golf bag leaned a little on the hefty side, and good thing I had grown used to it over the past year. I'd carried it eighteen holes across the Ahwatukee Golf Club plenty of times, not that I minded. Walking helped me to gauge the slope of the fairways a lot better than driving a stupid golf cart.

The tournament against Hamilton High was being held at Ahwatukee, another plus, since it was the only course I'd ever played. I knew every hill, every tricky sand trap, every mesquite tree and every hazard. I even knew where the cactus wrens and hummingbirds built their nests in the saguaros and paloverde trees on the fairways. Simply stated, I could play the course blindfolded.

Even so, I fidgeted in my seat, waiting for the others to board. It was almost two o'clock, and I wanted the tournament to begin already. I wanted to get to the course. I tried to concentrate on the English book between my hands, but my eyes glazed over the same page, again and again.

One minute before two o'clock, Henry Graser climbed aboard the bus, followed by Zack Fisher and Troy Bean. They talked animatedly and breezed by me like I was invisible. I pretended to stare out the window. Naturally, they chose the empty seats at the back of the bus.

My temples pounded as I stared at the emergency-exit instructions above the bus driver's seat. I had it memorized. *In case of emergency, remain seated...*

In case of emergency, throw your body through the glass and don't stop running till you reach the next galaxy... Okay, I made that part up, but I was certainly thinking it might be necessary.

Then Ryan Berenger climbed the stairs. He boarded casually, his eyes hidden behind dark sunglasses, enhancing his blondness all the more. I turned toward the window like I needed to shield my eyes from an eclipse and waited until Ryan's footsteps faded into the bowels of the back of the bus. Then I remembered to breathe. What was it about him that was so irritating? Being his partner for a whole afternoon would be pure torture.

Mercifully, Coach Lannon barreled aboard the bus with Scott Paterson, Bob Bernacchi and Dan White trailing behind him. Like the rest of the boys, they darted for the back, too, barely glancing in my direction.

Once everyone was seated, Coach Lannon made a dramatic show of looking at the back of the bus with one hand over his eyes.

"What are you boys doing way back there?" It really wasn't a question. "Get up here!"

I didn't turn to watch them fill the closer seats, but my skin prickled as I listened to their sluggish footsteps.

"Berenger, you sit up here with Fred." He patted the back of my seat. "Get better acquainted. You're partners today."

Don't remind me.

Somebody snickered in the seat behind mine as if Ryan had lost a bet.

As Ryan slid into the seat, I scooted closer to the window, putting as much distance between us as possible. Only six inches separated us, the closest we'd ever been, if you didn't count the cake incident. Still clad in sunglasses, Ryan faced forward and then rested clenched fists on his knees.

Nice.

I faced forward, too, trying to ignore Ryan, wishing that Coach Lannon would say something—anything—that would make the bus move faster. Once I started playing golf, everything else would disappear, even Ryan and his permanent scowl.

The coach proceeded to call out tournament pairings. "Graser, you're with Bean. Bernacchi, you're with White." He glanced down at his clipboard. "And, Fisher, you're with Petersen. You'll be assigned to your Hamilton High twosomes once we get to the course. Understood?"

Everyone nodded. A few mumbled and muttered.

"Just a reminder that the Ahwatukee Golf Club is a par 72. The first hole is a par 4 with a dogleg right. Don't forget there's water on the third and sixth holes. Nothing any of you can't handle. I played the course last weekend and the greens were running fast, so don't go heavy on your putts. Remember—slow and steady wins the race. Control is essential."

So far he hadn't said anything that I didn't know. I'd shot the course under par a couple of times. Getting par wasn't impossible, but it wouldn't win tournaments.

"Questions?" he asked.

Ryan raised his hand.

The coach nodded at him. "Ryan? And would you take off those glasses? Who are you trying to channel—Brad Pitt?"

Ryan smirked, but I saw his cheeks flush a little.

Good, I thought. *He's embarrassed himself. He should be embarrassed.*

Reluctantly, Ryan removed his sunglasses, letting them dangle against his chest on the end of a black leather strap. "What about giving up strokes, Coach?" He paused and tilted his head in my direction. "Shouldn't we have to give her, say, two strokes every nine holes to keep the play fair?" His tone was equal parts annoying and condescending. I could tell he was trying to sound like he was doing me a favor by asking.

I knew better.

Every part of me prickled with red-hot, sizzling anger. Ryan was totally messing with me. He was trying to psyche me out.

Coach Lannon's chin pulled closer to his chest. His voice stayed calm, almost as if he'd been expecting this, but I could tell Ryan's question made him angry. With a tight smile, he said, "Are you referring to Fred?"

Ryan nodded. "Well, yeah. She's the only girl on the team." He turned sideways to acknowledge the rest of the bus, getting a few supportive laughs.

"Glad you noticed," the coach said, pulling at his chin. "So you think we should make special accommodations for her?"

Ryan shrugged. I hoped it wasn't my imagination that he paled another shade.

"That's interesting, Mr. Berenger. I think I already know her answer, but why don't you ask her yourself?" He folded his arms and glared down at him. "Why don't you ask Fred if she wants special treatment at the tournament—because that is what you're asking, isn't it?"

Out the corner of my eye, I watched Ryan's Adam's apple travel up and lodge at the top of his neck like a peach pit. Clearly he hadn't expected that. He turned to me, looking a bit like he was afraid to take me straight on.

My eyes met his, challenging him—goading him to look away. I wanted him to ask me his stupid question almost as much as I wanted to tell him my answer. I didn't lower my gaze, even though every part of me wanted to. My hands were trembling, so I wrapped my fingers around the edge of my seat.

Ryan's face registered something I'd never seen before. For less than a heartbeat, it looked like respect. But then the flicker vanished, leaving the old Ryan Berenger in his place.

"I guess she doesn't," Ryan mumbled. "Forget I even asked."

With pleasure.

Neither of us said a word as the bus grew so quiet that we could hear the freeway traffic through the windows.

In a low voice, Coach Lannon finally interrupted our stare-down and said, "I believe you have your answer, Mr. Berenger. Now, can we close the chapter on Fred and her participation on this team and win a tournament today?"

My fingertips ached as they gripped the edges of my seat. It took all of my willpower not to throw Ryan Berenger out the window.

As soon as the bus pulled in front of the clubhouse at the Ahwatukee Golf Club, Ryan bolted off the bus after Coach Lannon, taking a blanket of heaviness in the air with him.

I pretended to fiddle with the button on my golf glove as I waited for everyone to leave the bus. The other boys filed past me with sideways glances, saying nothing. When I was finally alone, I sucked back a steadying breath and reminded myself why I joined the team, why I was at the tournament. Most of all, I reminded myself that I needed to win.

Outside the bus, Coach Lannon handed everyone their golf bags and a tournament scorecard before we all walked to the first tee. The Hamilton High bus was parked next to ours, and it was already empty.

The first tee was on an elevated hill, just past the clubhouse. All eight members from Hamilton High and their coach waited for us behind the tee box. They were dressed in matching green golf shirts and shorts, one face paler than the next. The coach waved at Coach Lannon and then tapped his wristwatch.

But everyone's eyes weren't focused on Coach Lannon or the Lone Butte High School players who trudged to the tee box in groups of two and three. Everyone's eyes were fixed on me and my plaid golf bag. Trust me, it was not my imagination.

I figured this would happen. When I hadn't been able to sleep last night, I'd practiced how to handle the unwanted attention. I had promised myself that I would not blush, I would not lower my eyes in embarrassment, and I would not fidget with my hands. I had planned to walk right up to the other boys and pull out my driver like it was a sword, challenging anyone to doubt my skills with my first drive. That was how I'd practiced it in my mind. It had worked well in the safety of my bedroom. But here's what really happened...

With my golf bag slung across my right shoulder, I walked alone up the tiny hill to the front of the first tee. I stuffed my hands in the front pockets of my new shorts to keep them from shaking. Sweat began to form behind my ears. My eyes alternated from scanning over sixteen curious faces to assessing the toes of my tennis shoes. Dryness invaded my throat as if I'd just swallowed a glass of sand.

Coach Lannon dropped back and walked alongside me for the last few yards to the tee. I was never so happy to be near him.

When we reached the other players congregating at the top, I hoped that no one would ask me to speak. I'd forgotten how, especially since every pair of eyes—blue ones, green ones, brown ones, some hidden behind sunglasses—tracked every movement and studied every inch of my body, clearly wondering if I was some sort of joke.

Some probably hoped I was.

Then there was my golf bag. Everybody gawked at that most of all, like it had just dropped from a spaceship pod.

A handful of the parent spectators stared, too, although more discreetly. I pretended not to notice them as I scanned the fairway for Dad. I hoped he was somewhere close on his work cart. There was some comfort in knowing that he breathed the same air.

"Coach Nickerson," the coach said, breaking the silence on the tee.

"Larry," he replied with a head nod. "Hey, boys." He paused, face frozen, while I waited for it. "And..."

Coach Lannon finished his thought. "Let me introduce you all to Fred Oday," he said, answering the obvious question. He placed a heavy hand on my left shoulder and pressed down. "The newest member of our team."

Member. Team. *Right.*

Coach Nickerson nodded at me, stared a second longer than he should have and then, thankfully, lowered his tanned face to the clipboard and began to call out the tournament foursomes, checking off each one with a flourish of his pen after he announced them. Teeth clenched, I waited for my name to be called.

"Berenger. Oday," Coach Nickerson said. "You're with Bellows and Frazier. You're up last."

I exhaled. Last was good. Last meant that Ryan and I would be the last to tee off from the first hole and the last to finish the eighteenth hole. I figured that my nerves would have settled to something below Richter scale proportions by then.

To stay focused, I pulled out my driver and a fresh white tee from my bag. I stood a safe distance from the tee box for some practice swings. Small bonus: the school provided each player with a sleeve of brand-new golf balls and a water bottle. As I waited for the first few foursomes to tee off, I noticed the small crowd of spectators hadn't moved, including one guy with graying sideburns and a palm-size notebook. He stood by himself underneath a mesquite tree. The man jotted something down and continued to watch me when he thought I wasn't looking. Odd.

Focus, Fred. Focus, I reminded myself, half pretending to watch the other players tee off. I couldn't concern myself with the stares from spectators or players. Surely the novelty of a girl on an all-boys' golf team would wear off eventually. Wouldn't it? And why did it have to be such a big deal? Didn't girls play on boys' teams in other schools? I had read once about a girl on an all-boys' football team. That had to be a thousand times weirder.

Coach Lannon finally called out our names. "Berenger, Oday, Bellows and Frazier. You're up next. Hamilton will tee up first."

I grinned inwardly. Even better.

I grabbed my club and my bag and walked behind the first tee to give the Hamilton players room to swing. The tall one with the reddish hair was up first. I noted that their swings weren't half-bad. They both smacked the ball solidly with their drivers, but both balls hooked left down the fairway, narrowly missing a thin strip of rocky desert that lined both sides of the grass. It was a par-4 hole so they had to get to the green in no less than three strokes to have a chance at par. Their grimaces after their opening swings reflected their challenge at achieving par.

Then it was Ryan's turn.

Ryan pulled out his driver, a sturdy club with a shiny metal head. *It was probably custom-made,* I mused.

He took two practice swings. His swing was nice. Solid. Smooth. I tried not to gawk at it too much at practice, but now, as his partner, I didn't have much choice.

Ryan approached the ball, bent his knees, lowered his head and adjusted his hands on the club. Then he pulled back the club above his shoulders. The ball cracked into the sky, sailing far across the fairway but veering right. It was a strong shot, but it rolled near the desert's edge. Ryan smacked his club against the ground when the ball landed. It hadn't gone where he wanted. He glared at the sky, angry.

Again I smiled inwardly. *Serves him right,* I thought. I knew that strip of desert where his ball had landed. The ground was hard and blanketed with tiny rocks and cactus needles. It wasn't easy hitting a ball out of the desert, even from the edge. I figured he'd scuff one of his shiny irons before he'd get his ball back on the fairway. I should have felt bad for him.

Finally it was my turn, and the tee box turned eerily quiet. It was as if everyone suddenly sucked in a collective breath. The only noise came from a few crows flying overhead. I tossed my ponytail over my shoulder so that it rested down the middle of my back and out of my way. I took a few practice swings to calm my nerves and loosen my shoulders. Then, like the others in my foursome, I approached the ball, bent my knees, lowered my chin and adjusted my grip. I took one last look at the flag on the green in the distance. It fluttered as if it was waving at me. From the tee box, it didn't look any bigger than a white sail from a boat in the middle of a lake. I inhaled a final, steadying breath, lowered my head and swung.

As soon as my clubface struck the ball, I knew where it would fly. I knew by the sound—loud and solid like a crack of summer thunder. The ball flew high into the sky and then sailed down the middle of the fairway, rolling straight for the green. It didn't go the farthest, but it went as straight as an arrow and stayed comfortably clear of the rough. In one stroke, maybe two, I was certain that I'd reach the green.

After my turn ended, several spectators gasped behind the tee box.

I nodded politely to the tiny crowd when they clapped, just like I'd seen golfers do on TV. Then I returned the club to my bag lying on the ground at the edge of the tee box. I picked it up, hoisted the strap over my shoulder and trotted off behind the others in my foursome, wiping the thin line of sweat on my forehead with the back of my hand. My pulse still raced from the adrenaline rush of a well-placed tee shot. I offered a silent thank-you to the sky for not embarrassing myself. The first shot was always the hardest.

Ryan was the first one to march down the fairway. One of the Hamilton High players, oddly, waited for me to catch up.

"So, you're a girl," the boy said to me with a smirky smile that dimpled both of his cheeks. Gangly with reddish-brown hair and freckles that matched, he made it difficult not to return that smile.

"Um, yeah?" I said, biting down on my lip.

"I didn't know girls were allowed in this division."

My shoulders shrugged. "I guess they are now."

"I'm Nate. Fred, right?"

"Yep, that's my name,"

"Strange name," he said.

"So I've been told." *A few hundred times.*

As we continued down the center of the fairway, his eyes drifted from the top of my head all the way down to my shoes. I pretended not to notice. "Where'd you learn to play?" We walked toward my ball. It was perched perfectly above a tuft of fairway grass, straight in front of the putting green.

"Here." My tone was matter-of-fact. I looked from the ball to the green and judged it to be roughly 120 yards.

"Your parents are members?" Like most of the other players, he wore sunglasses, but it didn't take bionic eyes to see the surprise behind his eyes.

"Sort of." I stopped. Grimacing, I lifted the heavy strap and dropped my bag to the ground. I rubbed my shoulder where the strap cut across. Then I pulled out a seven-iron.

The other players stood next to their balls, leaning on their bags, waiting on me. Since I was farthest from the hole, I went first. Just like at the tee box, I took two practice swings and then approached the ball to swing my iron. The ball sailed straight into the air and landed just below the green. I frowned. I'd wanted it closer. Now I had only two strokes to make par.

The other boys hit their balls. Ryan's ball landed on the green while Nate and his partner overswung and sent their balls sailing over the hole like errant water jets. They all proceeded toward the flag. Walking along the cart path, a small group of parents, along with the gray-haired guy with the notebook, followed my foursome. Coach Nickerson drove along in a golf cart, stopping to watch while feverishly jotting notes on his clipboard before speeding ahead to monitor the next group.

I pulled out my wedge and pitched my ball right up onto the green, exactly as I pictured it in my mind. It landed with a satisfied *plop* and rolled within two feet of the hole. *Easy putt,* I thought, relieved. Someone on the cart path clapped, but I didn't turn. I didn't want to break my concentration. I was too busy picturing how I would sink the ball into the hole with my putter, just as soon as the other boys landed their balls onto the green.

I marched straight up to my ball and marked its spot with a penny, my marker, and dropped the ball in my front pocket. All of the other boys used gold and silver markers, probably engraved with their names like everything else. I should care but I didn't. Not when I could taste the par I was about to make while the other boys in my foursome would be lucky to bogey. My fingertips tingled around my putter, waiting.

Ryan reached the hole in two strokes, but he had a long putt. The Hamilton High boys reached the hole in three strokes but with shorter putts. I was the only player with a reasonable chance at par. At the end of the cart path closest to the green, Notebook Guy scribbled furiously across a page.

Ryan putted first. His putter made a high-pitched *clink* when he struck the ball. The ball rolled several feet past the hole, and I smiled inwardly again even when I knew I should have been more supportive. Nate made his putt, making par; his partner did not. I waved on Ryan to make his putt. He sank it, saving par.

And then it was my turn. Notebook Guy stopped writing long enough to watch me. I took two practice swings, my habit before every hole, studied the green and looked for ruts or curves that would interrupt the line of my ball. Then I approached the ball, closed my eyes briefly and pulled back my old putter. It didn't make the pretty tinkling sound that Ryan's did, but a fancy putter didn't matter when your ball rolled confidently across a green, caught the edge of the cup and then dropped right in as if there was no other place for it to go.

Lone Butte High School won the hole.

RYAN

CHAPTER 14

I SHOULD HAVE WAITED FOR FRED and walked with her to the second hole to discuss strategy, but I couldn't. Graham Frazier was too busy yapping in my ear.

"Jeez, a girl on your team. That's pretty brutal," Graham said to me as if our team should be embarrassed. "I bet Seth was pissed." He grinned as he chomped on an enormous piece of gum, spitting as he talked. My nose wrinkled from the overwhelming smell of peppermint.

I knew Graham was trash-talking, just like Nate was probably doing to Fred. I watched him gab to her on the fairway. The Hamilton High players were known for it. And why not? It worked. They'd succeeded in whipping our butts the past two years.

I noted with some satisfaction that Nate's charms didn't seem to be affecting Fred. It was like she was in a parallel universe with her frozen expression. Her eyes never stopped scanning the fairway. I bit back a satisfied smile. Her disinterest must have been driving Nate crazy, never mind that her swing had so far been pretty near perfect. She hadn't given up a single shot. Nate and Graham had to be worried.

Oddly, Fred didn't seem to notice that her golf bag had gained at least ten pounds since this morning. How could she not notice? I wished she would. I'd almost told her about it during the bus ride, but my words had come out all wrong. Instead of telling her about the bricks, I'd made up a lame question and a roundabout way of getting her some strokes on her score. I didn't see how she was going to make it through the tournament without a little help. *I am such a tool!* If I had just been honest about the bricks, maybe we could have had a good laugh and moved on.

I caught myself before my emotions went whack and ruined my game. I shouldn't be thinking that way about Fred. I shouldn't be thinking about her at all. It was wrong, all wrong. Because of her, Seth had lost his spot on the team. I should despise her, not defend her. Let her fend for herself and find her own way.

"Maybe Fred is just having a little bit of beginner's luck?" Graham snickered over his shoulder at Fred and Nate. He blew a wet bubble with his gum.

I nodded and forced a tight smile when I really wanted to take my club to Graham's slimy mouth.

"Hey, is she Indian?"

I didn't answer.

"Never seen an Indian girl golfer before. That's a new one." He paused. "What's the next hole?"

"A par three," I said without looking at him. Suddenly walking alongside Fred didn't sound so bad. At least she was quiet. I glanced casually at her as she stood in the next tee box, staring down the fairway, probably picturing where she was going to place her next drive.

"You're up first," Nate said to Fred as the rest of us dropped our bags and began rummaging for the appropriate club.

Fred pulled out her driver again. The handful of spectators from the first hole had grown larger, and they weren't watching us. Everybody's eyes were drilled on Fred. If she was bothered by the attention, it didn't show. There were a couple of parents, a few students from school, a reporter from the school newspaper and some older guy with a notebook. He seemed to be particularly interested in Fred. A college recruiter, maybe, but that didn't seem right. It was too early in the season.

Fred tossed a few blades of grass in the air, checking for wind direction as the green slivers floated to the ground. Then she wound the end of her ponytail in her right hand as she squinted across the fairway and pursed her lips. Her hair wrapped like a silk rope around her finger, all black and shiny. The breeze lifted the wispy strands around her face as everything around her moved in slow motion: the branches from the mesquite trees, the wave of the grass, even the way the sleeves of her golf shirt fluttered at her elbows. Just like at the golf store when she had fingered the white pair of shoes.

I blinked, reminding myself not to stare. And to seriously get a better grip on reality.

I watched Fred approach the ball one final time. She took her typical two practice swings. Then she pulled back her long driver above her shoulders and swung, bending her elbows at exactly the right angles. Her ball made a perfect arc into the sky before landing in the middle of the green. Another straight shot. The spectators clapped quietly. They usually never clapped.

"Good shot, Fred," Nate said, and my jaw clenched from the sound of his voice. I didn't trust Nate.

I swung next, followed by Nate and then Graham. Only Fred and Graham reached the green on their first shot, but Graham had the longer putt.

After teeing off, I quickly slipped my club into my bag and then caught up to Nate and Fred as they started down the fairway, my clubs clanging around in my bag as I jogged.

"I need to talk to Fred," I said behind Nate. He didn't get the hint. *"Alone,"* I added, walking between them, forcing Nate to pull away.

Nate finally pulled back but not without flipping me the finger.

Fred adjusted the strap higher on her bag, but she didn't stop. Her eyes stayed focused on the fairway, the greens, anything but me. I might as well have been invisible.

"You should watch what you say to Nate," I told her as soon as Nate left us.

Fred's neck pulled back. "Why?"

"Because he's trying to mess with your head."

Fred shook her head as if I was crazy. "He's only being nice."

"*Nice,*" I sputtered with an automatic eye roll. "Sure," I said.

But her voice got louder. "Yeah, *nice.* You've heard the word, haven't you?"

"What's that supposed to mean?"

"Exactly what I said." We approached the ridge just below the putting green where my ball had landed.

I sighed. I tried to concentrate on my ball, on the next swing—anything but Fred Oday—as we rested our bags next to my ball. Then Fred rubbed her right shoulder, exactly where the strap cut across her chest. I cringed inwardly, knowing why.

Nate's ball was farthest, so he swung first.

"Everything isn't what it appears to be, Fred," I whispered, "especially at tournaments."

"Tell me about it," she muttered.

"With the Hamilton players, I mean," I added quickly. "They'll do and say anything to win."

"Maybe not today."

"Don't bet on it."

Fred leaned against her bag. "Why are you so concerned? Why are you talking to me all of a sudden like you care? You've been glaring at me all day. All week."

I pulled back. *She noticed?*

"I think it's you I need to worry about," she said, and I should have told her she was right.

Instead, I dragged my tongue across my dry lips. "Maybe I want to win, too," I said, lifting my bag onto my shoulder after Nate swung at his ball. It dropped on the far end of the green, giving him another long putt he'd be lucky to sink with one shot.

Fred chuckled. "Well, that's the smartest thing I've heard you say all week." She rotated her right shoulder.

I looked from Nate's ball to Fred and then to the bottom of her sagging bag. How did she not notice? I had the urge to tell her about the bricks, but when it came right down to it, I couldn't do it. Because if I did, then Fred would think I was worse than Nate Bellows or any of the other players on the Hamilton High team.

And she'd be absolutely right.

Fred

CHAPTER 15

WHEN COACH LANNON SPED down the path in his golf cart, the grin stretching across his face was touching both of his ears. Lone Butte High School was ahead of Hamilton High by two strokes, a first. And it was due mostly to my two birdies on the third and sixth holes. The coach grinned like he already tasted victory.

I should have been beaming, but I couldn't. By the time we'd finished the seventeenth hole, I was ready to pass out. My skin was flushed all over like I had a killer fever.

As Coach Lannon approached Ryan and me, his smile faded. "What's the matter?" His eyes darted to Ryan, as if Ryan had done something wrong.

Ryan swallowed as he and I stepped alongside Coach's golf cart for what seemed like an inquisition. My bag landed heavily on the pavement.

"Just kind of warm today. I'm a little out of breath." I forced a tight smile as I leaned against my bag and rubbed my shoulder. I didn't want him to think for one second that I was giving up, not when Lone Butte had a decent chance at winning the tournament. *Just one more hole,* I reminded myself. *Just one more. You can do it.* If I wimped out and didn't finish, the boys would have one more reason to label me a fluke. Or worse.

"Take another water bottle." The coach reached behind the seat in his golf cart for the cooler. "Here." He handed me a new bottle. It felt deliciously cold against my fingers, and I pressed it against my forehead, savoring how the droplets cooled my skin. "Why didn't you call me on your cell?" the coach said, looking between Ryan and me. I wasn't sure whose cell phone he meant me to use.

I dragged the back of my hand across my lips, letting the cool water coat the inside of my throat. "I forgot mine at home," I lied. *Along with my private jet.* "I'm fine. Really. The water helps. Thank you." I took another long sip and then massaged my right shoulder with my thumb.

"What's wrong with your arm?" He continued to scrutinize my every move.

"Nothing," I lied again. "It'll be fine."

The coach's eyes narrowed. For a second he reminded me of Dad. That's how Dad would have looked at me, too. To be honest, I was a little touched by it even as I was within inches of a full-blown heatstroke.

"Really," I added.

Coach Lannon's lips pursed as he considered this. "Okay, then. If you say so. You're up next on eighteen. The last foursome just drove from the tee. Not too much longer now. Hang in there, Freddy." He lifted his sunglasses back on his face and then turned the golf cart around. "You, too, Ryan," he said over his shoulder. "And keep an eye on her."

RYAN

CHAPTER 16

FRED AND I WALKED ALONGSIDE each other to the eighteenth tee box.

I had to slow my pace. Walking had become an effort for her because of her bag. It practically dragged behind her across the fairway.

"Fred, there's something I need—" I blurted, but Graham yelled at me from the tee box.

"Berenger!"

I turned reluctantly and lifted my sunglasses. I was tempted to flip him off.

"You're up!" he said impatiently. "It'll be dark soon. Coach just said we gotta move faster."

I let my sunglasses drop to my chest and squinted at the darkening horizon behind Graham. Slivers of purple and orange framed the top of South Mountain. In less than an hour, it would be too dark to play. We were running out of time.

Fred panted beside me till we reached the tee box and our nervous Hamilton High partners. Clearly Fred had not made their day any easier, and frustration seeped all over their faces.

Fred's bangs stuck to her forehead. She ran a finger through them, lifting thick strands off her skin. Guilt hammered at my temples as I watched her struggle with the heat.

"You go first," I told her. "I need..." But then I stammered. "I need to figure out which club to use," I added lamely, fumbling with my bag. Even though on the final par-4 hole of the course, it was pretty clear which club I would use.

Fred nodded and trudged up the hill to the top of the last tee box, her driver clutched in her right hand. With her other hand, she massaged the shoulder that had been carrying the brunt of her golf bag all afternoon.

At the bottom of the tee box, I was alone. All eyes were glued on Fred. Quickly I grabbed her bag, gathered all the club shafts with both hands and dumped them in a pile on the grass. Then I turned the bag on its side. It was almost as tall as I was. With one eye on the tee box, I began to shake it from the bottom, coaxing out the three heavy bricks. The first two tumbled out easily and crashed into the grass; the third one got stuck underneath something at the bottom.

"Stupid bag," I mumbled, shaking it harder. If only Fred had owned a newer one, there'd have been no room for three oversize bricks. I set the bag on its side again and bent down on one knee. My arm reached in all the way to my armpit. My fingertips grazed one end of the brick. It scraped against my fingers like sandpaper.

"Berenger!" Graham boomed again from the top of the tee box. I stretched my arm another inch, wincing, as I squinted against the sunset.

Almost got it, I thought just as the crowd from the other side of the tee box clapped. Fred must have hit another awesome drive straight down the fairway. If I hadn't been wrestling with a brick, I might have smiled.

Just as I opened my eyes and pulled out the third brick, someone said my name. It was like a whisper.

"Ryan?"

My eyes popped open, but the sun still blinded me, despite my sunglasses.

"What are you doing?"

My body froze. Sweat dripped down into my eyes. I sat squatting on the ground with a red brick in one hand and two more stacked next to my knees.

Fred.

I squinted up at her. The sun behind her back turned the tips of her hair all crimson.

Her voice got louder. "What are you doing?" Her speech slowed. "With. My. Bag?"

She bent down on one knee so that we were eye level. The whites of her almond-shaped eyes grew wide as they drifted from the brick in my hand to the others stacked next to me.

I panicked, trying to come up with some reasonable explanation.

Finally, I stood, rising one agonizing vertebra at a time. My own gaze dropped to the ground along with the third brick in my hand. I let it crash to the grass against the other two. It cracked in half. Carefully, I lowered my voice to mask its rawness. "I can explain," I said as I looked down at Fred, still kneeling.

Fred's head started to bob. "How could you..." Her voice rose with disbelief as her lower lip started to tremble. Her eyes bounced from the bricks to me and back again. "Why do you hate me so much?"

My shoulders caved forward, her words hitting me like a gut punch. My mouth opened but then snapped shut. For once, coming up with the perfect lie wasn't so easy. And the betrayal that filled Fred's face shamed me more than words. I was a shit and Fred knew it.

"Berenger!" Graham thundered again.

Fred's voice cracked. "You're up." She nodded her chin over her shoulder at the tee box. "You'd better get going." Without looking at me, she gathered up her clubs and slipped them carefully into her bag, one by one.

It was difficult to turn away and march up the hill to the tee box as if nothing had happened.

Lone Butte High School was about to win its first tournament against Hamilton High in two years, thanks to a quiet girl with mismatched clubs and a plaid golf bag, but I hardly felt like celebrating.

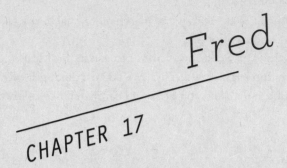

Fred

CHAPTER 17

"I MAY HAVE TO QUIT," I told Dad after the golf tournament.

We sat outside our front door on white plastic chairs, watching what was left of the day as it faded behind the Estrella Mountains. Our two Labs lay with their round snouts buried between their paws, nestled at our feet. I fiddled with a new golf ball, tossing it absently between my hands. I hadn't lost a single ball during the tournament, not like some of the boys who put new balls into the water or deep into the desert. There was almost as much satisfaction in that as winning the first tournament of the season. But after what had happened, I thought maybe it would be my last. The boys on my team, Ryan Berenger in particular, were pure evil. I didn't need them. I had enough problems.

But Dad's eyes narrowed. It was impossible to ignore them. They crinkled in the corners like they always did when he was troubled. He studied my expression like it was some kind of riddle to be solved. He'd been watching me—studying me—ever since he'd found me at the van after the tournament. I'd sat on the back bumper, waiting for him with my head in my hands. When he'd asked me what was wrong, I'd replied, "Tired. Just tired." And I was—dead tired. But it was so much more than that, more than I could put into words.

Finally, Dad said evenly, "What's changed since yesterday?" Ignoring him a second longer was not an option.

"Nothing," I said. "That's the problem. The guys don't want me on the team. I can feel it. I'm not part of their little country-club clique. They've been playing together forever, and I'm the outsider. Always will be." I didn't dare tell him they'd sabotaged my golf bag. That would make him angry and upset and wouldn't change anything. Worse, he'd tell Trevor, and there was no telling what my brother would do. Besides, I was more irritated with myself than anything. How was it that I'd carried that dang bag for eighteen holes and hadn't realized something was wrong with it? Was I that clueless? And how nice of Ryan Berenger to grow a conscience—on the eighteenth hole! They'd all probably enjoyed one great big collective laugh over the whole thing on the bus ride home. I'd have walked home on my hands and knees before I'd ridden back with any of them on that claustrophobic bus.

"Only two weeks ago the golf team was all you wanted. Now you've had a change of heart? Already?"

More like a close encounter with a heart attack.

I exhaled with the weight of all the bad thoughts taking space in my head. I stared up at the Estrella Mountains, wishing that everything would fade away. "I don't know, Dad." I looked straight into the sunset. "Maybe you and Trevor were right. Maybe being on this team is a bad idea."

Dad snorted. "For you or them?"

I didn't answer. I sank lower in my chair. The Lab at my feet lifted its head.

"Well?" he prodded.

"I guess for them. All I wanted to do was play. I wasn't expecting special treatment. That's the last thing I want."

Dad chuckled. "So, play. Enjoy. Have fun for once." He leaned forward in his chair. "Pretend those boys are invisible. Or," he said slowly, "you could try to fit in."

My eyes widened. *Fit in with a bunch of spoiled white boys? It would be easier to pretend I'm Princess Kate.*

"What happened today anyway? You won, right? How bad could winning be?"

My hands began to fidget. I tossed the ball between them to give them something to do. "Is Trevor coming home tonight?" Maybe talking with Trevor would help.

"Don't change the subject." Dad leaned forward. "What happened today? What aren't you telling me?"

My shoulders shrugged indifferently, but it felt forced. "Nothing that would surprise you."

A flock of doves cooed in a paloverde tree behind the trailer, filling the heavy silence. Somewhere in the distance, a coyote howled, and the dogs sauntered away to investigate. I closed my eyes, letting the soft breeze brush my cheeks. It was good to finally feel cool air again. Inside the trailer, the summer had dragged on far too long.

"You can't give up so easily, Fred," Dad said. His words surprised me. "Besides, I don't think that coach of yours would let you quit if you tried." He chuckled and shook his head when my eyes opened to look at him. "I thought the coach's eyes were going to pop out of his head from excitement when I saw him standing next to the bus."

"Yeah," I said. "They sure did." Although that's not what I remembered. I only remembered watching Ryan sulk his way back to the bus, his usual scowl plastered across his face, ignoring anyone's attempts at conversation. He'd never even apologized for the bricks. Not really.

"Practice tomorrow?"

"No." I rubbed my right shoulder, making a circular motion with my thumb. The muscle still throbbed where the golf strap had cut across my skin. A day off would be a good thing, but I was still going to try to play the Ahwatukee golf course on Saturday. The golf pro at the clubhouse usually let me walk on and play for free if it wasn't too busy.

"When's your next tournament?"

"Wednesday."

"Where?"

"Some country club on the west side. We play Glendale High, I think." The tournament schedule was in my nightstand next to my bed. I checked it every night. I had it memorized.

"So, now you're not giving up?" Dad tilted his head in a way that said he already knew the answer.

I smirked. "Guess not."

"Good." Dad rose from his chair just as Mom appeared at the screen door.

"Fred?" she called through the screen.

"Yeah?" I said.

"Can you tell me why a sports writer from the *Arizona Republic* is on our phone? He wants to speak with you."

My eyelids froze open. I turned a fraction toward Dad without blinking.

"Well?" Mom prodded. "He says he wants to talk to Fred Oday, the girl golfer he watched play today for Lone Butte High School." The ripped screen door creaked open and then slapped shut. "Someone want to tell me what the hell's going on around here?" Her arms crossed over her chest as she stood on the stoop.

Dad's mouth pulled back. Then he smiled crookedly at me. "Guess it's time we tell your mother what you've been up to. The cat's out of the golf bag."

For the first time all day, I heard myself laugh. But it was fleeting.

"Your daughter is an official member of the Lone Butte High School boys' golf team," Dad said, following behind me. He didn't bother to hide the proud tone in his voice.

"Golf team? Boys?" Mom stepped down a stair.

"Yeah, Mom," I said. "I'm on the team this year."

"Well, isn't that the dumbest waste of time," she said, her eyes wide, her head shaking.

My lips pressed together as I reached for the screen door and then the phone in the kitchen. I needed to get as far away as possible.

Would it ever be far enough?

RYAN

CHAPTER 18

I WAS RUMMAGING FOR a microwave dinner in the freezer when Dad breezed into the house from the garage.

I didn't turn when his keys slid across the countertop behind me. We hadn't spoken since the day I caught him holding hands with the family's hairstylist. And it if it were up to me, I'd keep it that way.

"Hey, sport," Dad said.

My jaw clenched.

"Where's your mom?"

I counted to three. Slowly. "Still at work, I think," I said without turning. My fingertips burned from holding three different frozen microwavable dinners—mac and cheese, chicken burrito and meat loaf. I chose the burrito and tossed the others back inside the freezer.

Dad put his briefcase on the tile floor and moved closer to the counter. His blue tie hung over his right shoulder. "Sorry I couldn't make it to your tournament today. Trial ran a little longer than I thought it would."

My shoulders shrugged. I hadn't expected Dad to show. Why was he apologizing? He hadn't made it to a tournament in two years. I closed the refrigerator door and padded across the tile in my bare feet to the cupboard next to the sink. I reached for a plate.

"How'd you do?"

"We won," I said without enthusiasm, still avoiding his gaze. Mostly.

Dad's eyes widened with obvious surprise. "Well, now." He chuckled, slapping his hands together. He fist-pumped in my direction but I ignored it, pretending that my hands were busy with the intricacies of tearing open the frozen dinner. "That's fantastic!" Dad said anyway. "How many strokes?"

I sighed inwardly while I took the time to search for a microwavable plate. Unfortunately the cupboard was loaded with stacks of them. "Two," I said.

"Wish I could have seen it." He sighed. "How'd you do?"

"Five over par," I said reluctantly. The more information I offered, the more questions he'd ask.

Dad's mouth pulled back in a grimace. Not good. "Five over par?" Not exactly what he'd hoped for. "Any big winners on your team?"

I slit open the cardboard package with a knife. I placed it in the microwave and set the timer. "Yep," I said.

Dad's eyes bulged. "Well, are you going to tell me?" His hands moved to his hips. "Was it Seth? Zack?" Dad knew all the players on the team. All of their parents belonged to the same country club.

I sniffed. "No," I said, leaning against the counter. "A new kid on the team."

"Who?" His voice got louder.

"Fred Oday."

"Oday, Oday," he said, eyes narrowed, thinking aloud. "Do his folks belong to the club?"

I chuckled darkly. I remembered a man approaching the van where Fred had sat after the tournament—the same rusted van that had idled behind me the first day of golf practice. The man's hands had been dark like river rocks and his overalls covered with grass stains. They'd climbed inside the van together like they knew each other. "I don't think so," I said finally.

"Humph," Dad said, surprised. "Well, you should invite him out one Saturday to play with us. I'd like to meet this rising star."

I couldn't help another air-chuckle. It felt all wrong and all right at the same time, especially when I pictured Dad's stunned expression if I were to bring Fred Oday to the club for that round of Saturday golf. I'd almost give up my Jeep just to see it.

Dad looked across the counter at me like he wanted to ask something more but decided against it at the last second. He reached for his briefcase and then turned for the stairs.

"Hey, Dad," I said.

Dad stopped. "Yes, son?"

"I saw you at the mall the other night."

His back straightened. "Yeah?"

"I saw you."

He chuckled. "Yes, I gathered that. Why didn't you come talk to me?"

"I saw you with Stacey What's-Her-Name. The lady who cuts our hair."

His eyes widened, surprised. "Yeah? So?"

"So?" My eyes widened like his. Not quite the reaction I expected. "You were holding her hand."

Dad laughed a little nervously. "Look, we were talking about her bankruptcy. I'm helping her file papers."

Okay, that was a new one.

Dad's voice grew louder. "I don't know what you think you saw, but I don't appreciate your tone or the implication. If you've got something to say, then spill it."

I wanted to believe him, but I didn't. Maybe it was because he was never around anymore. Maybe it was because I was feeling like such a shithead. "Forget it."

Dad turned away with a heavy exhale.

"Hey, Dad..."

"Yeah?" He stopped, his tone sounding more tired than before.

Instead of pressing him on Stacy, I switched topics. "Would you mind if I invited a few friends over Friday night?"

Dad's lip curled in obvious relief. "Don't see why not. Your mother's at a conference all weekend and I'll probably have to work through Sunday." He made a show of dragging his hand over his chin like he really had to mull it over. But then one corner of his mouth turned up in a lopsided smile. "Not too loud, though. Okay?"

"Sure, Dad," I said with mock obedience. "Not too loud."

The next morning, I searched for Fred before school.

Since there was no golf practice on Fridays, I figured she wouldn't be hanging by the gym or lugging her golf bag into Coach Lannon's office. And unless she was hiding in the girls' locker room, I was determined to find her. I'd decided last night that we had to talk. Ignoring her not only made everything worse, it backfired. Big-time.

After I parked my Jeep in the student lot, I walked through the courtyard where everyone met up before the first warning bell. I squinted across dozens of student clusters but didn't see her. But then I realized that I'd never seen Fred chillin' in the courtyard, at least not since I'd started paying attention.

I made one fast loop around the outside of the school, waving at a few of my friends, but not slowing long enough to talk. Fred wasn't anywhere outside. That much was certain.

I moved inside. I proceeded first toward the cafeteria, passing Sam Tracy and Peter Begay outside a row of lockers. I thought about asking them but decided against it, especially when I was pretty certain that the big dude glared at me.

Still anxious to find her, I jogged across campus toward the library. Just my busted luck: yesterday Fred Oday was everywhere. Today, she'd disappeared.

I reached the double-glass library doors in minutes. Breathing heavily, I scanned the wooden tables filling the middle of the room. They were all empty, except for the usual dusty reference books that no one ever opened. The room was so quiet that I could hear the soft hum of the librarian's computers behind the empty reference desk. I checked the two rows of cubicles closest to the library stacks. They lined the entire side of one wall. I walked down the middle, my eyes bouncing back and forth over the gray cubicle walls for the tops of any heads with shiny black hair. Most of the cubicles were empty, too.

I sighed glumly when I reached the end of the row. I really wanted to talk to Fred before class, and this was my only chance.

Then I saw a flash of something black in the corner cubicle next to the book stacks marked *Ww–Zz*. I jogged closer, and my breathing quickened all over again.

It was Fred.

With her back toward me, she huddled over a thick book and scattered notebooks.

My throat turned dry.

A strand of her hair twirled between the fingers in her left hand as she tapped her book with a pencil in her right.

I pulled back my shoulders. "Fred?"

She jumped in her seat and turned.

I lifted my palms. "Sorry. Didn't mean to freak you out."

One hand pressed against her chest. "Ryan?" Her eyes widened. "What are you doing here?"

"Got a minute?" I swallowed again. Hard.

She nodded reluctantly. I hadn't exactly given her a choice.

I bent down next to her chair so that our eyes were level. "I need to talk to you."

Fred pulled away, as far as her chair would allow. "Um, okay." Her voice was unmistakably cautious.

My eyes darted to my watch. The bell was going to ring any second. "I just wanted to tell you how sorry I am. About your bag, I mean. I never really got the chance to tell you yesterday. Anyway, what we did was stupid. And lame. We shouldn't have done that." The words tumbled out a little faster than how I practiced.

Fred blinked. "We? Who's we?"

My lips pressed together. There was no way I could keep this from her, especially now. "Me and Seth," I said finally. I seriously needed some water.

"Seth Winter?" Her eyes narrowed. "What's Seth got to do with this?"

"Don't you know?" How could she not know? Everybody knew. Everybody knew ten minutes after Coach Lannon had kicked him off the team.

But Fred shook her head, confused. "Know what?"

"You took Seth's spot on the team. He got axed."

Her eyes narrowed.

"You know, kicked off the team?" I added.

Then her eyes began to blink faster. Finally she nodded. "Okay, now I get it," she whispered. "I didn't know. The coach didn't tell me—"

"But that doesn't mean what we did was right," I said quickly. "I wish we hadn't done it. It was really lame. I'm sorry." My chest lightened just saying the words.

"But why did you wait so long to tell me? I almost passed out on the ninth hole!"

My knees began to ache a little from stooping. I stood when they started to tingle. Fred's gaze traveled up to meet mine, making it harder for me to concentrate. "I thought about it—telling you, I mean—but I didn't. That's all I can say. It was wrong and I'm sorry. Really, I am. I wanted you to know." Jeez, I was yapping like Graham Frazier.

Fred turned in her chair so that she was facing her book, long enough for me to catch my breath. I watched as she fidgeted with a page, and I wondered if I should just leave.

But then I said, "I also wanted to invite you to a party tonight. To try to make up for it."

Fred turned, her eyes widening with more surprise. "Is this another joke?"

I shook my head and bit back a nervous smile. "No joke. Totally serious this time."

"But...why?"

"Why?" I said, drawing back. "Does that mean you'll come?" She didn't look convinced. Smiling at her question probably wasn't helping.

She raised her chin. "Where is it?"

I bent down to my knees again, almost collapsing with relief. I picked up the pen resting next to her. "My house." I motioned for a page in her notebook.

She surprised me again and passed me the whole notebook, slowly at first, like she was having second thoughts. And then she just pushed it toward me.

I wrote my address on the corner of a page. "Will you come?"

Fred cleared her throat. "I don't know. I'll...I'll have to check my schedule."

My eyebrows lifted. "Okay, that's cool. Bring your boyfriend, if you want."

"Boyfriend?"

"Yeah. Sam. The big dude. Isn't he your boyfriend?"

"No. Why would you say that?"

My shoulders lifted at the news. "Oh, I just figured. He's always walking with you. You know, before school, I mean." Great. I was starting to ramble again.

"He's not my boyfriend."

I drew back a breath. "Well, I really hope you can make it. It'll be awesome."

"I'll...I'll try" was all that she'd promise before her eyes narrowed again. "Why are you being so nice all of a sudden?"

I stood, adjusted my backpack higher over my shoulder and said, "I'd just like a second chance. I figure we're on the same team. We might as well be friends."

Fred's lips turned up in one corner, just a little.

That had come out best of all, and I hadn't even practiced it.

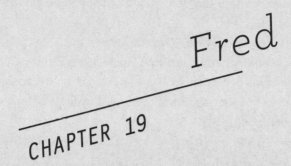

Fred

CHAPTER 19

I HAVE TO CHECK MY SCHEDULE?

I walked to English class dazed. *Please tell me I didn't really say* schedule.

I groaned inwardly as I stared into a sea of bodies, all struggling to swim upstream to their next class while I rehashed my library conversation with Ryan.

A warning bell buzzed throughout the school, grounding my attention. I had forgotten which warning bell, which class period and basically where I needed to be. I might have even forgotten my own name. So I simply kept walking, cocooned by backpacks and shoulders, the Lameness That Is Me song on replay in my head. *I suddenly have a schedule? I have appointments? Why did I say that to Ryan?! Please, Fred. Get over yourself. But Ryan Berenger actually thought I had a boyfriend....*

My internal chastisement skidded to a halt at the sound of a certain breathless voice somewhere in front of me. It squeaked, more noisily than all others, obviously loud on purpose. I tiptoed a few steps to locate its blond head. For once, Gwyneth was talking about something that compelled my attention.

"I'm pretty sure Ryan's going to ask his parents if I can come to his family's cabin over Thanksgiving. They go every year."

My stomach tightened.

"That is so cool," another girl gushed. "Do you go every year, too?"

"I'd like to," Gwyneth said, "but you know Ryan."

No, I don't. Just when I thought I knew Ryan Berenger, he'd hook a piece of his personality off the fairway and into the weeds. Like inviting me to a party out of the blue. I walked faster, eager for more eavesdropping.

I had to wedge between two freshmen who were walking directly behind Gwyneth and her other blond-headed friend. "Sorry," I muttered to the boy on my left as I accidentally knocked the backpack off his shoulder. "I'm late for class."

I finally pushed my way directly behind Gwyneth, close enough to smell the wake of the grapefruit gum snapping in her mouth.

"Anyway," she said, "I'm pretty sure his parents expect me to bunk with Riley but *so* not happening. Ryan and I have other ideas." They started to giggle, and my stomach lurched.

Ugh.

What did Ryan Berenger see in this girl? Was he sleeping with her? Gah! I didn't even want to picture that. Why did he want to be in the same time zone as Gwyneth? My mind drifted to a whole bunch of brand-new questions.

Before I knew it, I found myself in English class, seated in my usual spot.

My gaze dipped nonchalantly to my watch, and I wished the hands would move faster.

Somewhere in the back of the room, Ryan was sitting at his desk, listening to Mrs. Weisz's lecture on nineteenth-century literature. I wondered if his mind was drifting like mine to places it shouldn't. I imagined that every so often his gaze might sweep across the back of my head, and my skin tingled all the way down to my toes at the idea without my really understanding why. But then I reminded myself that this was the same boy who dated Gwyneth Riordan and who'd planted three bricks in my golf bag as a joke.

Some joke.

And then, oddly, I pressed my palm against my mouth and smiled into my hand. At least he'd apologized. And personally invited me to his party.

With my other hand, I doodled a golf shoe in the margin of my notebook, trying to make a show of pretending to listen to Mrs. Weisz's lecture even though what I was really trying to figure out was how in the world I could show up to Ryan's party. Would anybody talk to me? Would he? Would I have a good time? Wouldn't it be wiser to snag a shift with Mom at the restaurant instead? My brand-new golf shoes were finally within reach of my wallet. Convincing Dad to let me drive the truck into Phoenix on a Friday night would require superhuman persuasive skills, too.

I frowned at my options and sank lower in my seat. I wrote Ryan's name in my notebook and then quickly scratched it out. I nibbled on the end of my pen. Then I wrote, *Party?*

A party on the other side of Pecos Road with people I barely knew just didn't feel right.

But then, why did I ache to go so badly?

RYAN

CHAPTER 20

I PRETENDED TO WATCH Mrs. Weisz at the front of class when I was really studying the shape of Fred's head.

Her hair hung in soft waves all around her. Sometimes she'd move in a way that would spill her hair forward, exposing a smooth bare shoulder. And then someone would press that giant Slow-Motion Universe Button again.

Fred was the only one taking notes. Her fingers swept across her notebook, and she paused every few minutes to nibble on the tip of her pen. I figured her penmanship was probably as perfect as her name on that *Gatsby* book, each letter slanted and curved at all the right angles.

"What's she droning on about?" Seth nudged me with a sharp elbow.

"Huh?" I turned. For a split second, I thought he meant Fred. But Fred wasn't talking. "No clue," I said finally, turning my attention back to the front again. And Fred.

"Awesome," Seth replied wryly. "Big help."

I ignored him. I was too busy wondering for the hundredth time whether Fred Oday would show up at my party. Part of me was pretty sure she wouldn't. And who could blame her? But then the anxious part of me wished she would. Bad. *Real* bad.

I'd already told Seth that the joke was an epic fail. The news had seemed to bother him, but I figured Seth would get over it. He was always playing jokes on people—friends, family, even our math teacher, Mr. LaFruit. Freshman year, Seth had replaced all of Mr. LaFruit's whiteboard pens with permanent black markers and blamed it on Troy Bean. The sad thing was Mr. LaFruit believed Seth. Teachers always did. He had that kind of innocent face that no one ever doubted, especially teachers. Me, on the other hand, I always looked guilty whether I did anything or not. Just ask my parents.

Seth knew about the party tonight, and of course he was invited, but I hadn't told him I'd mentioned it to Fred. Yet. Knowing him, he'd go a little ballistic at first, but then he'd accept it. I'd get him to see that we owed it to her. Anyway, I figured I'd wait to see if she even showed up. Given Seth's lame hazing joke with the bricks, I had my doubts.

Seth nudged me again with his elbow.

"Mr. Berenger? Mr. Winter?" Mrs. Weisz snapped.

I blinked to attention.

Mrs. Weisz was gripping both sides of the podium like she wanted to hurl it out a window.

Thirty heads swiveled to the back of the room, even Fred's.

"Is there a problem back there? Do you have a question?" Mrs. Weisz's tone was majorly doubtful.

"No question, Mrs. Weisz," Seth said. His eyes blinked wide with innocence.

That usually softened the blow. For him.

"I was just asking Ryan for a pencil," Seth added.

"Well, Mr. Berenger?" Mrs. Weisz tilted her head.

"Yes, ma'am?" I said.

Her eyes rolled at me. "Do you have a writing instrument that you could lend to Mr. Winter?" Her thumbs tapped the podium. "Something we usually call a pen or a pencil."

A few students snickered.

Seth snorted behind his hand, his face conveniently shielded behind Harry Graser's ba-dunk-a-dunk head.

"Um. Yeah, sure," I mumbled, reaching into the backpack underneath my chair. I tossed Seth a blue pen and then looked back at the front of the room. Part of Fred's face peered at me over her bare left shoulder. I couldn't see her mouth.

But from the way her black eyes sparkled, I was sure she was smiling at me.

I felt my own mouth smile in return, just a tiny one, before Fred turned around again. I wasn't sure if she caught it.

Then I looked at Seth. He was glaring at me. "Who are you smiling at like an idiot?" he whispered.

My smile faded instantly. *What?* I mouthed at Seth. But I felt my cheeks burn.

Seth's eyes narrowed as they darted from me to the front of the room and then back again. "Are you bent?" he said.

I didn't reply. But then, I didn't need to. He'd caught me smiling back at Fred.

Uncomfortable, I sank lower in my chair and absently drew a feather in my notebook. I was in deep already.

The hands on the kitchen clock wouldn't move fast enough.

I looked at it again while I paced across the tile. It was 6:30 on Friday night, and Dad still hadn't left for work yet, if that's where he was really headed.

He'd already informed the whole family that he needed to drive to downtown Phoenix and finish drafting a few more legal briefs. It was the usual excuse, especially when Mom was out of town.

But I didn't care, not really. As long as he was long gone before my friends arrived. Mom had left for some conference in Tucson before anyone had gotten home. She'd put a handwritten note next to the phone along with cash for a pizza or takeout, signing her note *MB* as if we wouldn't know who left it. And I could pretty much count on Riley to spend the evening in her bedroom, surfing on her laptop. It was turning into the perfect ripper.

Getting Dad out of the house was the final hurdle. And he wasn't making it easy.

Dad barreled down the staircase dressed in casual pants and a golf shirt. "Sure you don't want to order a few pizzas or something for your guests?" he asked as he reached for his car keys from a hook next to the kitchen door. He turned to place two crisp twenties next to the phone. I didn't bother to tell him that Mom had clipped two twenties to her note.

Instead, I poked my head inside the pantry next to the refrigerator. "Maybe," I said. "But there's plenty to eat here, too." *Along with the case of beer in the basement refrigerator.* "Maybe later," I added, so that Dad wouldn't return the bills to his wallet.

"How many friends tonight?"

"Not many," I said casually. "Six or seven." *Make that twenty.*

Dad smiled, pleased. "Is Seth invited?"

"Yep."

"Good. I like Seth. Nice kid. Haven't seen him in ages."

'Cause you're never around, I wanted to say. But tonight, the only thing I needed him to do was walk to the garage, climb into his car and leave me alone till Monday morning.

Dad's keys jingled in his front pocket.

Finally.

My jaw unclenched.

Dad's lips twitched like there was something more he wanted to say but had forgotten. Or forgotten how.

Dad turned for the garage.

Almost there.

But then he stopped. He cleared his throat. "Not too late tonight. Okay?"

I sighed inwardly and did my best to display the appropriate

Obedient Son skills. "Right, Dad," I said quickly—too quickly. I was ready to burst. "Not too late. Got it."

Dad smirked at my uncharacteristic attempt to be helpful. "And don't be too loud if you go outside. Don't need any angry neighbors."

"Sure, Dad," I said.

"Call me if anything comes up."

I took a few steps toward him, coaxing him toward the garage door with my body. "Will do," I said. Another forced smile.

"Well, okay, then. I'll see you later—"

The doorbell rang.

Dad's face brightened, and my jaw clenched all over again. "I'll get that," he said. "Might be Seth. Wouldn't hurt to say hello, right?"

"No, Dad," I moaned. "That's okay. Really. I'll get it." This was so not cool.

But Dad was too fast. He marched to the front door with me trailing behind, my eyes burning holes in the back of his head. *Why couldn't he just leave when he said he would? Why the sudden interest in my life?*

Dad unlocked the heavy wooden door and pulled it open. I stood just behind him.

"Hi," said a voice that most definitely did not belong to Seth.

"Yes?" he said guardedly, like he was greeting a salesman selling water softeners. "Can I help you?"

"Is Ryan home?"

"Ryan?" Dad turned sideways to make room for me. We stood shoulder to shoulder in the doorway.

I felt my cheeks tighten, then flush, just a little. "Dad," I said as I dragged my tongue across my lips to coax them to move. "This is Fred Oday. The new player on the golf team I was telling you about." Beside me, Dad's entire body stiffened. Then I heard a gush of air.

"Oh..." Dad cleared his throat and opened the door, still hesitant. "Um, well. Won't you come in?" It was an uncomfortably weird welcome.

Fred glanced at Dad and then me like she was having second thoughts. Her shoulders rose a little higher when she walked through the door, like they did at school. Tonight, though, she couldn't hide behind a golf bag.

Dad continued with his nervous throat-clearing before shifting from one brown loafer to the other. I'd rarely seen him at a loss for words.

"Hi, Fred," I said once I got control of the nervous grin stretching across my face.

Dad had been bugging me about meeting the new star of the Lone Butte High School varsity golf team. Here was his chance.

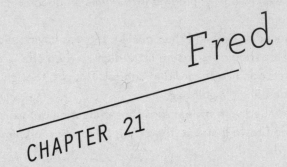

Fred

CHAPTER 21

COMING TO RYAN'S PARTY was a mistake. The nervous flicker in his dad's eyes confirmed it. Yep, I should have stayed on the other side of Pecos Road.

I'd seen that look before, unfortunately. Tons of times. Like the first day of freshman year when I'd sat alone in the cafeteria. Or when I went inside shops at the mall and didn't buy anything or, worse, lingered around a display case. Until recently, I'd seen that look at the golf course, too. The one that said I was welcome, but not really. Kind of hard to describe. But when it happens to you, you'll never forget it. It washes over you like a wave, pulling you lower like an undertow just because it can.

Ryan hadn't given me his phone number, only his address, and he hadn't specified a time so I'd taken a chance on driving into Phoenix just before it got dark, mostly to appease Dad. I was still weaning him from worrying about my night driving. Fortunately he was too tired to put up much of a fight tonight and had simply pressed the keys into my hand after giving me an abbreviated version of his *It's Not Your Behavior I'm Worried About, It's Everyone Else's* speech.

I'd parked near the corner and across the street, as far from the streetlamp's orange spotlight glow as possible.

I hadn't counted on meeting Ryan's father.

"So, Ryan tells me you're quite a golfer," Mr. Berenger said as he followed Ryan and me into a kitchen that was as big as the one at the Wild Horse Restaurant.

My gaze swept over all the cherry cabinetry and stainless-steel appliances. It was like walking into a department store. "Um, yes, I like to play golf," I managed numbly. My eyes landed on a lighted glass refrigerator that held nothing but wine bottles. There must have been at least fifty stacked inside.

"Your parents belong to the club?"

I paused and tried to control myself, pulling my shoulders back. "My father works at the club."

Mr. Berenger leaned against a granite countertop. It gleamed like wet river rock, and I fought the urge to run my fingertips across it. There wasn't the slightest smudge anywhere. "Oh, really?" He was intrigued. "Is he the pro?"

I swallowed. "No." I refused to let my gaze lower. "He's the groundskeeper."

Ryan's eyes flicked between us, and I got the sick sense that my answer pleased him.

"I see," Mr. Berenger replied in a small voice. He cleared his throat again and suddenly peeked at his gold wristwatch. "He must be quite a golfer, too? Like his daughter?" He said it like a question.

I smiled. "Not really. He's usually too tired to play after work."

"So, where'd you learn?"

"On the driving range." I paused. Then I answered the next question before he could ask it. "I just kind of taught myself by watching other people."

"You're kidding?" Mr. Berenger said, wide-eyed, the first honest reaction he'd had since I'd stepped through the front door.

I shook my head. "Not kidding."

"No lessons?" He said it like it was mathematically impossible.

"Not one."

Mercifully, Ryan said, "Dad, don't you have to be at work or something?" He did a head tilt toward the door off the kitchen, and I sucked back a tiny breath. "I really have to get ready for the party. You know, no parents allowed."

Mr. Berenger's palms lifted up. "Sure, son. Sorry, Fred. Didn't mean to hammer you. It's just that being a girl on a boys' varsity golf team—well, you got to admit it's kind of...different."

I nodded and smiled, but the sentiment was forced. Mr. Berenger didn't need to tell me about different. I had a Ph.D. in different. "I'm only on it because the school doesn't have a girls' team."

"Maybe next year."

"Yeah," I said. "Maybe next year."

Mr. Berenger's eyes darted to his watch one final, painfully long time. It was like he was having second thoughts about leaving. But then he waved goodbye and strode toward the garage door. "Have fun, kids. Don't forget what I told you, Ryan, about the noise." He threaded his car keys through his fingers. And then he was gone.

The air felt infinitely lighter.

Ryan turned to me. "Jeez." He rolled his eyes. "My dad's a lawyer. He's used to asking a lot of questions. It's kind of annoying. Sorry about the third degree."

I shrugged instinctively. "Sorry I showed up early."

He took a step closer and stuffed his hands in the front pockets of his faded jeans. "Don't be. I'm glad you came. I wasn't sure if you would."

I swallowed back the dryness in my throat. Ryan looked kind of cute, standing there all apologetic. I hadn't expected him to say that he was glad to see me, and I wasn't entirely unhappy to hear it either.

"Thirsty?" He turned to a refrigerator that was as tall as he was and five times as wide.

"Yeah."

"Beer? Coke? Water?"

"Water is good," I said quickly.

Ryan lifted a clear compartment inside the refrigerator door built especially for water bottles—stacks of them, and not the generic kind either. I'm pretty sure my mouth hung open a little. "Wow," I gushed.

"Wow, what?" Ryan turned, opened a water bottle and handed it to me.

"Wow," I stammered, summoning something better to say. "I'm sure thirsty."

Ryan chuckled. "Well, you came to the right place."

"I guess." I took a sip. "Can I help with anything?"

"Nope." He reached back inside the endless refrigerator and pulled out a shiny beer can.

My eyes narrowed automatically at the can. How I'd grown to loathe the sight of their flashy pretty colors and fancy letters.

"Something wrong?" He popped the tab back and lifted the can at me. "What? You don't drink?"

"Not...not usually," I lied as he opened a bag of potato chips and poured them into a silver bowl.

"Well, maybe later." He smiled, taking another sip. "Want to go wait outside? Everyone will be here in a little bit?"

"Sure," I exhaled. "Outside." *Where it should be easier to breathe.*

I followed Ryan past a wall of windows to a patio surrounded by desert that looked like a photograph, the kind you see in magazines and on postcards. The yard was more manicured than a golf course. All of the mesquite and palm trees dotting the rear fence were perfectly trimmed, along with the red oleanders and the sage bushes. They lined all of the flagstone pathways like giant mushrooms. White, twinkling lights peeked from every tree. Ryan pressed a button on a wall switch to light up a swimming pool that shimmered like turquoise. I stepped near the edge and peered at my reflection.

"Wow," I whispered again as Ryan jogged over to another wall switch next to a cabinet that held stacks of white towels. Each fluffy towel was perfectly folded.

The only thing missing was the desert smells that I was accustomed to—creosote, honeysuckle, sweet red earth baked all day from the sun. Here the air tightened around every one of my ribs whenever I breathed. Even the breezes moved differently, thick and confused, as if they were waiting to escape.

"What kind of music do you like?" Ryan said as he fiddled with another row of switches and buttons. Suddenly voices and guitars filled the backyard. They came from everywhere—the ground, the trees, the skies.

I swallowed. "Um, music?" I didn't have much time for music, not with homework and practice and weekend shifts at the restaurant. "Anything, really," I said, although that was a lie, too. I'd have bet Ryan never listened to—had never even heard of—Native Radio.

"Anything, huh," Ryan said, making a face as he switched through the channels. "How about this?" Electric-guitar music invaded the air. "This is one of my playlists."

"Playlists?"

"On my iPod?"

"Oh, yeah. Right," I answered over the music. Just because I didn't have my own iPod didn't mean I'd never heard of them. "This sounds good."

Ryan turned down the volume just before the doorbell rang. He frowned but said, "Good timing." The doorbell sounded hollow, like church bells. He held my gaze till the bell completed its little tune. Then he jogged back through the sliding glass. "I'll be back in a sec."

I fidgeted with the label on my water bottle while I walked one fast loop around the patio, mostly to calm my nerves. I wouldn't have minded a few more minutes with Ryan, alone. Maybe then I could have asked him a few questions for a change, like how many brothers and sisters he had or where he'd learned to play golf. The only thing I knew about Ryan Berenger was that he sat behind me in English, had a beautiful golf swing and parents who took him to fancy restaurants. And, for some bizarro-land reason, he compelled my attention despite my best efforts to ignore him.

I finally sat down in one of the white wicker chairs around a glass table facing the pool. I took a few more steadying breaths of the heavy air as I waited for the rest of Ryan's guests.

Just don't say anything stupid, Fred, I told myself. *Better yet, don't say much at all. You're pretty good at that.*

By the time the first few arrived, I'd almost completely peeled off the wrapper around my water bottle. I stuffed the sticky mess into the front pocket of my newest pair of jeans just as Seth Winter and Troy Bean bounced through the back door. Two girls I recognized from yearbook photos walked behind them. Seth held a brown paper bag in his arms.

Seth Winter. I wanted to crawl underneath the table.

"Whoa," Seth said the moment our eyes met. His blue ones widened to the size of quarters, enough to show that his pupils were dilated and glassy. The girl walking behind him bounced off his heels when he pulled back in midstride. But then he lifted his chin and grinned.

I didn't like his smile.

"Well, there. *Hola,* Pocahontas—I mean..."

My stomach tightened.

But Seth quickly faked a grimace. "Fred," he said finally.

"Winter!" Ryan said. He frowned at Seth as they stood in the doorway. Ryan nudged Seth's shoulder, hard, but not enough to knock him over. I wished he had.

Seth made a show of mock pouting as he lifted sheepish eyes from Ryan back to me. "Why didn't you tell me?" he said to Ryan with a frozen smile. There was more than playfulness behind his words and his glassy smile.

"Cram it, Seth," Ryan added but with a dark kind of chuckle. He ripped the bag from Seth's arms and placed it on the table where the items rattled against the glass top. He pulled out a bag of potato chips, another six-pack and an opened bottle of vodka, and lined them up on the table.

"From my old man's stash," Seth said, grinning and still studying me. I wished he'd stop. His eyes traveled across my face and then down toward my shoes and up again. It lasted less than a heartbeat, but it was enough to prickle every inch of my skin. Then he added almost as an afterthought, "Graser was behind us on the freeway." He nodded over his shoulder. "Should be here in a few."

I'd hoped that was the end of Seth.

Someone turned up the music so that everyone had to yell around the table to be heard.

I continued to fiddle with my water bottle, pretending to be interested in their conversation as Seth dragged back a chair across from me. Something about someone's new car. All the while, I could feel Seth's eyes on me, challenging me to look back at him when he knew I wouldn't. My forehead began to throb from the mental game we played, and I jumped when Ryan sat beside me. It seemed like hours had passed since I'd last seen him instead of a handful of minutes.

No one introduced me to the other two girls, but one of them answered to Tiffany. She looked like a Tiffany, and I recognized her from gym class. They sat across the table but didn't acknowledge my existence, which was fine. I'm not sure what we would have talked about.

I placed the water bottle below the table and between my legs as Tiffany lined up vodka shots with pale pink fingernails and white tips that presumably had never seen the bottom of a sink full of dirty dishes. Her fingernails matched her lipstick. I kind of liked the color and wondered if it would look as nice on me.

When there was a brief pause between songs, the somber doorbell filled the air again. No sooner had the sound ended when a new voice filled the kitchen. "Who drove the Tenement on Wheels parked out front?" the voice yelled through the opened patio doors. Like Seth's, her words slurred. Tiffany and the other girl began laughing again, more loudly than before. Seth joined them, in between a vodka shot and a swig from his beer can. He made an obvious head tilt in my direction.

My breathing stopped.

The girl from the kitchen laughed again, a high-pitched sound that was sharp enough to compete with the electric-guitar music in the backyard speakers. I recognized her voice immediately. It belonged to Gwyneth Riordan. I was starting to hear her voice everywhere. Of course she would be invited to her boyfriend's party.

My stomach sank a little more.

Gwyneth sauntered through the glass doors, smiling. But the grin turned icy just as soon as her eyes met mine. Like Seth, I didn't have to be a psychic to read her mind: *What's she doing here?* her eyes demanded of everyone seated at the table. Everyone but me.

Then I remembered Ryan was sitting next to me with his arm draped casually across the back of my chair.

Seth laughed again, forced this time. For Gwyneth's benefit? His nervous laughter filled a few seconds of uncomfortable silence. "Yeah, I saw that, too." Seth tossed back another shot and slammed the glass on the table.

I pressed my hands against my stomach. They were discussing Dad's van.

"Better make sure we lock our cars tonight," he continued. "This neighborhood's going to shit." Then his eyes landed on me, and I felt the undertow begin to pull me lower.

"Stop it, Seth," Ryan said over the laughter, but there was a seed of a grin in his voice. That made everything worse.

"Hey, when are we going in the hot tub?" Tiffany asked, her words slurring.

Hot tub?

"I didn't bring a bathing suit," I blurted, turning to Ryan.

Everyone laughed, Gwyneth loudest of all. She walked closer. "Oh, I'm sure we could find you a nice one-piece from Riley's closet, right, Ryan?" Her thick eyelashes batted with mock helpfulness.

"Stop it, Gwyneth," Ryan said. I had some satisfaction knowing Ryan was the only one not laughing. But from the corner of my eye, I noticed that the corner of his mouth did turn up.

"Seriously, Fred," Gwyneth said. "That *is* your name, isn't it?"

I nodded.

"By the end of the night, bathing suits are pretty much optional," she added, looking over my head to Ryan with a grin on her face that said they shared some kind of a secret. The people at the table laughed again.

My insides lurched. What was it about white people and hot tubs?

Then I turned to Ryan. "Where's your bathroom?" Breathing became difficult. It was like duct tape was pulled tight around every single one of my ribs.

Ryan leaned closer. His breath smelled like beer. "Just off the kitchen, underneath the stairs."

The table turned quiet as I stood away from my chair. I kept my eyes lowered. I really didn't want to watch six pairs of eyes tracking me.

"I'll go find you a suit," Gwyneth said, again with the fake sisterly voice, but I ignored her. "Don't worry. It won't show—" her eyes drifted to my boobs, or lack thereof "—much."

She stepped away from the back door so that I could pass. It was an effort for me not to leap through the opened door.

I not only wanted to leap. I wanted to run.

It seemed like I walked forever before I finally found the bathroom underneath the stairs. The light was already on, and I quickly closed the door, locked it and then braced both hands against the edges of a marble sink. Ice-cold, the stone jarred my skin. I took several deep breaths, waiting for my heartbeat to slow, even as laughter from the back patio floated beneath the door between pauses in the music.

It was like a nightmare.

Slowly, I raised my head and opened my eyes. A row of round, overly bright lights surrounded the upper half of an oval mirror. I stared back at my reflection and touched my cheek. My skin burned at the contact. The corners of my eyes were moist with tears, and my lips were dry. I bit my bottom lip to keep from crying. The last thing I needed was to cry inside Ryan Berenger's house.

I turned the silver faucet, and cool water rushed between my fingers. I lowered my head and patted my fingers against my face, soothing the heat on my cheeks. I shut off the water and stood straight again. Forcing three long breaths, I ran my fingers through my hair, so that it hung loose behind my shoulders.

Then I turned out the light and opened the door. Instead of walking toward the back door, I walked toward the front, the balls of my feet barely touching the tile.

"Fred?" Ryan's voice stopped me at the door.

Reluctantly, I turned around. "I need to leave." My voice had all the signs of cracking.

Ryan crossed the foyer and stood below a chandelier that sparkled like a wedding cake. He reached out and lightly grasped my elbow. His fingers were warm. I really wished he hadn't touched me. "Why?" he said.

"I promised my dad I wouldn't be late," I said quickly as tears began to build behind my eyes. Someone coughed from the top of the landing. My gaze darted up the stairs. A girl with a blond ponytail smiled at me, but her smile was apologetic. She had Ryan's smile. Surely she was his sister.

"Riley," Ryan said. "A little privacy. Do you mind?"

Riley's small shoulders slumped forward. Then her slender body shot up to a standing position before she pirouetted off the stairwell and into the shadows without a single word.

Ryan returned his attention to me. Softly, he said, "But you just got here. Party's just starting."

"I didn't bring a bathing suit."

"I know."

"And I'm not a big fan of hot tubs."

"I got that. It's okay, Fred. You don't have to do anything you don't want to."

"I know. That's why I need to go, Ryan. Sorry." *This was a mistake.*

But he didn't let go of my arm.

My eyes dropped to his hand at my elbow. "I need to go *now*," I said and tugged against his hand so that his fingers opened like flower petals.

Ryan frowned. His hand fell heavily against his leg. "Look, I'm sorry about what Seth called you. If that's why you're mad...." And before his next breath, he added, "I told him not to say that. I should have said something. I'm sorry."

My eyes widened with disgust. "He's said it before?"

Ryan's eyes dipped sheepishly, just as Seth's had done. "Yeah."

"A lot?"

He exhaled. "A couple of times."

I chuckled darkly. "Guess it's kind of funny, then." My voice caught between breaths. "A big joke." *I'm a big joke.*

"Fred," he said, scratching the back of his head. "It's not like that."

"Like what?"

Ryan paused, considering this. "It's just Seth. That's how he is."

"Impressive."

"Fred." Ryan reached without touching me, but I'd already made it to the door. "Wait."

"I've got to go." I opened the door and stepped outside. "I should never have come. Bye, Ryan."

Ryan stayed silent. This time he didn't try to stop me.

I jogged down the flagstone path to the sidewalk. I didn't look back. And I waited until I was inside the van before I allowed myself to cry.

RYAN

CHAPTER 22

"DID SHE LEAVE?"

I heard Gwyneth's quick footsteps before I heard her voice. I was waiting in the opened doorway, watching Fred climb into her van. The driver's door creaked loudly enough for me to hear. My head wanted to go after her, but my feet stayed planted in the doorway.

"Please say yes," Gywneth added with a forced chuckle meant to get me to laugh.

But I couldn't. I felt like a tool. Again. "Stop it, Gwyn," I said, finally finding my voice.

Gwyneth wrapped her arms around my waist, and my entire body stiffened. Her hands were ice-cold. "Why'd you invite her anyway?" she said, pressing her mouth against my shoulder.

I continued looking down the street, the warmth from Fred's skin still lingering on my fingers. Her van eventually started up on the third try. For a second, I kind of wished that it'd stall. Then she'd have to come back.

"Well?" Gwyneth prodded. She let her arms drop, and it was easier to breathe again, although just barely.

"She's okay," I said finally. "I like her."

Gwyneth's tone grew sharper. "You mean, as in you *like* her?"

I sighed. I wasn't about to explain everything to Gwyneth. She wouldn't get it. "She's just a friend." I finally turned to face her.

Gwyneth's eyes narrowed. "But we're your friends." She made a circle with her finger. "Seth, me, Henry, Zack. Right?"

I didn't say anything. Yeah, they'd all been my friends forever, but this was different in ways I couldn't explain, least of all to Gwyneth.

"Right?" she asked again, her tone sharper.

I nodded.

Gwyneth licked her lips. They were still pink and shiny. "And us..." she started but then hesitated. "We're still tight. Aren't we?"

It was as if someone had stuffed my throat with a towel.

"Ryan?" She tugged on my arm, kind of helplesslike, at least for her. Oddly, my chest tightened. I wasn't making this easy for anybody.

Fred's van drove down the street, chugging like a diesel truck. Gwyneth looked around me and glared at the dark street.

"Jeez," Gwyneth murmured. "Nice ride."

"Stop it." I closed the door. "Leave it alone."

"Chill, Ryan," Gwyneth snapped back. "Can we just get back to your party?"

"Yeah." I sighed, and despite knowing better, I draped my arm across her shoulders, mostly because I wanted to get away from the door.

We walked down the hallway and through the kitchen where the music was cranked so loudly we wouldn't hear each other.

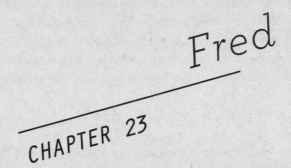

Fred

CHAPTER 23

WHEN I GOT HOME FROM RYAN'S party, Trevor and Sam Tracy were seated outside the trailer on plastic chairs. Trevor was drinking a beer, the silver can shining underneath the glow from the front-porch light.

Before I got out of the van, I wiped my nose and ran my fingers through my hair. If I was lucky, I could make it to the front door without stopping.

"Hey, Freddy," Trevor called out. "Look who stopped by." It was impossible not to notice Sam. It would be easier not to notice the sun.

"Hey, Sam," I said brightly. Too brightly. I kept walking.

"Wait up. Can't you hang for a minute?" Trevor said. "Sam walked all the way over here to visit."

Now I had to stop. Sam probably lived a few miles from us. So I swallowed and then spun around. I walked to where they sat and plopped down on the only other chair. It happened to be right next to Sam. "Hi."

He smiled. "Fred."

"Where've you been?" Sam asked.

"Nowhere." I let my hair spill forward on my shoulders. It was hard to sit still.

"Dad said you went to a party," Trevor said. "I'm surprised he let you drive by yourself."

My teeth clenched. I wasn't in the mood to be smothered. "Well, he did."

"Lots of crazies on the road, Freddy," Trevor said, switching to the Overprotective Big Brother Voice that drove me nuts. "Two psycho white boys in a monster truck almost ran me off the road the other night."

My jaw dropped. My brother was overprotective, but he was the only brother I had, the only one I wanted.

"Did you get a plate number?" Sam said.

"Couldn't," Trevor said, taking a sip from his can. "I was too busy trying to avoid being roadkill."

"What'd they look like?" Sam said.

Trevor's lips sputtered, remembering. "High school kids, driving daddy's brand-new wheels. Blond Ken dolls. Think they're The Shit. You know the type."

Sam nodded, and my entire body stiffened. If Trevor had said they'd been driving a Jeep, I might have vomited the dinner I was too nervous to eat.

"You probably know 'em," Trevor said, his gaze sweeping between Sam and me. "I'd bet my motorcycle they go to your school."

I started to stand, anxious to bolt for the trailer. I didn't know how much more I could take before my head would explode. From Trevor's inquisition and boys running my brother off the road like it was a game to the sad fact that I'd been foolish enough to think that Ryan's party would be special, my insides raged like a dust storm.

"Wait, Freddy," Trevor said, reaching out to stop me. "Tell us about this party. Seriously. What kind of party?"

Trapped, I sank back into my chair. I really didn't want to explain. I barely wanted to think about it. "Yeah, it was just a thing. A golf-party thing."

"Where?"

I sighed. "Ryan Berenger's house."

Sam bristled beside me. "What's he drive?"

"A Jeep," I said quickly. Relieved.

Trevor's lips sputtered. "Spoiled white kids. What do you want with them?"

"We're on the same team," I said.

"That doesn't mean you have to party with them. Or does it?"

I shrugged my shoulders. After tonight, that didn't seem possible.

Trevor took a swig from his beer and crushed the can between his fingers, his eyes bouncing between Sam and me. "You guys hungry? I'm thinking about heating up a pizza."

Sam nodded, but I said, "I'm not hungry."

"More for us, right, Sam?" Trevor winked. "I'll be right back."

After Trevor trotted off to the kitchen, Sam said, "So how was it?" filling the silence. "The party, I mean." I could tell that it bugged him as much as Trevor, maybe even more, that I'd gone to the stupid party.

My temples began to throb. I really didn't want to talk about it. "It was fine." I got up and walked to my putting green.

Sam followed behind me. "If it was so fine, why have you been crying?"

I froze just for a second before I kept walking. "Have not."

"Have, too. Your cheeks are all wet." Then he paused long enough for a long inhale. "I'm only going to ask you once, Fred. Did any of those dudes do anything to you?"

"No," I blurted. "And you've got to stop this, Sam. Stop baby-sitting me. Between you and my brother, you're both driving me crazy." I reached for my putter, which was leaning against the house, but Sam's hand was over mine before I could grab it. His palm was hot.

Slowly, I slipped my hand away from his and began to walk toward the road. Away from the glow from the front-porch light. Away from everybody. I didn't want Sam to see my face. I didn't want to admit what he already knew.

"Hold up." Sam followed behind me.

But I kept walking, the desert crunching below my shoes.

"You can tell me, you know. You can tell me anything."

"I know," I said, and that was true. I'd known Sam Tracy my whole life. We were the same age, had gone to grade school together. Our parents had gone to high school together. Sam had always been so nice to me, so protective. Like family. Like a brother.

He pulled back on my shoulder, stopping me before I reached the dark road. "Then why won't you tell me what really happened?"

I turned to face him, his hand still heavy on my shoulder. "Because it's stupid."

His hand squeezed my shoulder. "You're the smartest girl I know, Fred. You're not stupid."

I choked back a sob, searching for his eyes in the dark. Everything blended into the night around him except the whites from his eyes. "My stupidity might surprise you."

Sam inhaled loudly.

And the next thing I knew, he reached for my other shoulder. He pulled me closer. Then he bent lower and kissed both of my cheeks. They were still damp. It was like he wanted to kiss the tears away.

I swallowed, hard. "Sam..."

But he said nothing.

"Sam," I said again, but the third time he leaned in, he covered my mouth with his.

My eyes popped open.

His lips pressed against mine, waiting. He pulled me tighter.

I couldn't stop myself. His lips were soft. I reached my arms around his neck and felt his muscles respond underneath my fingers. His whole body warmed against mine, and he pulled us closer.

Every inch of me knew what we were doing was wrong, but I couldn't pull away. The sky was dark, his body hugged mine like a blanket, and he wanted me. Somebody wanted me. And in that moment I needed somebody, too.

As soon as the sun came up the next morning, I drove with Dad to the Ahwatukee Golf Club. I'd barely slept, didn't want to sleep, especially after my kiss with Sam. We'd crossed a line, and I wondered if we could ever find our way back. When I'd driven him home, neither one of us had said anything to fill the awkward silence.

Practicing golf would be good. I needed something that I could control.

After Dad parked the van, we climbed into his work cart parked alongside the maintenance office. He gave me a ride to the driving range. I sat in the back of his cart next to his rakes, brooms and shovels.

"See you right back here around five o'clock." Dad forced a smile, but his eyelids were red and puffy from lack of sleep. When Mom had returned home from work last night, she'd proceeded to keep everyone awake as she'd finished an entire bottle of red wine. I'd tried to block out her voice beneath the pillow on my bed, but Dad didn't have it as easy. Between glasses, Mom had rattled off the usual list of regrets and complaints, that she hated her job and why shouldn't she pack the van and drive to San Diego and live on a beach and collect seashells. By the time she had reached the end of the bottle, she had pretty much declared that she hated everyone, herself especially.

"Sure you'll be okay?"

I smiled at Dad. He always said that. And I always replied with the same answer. "Yeah, Dad. I'll be fine." I was used to being fine because there was no point in being anything else. "I need to practice for the tournament next week. Remember?"

"Stop by the pro shop. John should be able to get you a walk-on, but not till later." John Dieter was one of the club's pro golfers.

He always let me play for free near the end of the day if it wasn't too busy.

"Okay, Dad." I flashed him another reassuring smile. "What about you? You okay?"

"Me?" Dad brushed off the question. His lips sputtered. "Don't worry about your old man."

My throat tightened when Dad smiled back. The corners of his eyes crinkled more deeply than yesterday. He looked markedly older, somehow. Sadder. My own heart ached, looking back at him.

"Okay, then." He turned toward the course and the day that wouldn't end without him. "If you need anything, Murray can always reach me on the two-way."

"I know. I'll be fine. Don't work so hard. You look...tired."

Dad lifted his hand, brushing off my concern. His lips sputtered before his rough palm cupped my cheek. Then he hopped into his work cart and drove down the path to the maintenance office. The next time I'd see him, he'd be covered in grass clippings and smelling of wet mulch. Someday I wanted to do something so big that Dad wouldn't have to toil all day on a golf course. Someday...

I sighed before turning my attention to the driving range. The range stretched as long as a football field and was equally as lush. And it was completely empty, except for the usual birds, jackrabbits and hungry coyotes.

I was the first person there. I usually was on Saturday mornings. With my golf bag threaded over my right shoulder and the handle of a metal bucket of practice balls hanging from my left hand, I trudged to the farthest slot on the ridge overlooking the course, my favorite spot. It was closest to the mesquite trees and provided shade in the afternoon.

When I reached the spot, I balanced my bag against the stand, placed the bucket next to it and pulled out my driver. I palmed the club's face, all chipped and pockmarked from years of use. And just like always, I closed my eyes and took a few practice swings, enjoying the brush of the cool morning air against my cheeks. I swung my club back and forth like a pendulum. It felt good. It always felt good. I waited till the movement loosened all of the muscles in my back and shoulders.

One swing, then another.

Back and forth.

Quickly, my body began to relax.

Because I was alone, I started to hum softly with my eyes closed. More practice swings.

Back and forth. Back and forth...

"Pretty song."

My arms froze midswing while my eyes popped open.

"Sounds kinda sad, though."

"Ryan?" I turned as my arms dropped.

Ryan Berenger stood a club's length in front of me with his bag strung casually across his back.

"Where'd you come from?"

A careful smile lifted his lips.

My own lips felt like rubber and worked about, as well. "What are you doing here?" I leaned against my club like it was a cane, trying to act casual but failing miserably.

His chin lifted. "Tell me where you learned that song and I'll tell you."

I choked back a nervous laugh. I had no intention of sharing anything, especially after last night.

But he smiled that smile again, the one that made my knees a little wobbly. "Come on, tell me."

I caved too easily. "My mother used to sing it to me." After I said it, I hated myself for sharing something so personal. And it sounded lame. Of all the songs I could have hummed, why that one?

"It's pretty."

My lips pursed, suspicious. "Yeah, you said that. Now tell me what you're doing here."

"Aren't I allowed?"

I shrugged indifferently, but I was still beyond curious. I figured he and his friends had partied all night long. How could he manage golf at the crack of dawn? "Go for it. There are plenty of open spots." I waved at the rows between us and then turned toward my bag to avoid his eyes. But then I heard his footsteps across the grass, his bag jingling. He didn't walk away like I'd assumed he would; he walked closer.

My knees wobbled again.

"Mind if I practice next to you?"

I raised my eyes in more mock disinterest and then began to fumble for something in the front pocket of my golf bag. A brown sack with a cheese sandwich plopped out, along with a water bottle. I stuffed them back inside and then pulled out a tee.

"Plan on being here long?"

"As long as it takes." I exhaled without looking at him. I teed up my first practice ball.

"Seth and I were supposed to tee off at 8:30, but he couldn't make it. He's kind of hungover from last night."

I rolled my eyes. *Seth.* I was beginning to loathe even the sound of his name. "Color me surprised."

"Anyway, there's a spot in my foursome at 8:30. Wanna play? If you don't, it'll just go to waste."

"I didn't bring enough money—" I said before I could stop myself. Money wasn't the issue.

"Don't worry about the green fees. My dad's already paid for them. Hey," he added amiably. "It's the least I can do, especially after last night, right? Sorry I was such a jerk." He smiled, but his eyes flashed with a shade of sadness, even desperation. So unlike him. But it faded in the next heartbeat, like he wanted—needed— to hide that part of himself.

I inhaled, considering my options. Did I really want to spend four hours with Ryan Berenger and his friends on a perfectly good

Saturday? "I don't know..." I hedged. The more I thought about it, the worse the idea sounded.

"Oh, come on, Fred. Play with me. It's just golf. I promise I don't bite. Not usually." He grinned.

I had to stop my own smile, and I'm pretty sure my traitor cheeks flushed.

Still, I made a show of pressing my lips together and considering the offer. I couldn't believe that Ryan Berenger was standing before me dressed smartly in khaki shorts and a blindingly white golf shirt with a perfectly pressed collar at such an early hour on a Saturday morning. I figured him for the type who'd sleep till noon, at which time a maid probably delivered him waffles in bed.

"My dad even throws in lunch at the clubhouse." His grin spread wider along with his arms. He sensed me weakening. "Can you find a better deal than that today?"

My vision blurred a little as I fought against my own grin. I rubbed my shoulder like I was cold, even though it was already eighty degrees in the shade.

"Fred?" he begged when I didn't answer. His brow even furrowed a little.

"Okay, okay. I'll play. But I should probably warn you that I'm not much for small talk."

Ryan smirked, and his chest caved forward like he was relieved. "That's okay. I'm counting on it."

Somebody pinch me.

I sat alongside Ryan in the golf cart, alone, as he drove us to the first tee to join up with the rest of the foursome.

Along the way, he stopped the cart outside the clubhouse, leaving me by myself. I watched him talking to the golf pro through the window. He leaned his forearms against the window, and I couldn't help but casually admire the broadness of his shoulders. My eyes drifted lower. It was hard not to.

When he returned, I looked away, just for a moment. Until he shared the news. "Sorry, Fred. It's going to be just you and me."

"Just us?" My eyes narrowed. "What happened?"

"The other two in our foursome canceled. Weird, for a Saturday."

"Yeah, weird," I said. Very weird.

"We'll just finish faster." He smiled. "The pro said we could go ahead and play."

I'd have been lying if I said I was disappointed. More than anything, I was supremely glad that we weren't teaming up with any of the players from Lone Butte. It was bad enough that I had to endure them during the week, and I was pretty sure they felt the same way about me.

Ryan drove the golf cart to the first tee, and we both climbed out to retrieve our drivers. Already wearing my golf glove, I took my club and walked silently to the tee box with Ryan beside me. This early, the course was quiet. Too quiet. I could hear myself breathing through my nose.

"You first." Ryan motioned to the tee box.

I bent over to tee up my first shot before stepping back for a few practice swings. And caught Ryan's gaze in my periphery, the slightest smile lifting his lips. He was watching me—maybe even studying me—and I wanted him to, mostly because I craved to know why. What was so compelling about me? Was I simply a golf swing to him? Or was I something else? I pushed away jumbled thoughts by inhaling a deep breath with each practice swing. But I'd be fooling myself if I said my curiosity about Ryan didn't consume my almost every waking thought.

Deep breaths didn't help. This was turning out to be harder than I'd expected.

I couldn't help but wonder if I was measuring up to his expectations. Or if I even wanted to. I had to remind myself for the zillionth time that Ryan was the type who chased after the likes of Gwyneth Riordan and girls with 90210 names like Madison and

Alexandra. He threw drunken parties and got naked with them in hot tubs. Today was all wrong. Why did he have to find me at the driving range anyway?

At least I could get in a round of golf. And stop overanalyzing everything.

Without so much as a glance in his direction, I stepped up to my ball, lowered my forehead and bent my knees. I swung my club, closed my eyes, and listened to the sharp, clear sound of the ball when it left my club. Normally I closed my eyes only on my practice swings, but with Ryan so close, this was the only way I could concentrate.

"Good shot!" Ryan said after the ball went sailing into the air.

I opened my eyes and watched the ball fly across the sky and land in the middle of the fairway.

"Do me a favor?" Ryan said.

"Okay." I pulled the tee out of the ground.

"Watch my swing. Tell me what's wrong with it."

Wrong? Is the color of the sky wrong? What could be wrong?

"Uh...okay," I stammered and then stepped away from the tee box to give him enough swinging room.

Ryan bent over to tee up his ball. His blond head gleamed in the morning sun. I liked how his hair was always slightly disheveled, never perfect. He stood, legs together, studying the fairway. His lips always pursed when he concentrated. Then he spread his legs apart and took three practice swings before adjusting his black sunglasses one final time. His little ritual. Kind of like mine before I struck a ball.

I had to remind myself to focus on his swing. My pulse started racing when I realized that Ryan would expect me to say something helpful, something coherent.

Come on, Fred. Pull it together!

Finally, Ryan swung his club, and I sucked back a breath. His ball sailed farther than mine but not as straight. It sliced slightly to the right before landing on the edge of the fairway. A decent shot, but not great.

Ryan grumbled. He let his club thump to the ground like it was a heavy bowling ball. "Well?" He frowned in the distance at his shot.

I cleared my throat. "It was a good..." *And you looked amazingly hot swinging your club.*

"But?" He walked toward me and let his sunglasses drop to his chest. My heart raced faster as his glasses dangled at the end of the leather strap.

"Well..." *Here goes.* "You raised your head before you completely followed through. And you might be gripping your club too tightly." I grimaced at him apologetically.

Ryan's head began to bob slowly, as if I'd just shared the world's greatest tip in, like, ever. "Yeah," he said, pausing the head bob to let a smile slowly stretch across his face. "I think you're right. Coach is always getting on me about that." Another heavy sigh. A happy one? "Jeez, I really have to stop that."

Everything was going well, but then I had to blurt out, "Next time, why don't you try closing your eyes on your practice swings. Picture your swing. Picture where you want the ball to go."

His chin pulled back. "Seriously?"

Why'd I say that? "Yeah." I climbed into the cart, avoiding his gaze as I spoke. "Close your eyes and then let your body do the rest." I braced myself to be chided.

But Ryan didn't laugh. "Okay." His tone turned serious as he climbed into the cart beside me. "I'll try that."

I couldn't look at him. I'd sounded so cheesy. *Close your eyes and then let your body do the rest. Really, Fred. What were you thinking?*

"Thanks. You're sure you've never had lessons?" The cart started humming beneath our feet as we drove to the next hole.

"Positive," I said, turning. Looking at him, sitting so close, I squirmed as heat rushed up beneath the buttons of my shirt.

Ryan smiled.

I gripped the side handle on the cart so that I wouldn't fall out.

It was going to be a long morning, certainly different from the one I'd planned.

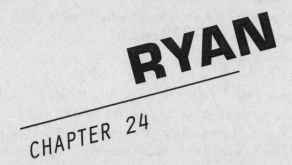

RYAN

CHAPTER 24

I WAS FEELING LUCKY WHEN I found Fred alone at the driving range, although luck didn't have much to do with it.

I'd remembered something Coach Lannon had said after the tournament last week during the bus ride back to the school: *You guys should spend your Saturdays at the driving range like Fred, practicing. She must plow through six buckets of balls, at least. If it wasn't for her, we would have lost this tournament. And it was ours to win this year.* Most of the guys had bristled at Coach Lannon's assessment, even me, but that was last week. Last week I was doing everything possible to ignore Fred Oday's existence.

Now she had become impossible to ignore. She was everywhere, even when she wasn't. I hadn't been able to stop thinking about her for longer than five minutes, and I wasn't exactly sure why. Suddenly I had become curious about everything—like how she got so good at golf, where she lived, who she hung with, what she thought about and why her hair always smelled soft and sweet like the desert. It was embarrassing, really, and I hadn't told anyone. How could I? Who'd understand it if I said that Fred Oday was different in all the ways that were beginning to matter?

At the ninth hole, just as the course started to fill with golfers, the woman who drove the beverage cart finally stopped alongside us, her silver cooler loaded with cans covered in ice. My mouth watered just looking at it.

"Thirsty?" I asked Fred when the beverage cart stopped.

Fred shook her head. "I brought water."

"Come on. Do you like Coke or root beer?"

Fred's lips twisted. "Okay. Root beer, then."

"Two root beers," I told the lady, reaching for my wallet. She handed each of us an ice-cold can. Fred pressed hers against her forehead. I figured her head must get pretty hot with all that hair.

When she left, I said, "Wish I could have bought two beers."

The brightness in Fred's face faded, and I wanted to cram the words back into my big stupid mouth.

Lame, Berenger. Totally lame.

"So, you don't drink?" I popped my can, anxious to prove that I wasn't the tool that she obviously thought I was.

Fred shook her head and looked away, distant again.

"Why?"

She wouldn't face me and fiddled with her can. "Cuz I don't like it."

"So, you've tried it?" I asked her carefully.

Her chin lifted. "A sip or two." She turned, finally.

"Don't like the taste?"

She nodded. "Or the smell."

"Oh. Well, that's cool."

A nervous giggle rumbled in the back of Fred's throat, surprising me. "That's cool?" Her eyes widened. "I've seen what it does to people."

I watched my reflection flicker in her eyes. I wondered if she was referring to me, but Fred had never seen me drunk, and for that I was supremely grateful. "You mean like some of the guys at my party." It wasn't a question.

"Your party." She paused, a crisp edge to her voice that I hadn't heard before. "And other places."

Real pain clouded Fred's eyes when she said *other places*. On the reservation, I assumed. It bothered me to see the hurt in her face, her eyes, and at the same time I wanted to understand. I found myself anxious to know everything about her. Just when I had almost worked up the nerve to ask, she sighed impatiently and glanced at the foursome gaining behind us. They had almost reached the green. "Come on, we better get going." Fred started to climb out of the cart, but I held her back. Her eyes dipped to where my fingers clutched her forearm.

"Sorry, Fred," I said quietly.

"For what?" Her eyes met mine.

"For making you mad. Again. I didn't mean to."

Fred sighed again. "I'm not mad. I'm just not much for small talk, remember?"

I paused and then made a teasing face. I released her arm, reluctantly. Her skin brushed like satin against my fingertips. "So you've told me."

"It's your shot." The lightness returned to her voice.

We walked side by side to where our golf balls had landed in the middle of the fairway, only a few yards apart this time.

Fred

CHAPTER 25

WHEN RYAN REACHED FOR my forearm, I thought my breathing would stop.

I really hoped he hadn't noticed that my skin was on fire, and not because it still felt like August in late September. My body temperature had absolutely nothing to do with the weather and everything to do with Ryan Berenger. Just one look from him gave me goose bumps. Could another person truly cause that?

I was having such a good time playing golf with him that it surprised me.

But why'd he have to bring up drinking? Drinking was something that I did my best to forget, especially when I could avoid it. I doubted his mother sat around their perfect backyard wearing her sparkly birthday necklace and tossing empty beer cans into their manicured flower beds, reminding Ryan that the best he could hope for was a trailer and a waitressing job.

"Your turn." I nodded at his ball. Since he'd tried my little trick and started closing his eyes on his practice swings, he'd been hitting straighter drives. A small part of me wondered whether at first he'd sliced the ball on purpose to get my attention, to get me to look at him. If only I could tell him that it wasn't necessary to ask for a golf tip. I'd have done it anyway.

Ryan hit his second shot so that it landed squarely on the green.
"Great shot," I said with my hand over my eyes to block the glare.
"Thanks." He smiled at me. "Your turn."

I walked over to my ball and took my two usual practice swings.
"You mind watching my swing?" I said casually without really looking at him. "I'm having trouble with this nine-iron. Tell me what I'm
doing wrong?" Not completely untrue but not completely true either. For the first time in my life, I felt a little bold. Totally unlike me.

Ryan took a step closer. "Sure," he said. He looked eager.

I lowered my forehead and bit back a guilty smile.

I gripped the club, lowered my chin and bent my knees. Then
I swung the club and lifted my head, a moment sooner than necessary. The ball sailed into the air and bounced next to the green
instead of on it. I made a frowny face.

"What happened?" Ryan walked onto the tee box. "I've never
seen you do that before."

"What?" I said, careful to maintain an innocent tone. Jeez, I was
acting like such a girl!

Ryan chuckled. "You missed a green!"

"Hey, I'm not perfect, you know." My head tilted to one side.

But Ryan chuckled again, still watching me from behind his sunglasses. From the way his smile turned up on one side, I thought
he might disagree. Did he seriously think I was bordering on perfect? At least special?

"Keep your head down on your swing," he said, not bothering
to hide his smirk.

I smiled sweetly. "I'll try to remember that."

Then Ryan laughed, and I couldn't help laughing, too. It felt so
good. It was like a dream. The day—life, the sun, the air—everything began to feel so unbelievably good. I wanted to stay wrapped
inside it.

We finished playing the back nine less seriously than the front
nine. We went from a formal round of golf to something resembling

miniature putt-putt at the mall. The only things missing were the windmills, lazy rivers and rubber ducks. We used our golf clubs like pool cues when we weren't using them like hockey sticks.

"Good thing Coach Lannon isn't watching," Ryan said. "He'd freak."

For the rest of the morning, we didn't keep score or stress about missing short putts or long drives. Ryan wasn't loud or nosy; he wasn't overly talkative either, although he did enough talking for the both of us. I liked that. I liked that he had less of an edge away from school and his friends. He could be sweet and funny. I could stay pretty comfortable around him, almost enough to be myself.

We switched clubs and experimented with using drivers as putters and putters as drivers. I even let Ryan make a crack about my golf bag. I had it coming. "This looks like my grandmother's couch," he said, examining it, and I tried to look mad but he made me laugh till my ribs ached.

Around the thirteenth hole, the ranger yelled at us for slowing the play, and we both had to bite down on the insides of our lips to keep from laughing. And getting kicked off the course.

By the eighteenth hole, I didn't want the day to end. It had been one of the best days that I could remember in, well, forever. If Ryan had suggested playing another round, I would have happily agreed, no matter how badly my arms throbbed.

Instead, he said, "How about lunch?"

I said, "Yes," before he finished asking. I'd never had lunch at the clubhouse before. It was reserved for members only. Never mind that it was the world's biggest luxury to be waited on by someone else for a change, complete with linen napkins and crystal water glasses and everything. I couldn't refuse.

We both ordered cheeseburgers as thick as hockey pucks. Ryan insisted that I try the vanilla milk shake. "If I get one, you've got to get one, too," he told me. I ate every morsel, including all of the French fries and the enormous pickle that accompanied my plate.

"Finally," Ryan said as I bit into the pickle. The juices exploded inside my mouth. "A girl with an appetite."

"What?" I said. "A girl can't eat?"

"Exactly," Ryan said.

At last, Ryan signed a receipt left on our table. "Do you need a ride home?"

"No," I said quickly. *No way.* "But thanks anyway."

"How will you get home?"

"My dad. He gets off his shift at five."

"But what will you do till then?"

My shoulders shrugged. "Practice some more. On the driving range."

"So this is how you spend all your Saturdays?"

I nodded. "Mostly, although the day usually doesn't include lunch at the clubhouse."

"No wonder you're so good."

I felt my cheeks turn hot. "Practice never hurts."

"Obviously."

Ryan leaned back in his chair, studying me again. I guess you could say I was starting to get used to it. The window behind him overlooked the golf course, framing him like a photograph in perfect greens and oranges. "You really are serious about your golf. I thought I loved golf, but I am nothing like you. Not even close."

I looked back at him, and my smile tightened, just a little bit. I wasn't ready to tell him why I left home every chance I got. Golf just happened.

"But I don't mind driving you home—"

My eyes widened. "No!" I paused and then swallowed, before he thought I was a lunatic. "I mean, that's real nice of you, but thanks. My dad kind of prefers that I wait for him. It's sort of become a ritual."

Ryan's chin pulled back.

"You know," I said, "gives us a chance to talk and stuff."

Ryan sighed heavily. "No, I wouldn't know." But then he leaned forward and crossed his arms on the table. In a softer voice, he said, "I really had fun today, Fred. Thanks for playing with me."

Instinctively, I leaned forward, too, our elbows only inches apart. "Me, too. Thanks for asking."

"Are we cool?"

"Totally."

Then Ryan dipped his head, and his eyes flashed behind me, like he'd seen a werewolf or something. "Oh, no," he moaned. He sank lower in his chair so that my head could hide him.

"What?" I turned.

"Don't turn around."

Too late.

"Dammit," Ryan exhaled. "It's Zack Fisher and his dad."

A sour taste rolled up my throat. Why did it feel like we were doing something wrong? Like I was wrong?

"Great. He sees us." He exhaled through clenched teeth. Another soft moan. "And he's coming over...."

"Probably time for me to go," I said, but I had no idea how to leave. My body was frozen to the chair.

Ryan thrust out his hand, covering mine. "No!" The water glass next to my hand wobbled, and his voice softened. "I mean, *no*. Just wait. I'll deal with Fisher."

I looked down at Ryan's hand, covering mine, confused. Waiting. Did he realize my fingers had begun to shake?

Then I glanced over my shoulder again, just slightly.

Zack waved, the curls bouncing about his head. When his gaze met mine, his eyes widened with that same look of horror in Ryan's eyes. Zack stopped so abruptly that the toe of his dad's golf shoe caught his ankle.

Ryan chuckled a little at their impromptu floor show, but I didn't share in the amusement. Was Ryan embarrassed to be seen with me?

I looked back at Ryan, a dozen new questions filling my brain, then down at our hands, then back into his eyes. Confusion. Frustration. Pure agony.

Ryan's gaze met mine. He didn't release our hands.

My breathing stopped. I needed water but didn't—couldn't—slip my hand away from Ryan's, even though I knew with every brain cell that I should. "Is it a problem seeing Zack?" The words stung inside my mouth.

The tightness in Ryan's face began to fade. "It's always a problem seeing Zack."

"Why?"

Ryan chuckled again, but this time it was forced. "Because he's got the biggest mouth in the galaxy."

I was afraid to look behind me again. I wished Zack had never come to the clubhouse, but maybe it was better that he had. At least now I knew Ryan didn't want anyone to know about us, if there was an *us*. My voice wavered. "Is he still here?"

Ryan sat higher. "No. His dad yanked him out the door. Probably late for their tee time. Lucky us."

Lucky me.

"You doing anything tonight?" Ryan asked suddenly, and I'm pretty sure all the blood drained from my face. My emotions jumbled and wound together like a ball of rubber bands. I didn't know which one to pull at first.

When I looked down at our hands again, Ryan sat back, releasing mine as if finally realizing that he'd been holding it. My head went a little dizzy. "Tonight?"

Ryan smiled again, the crooked kind that made breathing difficult. "Yeah, it's Saturday night. Do you...go out?"

Normally I try to work, I thought, but I didn't dare say that. Then I would have to tell him where, and that would only dredge up a really ugly memory involving me, him and a gooey slice of mesquite-honey mousse cake.

"Um, sometimes," I said in a casual voice. *Make that never.*

Ryan cleared his throat. He wasn't letting it go. "Well, would you like to go out with me? Tonight? Maybe see a movie at the mall?"

I stared back at him numbly. *Like a date?*

I looked at him without really looking at him. Urgently I ran through a laundry list of logistics in my head: (1) I would have to make sure I wasn't offered a shift at the restaurant. Turning it down would only piss off Mom; (2) I would have to borrow Dad's van, which had less than a half tank of gas; (3) I would need to cajole Dad for permission—and Dad had barely slept last night; and (4) What about Gwyneth Riordan? Weren't Saturday nights usually reserved for girlfriends? The Gwyneth Situation nagged at me most of all.

"Well?" Ryan winced, lowering his chin as if he was bracing himself for a *no.*

"Um, I don't know..." I said finally.

"I could pick you up—"

"No!" I said again, interrupting him. "I mean, that's not really necessary."

"We could just go somewhere and talk if you don't like movies."

"Go somewhere?" I blinked away the dryness beginning to cloud my eyes.

"Yeah, it's been fun talking to you today. I guess..." His head tilted as his shoulders lifted. "I guess I'm not ready for it to end." Then his cheeks darkened, and I felt a relieved smile stretch across my face. That might have been the nicest thing anyone had ever said to me in the History of Ever. My skin turned warm and tingly again, all the way down my back.

I heard my own voice say, "I like talking to you, too."

Ryan's face brightened, as if what I'd said surprised him. His eyes lowered to my hands, and for a moment I thought he might reach for mine again. I wished he would. I wanted those goose bumps.

But then I had a better idea. "Do you know where Pecos Road ends? At Chandler Boulevard? There's a barbed-wire fence at the end."

Ryan nodded, but his eyes narrowed. "Yes," he said slowly.

"Meet me there at eight?"

He blinked. "Can't I come pick you up?"

I swallowed. "No, that's okay. I can get there myself."

"In your van?" His tone turned doubtful, but I ignored it.

"Something like that." By eight o'clock, Dad would be sleeping, and if Mom was home, she'd already be well into her first six-pack and wouldn't notice I was gone. She'd think I was in my bedroom, reading. It could work.

It *had* to work.

"Okay, then," Ryan said as he rose from his chair. "Eight o'clock. I'll be there."

I smiled up at him, every inch of my skin still tingling from my forehead to the tips of my toes. My hands reached underneath the table and pressed against my stomach when it started to do flip-flops.

RYAN

CHAPTER 26

JUST BEFORE I DROVE AWAY from the golf course, I texted Seth. I didn't want to call his cell because I knew what he would say, and I didn't want to hear it. I'd deal with it later.

Dude. Cant make it 2night. Sry. 2hungover. TTYL.

It was probably the first time in two years that we wouldn't hang on a Saturday night. I knew Seth would be pissed, but I figured Gwyneth for full-blown furious. Unfortunately I'd have to talk to her at some point, but I didn't expect her to understand either. I wimped out and texted her, too:

G. Sry. Have 2 do somethng with the fam 2night. Later. TTY Mon.

Lame? Totally. But my head was buzzing. I couldn't wait to see Fred. There was something about her that pulled at me. I was done fighting it.

Could another person make you feel so different? Better?

When I got home from the golf course, I was in such a good mood that I wasn't even upset that Dad was sitting in front of the television watching a football game with a beer in his hand and wearing the faded University of Arizona sweatshirt he loved so much. Usually when Mom was away for a weekend, Dad prepared for a trial 24/7. Those were the best weekends ever.

"Hey, Ryan!" Dad called out in a playful voice that made me wince. Dad's arm draped across the couch. "Wildcats are playing the Sun Devils! It's the biggest game of the year!"

"I know, Dad." I moved to the refrigerator for a soda. I couldn't match his enthusiasm for the game. It wasn't that I didn't like football. It was just that Dad would start listing all the clubs and fraternities he'd want me to join when I went—if I went—to the U of A.

"Come watch the game with me!" He raised his beer can like we were frat brothers.

"Can't," I lied.

"Can't watch your future alma mater with your old man?" Dad looked stunned, as if we watched games together all the time. There'd been a time when that was all I'd wanted—just a fraction of his attention.

"Sorry," I said from behind the refrigerator door. "Got plans. Got to get ready."

Dad shot up from his leather lounge chair, the springs creaking from his weight. He swaggered into the kitchen. "Well, I'm sorry, too. Sorry I couldn't make it for golf today."

I guessed *sorry* was better than nothing. If only it meant something.

"S'okay, Dad," I said without looking at him. I really wished he'd stop apologizing. Missed tee times had become the norm. And everything was cool, as long as his secretary kept calling the clubhouse every week to make my Saturday tee times on Dad's behalf. I probably heard more from her than Dad.

"So, did you play with Seth?" He grinned like he already knew the answer.

I turned, considering his question. "Nope," I said, purposely evasive. It seemed wrong sharing anything with him about Fred. But it sure was tempting.

Dad's eyebrows lifted. "Henry?"

"Nope," I said again, popping the cap to a Coke. I waited for the fizz to stop and then slurped the foam, hoping he'd go away.

But Dad wouldn't let it go. He chuckled. "Well, are you going to tell me?" He leaned against the counter when his tone turned noticeably sharper. "Or do we keep playing word games?"

"Fred Oday," I said simply. It felt good to say her name. "I played with Fred Oday."

Dad made a face as if he'd heard me wrong. "The Indian girl?"

I cringed. "Yeah."

"Humph." His brow furrowed. "You really think that's a good idea?"

"What do you mean?" I said, but then wished I hadn't.

Dad shook his head like the answer was obvious. "You know, playing with a girl and all."

"You mean an Indian girl? Or just a girl?" Dad knew that I'd played with Gwyneth once, and that had been perfectly fine with him. Dad, in fact, had encouraged it, paying for her tee time and everything. I wondered what would happen if I told him that he'd paid for Fred's tee time today, too? Gwyneth had been a golf-course nightmare and had never stopped complaining about how hard it was to hold a club, how her arms ached, how hot the air felt. She'd complained about everything. I hadn't been able to wait for that afternoon to end.

Dad's lips pursed. "That's not what I mean, not exactly." He braced himself against the counter. "I just mean it might be better if you play with your friends on the team—Seth, Troy, Henry and the others. They'd probably give you a better game. Better practice."

"Dad, Fred Oday *is* the best player on the team. We could go to the state championship because of her. Don't you get it? You should see her drive a ball," I said, knowing full well that would never happen.

But Dad rolled his eyes like I was a little bit crazy. "Just because she played well in one tournament does not a champion make," he clipped in his best know-it-all, professorial voice.

I bristled. "I've got to get up to my room." I swallowed back building anger.

"Sure, sure." Dad lifted his palms. He must have seen the aggravation in my eyes. "Whatever you need to do. I just thought we could spend some time together. Talk. Catch up. That kind of stuff."

I swallowed, hard. "Sorry, Dad. I already made plans. It is Saturday night, you know." I began to walk away.

"S'okay. Bad timing. My mistake." Dad walked after me toward the stairwell. "Well, what do you have going that's so important?"

"I'm meeting Fred."

Dad crunched the beer can in his hand.

I forgave myself for grinning just a little.

Fred

CHAPTER 27

"WHERE ARE YOU GOING?" Trevor asked in the kitchen where he was watching a television propped on a dictionary next to the refrigerator. The antenna had a wadded ball of tinfoil wrapped around the tip.

"Shh!" I said, my eyes darting between Trevor and our parents' bedroom. Their bedroom shared the wall with the kitchen, and the wall was as thin as cotton. "You'll wake Dad." I was drying dishes from the sink.

Trevor chuckled. "Doubt that. He didn't even eat dinner, he was so tired."

"I know. I put chili and fry bread in plastic wrap for later."

Trevor wiggled his fingers at me, fanlike. "So, Freddy. Come on. Tell me where you're going. What's on your social calendar for this evening?" Obviously he could tell from my clothes that I wasn't going to be spending the next three hours in my bedroom. He'd probably also noticed that I'd used a little of Mom's mascara and some lip gloss. Totally not my usual Saturday night attire.

"I'm meeting some friends."

"Who?"

I didn't answer.

"Rez kids?"

"Yeah," I lied. If I told him the truth, he'd freak and get all annoyingly older-brotherly protective.

"Well, who?"

I sniffed, avoiding his gaze. "Yolanda, Kelly, Pete and Sam."

Trevor grinned. "Big Sam? I think he has a crush on you."

I avoided his gaze. "You need to stop encouraging him. Sam and I are just friends." I needed to talk to Sam, too. I just needed to find the right time, the right words. Why had I kissed him? Why did he have to be so kind?

Trevor laughed. "I think every girl on the Rez over the age of thirteen has a full-on crush on him. Why don't you?"

"'Cause I've known him since kindergarten."

"So?"

"*So?*" My eyes blazed at him. "So I was there when he spit up milk during class in the first grade. I remember when he cried in the third grade after Yolanda pulled his pants down when he hung from the monkey bars. That's why. For starters."

Trevor laughed, harder.

"He'll never be anything more to me than a friend." I paused. "And that's another thing. You can tell him to stop following me around at school like some kind of bodyguard."

Trevor's lips sputtered. "I have no idea what you're talking about."

"Sure you do."

He shook his head. "Sure don't."

I exhaled loudly before reaching for my jacket on the kitchen chair. I didn't know whether to believe him, but I didn't care. I was more concerned with leaving the house on time.

"At least tell me where you're going, in case Dad wakes up and asks."

My nose had to be growing a mile long. "By the Estrellas," I lied again, avoiding his gaze as I turned back toward the refrigerator and pretended to look for something else to eat even though I was still full from the cheeseburger at lunch.

"A bonfire?"

I pirouetted around and forced a smile. "Something like that."

"Want a ride on the bike?"

"Nope. I'm going to walk." Fortunately it wasn't a long walk to the Estrellas or to the end of Pecos Road. A mile at most in the desert. Trevor and I had done it so many times that we could do it with our eyes closed on a moonless night if we had to. We knew our corner of the Rez better than anybody. We knew which washes raged during the monsoons and all of the flat dirt paths that snaked around the endless sage and saguaro. Besides, with the stars and a half-moon to light the way, it'd be like walking underneath strings of Christmas lights.

"Okay, but don't forget the flashlight," Trevor said in his big-brother voice. "Just in case."

"I won't," I said as my shoulders began to loosen.

Finally.

I'd survived the evening's second hurdle. The first had been learning that Trevor would be staying home till midnight and could entertain Mom if necessary before he had to work his night shift at the gas station. Fortunately, Mom would be too tired to notice me missing and too drunk within thirty minutes of arriving home to care. And Trevor would keep her occupied outside long enough so Dad could sleep.

My eyes darted to the clock on the green stove. The second hand ticked so loudly that I heard it over the television. "I better get going," I told Trevor. "There are leftovers if you get hungry."

"Thanks, Freddy," he said before turning back to some old rerun with motorcycle cops. "Say hi to Sam." His eyebrows wiggled as he got up to slap the television on its side when the screen turned fuzzy.

Relieved, I practically skipped to the front door, pushed open the screen and bounced out the door into the cool desert.

I couldn't be late.

I had no idea why I'd agreed to meet Ryan at eight o'clock. I really should have my head examined.

Why would someone like Ryan Berenger want to spend time with someone like me? Alone?

He should be spending Saturday nights with his girlfriend. Not girls named Fred who lived on the other side of Pecos Road.

It was just that we'd had such a nice time on the golf course. Ryan was so surprisingly funny and attentive. At least, he had been when I'd been able to focus. Half the time, I'd barely heard a word he'd said, even when he'd talked about golf and last year's tournaments. I should have been concentrating, especially when he'd told me about the other golf teams, the best and worst players, the tricky courses on the tournament schedule, filing away all information for future use. Instead, I'd been too busy pretending *not* to be studying the back of his head, his jaw, the way his shoulders rippled when he swung his club, his perfect smile and his eyes, the color of a morning sky.

Was there more to Ryan Berenger than I'd realized?

Once in a while I'd caught him studying me, too, but he'd quickly lowered his chin and pretended to fiddle with the rubber grip on his club or the silver button on his glove, biting back a nervous smile. It had been kind of sweet. Those had been the silent moments when my knees had almost buckled. Other than Sam Tracy, I'd never had a boy's eyes sweep over me before. Like he wanted me. Like I was special. The difference between Ryan and Sam was that I wanted Ryan, even though there were a hundred perfectly logical and sane reasons not to.

My feet barely touched the ground. I felt as if I could fly all the way to the end of Pecos Road.

RYAN

CHAPTER 28

I RACED DOWN PECOS ROAD with the windows down. The radio was blaring, but the dry wind whipping through the Jeep's plastic flaps drowned out most of it.

My foot pressed harder on the accelerator the farther I got from Phoenix, and I passed only a handful of cars traveling in the opposite direction. The air even tasted lighter. I caught my smile in the rearview mirror.

"You're a complete idiot," I said aloud, laughing to myself.

When I reached the end of Pecos Road, the only thing that separated my front bumper from the Gila River Indian Reservation was decades-old rusted barbed wire. I shut off the engine, even the radio, and the world grew so still that silence became its own sound.

I left the headlights on, though. They shone across the desert over endless saguaro and paloverde, casting frozen shadows. If you didn't know you were staring straight into the desert, you might have thought you were gazing over the heads of giant soldiers. On Mars.

I reached for the roof bar and pulled myself out of the Jeep. My shoes slapped onto the pavement.

Then I walked toward the headlights, my footsteps filling the air. I leaned against the hood, waiting, staring out into the desert. Just as I pushed back, my breath hitched. Fred walked out of the darkness into the headlights' yellow path like she'd just beamed down from a cloud. I'd never even heard her approach.

"I don't believe it." I lifted off the hood, mesmerized.

"I told you I'd be here," Fred said, switching off her flashlight, squinting against the headlights as she crossed from the desert onto Pecos Road. The waist-high barbed-wire fence that separated us had been trampled down in most places. She found a low spot to cross over.

I met her at the first opening in the wire and extended a hand.

"I saw your headlights from the wash. Didn't even need my flashlight. Nice assist." She took my hand, only for a moment, and then hopped over the broken wire.

"You're welcome," I said as her hair and eyes blended against the darkness. "Fred?" I swallowed.

"Yes?" She looked up at me, and my knees wobbled.

"You are officially the coolest girl I know. I don't know a single girl who'd walk across the desert in the dark. By herself."

Fred chuckled. "I've done it lots of times." Her tone was far from boastful. I was learning to like that about her. A lot.

"Really?" I said.

"With my brother," she added quickly. "Usually."

"You know, it wouldn't have been a big deal to come pick you up at your house."

She shook her head and placed her flashlight on the hood of the Jeep. "No." She rubbed her hands together as if she was cold. "This is way better."

"What's wrong with coming to your house?" It tugged at my gut that maybe I embarrassed her or something. Did her parents hate white guys?

Another shoulder shrug, and she looked behind her into the desert. "This is just easier."

"But what about animals?"

She surprised me again. "The coyotes are skittish. And the jack-rabbits don't bother anybody."

"Rattlesnakes?"

"If you leave them alone, they'll leave you alone."

"Bobcats, then. You hear about attacks on the news. Sometimes."

"That's rare. Besides, they stick to the high rocks." She nodded over her shoulders at the Estrellas, but it was too dark to see their jagged peaks.

I chuckled, still watching her. "Well, that's good to know. Are you cold?" I said as her hands crossed over her chest. She wore a bright white T-shirt underneath a blue windbreaker.

But Fred shook her head.

"Thirsty, then?"

"Yeah," she said carefully, "a little."

I reached into the backseat of the Jeep and pulled out a cooler big enough for a six-pack.

Fred peered over my shoulder.

"Don't worry. It's just root beer. You liked it today, remember?"

Fred's smirk turned into a tiny smile. She nudged me with her shoulder. "Yeah."

I took out one can from the cooler and popped the top. "Here. Drink this."

"Thanks." As Fred took the can, a green glow shimmered into the sky about a block down the road. It looked like the glow from a dashboard or maybe a dome light in the front seat of someone's car. "Who's that?" she whispered.

I looked over my shoulder. The truck must have just pulled off the road. "Don't know. But people come here to park all the time."

"Park?"

I paused, reading her face. She really didn't know. "You know, Fred." My mouth pulled back, embarrassed. *"Park."*

"You mean, like car trouble?"

I cough-chuckled and then snapped open another can of root beer. "No, that's not what I mean. I mean I think they just want to be alone." This time I tilted my head, waiting for her to catch on. Seriously, was she that naive? It was curiously refreshing.

After a few more seconds, Fred's lips pulled back, and I had the sudden, incredibly impulsive urge to kiss them.

"Oh," she exhaled. "Right. I get it."

I laughed with her and tried to blink away the thought of kissing her. But it was never too far from the center of my brain.

"Come on." I pulled on her elbow. "Let's sit in the car. I brought a few CDs. Thought maybe you might want to listen to some music."

"Sure. Music would be good."

But when we sat in the Jeep, I forgot all about putting in a CD. I was too busy thinking that my thigh was an inch from hers. My shoulder was brushing up against hers.

"Fred, mind if I ask you something?"

"Sure." She turned toward me, and her knee pointed at my thigh, making breathing a little difficult.

I blinked and tried to erase all thoughts of placing my hand on her leg and pulling her closer. "I know this sounds lame, but I think we've met before."

"Yeah, I know," she said. "We had freshman English together."

I smiled. "No. Not that. I'm talking a long time ago."

"How long?"

"Fourth grade."

"But I went to school on the Rez—"

"I know. But don't you remember when a busload of white kids from Kyrene Elementary invaded your school?"

In the glow of the dashboard, Fred smiled. She nodded, once.

"And we all sat around in a big circle while this old dude with braids—"

"George Trueblood," she corrected me.

"Yeah, well, he told us stories for what seemed like a million hours. My legs almost fell off from sitting so long."

"You didn't like the stories?"

I paused. "I liked the stories. But I think I was too busy trying to get your attention to care."

Fred's chin pulled back. "Me? How'd you know it was me?"

"Did you wear ponytails back then?"

"Yeah, but so did just about every girl in my school. Yolanda, Kelly, Wil—"

I lifted my hand to her mouth. "But did you have a space between your teeth?"

Fred laughed, and I felt her breath against my palm. "Yeah. I used to, but my teeth grew together, thank god. But are you so sure it was me?"

"I think so." My hand fell to her leg. "It had to be. You smiled right back at me. Don't you remember?"

"I remember the bus. I remember a bunch of kids. But we got a busload every year. I think it was to try to show the kids on the other side of Pecos Road how the Indian kids lived." Her nose wrinkled, and I wanted to lean over, badly, and kiss the tip of it. "We really didn't like those field trips very much."

I pulled back. "Why?"

"It felt like being an animal in a zoo or something. I mean, we had school, ate, dressed, lived, just like everybody else, except we lived on a reservation. We never really understood the attraction. Did you all think we lived in tepees or something?"

"Sort of."

"Figures." Fred chuckled.

"How come you never visited our school?"

"Field trips cost money."

"Well, if the reservation is no big deal, how come you won't let me come pick you up at your house?"

Fred pulled her long leg down and slowly swiveled forward,

her gaze fixed on the dashboard. "It's kind of complicated at my house at the moment."

I put my arm along the top of the seat, wanting desperately to reach for a strand of her hair. And wanting her to turn and face me again. "Join the club."

"You, too?"

"Totally."

"Your mom?"

"My dad," I said, feeling a heaviness return to my shoulders, despite the nearness to Fred. I almost wished I hadn't said anything. But then I heard myself say, "It's like my dad and I don't know how to talk to each other anymore. And when we do, it's total crap."

"But your family seemed so perfect at the restaurant—" Fred's hand flew to her mouth. "Oops."

I bit back my grin. "So busted."

"I am?" She cringed behind her hands.

"Totally."

"How long have you known?"

"I remembered you from the fourth grade. I think I could remember you after you dropped a piece of cake in my lap."

Her clasped hands fell to her lap. She turned again in her seat, her kneecap touching my thigh, and my heart began to beat faster again. My fingertips brushed her silky hair. "Sorry about the pants," she said.

My grin spread, and I couldn't help but laugh out loud. "Finally, Fred. I was wondering when you were going to tell me. I can't believe you waited this long. I'm impressed!"

Fred smirked.

"The cake in my lap was the highlight of the dinner. Did you do it on purpose?"

"No!" She laughed.

"Sure you didn't," I teased.

"When did you realize it was me? I really thought you didn't recognize me."

"Oh, I don't know. I think I realized it the next time I saw you in English."

"Why were you in such a bad mood that night? You were practically breathing fire. I should have spilled water on you. Was the food that bad?"

My smile faded. "You don't know my parents."

Fred leaned closer, placing her hand on my thigh, and my body temperature began to explode. "My dad always says there's nothing that can't be fixed."

I inhaled, trying very hard to slow my heartbeat. "He's never met my family."

"If it makes you feel any better, mine's a piece of work, too."

"Not perfect?"

"Hardly."

"Then I guess we do have something in common." In a weird way, I got the feeling she was happy to hear that, even if we were comparing family dysfunction.

The Jeep grew silent. I was pretty sure Fred had stopped breathing. I knew I had.

Carefully, I edged closer, just an inch at first and then another, till finally my arm was completely wrapped around her, and her head was nestled against my shoulder. It felt so good, the closeness. I had wanted to reach for her, to touch her, all day.

Her breath warmed my neck. Slowly, I lowered my chin so that it brushed the top of her head. My eyes closed as I listened to our breathing, her heartbeat and all the corny things that scrolled through my head. I wanted to say something lame, like how her hair smelled as sweet as the desert, because that was how she made me feel—alive and special. Even when I didn't deserve it.

I'd never said anything like that to a girl before. "Fred." My voice cracked from too much silence.

But Fred didn't answer. Instead, she turned her face upward to meet mine. The tips of our noses brushed against each other. Hers was warm and soft. Like her hair. Like everything about her.

I took a chance and lowered my mouth toward hers till we were a breath apart.

She didn't pull away.

Then I very gently pressed my lips against hers. Soft and curious at first. Then I pressed harder.

When Fred kissed me back, my universe cracked open.

The other parked car screeched in reverse across the pavement, its headlights flashing across ours, before racing in the opposite direction.

We barely noticed as our kiss grew deeper.

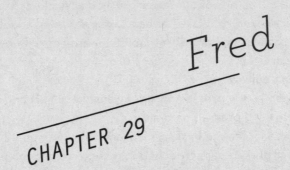

Fred

CHAPTER 29

I DIDN'T KNOW WHAT TIME it was when I headed back home across the desert, but it was late enough for the moon to have dropped behind the Estrella Mountains.

It wasn't easy convincing Ryan to let me walk home either. It was barely a mile, I assured him, compared to at least twenty if we drove all the way down Pecos Road, got back onto the freeway and then drove another ten miles onto the Rez off the next freeway exit. It would have been like driving in a complete circle when all you really needed to do was walk to the center.

"Let me at least drive you through the desert, then?" he insisted as we leaned together against the hood of his car. "My Jeep can handle it. It's four-wheel drive."

"No. If the Tribal Police catch you, they'll arrest you for trespassing." That was only partly true, although I made it sound as if there was an army of Tribal Police patrol cars on the Rez when really only a handful existed. What I wanted to avoid was introducing Ryan to my most assuredly drunk mother. There was no telling what she would say if she caught us on the doorstep. Ryan would have been as out of place at our trailer as a stretch limousine.

Despite my protests, Ryan insisted on keeping his headlights shining over the desert as I walked back home. Halfway through the desert when I stopped to look over my shoulder, I could still see his headlights, a reminder that we were connected by a beam of light and his concern. The headlights were as bright as stars. I kept glancing over my shoulder, watching them, until they turned the size of fireflies. I had a crazy stupid happy grin on my face the whole way home.

When I finally got home, the house was so quiet that I could hear the reliable tick of the second hand on the stove clock in the kitchen. I crept into my bedroom, barely letting the screen door squeak. In the darkness, I looked up at the sky from my bedroom window, still smiling. When the curtain fluttered, I was treated to a blanket of stars. Just like I always did, I found the Big Dipper. Then the Little.

As I gazed out the window, my fingertips brushed over my mouth, cheeks, neck, all the places that still tingled from Ryan's kisses and warm hands. His fingers, like his kisses, were gentle and curious. Nothing like I expected. When I closed my eyes, I could still see him, feel him, his arms wrapped around me, his hands pressed against my skin, mine against his, exploring each other. When I kissed Ryan Berenger, I swear I saw more stars than all the stars in the sky.

I vowed that I would never forget this day—this night—for as long as my ancestors allowed me to live.

It had been the happiest, most perfect day. And it had happened when I least expected it.

The rules have changed, haven't they?

That's what I thought as I walked to the school library on Monday morning, just like I always did, after dropping off my golf bag in Coach Lannon's office. Sam called to say that he and Pete would catch a ride with Kelly and Yolanda, but, other than that, it felt like your basic Monday.

But...was it?

The day might have felt the same, but I felt completely different, almost like a person reborn. My heartbeat pounded louder, stronger. I didn't walk so much as glide. The sky smelled fresher, the air felt lighter. Whenever I touched my face, my lips were turned up in a goofy smile. Jeez! Would anyone else notice? Was my happiness that obvious?

I'd wondered all weekend whether Ryan and I would eat lunch together in the cafeteria. I couldn't wait to see him again.

What about English?

Would we sit together in Study Hall, too?

And what about golf practice? Surely we'd practice alongside each other, wouldn't we?

Or—and this was the part that frightened me the most—would everything in my life stay exactly the same? If it did, then Saturday night never happened. It might as well have been a dream. My chest tightened, imagining such a cruelty. And for an instant, my goofy smile faded.

I just had to find out. I had to know.

With my backpack threaded over my shoulder, I opened the door to the library and breezed by the empty library desk. Then I walked along the quiet row of mostly empty cubicles until I reached the last one at the end of the stacks. It had been my pre-first-bell hiding spot for the past two years, one month and three days, but who was counting?

When I reached my usual spot, I almost swallowed my tongue. That's because I was about to trip over the tops of Ryan Berenger's Converse tennis shoes. They were crossed at the ankles and sticking outside the cubicle entrance like tree branches.

"Hi, Fred," Ryan said.

Fred. I loved the way he said my name. It almost sounded pretty.

My stomach dropped, but in a good way. I could barely mouth, *Hi.* I had to blink, just to make sure he wasn't an illusion.

"Thought you'd get here earlier." He stood slowly and dangerously close, making just enough room for me to squeeze into the cubicle.

Instant body heat.

Ryan had to have felt it, too. His mouth twisted into a shy smile so breathtakingly beautiful that my body swayed.

Finally, my vocal cords caught up to my brain. "I had to drop my bag off in the coach's office." I laid my backpack on the desk and reached for the zipper, grateful for something to occupy my hands.

"Want to work on English before Homeroom?"

"English?" *What's that?*

Ryan nodded. He wedged around me to squeeze outside the cubicle. More heat, followed by enough electricity to power half the country. "I'll get another chair."

Please don't, I wanted to say. *Please stay.* Instead, I said, "Okay," quietly inhaling the minty shampoo scent from his still-damp hair. Some of the blond ends were clumped together with moisture. I wanted to run my fingers through his soft waves like I had Saturday night.

Ryan found another empty chair and wedged it inside the cubicle. There was barely enough room for one chair, let alone two, and that was perfectly fine by me. Our thighs melded together as we sat alongside each other, warm and secure.

"Have you written your paper yet?"

I nodded, although I hoped he wouldn't ask what I wrote yesterday. Gazing into his eyes, I couldn't remember a single word. I wasn't sure I remembered the instructions.

Ryan threaded his fingers through his hair, and I wished that I were that hand. "I didn't." He sighed. "Maybe we could get together this week and work on it? I could really use your help."

I nodded again, numbly. *This week? Work on it? Work on what? He wants to do homework together? With me?*

When I didn't answer, Ryan reached for my hand, just about putting me over the top on the emotional scale. It was like I'd ridden to the highest point of a roller coaster, the wind swallowing my breath. Another second and I'd start screaming with my arms over my head. Then he placed his other hand over mine like a sandwich. "Fred...you're shaking. Are you okay?"

I managed a small nod. I wished I could tell him how happy I was, but the words wouldn't come.

By the way his smile turned crooked, though, I figured he already knew. "Good," he said as he squeezed my hand. "I thought about calling you yesterday, you know."

My stomach fluttered all over again. "You did?" My voice squeaked with more surprise. I would have loved a call from Ryan yesterday. I couldn't stop thinking about him all day.

"You're not in the book."

"What book?"

"Phone book."

"Oh." Quickly, I took the blue pen from the front pocket of my backpack and wrote down my phone number.

"Your cell?"

"No," I said without looking at him. "It's to the phone in our kitchen." *And it works, so long as my mother pays the phone bill.*

He put his arm behind the back of my chair. "You don't mind if I call you at home?"

"Call anytime." I tried to sound casual, but I was so not good at sounding casual. I wasn't good at sounding like anything.

Ryan let out a breath like he was relieved. Or surprised. "I really had fun on Saturday," he said, reading my mind. "The whole day, I mean. Not just at Pecos Road."

I felt my cheeks blush, remembering. I remembered every kiss, every touch, every second, every breath. I put down the pen, just in case he wanted to hold my hand again. "Me, too," I said. There was so much I wanted to tell Ryan, if only I had more nerve. *Me, too* hardly described it. I wished I could tell him how the mere sight of him made my stomach do flip-flops, how being close to him made every inch of my skin tingle. If he was patient, I'd tell him everything. *Everything.*

"I brought you something." He leaned forward for his backpack. I leaned forward, too, curious.

From the top pocket, he pulled out a rolled-up *Arizona Republic,* the sports section. He laid it over the opened notebook and turned to page three.

"I wasn't sure if you saw this, but your picture is in here, along with a blurb about our win last week." He turned, his face so close to mine that I could see a tiny freckle on his nose. "It's a pretty good picture."

"What? Me?" I broke away from Ryan's gaze to smooth the newspaper. On the bottom of the page, there was a black-and-white photo of me standing on the fourth tee at the Ahwatukee Golf Club. I remembered the hole well. I had just swung my driver and was staring down the fairway, waiting for the ball to drop, hoping it would miss a gigantic sand trap. I didn't remember any camera or flashes. The caption read Fredricka Oday from the Gila Indian River Community, Lone Butte High School Varsity Golf Team. I wondered if anyone from the Rez would see it. I didn't know anyone who got the newspaper delivered.

"Ugh. They used my full name."

Ryan smiled. "I like it. It's different."

"You can't be serious."

"Totally serious."

I bit back a smile. Ryan Berenger continued to amaze me. "Who took it?"

Ryan didn't answer. Instead, he said again, "Pretty picture, too," smiling at me sideways until the heat turned up in my cheeks. "Looks like you're getting famous around here," he teased, and my skin burned hotter. I finally smirked at him and wrapped my hand around his arm.

Then I studied the picture again. "I don't remember a photographer. Someone from the paper did call my house, but he only wanted to know how long I'd been playing golf. He said he'd try to come watch one of our tournaments but didn't make any promises." *Never mind that I've never been in a newspaper before.*

"You'll get used to it, especially when you keep winning."

"*If,* not *when.*"

"No way," Ryan chuckled. "You'll keep winning. I've seen you play. And I have a good feeling."

I sat higher in my chair and beamed back at him. I could feel my lips curving upward again, into that goofy, deliriously happy smile. I bit down to stop it.

The rules have changed.

The first warning bell rang.

"Damn," Ryan muttered, frowning at the wall clock. "We gotta go."

"Yeah," I said, just as Ryan turned, leaned closer and then very gently pressed his lips against mine. His lips were soft and warm and his tongue parted my lips. It wasn't a dream.

My head spun all the way to Homeroom.

RYAN

CHAPTER 30

I WALKED FRED TO HER HOMEROOM before running halfway across the building to mine. I glided inside, skateboard-style, just as the bell rang, and ignored the Homeroom teacher's glare when my kicks screeched across the linoleum.

Too bad I couldn't switch to Fred's Homeroom. It would have delayed the inevitable for twenty more minutes. I seriously needed to talk to Seth and Gwyneth. I was dreading it, but they had Fred figured all wrong. And maybe they had me figured all wrong, too.

Seth sat in the last row. I slid into the empty seat beside him. I dumped my backpack underneath the desk and nodded, just as the principal started droning over the loudspeakers about Friday's football game and the upcoming Homecoming dance.

I cringed inside. *The dance.* One more thing I'd have to cancel with Gwyneth.

"Hey. Dude. Thanks for the blow-off on Saturday." Seth's smile was tighter than usual, every facial muscle triggered to snap like a mousetrap.

"Yeah, sorry," I exhaled.

"You missed a real ripper."

I nodded like I was bummed. But then my hand absently

scratched the side of my head. "Had some lame stuff going on at home."

"Really?" Seth's eyes widened just as mine darted to the desk in front of me. "Like what?"

I swallowed, considering this. I hadn't planned on telling Seth about Fred and me in Homeroom. I was kind of hoping to wait till after school, at least till lunch. "Oh, you know. Stuff. My old man wanted me to keep an eye on Riley while he was at work."

Seth chuckled. "Work?" His eyebrows arched, doubtful. "Since when?" Unfortunately, Seth knew all about Dad. I should have said something more believable, but his sudden inquisition was unexpected.

"You know," I said, eager to fast-forward past Dad's extra-curricular activities. "Whatever it is he does."

"You mean banging secretaries?"

I glared at him.

"That's too bad. Missed a ballin' party at Troy's." He made a drinking motion with his hand, but his eyes still had a crazy glint, like there was more to the story. Like the police had been called or something.

"So I heard," I lied and faked a conspiratorial grin. If only I could tell him that I hadn't missed a thing. I would have traded one hundred parties at Troy's for one Saturday night on Pecos Road with Fred. I couldn't get her out of my mind, and now I didn't want to.

"Gwyneth's pretty pissed at you. I'd stay clear till at least fourth period."

"Yeah, Gwyneth..." My voice trailed off. Back to reality.

Fourth period was Study Hall when we usually sat together and I half listened to her complain about one of her girlfriends or some teacher that she hated. That was when I planned to talk to Gwyneth. I wanted to break up with her, and I already felt pretty guilty about not doing it sooner. "Thanks for the warning."

"But I think she said something about meeting you after English," Seth added.

My shoulders slumped. I would have preferred Study Hall.

Seth paused. His eyes narrowed to tiny slits as he peered at me sideways. "Zack said he saw you at the club with Pocahontas." He paused again, oddly.

Zack. I had forgotten about seeing him and his dad at the country club on Saturday. Funny, it had bothered me then but now I didn't really care. Let him see Fred and me together. Let everyone see us together.

My mouth turned dry as Seth waited. Finally I said, "That's lame, Seth. You really shouldn't call her that."

"What?" Seth's voice challenged, as if he had been expecting me to defend her. "Pocahontas?" Two guys in front of us turned their heads, looked at each other and smiled nervously.

"Cram it, Seth," I hissed.

"Isn't she Indian? Or am I not allowed to say it?"

I ignored him.

"Something else you want to tell me?" he taunted.

"What is your fucking problem?"

"I don't have the problem." He paused. "You do."

Anger churned inside me like a tornado. Seth was stoking for a fight and impossible to ignore. I wasn't about to talk about Fred in Homeroom in front of a couple of nosy dudes.

Seth leaned closer when I didn't answer him. He lowered his voice. "Then let me say something." He jabbed his forefinger at me. "First, don't lie. I am not a tool. I know why you flaked out Saturday night. I *saw* you." It was as if he'd prepared for this. "I saw what you did."

I glared at him.

A glint of satisfaction settled on his face. "We both did."

"Who?" I blurted. But then I remembered the truck, the one that had peeled away in the dark.

"Gwyneth. We followed your ass to Pecos."

"You followed me?" My voice rose in disbelief.

Seth began to stutter. I hadn't heard him do that in years either. It only happened when he got really pissed. "And, s-s-s-second..." He stopped and drew in a breath to steady his speech. "Do you realize that you're screwing your life by hanging out with that Indian?"

My body froze. "Shut. Up. Seth," I said through clenched teeth. "Just shut up." By now, half of Homeroom was listening, or trying to. Fortunately, the overhead speakers were turned up pretty loud.

"What do you have in common with her anyway? Have you thought about that? And have you forgotten that she's the reason I'm off the g-g-golf team?" Seth began to stutter again. I knew that he also was itching to remind me how his dad had been killed, but, thankfully, he left that unspoken.

My nostrils still flared. I couldn't answer him.

"You know the only reason you're interested in her is because it'll piss off your dad. Admit it." Seth's eyes grew dangerously dark, daring a contradiction.

My breathing got louder as I drew it between my teeth, glaring back at Seth.

Seth lowered his voice. "Are you going to start hanging out on the reservation now, going to powwows and shit? Have you gone totally lame?"

"Shut *up*, Seth," I said. He was pushing me, and my fingers tingled as if they were on fire. I wanted to punch something. I shoved my fists between my legs. "Just shut up and leave me alone," I said as I waited for the next bell to ring. "You don't know what you're talking about."

The principal finally finished his announcements. I hadn't heard a single one. Students began to shuffle books and papers as they reached for their backpacks, stealing glances at Seth and me, probably wondering if there was going to be a fight. I saw a few reach for their cell phones.

"Sorry, dude," Seth said, his voice normal again. "But I'm your best friend. Somebody had to tell you."

"Stop talking, Seth," I said through clenched teeth. "Please." My forehead started to throb, and the curious stares around me didn't help.

But I couldn't flake off something that Seth said. Was I falling for Fred for all the wrong reasons? For an instant, a part of me wondered if he was right.

Maybe I should have left everything the way it was.

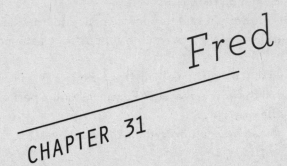

Fred

CHAPTER 31

I SURVIVED HOMEROOM AND FOUND my way across campus to English without hyperventilating. I didn't walk to English as much as float.

Along the way, I scanned the hallway for Ryan, trying not to appear too eager but unable to ignore the fireworks bursting inside me. I'd never been so exhilarated by a day that had barely begun.

I walked into English before the bell. Almost everyone was seated, including Ryan. He sat in the last seat in my row, his head partially hidden and lowered over an open book. He didn't look up when I entered, and I wondered whether to go back and say something.

Like *Hello.*

The rules have changed, I reminded myself. I could do that now. He was my boyfriend, wasn't he?

But then my eyes met Seth Winter's. He sat next to Ryan. He flashed one of his tight-lipped, icy smiles that made every hair prickle on the back of my neck. I had to wonder what Ryan saw in Seth. Could Seth ever forgive me for taking his spot on the golf team?

Then my eyes lowered to my seat, the empty one at the front of the row. There was a folded newspaper waiting on my desk, maybe the same one that Ryan had shown me in the library, and my stomach somersaulted all over again.

Quickly, I placed my backpack underneath my desk and slipped into the seat.

My smile faded when I found the photo on page three of the sports section, the same one where I was holding my driver on the fourth tee. Someone had used a black marker to draw a band around my forehead with feathers on each side. A crude Indian headdress.

My nostrils flared and my breathing quickened.

The photo turned cloudy the longer I stared at it. I had to swallow back the bile building deep in my throat. I folded and then crumpled the newspaper and stuffed it inside my backpack. I wanted to shred it into a million tiny pieces.

"Miss Oday?" Mrs. Weisz said. "Is something wrong?"

I froze. My eyes turned up. Then I remembered where I was. "Wrong?" I mumbled.

"Yes, wrong," Mrs. Weisz enunciated. "You keep rattling that newspaper. Do you mind?" Her eyes looked like they could bulge through her bifocals. A few students snickered behind me. One of them sounded like Seth.

"Sorry," I whispered.

"Thank you," Mrs. Weisz said with a flourish and then returned to writing assignments on the whiteboard. Her black marker squeaked across the surface.

Still struggling to control my breathing, I turned and peered over my shoulder at Ryan. I needed to talk to him. I needed to tell him about the newspaper. I figured he'd be as angry about it as I was. Instead of finding Ryan's eyes, I found Seth's cold, empty ones. That icy grin still plastered across his face.

I spun around and tried to focus. But concentration was impossible. All I could see was the clock above Mrs. Weisz's head. It was as if somebody had smothered the clock's hands in glue.

When the bell rang, I was one of the first students to stand. I grabbed my backpack, stuffed my books inside and waited for Ryan to walk down the row.

But Ryan sprang out of the back row in four long strides and was the first one to reach the door.

He didn't turn toward the front of my row like I'd figured he would. His head and eyes stayed lowered. He didn't acknowledge me in any way. I was invisible.

My throat tightened as I watched him dart toward the door without even a glance in my direction.

What is happening?

I had to talk to Ryan.

This can't be happening, this can't be happening, this can't be happening. This. Can't. Be. Happening.

And yet it was.

RYAN

CHAPTER 32

I COULDN'T LEAVE ENGLISH CLASS fast enough. It was like my head wanted to explode, and sitting next to Seth only fueled my pent-up frustration. I couldn't stop thinking about what he'd said: *You're only interested in Fred because you know it will piss off your dad.*

Was that why I liked her?

My mind raced throughout class, never once hearing Mrs. Weisz's lecture on Shakespeare.

As soon as the bell rang, I sprang from my seat and raced for the door, my backpack already threaded over my shoulder. I ignored Seth's "Hold up" call. Instead, I burst through the door and headed for the corner where I planned to wait for Fred, alone. She would have to go that way to reach her next class.

Except Gwyneth was already waiting for me outside the door.

She had one hand resting on her hip and her backpack threaded over her opposite shoulder. Her weight was shifted on her right leg like she'd been waiting awhile. And she was smiling at me, the tight-lipped kind.

I pulled up when I saw her. I had hoped not to talk to her till fourth period. Nothing was going the way I had planned.

"We need to talk." She grabbed my hand. *"Now."* Her fingers were dry and ice-cold.

She tugged, and I followed, grudgingly, to the corner where I had planned to wait for Fred. It had a perfect view of the English classroom door. Until people began streaming out of the rooms and brushed by us from all directions. It was like being in a fish tank. In a matter of seconds, the normally gray hallway erupted with color and voices.

I lowered my head toward Gwyneth so I could hear her, keeping one eye on the door to watch for Fred. "Yeah," I said, swallowing. "I need to talk to you, too." Her hair smelled like strawberry cough syrup, suffocating me.

"Me, first," Gwyneth said, predictably. Her chin lifted. She left her hand on my forearm and began to rub her thumb nervously against my wrist.

"You didn't call me back yesterday."

I swallowed. "Sorry."

"Where were you Saturday night?"

"Out," I said flatly. I wondered if I should tell her that I knew she and Seth followed me.

"With who?"

"With Fred," I said quickly.

Tears began to moisten Gwyneth's eyes. That didn't help. "Fred?" Gwyneth said it like it was impossible. Her shiny pink lower lip began to quiver.

Jeez. This is hard.

"Look, I know I should have told you. I'm sorry. But this thing with Fred and me..." I paused. My voice lowered. "It just...happened."

Gwyneth choked back a sob. "You lied to me!" She lifted her hand to her face, rotating between hiding her eyes and glaring at me. "You've been lying to me all along."

"I'm so sorry, Gwyneth. Please don't cry," I said, struggling for the right words but finding none. I mean, how do you get a girl to stop crying once the tears start flowing? "But I like Fred. A lot."

Oops. Totally wrong thing to say.

Gwyneth cried harder, muffling her sobs with her hand. She leaned on me like she was about to faint. I couldn't tell if she was being overly dramatic or was truly upset. "But what about Homecoming next month?" She sniffed against the back of her hand. "You promised."

Instead of answering, I closed my eyes briefly. I didn't even like school dances. Gwyneth's hand on my arm started to shake when I didn't say what she wanted to hear.

"Please, Ryan. Don't do this...." She leaned against me, squeezing my arm for balance, but then her voice changed. Peering around my shoulder, she half blurted, half laughed, "Oh, no. Look who's here...."

"What?" I turned.

"Skank," Gywneth said, loud enough for everyone in the hallway to hear.

Fred stared at us from across the hallway. Her lips parted slightly as her dark eyes pulled together, confused. Angry. They darted between Gwyneth and me. They took in Gwyneth's hand resting on my arm, her entire body leaning into mine. Fred blinked once, then twice. Her head began to shake.

"Fred," I said. But then my eyes traveled above her shoulders.

Sam Tracy appeared behind her, dwarfing Fred and just about everyone else. He didn't glare at me, but he didn't look like he thought very much of me either. He tapped Fred's shoulder, and she turned to him. He lowered his head to say something in her ear that I couldn't hear above the roar of voices filling the hallway. She nodded, and together they turned and walked down the hallway, surrounded by frazzled students trying to beat the next bell.

"Fred!" my voice roared. "Wait!" I shook off Gwyneth's hand.

But Fred didn't stop.

I abandoned Gwyneth and wedged my way through the crowd to reach Fred, jostling the people around me with my backpack. Someone even yelled, "Dude, chill!" but I ignored him.

Fred moved fast, and for a huge guy, so did Sam. I finally caught up to them right before they reached the next doorway. I pulled back on her shoulder till she had to stop. "Fred," I said again. "Hold up. Please."

This time, Sam spun around and glared at me, his black eyes shiny with bottomless anger. We were both breathing pretty heavily, and my heart began to pump in overtime.

"Hey, you got a problem?" Sam said, plucking my hand from Fred's shoulder. Then he replaced my hand with his beefy one. Like his belonged on her shoulder, not mine.

Fred finally turned, not because she wanted to, but because she had to. The three of us were causing quite a scene in the hallway.

I looked at Sam. "Can you just give us a second?"

Sam turned to Fred and frowned. But she nodded at him while barely looking at me. "I'll see you inside," she said to Sam.

Sam sighed and walked inside the room backward, glowering at me the whole time. I ignored him as students filed past us into the classroom.

"It's not what you think," I said. "With Gwyneth, I mean."

Fred shook her head. "Really?" Her eyes pooled with hurt. "You looked pretty cozy. And you ignored me in English." She looked at me like she was looking through me.

"Well, what's with Tracy?" I retorted. I hated that she was suddenly looking at me like I was some kind of stranger. "You two looked pretty tight, too." I wanted to swallow back the words, but my entire body was pumped with enough adrenaline to fill an Olympic-size pool. Seeing them together, Sam's hand on her shoulder, even for an instant, was like a punch to the gut.

"Sam is just a—" But then Fred stopped herself. Her chin lifted. "Sam and I date. Occasionally."

It was like someone split open my chest and yanked out my heart. I sure as hell wasn't expecting that. "Wish you would have told me that." *Before I fell for you. Hard.*

"Maybe it's better if you just leave me alone, Ryan. Maybe it's better if we leave each other alone. We made a mistake. This is a mistake."

"What?" My voice turned raspy. I couldn't believe what I was hearing. I went speechless, and my eyes dropped to her right hand. She clutched a piece of newspaper. It was wadded up into a ball inside her hand. But then my eyes traveled from her hand back to her eyes. They were still wide. Hurt. And suspicious. Finally, I took one step back and dragged my tongue across my lips, sensing the brick wall building around her heart. It might have been invisible, but I saw it as easily as I'd seen the rusted barbed wire at the end of Pecos Road. "Okay," I said, lifting my palms. "If that's what you want. But you got it all wrong. You got *me* all wrong."

Fred opened her mouth to say something, and for an instant my breath hitched with hope. But her lips snapped shut, and she said nothing before turning into the classroom just before the bell rang. I couldn't help but notice that Sam had saved the seat beside him with his backpack.

And now I was late for class.

Standing frozen in the hallway, I watched Fred till she took her seat next to Sam. She never looked back.

Behind me, Seth said, "Told you, dude. You should have listened. The girl is weird. And totally wrong for you." He paused, peering over my shoulder into Fred's classroom. "Indians always stick together. Don't forget that."

Still speechless, I walked with Seth to our next class as a familiar hollowness filled my chest all over again like it had never left. Whatever opening in the sky that I'd thought I'd soared through on Saturday night had slammed shut like a steel door right in my face.

Just like that.

Fred

CHAPTER 33

THE NEXT TWO CLASS PERIODS muddled forward in a hazy blur.

Teachers prattled on about hydrogen and mercury, and then their voices morphed into mind-numbing discussions about complementary angles and trigonometric functions. Normally I wouldn't have minded, but today it was all I could do to stop from snapping my pen in two. For the first time in my whole life, school held no appeal. I couldn't concentrate on a single thing. I didn't care about chemicals and angles and numbers.

Sam asked me what was wrong, but I couldn't tell him. I already felt terrible for using him, whether he realized it or not. I owed him an apology as much as I owed one to Ryan.

Why had I behaved like such an idiot after English? I'm sure there was a perfectly understandable reason why Ryan was holding Gwyneth Riordan in the hallway, right? It was just that it hurt so much seeing them together like that, so intimate.

At lunch, I walked quickly into the school cafeteria. The room buzzed with student voices, chairs scraping across the floor, trays slamming. The fried smells wafting from the kitchen mixed with the unease roiling in my stomach, and not in a good way. I had to press my palms below my ribs to hold myself together.

I stopped inside the entrance and scanned the room. My eyes swept the tables closest to the windows, a part of me hoping that I wouldn't find Ryan in his usual spot.

But there he was.

The sun streamed through the window behind him, brightening the tips of his hair but shadowing his face. He was surrounded by all of his friends, including Gwyneth. Still Gwyneth. Always Gwyneth.

I stood at the entrance, watching. Waiting for him to move.

But Ryan didn't see me—or pretended not to.

I should have marched over to his table, but my legs froze.

Then the room morphed from light speed to slow motion. All of the colors inside the cafeteria began to swirl and blur together, and the room went completely silent—at least inside my head. That's because I had to watch as Ryan placed his arm behind Gwyneth's chair like it belonged there. Like it had never left.

Nothing had changed. Everything that I thought had changed, hoped had changed, had returned to exactly as it was, as if it had been there all along.

My eyes turned cloudy, watching, and it was like the cafeteria started breathing for me, slow and heavy. Then my temples began to pound as everybody's faces blurred together in confusing patterns like they were one great big blob at the end of a kaleidoscope. My hands pressed against my stomach.

"This can't be happening," I muttered, fighting back nausea. It was like living inside a nightmare. It *was* a nightmare. Gwyneth must have been able to read my lips because she flashed me a triumphant smile. "This isn't real. I must be dreaming," I mumbled, blinking rapidly to clear my eyes. But then I let my mind think something even worse: *Ryan played me. He used me.*

My knees began to buckle, and I had to reach one hand for the wall. Just as I was about to leave, a hand pulled back my elbow.

"Fred?" a girl said close to my ear. Her voice was light and airy. Steady. Achingly familiar.

I blinked again.

"Are you okay?"

I didn't answer. *Am I okay?* The answer was too painful.

"Want to eat lunch with Yolanda and me?"

I focused on her face. It was Kelly Oliver. I'd never been so glad to see her in my entire life. Yolanda stood beside her, her eyes narrowing before traveling over my shoulder toward Ryan's table.

"Fuckers. Can't trust 'em. None of 'em."

"Watch your language, Yo. Not the time."

"Well, it's true. You know it's true."

Kelly rolled her eyes at her cousin. "Let's just eat, okay." Her hand wrapped around my arm like a soft blanket. "Come on, Fred. You're stuck with your homegirls today."

I nodded numbly as the room turned blurry again.

"Good," Kelly said, guiding me to a table that faced away from Ryan. "'Cause you look like you could use a friend."

RYAN

CHAPTER 34

AFTER LUNCH, I DECIDED to ditch school with Gwyneth and Seth. It hadn't taken much convincing from Seth. Ditching would feel good—anything to numb the hollowness that had crept back inside me. And erase the image of Sam's hand on Fred's shoulder. It had been there before. That much was clear. His eyes had told me everything I needed to know.

"I wanna get baked," I mumbled to Seth as I drove to my house to party. Really, I wanted to forget about Fred. And I totally wanted to forget about Sam with Fred. Good thing that Mom and Dad wouldn't be home till late.

"Me, too," Gwyneth chimed in from the backseat as she checked her cell phone for texts. Like Seth, she had returned to her old self. It was like the morning had never happened. Everything was forgiven; everything was forgotten. Like a blank slate. A do-over for everybody.

"I'm down," Seth said as he turned up the volume on the car stereo. The bass hammered like my temples, numbing my forehead. Seth slapped the back of the seat, startling me. "See?" He grinned at me from the passenger seat. "Now, this feels right, doesn't it? *This* feels good. Hanging, just us. What did I tell you?"

My shoulders pulled back, but I said nothing, pretending instead to concentrate on something in the rearview mirror. All I saw was my expression. It scowled back at me.

"Now, aren't you glad you listened to me?" It came out as a challenge. But I knew it had way more to do with Fred Oday than ditching school.

So I nodded, once, only so that he'd change the subject. Fred was the last person I wanted to talk about, especially with Seth.

"Good," Seth said. "Then let the chillin' begin." He howled out the window like a wolf and then cranked the music louder.

For the next four hours, we downed two six-packs from Dad's basement refrigerator and went through a pack of cigarettes hidden inside Gwyneth's backpack. Then Gwyneth suggested that we do a shot every time the DJ said the word *awesome* on the radio. In less than an hour, we plowed through half a bottle of Dad's best tequila. Dad would be pissed, but I didn't even start to care until half the bottle was empty.

And then I woke up in a daze on a lounge chair next to the pool with Gwyneth lying next to me, her arm draped like a weight across my chest. My throat felt like it had been rubbed with sandpaper.

Someone kicked my foot.

I stirred a little.

"Ryan!" someone hissed. She kicked my foot again. "*Ryan!* Wake up."

I licked my lips and tasted chunks of salt from the last tequila shot. My eyes opened, but the backyard was blurry. So was Riley.

Riley?

Riley stood over me, her skinny arms making a perfect triangle on the side of each hip. She was all pinks and whites, dressed in her funky dance-practice attire—leggings and a sleeveless T-shirt that stretched down to her knees. The colors burned holes in my eyes. "Go away," I mumbled before shutting my eyes.

"Can't," Riley said. "The Phoenix police are standing outside our front door."

My eyes popped open. I bolted upright but stopped short of standing when a sharp pain slashed across my forehead. It was like being clocked with a golf club. For a moment, everything went fuzzy and my body spun. I needed to spew.

Fortunately, Riley grabbed my shoulder and steadied me. "What should I tell them?"

"Why are they here?" I swallowed back the building bile and tasted too many cigarettes.

"Someone complained about the music."

I titled my head. The backyard was completely silent except for the hum from the pool fountain. "What music?"

Riley sighed, shaking her head. "The music that I just turned down. Jeez, Ryan. I could hear it down the street when I rode up on my bike. What were you thinking?"

I wasn't.

Below me, Gwyneth giggled groggily, and I looked all around the yard for Seth. He was missing. "Perfect," I said wryly. "Seth is always gone when I need his help."

"You're just figuring that out now?" Riley's eyes widened.

"Shut up, Riley."

"Well, they're gonna want to talk to Mom. Or Dad." I could tell by the way Riley's eyes stretched across her face that she was scared. And disappointed. Her gaze darted toward the glass table next to the back door. It was littered with silver cans and cigarette butts. I wished that she hadn't seen that.

"Don't worry," I said.

"Don't *worry?*" Riley laughed, the breathy, anxious, on-the-verge-of-hysteria kind. "What is wrong with you? Don't you know how mad Dad will be? And Mom will blow."

I rolled my eyes at her. Unfortunately, I'd had plenty of experience in the Pissing Off Mom and Dad Department. "Are they ever anything else?" I snorted.

"You don't make it any easier."

The front doorbell rang. Twice.

Riley started to twist into a pretzel. "What d'we do?" A veil of old cigarette smoke hung in the air. It would take more than air freshener to mask it.

Reluctantly, I stood, wobbling till Riley grabbed my arm. "Guess I'll go talk to them and give them Dad's cell number." My feet padded against the warm concrete. Riley trailed after me.

"Dad is so going to kill you."

That made me chuckle. "It'll just get added to the list." But then I swallowed, hard, as I braced for the worst.

At least everything was back to normal again. I only wished that *normal* felt better than it did.

Fred

CHAPTER 35

THE NEXT MONTH PASSED as cruelly as the Monday morning when all of the rules in my life were supposed to have changed.

Days and then weeks began and ended in alternating waves of slow motion and fast-forward, waiting for me to either catch up or slow down when I could barely manage either.

I slept and ate very little. One night Kelly and Yolanda showed up at our trailer in Kelly's pickup truck and pretty much forced me to go mall shopping with them, but even window-shopping didn't cheer me up. Then one Friday—or maybe it was a Wednesday—Sam worked up the nerve to ask me out on a date, but I had to say no, much to Trevor's disappointment, even after he offered the use of his motorcycle. Sam didn't press, but I was pretty sure he knew why I had turned into a total zombie. Unfortunately, the more my friends tried to draw me close, the harder I pushed away.

Concentrating in class became almost impossible, but I still turned in passable assignments and pretended to take notes. If the teachers were concerned, they didn't say. Last Thursday before school, when I dropped off my bag, I couldn't bottle everything inside me anymore. I just cried in Coach Lannon's office, and he didn't say a single word. He didn't ask any questions. He just let me cry into my hands while passing me tissues. But I think

he knew. Instead of prying, he hung close to me at practice, waiting, I guess, for me to say something, share anything. I wouldn't—
couldn't—say anything. I didn't know how to put into words the
pain that had torn my heart wide open, leaving it exposed. It was
easier to say nothing.

Golf was my only constant, and we'd won our last three tournaments. It was the only thing that I could truly control, and for that
reason I clung to it while everything else spun around me dull and
lifeless, just like it was the day before I'd kissed Ryan Berenger and
thought that I was special. At least he went out of his way to avoid
me at golf practice. He didn't even pretend *not* to look at me anymore. I had become as invisible as the wind again.

The other players still talked in hushed voices whenever they
were around me at practice or during tournaments, and once or
twice I'd clearly heard someone mutter "Pocahontas," but I was
too numb to put up a fight, even if the nickname burned like fire
inside me.

I hadn't uttered one complete word to Ryan since the Monday
morning we broke up—if you could call it that. We barely talked
at tournaments, even when you'd think teammates would at least
exchange niceties, like "good shot" or "you're up next." Ryan and
I did not. And that was just as well.

A single word from him would have summoned a new round of
tears, especially when I had to remind myself that I had never mis-
judged a person more in my entire life. Maybe Yolanda was right
about white people—at least white boys named Ryan Berenger.

"You're awfully quiet again today," Dad said when he picked
me up from school after practice. "Barely said a word to me on the
drive to school, too."

That was true. I hadn't felt like talking to anyone, even Dad.
"Just tired," I said, my excuse for everything lately, as I lifted my
golf bag into the back of the van. I'd slept in fitful spurts all week.
At least I'd have the weekend.

"You sure that's all it is?" His eyes, red around the edges, narrowed to tiny slits. "Something happen at school? At practice? You haven't been yourself, Fred. Tell me what's going on."

I closed the rear door. It slammed with a loud *clang*. Then I paused, my hand still clutching the door handle, trying to conjure up some nerve. With a deep breath, I walked around the van to the passenger door. "Yeah," I said with forced brightness. I climbed into the seat. "I mean, no. School is fine. Practice is fine." Golf practice was always fine.

"Well, I want you to take a break from golf this weekend," he said as the van chugged away from the curb. "You're not coming with me to work tomorrow and that's final. I want you to do something else." He turned to me, and his eyes grew uncharacteristically wide. "Anything else. You're practicing too much. Give golf a rest, Fred."

"And do what?" I chuckled and then wished I hadn't. Other than homework and golf, I wasn't exactly swimming in extracurricular options.

"Well, your mother said this morning they were short-staffed at the restaurant. Maybe you should take a shift with her. How's that sound? That would keep you away from your clubs for at least a day."

"Really?" I turned, feeling lighter. It'd been a while since the chef offered me a shift. He must be desperate.

Dad returned the smile. "Really. And a couple days away from the golf course will do you good."

"Maybe." I sighed, but then my shoulders lightened all over again when I remembered something important. Something I'd forgotten.

"See?" Dad said, studying my expression between checking his rearview and the traffic entering the freeway. "You're smiling. It's helping already."

I tilted my head toward him and smirked. Then I turned and watched the traffic from my opened window. I blinked into the wind, the warm air drying my eyes and brushing against my face.

The wind blew my hair so that it swirled around my head. I closed my eyes and imagined the most perfect pair of white leather golf shoes with soft pink piping.

Then I smiled inside.

How had I forgotten?

A couple more shifts at the Wild Horse Restaurant and I'd finally have enough money to buy them.

At least that was something.

"Please tell me you're joking."

"I'm not joking, Fred," Mom said as she tied a teal-blue sash around her waist in the Wild Horse kitchen on Saturday night. I wore the same uniform and had tied my hair in a single braid that stretched down to the small of my back. Mom fiddled with a few loose strands around her face and then tucked them into the bun pinned next to her neck. Around us, a dozen other waitresses and bussers raced through the kitchen carrying water pitchers and balancing round trays piled high with the evening's salads and entrées. Sam and Peter nodded at me as they wheeled a full tub of dirty dishes toward the sinks. Tonight just about every Lone Butte Rez teenager had snagged a shift at the restaurant.

"But why didn't you tell me?" I asked her.

"I didn't know till a few minutes ago," Mom said as she wedged a black leather order pad into the waistband of her pants. "Apparently they're expecting a large crowd tonight. You think they consult with me around here?" Her widened eyes dared a contradiction.

I swallowed, suddenly dizzy from the steamy kitchen heat and melting-butter aromas swirling around us. My temples pounded with fear. "But I can't do it."

Mom sighed like I was crazy. "Don't do this to me, Fred. You wanted a shift. I got you a shift. And you pick now to have a meltdown? On the busiest night of the week? And I don't have to remind you that if you blow it tonight, you can probably kiss a full-time job after graduation goodbye."

If only.

"This is your last chance, Fred."

My breathing quickened and my nostrils flared as my mind—my whole body—struggled for control. Instead, my eyes darted to the swinging door when it burst open from a busboy carrying a tray stacked with dirty dishes. The door swung wide enough for me to catch a glimpse of the table nearest the window.

"But they're kids from my school, Mom. It'll be too humiliating."

Mom snorted. "Yeah, welcome to my world. It's humiliating for me every time I come to work. Trust me, you get used to it."

My lower lip began to quiver before I could bite down on it. "But, Mom..." I moaned softly. I hated sounding like a child, but never in a million years had I expected to be waiting on a table full of kids from Lone Butte High School.

In my haze this past month, I must have missed the usual posters announcing a dance this weekend. Was it Homecoming? Girls' Choice? I barely noticed. Or cared. I never expected to go to dances and was too focused on avoiding Ryan Berenger and his creeptastic friends.

Of all the fancy restaurants in Phoenix, why did they have to come to the Wild Horse?

Mom yanked on my elbow hard enough to make me blink.

"Look, one of the kids' parents is friends with the chef. That's how they got a reservation. That's all I know. Now, you just stay behind me and do as I say. You won't even have to talk to them. I'll do all the talking." Her tone softened a fraction. "Now, we've got to go to work. They're in our section tonight. Can you at least manage that?"

I nodded stiffly.

"Good." Mom released my arm. She turned to a shelf just inside the kitchen door and picked up two water pitchers, handing one of them to me. "Try not to drop anything, Fred. Concentrate." Her brow wrinkled with new doubt. "Please?"

I took the pitcher with both hands. It was ice-cold and felt as heavy as the rest of my body. With my head lowered, I followed behind Mom and wished that I could die.

RYAN

CHAPTER 36

IN MY CHAIR NEXT TO GWYNETH, I pulled on the black tie at my neck. It had gotten tighter the moment we stepped inside the Wild Horse Restaurant.

The part about school dances that I despised the most, other than the lame dance itself, was going to fancy restaurants and pretending that all of the other diners weren't staring at us.

Unfortunately, the dinner was the part of the evening that Gwyneth loved most, even though it'd be a miracle if she ate a speck of anything. And I should have seriously paid more attention when she squealed about the dinner reservations yesterday at lunch. I'd only half listened to her, as I was prone to do. When our rented limousine had pulled up to the front door of the Wild Horse Restaurant, I'd felt sick all over.

Across from Gwyneth and me at our round table, Seth and Zack scanned the menus while Gwyneth, Sara and Kari discussed who was having the best after-dance parties and whether we should stop at the gas station on the reservation to buy tequila with Gwyneth's fake ID.

"Indians never check your IDs," Kari said. "All they care about is selling beer."

I sank lower in my chair as my eyes scanned the crowded restaurant. I was torn between wanting to see Fred and not seeing her at all. It was bad enough trying to pretend that I didn't want to talk to her, to touch her, every moment in school and at golf practice. The tournaments were even worse. My play in the past three tournaments had sucked while Fred had played as if she was on fire. I supposed she was over me with golf scores like that, if she had ever been into me at all.

I also wondered about her and Sam. A lot. He followed her everywhere—before school, between classes. Sometimes he even carried her backpack. He'd become like her permanent shadow. If I had tried to approach her, he'd have probably stuffed me into a locker or something.

Despite it all, I hoped that Fred's waitressing career had ended the night she'd dropped a slice of mesquite-honey mousse cake into my lap.

"Something wrong?" Gwyneth said to me, taking a rare pause from Sara and Kari. Since our quasi breakup a month ago, which had lasted all of five minutes, she'd been annoyingly attentive, as if she expected me to break up with her again at any moment.

I cleared my throat. "No," I said. *Yes. Everything.*

"Really?" Her eyes narrowed.

"Just wondering what to eat for dinner," I lied. My menu rested untouched in the middle of the table.

"Have you eaten here before?" Seth peered at me above the menu.

"Uh-huh," I mumbled. "Once."

Seth placed the menu on the table and grinned wide enough for my hand to tug again on my tie. "Really?" Seth said. "Me, too. Once. With my parents." His tone turned innocent, enough to get my attention. I knew that tone. It was the opposite of innocent.

"Well, if we ever see our waitress, it'll be a freakin' miracle," Gwyneth said behind her hand in a singsong voice but plenty loud enough for everyone at the table to hear. "My dad promised we'd get the VIP, but so far..." Her mouth pursed with impatience.

I ignored her. There was no pleasing Gwyneth. Instead, I glanced across the table toward the back of the restaurant just as the rear doors swung open. "Oh, no," I mumbled.

"What's wrong?" Gwyneth said.

A lady approached our table with a tight but friendly smile. It was the same waitress from Mom's birthday dinner.

"Good evening, kids," she said. "Welcome to the Wild Horse. Enjoying a dance tonight, I see. You all look so nice." She smiled at everyone at the table, not too brightly or loudly, but in that way that said she wouldn't be an intrusion.

My breathing stopped when Fred stepped around her.

With lowered eyes, she began filling our water glasses with an enormous pitcher. She started with Gwyneth.

"Oh?" Gwyneth said before biting down on her lip to stifle a giggle. Her eyes blinked wide as she tracked Fred's movements. Then her hand proceeded to cover her smile as Fred reached for her empty crystal glass.

If our waitress noticed, she said nothing, while Fred moved silently around the table. The older lady proceeded to list the chef's entrée recommendations. No one really paid any attention to her, least of all me.

"The chef recommends the braised lobster tail with avocado mousse or the Sea of Cortez seviche..." the lady continued as I watched Fred finish pouring water into the glasses. Her hands shook, but only a few drops spilled onto the white linen tablecloth, mostly because the water pitcher was as bulky as a goldfish bowl. It was crammed full of ice and lemon slices.

Fred saved my water glass for last. Instead of having her reach into the center of the table, I handed her my glass, and for an instant our fingers brushed. Hers were cold from holding the pitcher.

"Hey, Fred," I said quietly as the waitress continued to rattle off the specials in the background.

"...grilled tenderloin with onion pearls, marinated duck breast in a wine reduction sauce..."

Fred's eyes flickered at the touch of my hand but only for a moment.

"I'll be back in a few minutes to see what you've decided," the waitress said. "Can I bring you some freshly baked olive bread?"

"Is this bottled water?" Seth asked Fred, pointing a silver fork at his glass. The way he tapped it against the glass made my teeth clench.

The waitress pulled her shoulders back. "It is filtered water, sir. Would you like us to bring you something else? A bottle of sparkling, perhaps?"

Seth shook his head and took another long sip. "No, this is fine. Can I get some more?" He shook his half-empty glass at Fred, and her cheeks darkened to a deeper shade.

I wanted to reach for the water pitcher and dump the rest in Seth's lap.

Carefully, Fred moved alongside Seth. Seth placed his glass in the center of their table. Fred's lips twisted as she reached across him for the glass. Her hands shook, and my chest tightened. I was afraid she'd drop the glass.

As soon as Seth's glass was full, Fred turned and walked in the opposite direction with her empty water pitcher. "And some bread!" Seth called after her. "Please?" he said with that perfected wide-eyed innocent look. He turned it on the waitress, too, but she nodded at Seth with a strained smile beneath flared nostrils.

"I'll be back in a few minutes to let you decide on dinner." And then she was gone.

Gwyneth giggled as soon as we were alone. "*Awkward!*" Her eyes bulged with delight.

"Jeez, I think just about every Pocahontas from school works at this place," Seth said, nodding toward the table across from us. "I recognized two more over there."

"What is your fucking problem?" I glared at Seth.

Seth's grin faded. "No problem," he said, blinking slowly when he realized that I wasn't laughing. "Just making an observation."

"Did you have to act like an asshole?"

Gwyneth's giggling ended abruptly as Seth leaned back in his chair. "What'd I do? I was just asking for water. And bread. Isn't that allowed in a restaurant?"

"No, you weren't. You were trying to embarrass her."

"Who?"

My nostrils flared. "Fred."

Seth's eyes opened wider. "So what?"

My breathing quickened. "How'd you know she worked here?"

Seth's lips fluttered. "I may have overheard her talking to one of the other Pocahontases. Besides, where else can they work around here?"

"Shut your mouth, Seth."

"Make me," he said, clearly enjoying his moment.

"You can't let it go, can you?" I said.

"Let what go?" Seth said, a maniacal grin blanching his face. "The fact that I got balled up and she got my spot?" He leaned closer to the table, his smile replaced with a sneer. "You're right. It still pisses me off. Would you be okay if it'd happened to you?"

I said nothing, and the rest of the table turned silent. I couldn't stop glaring at Seth. It was like looking across at a complete stranger, not someone I'd known my whole life.

But then Seth tried to laugh it off. "Hey, I'm only messing with you. Lighten up, okay?"

My throat turned dry. I suddenly wanted to be as far away from the table as possible. I scooted out my chair. "I'll be back."

Gwyneth grabbed my forearm, stopping me. "Where are you going?"

"To find the bathroom." I shook off her hand.

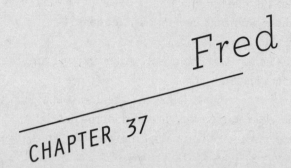

Fred

CHAPTER 37

RYAN WAS PACING OUTSIDE the front of the restaurant when I found him, his hands jammed in the front of his pants. Truthfully I had seen him through the front windows before I pushed open the wooden door.

He had offered Peter a twenty to find me. Peter didn't take his money but found me anyway. I didn't know whether to be flattered or annoyed by his persistence, but my brain knew better than to come looking for Ryan Berenger.

"What do you want, Ryan?" I said before the door had a chance to close. The air swirled, hazy and weird. I looked up at the sky and heard thunder rumble in the distance. "I've only got a minute." It was the first time I'd spoken to him in over a month. We were still paired at tournaments, but I'd kept my distance as best I could and focused on my strokes.

"I am so sorry, Fred," Ryan blurted. "I didn't plan this. None of it."

"*Now* you're sorry?" I heard my voice get louder. "Great timing, Ryan."

His hand pulled through his hair like he wanted to tear it off. His collar was completely open, his tie crooked. He looked a wreck. "I'm sorry about what Seth said, too. He didn't mean it."

"Really?" My chin pulled back. "Seems to me he's the only one being honest. I'll give him that."

Ryan paused. "What's that supposed to mean?"

My teeth clamped shut.

Ryan exhaled heavily. "Look, Seth was just having fun. The stupid kind. That's just Seth."

"And I see you continue to follow his lead like a puppy dog. Congratulations. Gold star for you." I turned for the door.

Ryan followed and pulled back on my elbow. "Fred, please. I want to talk to you. I need to talk to you—"

"There's nothing to say."

"You never gave me a chance to explain. About Gwyneth, I mean."

"I saw everything perfectly."

"No, you didn't. I was breaking up with her."

I laughed. "And yet you're here with her." I looked him up and down, all debonairly disheveled in his suit. "Going to the dance?"

Ryan exhaled. "I promised to take her a while ago."

I turned for the door.

He pulled back, harder. "Well, what about you and Sam? I thought you didn't have a boyfriend. And yet he follows you around everywhere."

"I've known Sam my whole life."

"I could say the same thing about Gwyneth."

"Well, you've picked a lovely girl." I looked down at his hand but said nothing, because what else could I say? It was true. Especially the part about Ryan in a suit and Gwyneth in a beautiful dress, together, at a dance. Sam and I and our pretend dates seemed secondary. And delusional.

He lightened his grip. "I know. It's whacked. It looks all wrong."

I laughed again, but the chuckle wedged deep in my throat, threatening to dredge up tears. I wasn't handling this well at all.

"Fred, please—"

"I've got to get back to work. Apology accepted, okay? But do me a favor and leave me alone." My voice cracked, and I immediately hated myself for it. Now was not the time to cry.

"Please don't cry, Fred," he said. "Please."

I pressed my lips together when the lower one started to quiver. I turned and covered my face in my hands.

"How did things get so messed up?" Ryan whispered.

Slowly, I uncovered my face.

Ryan wrapped his arms around me, and, for a second, I let myself sink against him, breathing him in, his minty shampoo and cologne. But it was over before it started. The door burst opened behind me. I instinctively pulled away, expecting customers leaving the restaurant—or worse, Mom hunting me down.

But then a flash of white and a whiff of the kitchen invaded my senses. Beside me, Sam's hands reached for the lapels of Ryan's jacket. In less than a heartbeat, Sam threw Ryan into the air and across the sidewalk like he was a pillow. Ryan crashed so hard against the cement that I worried he'd broken all the bones in his back. In his whole body. I didn't expect him to get up.

"Sam!" I yelled.

Without a word, Sam charged after Ryan.

I ran after him, trying to reach Ryan, but before I could get to him, Ryan was on his feet and lunging toward Sam's stomach, the whites of his eyes blazing with anger. He ran straight for Sam with widespread arms, surprising him. Surprising me.

Sam fell back, only for a split second, until he charged right back at him.

"Ryan! No!"

Neither one listened.

"You must be deaf, because I thought I heard her say, 'Leave me alone,' White Boy," Sam said, pulling his fist back for a punch.

I screamed as I leaped for Sam's arm. If he connected his fist to Ryan's face, there would be broken bones. And blood. Lots and lots of blood.

Crack! The sky flashed.

Then someone behind us yelled, "Hey, what the hell's going on?!"

In the next instant, bussers, waitresses, even customers flooded the sidewalk, wedging between Ryan, Sam and me even as the sky split open with lightning and thunder.

Someone pulled me back—Kelly, I think—as two guys pulled Sam off Ryan, even as they continued to throw punches at each other, some connecting, others missing.

Then the rain started to fall in gray sheets, mixing with the desert air. Customers ran for their cars.

Another lightning bolt.

The thunder competed with the thrashing and yelling that spilled into the parking lot. After a while, I couldn't tell who was fighting, who was hitting whom. My hair clung to my forehead like wet noodles as I stared, stunned, at a sea of moving bodies and loud voices.

I kept trying to get a look at Ryan, but people stepped in my way as Kelly dragged me back toward the door. Forget yelling. No one was listening to anybody. Anger and rage mixed with the rain, charging the air. Complete chaos, in the time it took to blink.

But then the headlights of a car appeared from somewhere in the parking lot, freezing the pandemonium like a camera flash. A limousine. It stopped parallel to the crowd. The door opened and someone was thrown inside. I prayed it was Ryan.

I didn't know what to do. I tried to run forward, but Kelly gripped my arm, tight.

"We better get inside. We're getting soaked," Kelly said. "Sam will take care of it."

Take care of it?

I turned to Kelly. "Sam'll kill him."

"Sam just tossed him in that limousine. He'll be fine. Safest place for him."

"Fuckers," said a voice behind us. Yolanda. "Told you they can't be trusted. None of those shit-faced motherfuckers can be trusted."

"Enough, Yo!" Kelly said.

"It wasn't like that," I started to say, still straining to see between the arms and legs. "He was trying to apologize." *And I wouldn't listen.*

With her arm still wrapped around my waist, Kelly and I walked through the door. "We gotta get back to work. Chef's gonna be pissed."

I didn't care.

Back inside the restaurant, I had no idea what to expect. It seemed that half the guests were still milling around outside, even as the sky opened up with rain.

When I returned to the spot where Ryan, Seth and their girl-friends had been seated, their table was abandoned.

"I don't believe this," Mom said behind me, her nostrils flaring. She proceeded to fill an empty serving tray with their un-used plates, napkins and glasses, not bothering to soften clanging silverware. "Our biggest table of the night. Gone." She tossed the last bread plate into the pile with a loud exhale. Then she turned sideways long enough to glare at me. "Happy now?"

I didn't answer.

Instead of numbness the following week at school, I felt embar-rassment. I didn't need a cell phone or bionic ears to know that the Saturday night fight was all anyone was talking about.

In the cafeteria, I'd overheard that cell-phone photos of Sam and Ryan were being texted around everywhere. Someone had said something stupid and cruel on Facebook about Sam. About me. Even about Kelly, the nicest person I'd ever known. I did my best

to tune it out but was only mildly successful. Like before, I clung
to golf, the only thing in my life I could control.

The following Thursday after lunch, the Lone Butte golf team
boarded a bus to the Glendale Golf Club. I sat alone in the first
row, my usual spot, facing the window.

Coach Lannon, mercifully, did not insist that Ryan sit beside me.

Ryan hadn't tried to talk to me since Saturday night, and that
was fine with me. If things had been weird before between us, they
were in-a-parallel-universe weirder now. At least he was leaving me
alone, which, I supposed, was better for everybody.

That didn't mean that I wasn't completely aware that Ryan
was sitting two rows behind me next to Zack Fisher with his iPod
jammed in his ears. The volume was so loud that I could hear electric guitar blaring from Ryan's earbuds two rows up. On Monday,
he'd had a welt on his cheekbone from Sam's punch, but now it
was just a pale purple bruise, like a birthmark. He kept some of it
hidden behind his sunglasses. Sam had a similar one on his left
cheek, so I supposed they were even.

Once everyone boarded, the driver pulled out of the parking lot
and Coach Lannon started to bark out pairings and tidbits about
the Glendale Golf Club course that he had scribbled on his clipboard.

"Don't forget there's water on sixteen."

"Watch out for the tricky sand trap in front of the third hole—it's
right in front of the green."

"Stay strong."

"Stay hydrated."

"Keep your heads down."

"Be the ball."

I listened to all of his cautionary words and watched his lips
move, but the only thing that mattered was this: "Fred, you'll be
paired with Ryan again. You two had the lowest scores last week."
In golfspeak, low was good.

I nodded at the coach, but I didn't turn to acknowledge Ryan. Following that breaking news, you could've cut the silence inside the bus with a chain saw.

Focus, Fred, I reminded myself a half hour later when the bus pulled up alongside the bag drop at the Glendale Golf Club.

Focus. You've got to focus.

I was the first person off the bus right behind Coach Lannon. I was also the first to grab my bag before walking to the first tee. Midway down the cart path, two men and one woman began asking me all sorts of nosy questions. They'd blocked the path with their bodies, so I had to stop.

"How does it feel to be the only girl on an all-boys' team?" asked the red-haired woman. She clutched a small notepad with a pen poised above it.

"Where'd you learn how to play, Fred?" asked the younger man. He was kind of good-looking in a shiny way, and I thought I recognized him from one of the local TV stations. Weirdly, he looked smaller in real life. He thrust a tape recorder the size of a pen underneath my chin.

"Planning any new strategies this week?" the older man asked. I recognized him from the first tournament, Notebook Guy with the gray sideburns. He'd called me "the girl with the golden arm" in the newspaper. It was one of the nicest things anyone had ever said about my swing—not including Ryan, of course.

My eyes jumped to each of them, unblinking, just as Coach Lannon caught up behind me.

"Whoa, whoa," he said, placing a heavy hand on my shoulder. "Can you save the questions for after we play?"

The threesome nodded reluctantly.

The coach stayed with me till we reached the tee box. "Don't mind those sports reporters, Fred. I'll keep an eye out for them. They're only doing their job."

I nodded. "But why aren't they asking anyone else questions?"

"They will. For now you're the novelty."

"Because I'm a girl?" *Or an Indian girl?*

Coach Lannon smiled and pushed his sunglasses above his forehead like he wanted to make sure I saw the meaning in his eyes. He leaned closer. "Because you're good."

I swallowed, considering this.

"Put it out of your mind, Fred, and just play golf." His voice turned softer. "Have fun out there, okay?"

"Okay, Coach." But I didn't plan to have fun. I planned to be the best. I planned to win.

The coach turned back down the path toward the bus and the other players.

I stood alone at the edge of the first tee box and began to fidget with my hands. But as soon as I gazed across the fairway, I completely forgot all about the reporters, Ryan and everything else.

There were twice as many spectators on the fairway as last week and most of them were staring at me, including Kelly, Yolanda, Sam and Peter. Even Vernon Parker was with them. Being a freshman, he had to have ditched school to be here. They all waved when I spotted them. Just seeing them turned my throat raw with an unexpected lump.

Kelly had told me yesterday during lunch that they were thinking of attending the tournament today but I'd thought they were only being nice. That would be like them. Because why would a bunch of Rez kids want to drive forty miles to watch a golf tournament, especially when golf was about as popular on the Rez as ice hockey? "We're planning to come if my dad can get my truck working by then," Kelly had told me. "We're proud of you. Everybody's proud. Don't forget that, Fred. My little sister even asked my dad for golf clubs! Said she wants to play like you."

There were a few other people from the Rez, including the most recognizable one: George Trueblood.

George Trueblood was sort of a legend on the Rez but mostly

in his own mind. He didn't claim to be Gila; he claimed to belong to all of the Tribes. He called himself a Pipatsje. He hung out most days at the Gila Community Center, didn't work much, but he didn't give anyone trouble either. He believed that he was an Indian Chief, and no one would ever tell him he wasn't. The elders let him lead parades, sit in the inner circle during community meetings, tell old legends and stories at the Rez school, and allowed him honorary positions that I was guessing he probably didn't otherwise deserve. Everyone loved George Trueblood. He'd even stayed in our trailer a few times when the desert nights grew too cold to sleep outdoors.

But the golf course was hardly the Rez. No one would understand George Trueblood like we did.

I cringed inwardly at his clothes and felt guilty in the next instant for my embarrassment. He was dressed in a buckskin jacket with fringe along both arms even though it still felt like August. A green-and-blue beaded band wrapped around his shiny forehead. His marble-black hair stretched down to the small of his black in a single tight braid. The strands were sprinkled with gray. On the Rez, I didn't give George Trueblood and his strange ways a second thought. Off the Rez, he stood out even more than I did.

"Here's a new sleeve," Coach Lannon said, walking back toward the tee. He handed me a box with three white golf balls.

"Thanks." My eyes swept over the crowd that had formed around the first hole. Every time I blinked, the crowd swelled. This week, Principal Graser was in the crowd, standing out in his blue suit. He and Coach Lannon exchanged a wave.

I threaded my golf bag higher across my shoulder, letting its weight balance as much as steady me. Then I squeezed the golf glove peeking out of my back pocket for luck.

Coach Lannon removed his visor and wiped his forehead with the back of his hand. "There's one other thing," he said.

I turned to him, waiting, expecting more news on golf pairings or something.

"The starter is telling me that the tall man over there insists on saying an Indian blessing before the tournament starts."

"His name is George Trueblood," I corrected him.

The coach paused. "Okay," he said. "Mr. Trueblood. But what d'you think? Would you like him to do it? Your call."

I swallowed, considering this, as my eyes drifted back to the crowd. They landed on my friends from the Rez. Normally our prayers and blessings were considered sacred and not shared outside the tribe, but I wondered if we should make an exception today. "Yes," I said, surprising myself. "Let him."

Coach Lannon glanced down at me and smiled. "Well, okay, then. You got it."

"A blessing can't hurt," I added, lifting my chin.

The coach tilted his head. "Can't argue with that." Then he turned to the starter and yelled, "Okay, Ron." He swirled his forefinger in the air.

Ron, the starter, wore a black-and-white-striped golf shirt. He motioned to George Trueblood.

I caught Kelly staring at me, trying to get my attention. She stood next to George Trueblood. Her shoulders shrugged apologetically, but I smiled back and shook away her apology with my head. *A few minutes isn't going to hurt anybody,* I tried to tell her.

George Trueblood stepped onto the fairway, one worn moccasin at a time. From a distance, his shoes looked like brown socks. He walked straight and held his chin high. When he raised his arm, the crowd turned silent. The fringe from his jacket fluttered downward like a dozen arrows. If his deep voice hadn't commanded everyone's attention, the sharp edges to his weathered face would have. Even the doves and the cactus wrens turned silent in the trees that lined the fairway—at least I imagined that they did.

"What's he saying?" someone whispered behind me.

"Hell if I know," another voice answered.

"He sounds like he's grunting," laughed another.

More chuckling.

Coach Lannon turned his head and glared. "Show some respect, boys."

I swallowed back an angry breath as I struggled to concentrate on George Trueblood's words. I'd probably heard them a dozen times. Even though I didn't understand everything, I certainly got his meaning.

"What's he saying?" The coach whispered beside me, his arms crossed over his chest.

I hesitated. But the coach nudged me again.

So I translated,

May the warm winds of Heaven blow softly on your house;
May the Great Spirit bless all who gather here.
May your moccasins make happy tracks in many snows;
And may the Rainbow always touch your shoulder.[4]

My eyes never left George Trueblood as he spoke. When he lowered his long arms, Coach Lannon turned to me and whispered, "Is he done?"

I nodded without looking at him and watched as people began to fidget along the fairway. A few even clapped, but clapping wasn't necessary.

George Trueblood turned to me. His expression smiled at me, even though his lips never moved.

I nodded at him, grateful.

"Finally," someone muttered behind me.

"Jeez, let's get started," said another.

The coach turned toward the voices and sighed with exasperation, shaking his head. Then he turned to me. "You and Ryan are up, Fred. Good luck."

The starter blew his whistle. Twice. The sound pierced the sky, and the people standing closest to him had to cover their ears.

---

4 Cherokee Prayer Blessing.

I strode to the top of the tee box, my expression frozen. I was determined to win this tournament. And I'd already played the first hole in my mind: I'd reach the green in two strokes.

I didn't even notice Ryan standing behind me till he spoke. "Fred," he said. "Do you—"

His voice sliced through my concentration. "Please don't talk to me, Ryan." I plucked my driver from my bag. "Let's just play golf."

Ryan lifted his palms and backed away a step. "I was just going to ask you if you wanted to go first," he said evenly.

"Oh," I replied in a small voice. But then I said, "I'd rather flip for it," finally looking back at him. It was the first time that we'd looked directly at each other since Saturday night. My eyes quickly swept across his face, long enough to notice his bloodshot eyes, the bruise on his cheek. Even his golf shirt was wrinkled.

Ryan won the coin toss, calling tails.

We were paired with two other players from Glendale High. They kept staring at me like I was some sort of freak. The golf-girl freak.

I walked the course alone, but the vast majority of spectators followed my foursome from hole to hole. Ryan didn't attempt to talk to me again. The only person who checked on me was Coach Lannon as he flew across the path on his golf cart tracking the team. My Rez friends didn't say anything, just gave an encouraging nod and smile here and there. That was all I needed.

By the ninth hole, I'd managed to par six of the holes and birdie two. I probably would have birdied three if I hadn't caught the eye of Seth Winter and Gwyneth Riordan on the opposite side of the putting green, directly in my line of sight.

On purpose?

You never knew with Seth Winter.

Gwyneth blue Ryan a kiss as he waited on the green behind me, and I felt my stomach lurch as I tried to line up my putt. I three-putted and cursed myself for losing my concentration. It would not happen again.

By the tenth hole, on a short par four, I got my first eagle of the day, and the crowd erupted in approval. "Fred Oday is in the lead," I heard people murmur as I walked the cart path to the eleventh hole. Even Ryan muttered, "Nice hole." I said nothing back, refusing to look at him. Instead, I searched the crowd for familiar faces—Kelly, Yolanda, George Trueblood, even Sam. When I found them, I smiled, and they waved their arms overhead, energizing me.

I birdied the eleventh hole and parred the twelfth and the thirteenth. For the next four holes, I blocked out all voices around me, even the few friendly ones. The world moved in graceful slow motion, and the colors blended together again at the edges, muted and wispy, as I found my rhythm. My only focus was the golf ball and landing it inside the hole with as few strokes as possible. My swing was the only thing I could control; it was the only thing that made sense. I loved it when I found my zone, and I was definitely inside its warm and calming embrace in this tournament.

After I sank my final putt on the eighteenth hole, Coach Lannon's voice was the first sound to break my trance. I blinked, and the world started to spin faster again. The colors turned sharper and more vibrant. I heard clapping, floating in my direction in waves. It was almost like I'd returned to my body from some far-off place.

"You've won, Fred. Again!" Coach Lannon roared. "And we're gonna win our fifth tournament, thanks to you. Can you say *state championship?*" He patted my back, harder this time, and I stumbled forward with only my right foot to keep me from crashing to the ground.

I forced a tight smile, mostly from the shock of the back slap, as the coach led me by my elbow to the white tent at the edge of the parking lot where each player was required to return a signed scorecard to the tournament officials. The three reporters with their notepads and tape recorders trailed a few steps behind us, closer than before. Ryan followed somewhere alongside me.

Just as we were about to enter the tent, the starter stopped us.

"Hold on, there," he said, pulling on the coach's left shoulder.

"What's up, Ron?" Coach Lannon said.

The starter cleared his throat, scratched the side of his head and then said, "There's been some talk among the players, Larry..." He avoided eye contact with me.

"Talk?" Coach Lannon's hand dropped from my back as he turned to face him. His chin lifted. "What kind of talk?"

The starter cleared his throat again. "Someone got a look at the girl's bag." He nodded at me, as if there would have been a question about which girl.

Coach Lannon chuckled. "Yeah? So it's a little *loud,* I'll grant you that. So what?"

The starter's head tilted. "It's not the outside, Larry. It's what's inside. Each player can only carry fourteen clubs. You know that. It's PGA regulation. I don't make the rules. I just follow them."

Coach Lannon blinked, slowly, like someone was waking him from his own private trance, too. Then he turned to my bag. It still hung over my shoulder. "Let me see your bag, Fred." His fingers fluttered at me.

I let the strap slip off my shoulder. It landed on the pavement in front of me with a heavy *thunk.*

The coach and the starter placed their hands on either side of it. "One, two, three..." Coach Lannon began counting. "Four, five, six," he said.

"Seven, eight, nine." The starter counted, too, tapping the tops of each club with his pen.

"Ten, eleven, twelve, thirteen, fourteen." They both paused.

My breathing stopped.

"Fifteen," they said in unison. Coach Lannon's eyes bulged like someone had just squeezed his neck.

"Wait a minute," I said, pushing the clubs around. My eyes locked on to all of them at once. I knew my clubs like I knew my own name. Each one was mismatched, a little rusty around the shafts, and scratched and pitted where they should be shiny and smooth. All except one.

In the middle, wedged between my irons, I pulled out a two-iron. It was long—too long for my height, shiny and barely used.

And I'd never seen it before.

"This isn't mine." I turned it in my hands. I knew the rules about the limits on clubs. And I knew you had to finish a tournament with the clubs you started with. I wasn't looking for an unfair advantage.

A crowd began to gather around us.

The starter tilted his head to the side, finally acknowledging my existence. "But it was in your bag," he said to me.

"You heard her, Ron," Coach Lannon said. "I believe her. It's not her club."

The starter sighed, pointed to the club. "But it was in her bag," he said again, as if the coach had a hearing problem. "I saw it with my own eyes. There's no denying it."

"This isn't right." Coach Lannon shook his head. The crowd began to murmur and fidget around us, making breathing difficult.

My forehead began to pound, and the pavement looked like it was moving. I let the two-iron slip from my hand. It clanged to the ground, and I watched until it stopped wobbling against the pavement.

Beside me, Ryan bent down to pick it up, startling me. I never heard his approach.

"You know our rules," the starter said as the crowd tightened another notch around us. "Fred will have to be disqualified."

Disqualified?

"Cheater," someone snickered behind me. "The Indian is a cheater."

That was even worse.

RYAN

CHAPTER 38

I PICKED UP THE TWO-IRON from the pavement after it slipped from Fred's fingers.

I wasn't sure if she knew she had dropped it. I wanted so badly to tell her not to worry, that it was just a lame golf tournament, but I lost my voice. Again.

Then I had to listen to the names people called her. They floated through the crowd like flies you couldn't swat. Whispers, mostly, but loud enough to hear.

"Cheater..."

"Disqualified..."

"Loser..."

"Indian cheater..."

I took a closer look at the club. It was a TaylorMade, smooth and shiny. Familiar. There was no way that Fred could have used this club. It was too long for her arms. She would have had to have been at least six feet tall to swing it comfortably.

The club wasn't hers.

Quickly, I slid my golf bag off my shoulder and balanced it in front of me. My fingers moved over the tops of my clubs, searching, moving, shuffling. Counting. One of the plastic sheaths in the middle was missing a club.

My pulse raced at the discovery. "Seth." My jaw tightened.

Then I looked across the cart path for Fred. She was already walking back to the fairway, her head lowered. Half the crowd continued to trail around her, including the three newspaper reporters.

"Fred!" I shouted, but she didn't turn.

"Shit," I muttered just as Henry Graser and Zack Fisher barreled down the cart path straight for me, their golf cleats clicking against the pavement. Grins stretched across their faces.

"Congrats, dude!" Zack said, slapping my shoulder.

"For what?"

"For first place!" Henry chuckled with excitement. "Word's already down to the ninth hole that Pocahontas has been eighty-sixed!"

I flinched at the casual way they mocked Fred. "Shut up, Graser."

Henry rolled his eyes. "You have seriously got to get over that chick, Ryan."

I ignored him.

Zack removed his baseball cap and wiped his flushed forehead with the back of his hand. "Turned in your scorecard yet?"

I swallowed. "Not yet."

"What are you waiting for?" Zack's eyes widened as they swept across mine.

I squinted over Zack's shoulder for another look at Fred. I caught only glimpses of her black ponytail and purple shirt through the crowd. Instead of Coach Lannon, she walked between two girls with coal-black hair, Kelly and Yolanda, girls I barely knew even though we'd been at the same school for three years. The tall Indian who'd given the blessing walked next to them, towering over everybody like a cottonwood tree. I recognized him instantly from years ago at the reservation school. He was exactly as I remembered, only with more gray hair. He carried Fred's golf bag over his shoulder. I watched them until they reached the top of the cart path. Fred kept slipping farther away from me, and I just let her go.

"Come on," Henry prodded. "Let's go." He motioned toward the tent.

Finally, I nodded at Zack, and all three of us turned toward the white tent without another word.

I couldn't hate myself more if I tried.

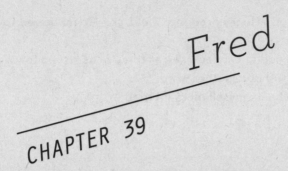

Fred

CHAPTER 39

I RODE HOME FROM THE GOLF tournament wedged between Kelly and Yolanda in the cab of Kelly's gray pickup truck.

Sam, Pete and Vernon sat with George Trueblood in the truck bed. He shouted greetings and blessings at the other passing cars and trucks on the freeway over the throaty roar of the truck's engine in a language that no one recognized. When I turned to look at them, Sam caught my eye and smiled at me, just a tiny apologetic grin, and shrugged his shoulders. Even though I was still angry at him for the fight Saturday night, I could never hate Sam Tracy. It would be like hating Trevor. I returned a sad smile because I hardly had the energy for a happy one.

"Don't worry, Fred," Kelly said for the second time, her arm draped over the steering wheel. "We saw you win. And we know you did your best. And you're still my little sister's hero. Nothing's gonna change that."

"But that wasn't my club in the bag," I said through still-cloudy eyes. "I won that tournament. Fair and square."

Yolanda snorted. "One of those white fuckers did it. Guaranteed."

Kelly glared across the seat at Yolanda. "Seriously, Yo. Do you ever hear yourself?"

"Can't help it," Yolanda said. "Those shits remind me of blood-suckers."

"Not helping," Kelly warned. "Enough with the drama, okay?"

"What?" Yolanda said. "You know it's true. They're just jealous." She paused. "Too bad we can't have our own Rez golf team. Wouldn't that be better, Fred?"

My head felt as heavy as a bowling ball. "Who would I play with?"

Yolanda didn't say anything. But I already knew the answer.

Kelly's voice turned softer. "We saw you, Fred. We watched you at every hole. We know you won that tournament. That's all that matters. That's what we'll tell everybody. They'll believe us." And by everybody, she meant everybody on the Rez.

"But I didn't cheat. I'd never cheat," I said, mostly to myself. I sank lower in the torn leather seat and sighed heavily, inhaling a mixture of stale cigarette smoke and peppermint. I said nothing for the rest of the ride home.

When Kelly dropped me off at my front door, the carport was empty. Only the Labs greeted us. George Trueblood carried my golf bag to the putting green next to the trailer. Sam hopped out of the back of the truck when I opened the passenger door, while everyone else stayed with the truck. Kelly pulled forward underneath a shade tree near the road to give Sam and me a little privacy.

I'd been expecting something like this—with Sam, I mean. We'd been kind of dancing around it the past few weeks.

Sam stood next to me on the stoop, his hands jammed in his front pockets. Finally, his eyes met mine, and he said, "You played real good today."

"Thanks." I swallowed.

He paused. "And I'm real sorry about Saturday night. I just lost it when Pete told me Ryan was waiting for you outside the restaurant. Then I saw him pull your arm..."

"You didn't have to hit him."

"I know."

"Or throw him."

"True."

Without another word, Sam sighed. Then he reached for my shoulders, lowered his head and kissed me. His kiss came at me fast, like a water blast, but then it lingered, sweetlike, just like it had that first time when everything changed between us. Slowly, he pulled back with his eyes still closed, like he was afraid to see my reaction. Finally his eyes opened, and he looked straight into mine.

I looked straight back at him.

"Anything?" He winced.

I swallowed and then allowed myself a breath. My answer was going to hurt. "No," I replied quietly. I did not see stars when I kissed Sam Tracy. My knees did not go all wobbly. My stomach did not do flip-flops. It would be so much easier if they did.

"Not even a little?"

"Sam, you're one of my best friends. I love you. You know that."

"But that's it, right? Just friends?"

I swallowed again. Then I nodded once.

His lips sputtered. "You really like that dude, don't you?"

I sighed, unable to answer. Everything was so messed up.

Sam paused. "Still friends?"

"Always."

"Well, I'm not giving up. You can't get rid of me. I might as well warn you now."

I smiled up at him, grateful to be loved so much. But my head was spinning.

With a heavy sigh, Sam stuffed his hands back in his pockets, tilted his head and began to walk backward toward the truck. "See you tomorrow."

I nodded just as George Trueblood rounded the corner of the trailer and met me at the door. He pressed something small and soft between my fingers. "For you, little sister."

I looked down at the palm of my hand. A white feather rested in the middle of it. My face turned up. "What's this?"

"A falcon feather," he said. "A reminder that your journey is long but not impossible."

"Isn't it?" I half laughed.

"Don't give up. You can't give up," he said over his shoulder, walking back to the truck. With one easy leap, his long legs landed back inside the bed next to the rest of the boys. His voice turned louder, at least for him. "You made us all proud today. Your journey has become bigger than you, Fred. Others live through you now. Don't forget that." He slapped the side of the truck, and Kelly dutifully put the vehicle in Drive.

"But—" I said.

George Trueblood just smiled as Kelly tooted the horn.

I watched the truck chug its way to the road. The Labs barked and chased it all the way to the edge of the driveway, oblivious to the dirt clouds swirling behind the mostly bald truck tires. I watched till everyone was completely out of sight. Only the sound of the phone ringing inside broke my concentration.

Mom must have paid the phone bill this month. I sighed with relief.

I stuffed the white feather inside my front pocket and reached for the door.

It was unlocked, as usual. I ran the three steps to the green wall phone in the kitchen.

"Hello?"

"Fred?" The voice was deep.

My eyes narrowed. "Yes?"

"It's Coach Lannon."

I closed my eyes, leaned all my weight against the wall and then very slowly sank to the floor, one muscle at a time. "Hi, Coach," I said with forced enthusiasm.

"I've got some strange news to report. It couldn't wait. Got a minute?"

"Sure," I murmured, unsure if I wanted to hear it. Had the judges found something else wrong with my bag? Did I forget to sign my scorecard? Was there another reason why I should have been disqualified?

"One of your teammates came forward," he started.

Teammates. That's a stretch. "For what?"

"To say that the club in your bag wasn't yours."

"What?" My eyes popped open. My voice filled the tiny kitchen. "Who?"

Coach Lannon paused like he was hesitant to tell me.

"Who?" I said again, sitting straighter against the wall. "I need to know. I have a right to know."

Coach Lannon exhaled heavily into the phone. "It was Ryan Berenger. I'm sorry to have to tell you this, Fred. I know he's your partner."

My brow furrowed. "Ryan? But that's not possible...."

"He told the judges when he turned in his scorecard."

"He confessed? But that would mean he's disqualified, too—"

"Correction." Coach Lannon drew out each syllable. "That means that *he's* disqualified, and *you* won the tournament."

Silence.

"Fred?"

I swallowed. "Yes?" I began massaging my temple, closing my eyes.

"Are you going to be all right?"

Hardly. "Um. Sure, Coach." But that was a lie. If anything, I was far from all right.

"Look, Fred, I may be a teacher and all, but I wasn't born yesterday. I've got two eyes."

I stayed silent, still processing.

"I know some of the guys have been giving you a hard time.

And I know what's going on between you and Ryan. I'm a little slow sometimes but not entirely blind."

Oh, god. I could barely speak. I didn't want to talk about Ryan with Coach Lannon. I could barely discuss him with Kelly and Yolanda.

"Would you like me to talk to the other guys? Maybe have a special meeting—"

"No!" It came out like a shout. "I mean, please don't."

He paused. "Let me know if you change your mind."

"I will." *Make that, never.* The last thing I wanted was some kind of intervention.

"Well, anyway, I just want to say how sorry I am. How hurt you must be, about Ryan."

"I'll be fine," I said, but it came out like a whisper.

"You don't sound fine."

"I am." I swallowed. "Really."

"Hmm," he said, unconvinced. "Well, maybe this will cheer you up...." He paused to exhale again. "I got calls today from recruiters from ASU and U of A. They're sending reps to the tournament next week."

"Why?" My eyes flew open again.

The coach laughed, and I had to move the phone away from my ear by about six inches. "Because they're interested in watching you play, Fred. You're making an impression. You hold your own against boys twice as strong. That's why."

"Oh," I said numbly. "That's nice." *That's nice?* That was the whole reason I'd joined the team. It was supposed to change my life. Unfortunately, it had, but in ways that I'd never dreamed.

"Nice?" He tsked at me like I was a child. "Anyway, I'll see you at practice tomorrow." Another phone rang somewhere in the background of his office. "Gotta run. Let's talk more tomorrow, okay?"

"But what about Ryan?"

"He's off the team. I didn't have a choice."

"But he's one of our best players."

Coach Lannon sighed into the phone. I could tell he wasn't happy about his decision. "I know, but the school has strict rules about cheating."

"But what if it was an accident? Maybe his club just wound up in my bag by mistake."

"Fred," the coach said slowly, like he had more bad news. "I'm sorry, but that was no accident."

"How do you know?"

"Because Ryan said so."

My throat tightened.

"Look, I didn't mean to lay all this on you. But I did want you to know that you won the tournament. That's all. That's what you should focus on. That's all that matters."

If only that were true.

"Okay, Coach," I said. I wasn't sure if he heard me.

"See you tomorrow." Coach Lannon hung up and I continued to stare numbly at the silver-speckled linoleum floor, the phone still pressed against my shoulder. I opened my palm for George Trueblood's feather.

Your journey has become bigger than you, Fred.

Finally, I blinked when my eyeballs turned dry.

The dial tone buzzed near my ear. Standing, I placed the phone back in its cradle.

Now I had no choice but to talk to Ryan, once and for all.

RYAN

CHAPTER 40

"WOULD SOMEONE MIND explaining to me why I just got a call from Coach Lannon kicking *my son* off the golf team? And he informs me in a *voice mail?*"

Angry blotchy red spots covered Mom's cheeks when I walked into the kitchen from the garage. She looked as stressed-out as ever. Her cell phone was still clutched in her hand, and she was pointing it at me. I hated when my parents talked about me in the third person, even when we were in the same room.

"What?" Dad had this panicked look on his face like we had just received instructions to evacuate the neighborhood or something.

"Great," I muttered to myself. The one night I needed them to work late like they normally did, and they picked tonight, of all nights, to pretend we were the Cleavers. And Coach Lannon. Why did he have to call Mom? She handled bad news about as well as Dad, despite dealing with worse at work. Strangely, she'd been calmer when the police had called Dad last month to report my partying at the house when I should have been in school. She expected that, I guess. Walking away with only a police warning had softened the blow. But an unexpected voice mail from a teacher or a coach? Mom went ballistic.

My car keys skidded across the kitchen counter, filling the silence.

Before I answered, I scanned the kitchen table. It was set for an actual sit-down dinner, with plates and folded napkins and everything. Not a microwavable box anywhere. There was even an orange candle burning in the middle that smelled like grapefruit. If it were any other night, it might have been...nice. For a change.

Riley sat cross-legged in her usual spot at the table, studying me. She twirled a strand of her hair between her fingers. When our eyes met, she smiled, an unspoken promise that she was on my side no matter how badly I screwed up.

I shot her a grateful smirk.

"Well?" Mom said, louder. "Can you explain what's happening here?"

"Can I take a shower first?" I said, even though I already knew the answer.

"I don't think so, young man. You're not leaving this kitchen until you tell me what is going on."

"Yeah," Dad said behind her, his hands on his hips. "Come on, Ryan. Talk to us." It was the first time that I'd seen them together since the birthday party at the Wild Horse Restaurant.

Cornered, I scratched the side of my head. "It's true," I said finally. "I got kicked off the team." My shoulders shrugged as if dudes got kicked off varsity sports teams all the time.

"Yes, Ryan. I gathered that," Mom said. "But *why?*"

I exhaled with the weight of the news. "I got disqualified from the tournament today."

Dad's gaze pulled back another notch. "Disqualified?" He said it like he didn't understand the meaning of the word.

"Seems one of my clubs wound up in my partner's bag." Another shoulder shrug. Truthfully, telling my parents didn't feel as bad as I'd thought it would. In fact, it felt pretty good. At least it was the truth this time.

Mom's face crumpled. "How did that happen?"

A nervous chuckle. "I guess I put it there."

"You put it there?" Dad said. "On purpose?"

I didn't answer.

"Do you realize what this might do to your chances for getting into U of A? Or any college?"

I shrugged my shoulders again. I hadn't given it a thought. College wasn't exactly high on my list.

"Do you realize the strings I'll have to pull for you now? How could you be so careless?"

My head turned numb.

"Who was your partner?" Dad asked.

I opened my mouth but then thought better of it.

"Who?" he prodded.

"Fred Oday," I said finally.

"That Indian girl?"

I nodded.

"I had a bad feeling about her," Dad said, turning to Mom. "But your son never listens to me. Never."

"*My* son?" Mom's eyes widened.

I knew that I should have stayed quiet, but I chuckled again. "Kinda hard to stay away from her, Dad. We're on the same team—well, were."

Dad turned his angry gaze on me. "Don't be flippant."

I knew it was weird and all wrong, but it felt good to disappoint him for once, at least when I meant to. I was finally living up to their low expectations. And Mom was so crazy pissed that she didn't know whether to speak or blink. Finally, she just gave up and covered her mouth with her hand while shaking her head at me.

"Well, I'm going to call the coach first thing tomorrow and get this whole thing straightened—" Dad began.

"No, Dad," I said, the only calm one in the kitchen besides Riley. "Don't do that."

"And why not?"

"Because I deserved it."

At least that part was one hundred percent true.

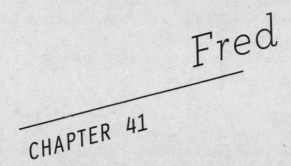

Fred

CHAPTER 41

THE NEXT DAY, I WALKED INTO Lone Butte High School alone and with real purpose. Not numb or embarrassed. Determined.

I scanned the faces in the courtyard and the hallways, even the ones that stared back at me like I was some kind of freak. After dumping my golf bag in Coach Lannon's office, I started searching for Ryan. The library and studying would have to wait. I needed to talk to Ryan before Homeroom and sort out this whole tournament-disqualification mess. Surviving the weekend without knowing the truth about the extra club would be impossible. I needed to hear it directly from him. He owed me that much. I'd make him owe me that much.

And the one time I was brave enough to troll among all the popular cliques in the courtyard turned out to be the one time that I couldn't find Ryan anywhere.

Typical.

Normally he was seated in the center of everything with Gwyneth Riordan hanging on his shoulder like she had a balance problem.

But, of course, not today.

I passed Seth Winter, though. He and Gwyneth stood near the courtyard fountain, whispering. I pretended to ignore their obvious glares as I passed. Clearly word traveled fast, even at an enormous school like Lone Butte. No matter what I'd accomplish from this day forward, I'd probably always be known as that crazy Indian girl who cheated at golf.

On the small chance that Ryan was hiding in the stacks, I checked the library cubicles, too.

Nothing.

I raced outside to the parking lot and hunted for Ryan's Jeep. It was usually parked in the first row near the middle. But a bright blue Volkswagen Bug with a sunflower wrapped around the antenna trespassed in Ryan's usual spot. I cursed the happy car before walking back inside.

The first warning bell rang, and I turned, reluctantly, for Homeroom. But then I realized that I'd see Ryan in English, and my pace quickened.

Time had to move faster today. It just plain had to.

After an excruciatingly long Homeroom, I walked to English behind a wall of students, mind-melding with the back of their heads to move their feet faster. *Faster, faster, faster!* I screamed inside my head.

I had already decided that I would ditch for the first time in my entire life if Ryan would agree to talk with me. The seven minutes between classes hardly seemed long enough to have one of the most important conversations of my entire life.

I waited outside the door to Mrs. Weisz's English class and watched students stream inside. My chest tightened as the hallway began to drain of students and clatter. I kept glancing from the wall clock inside the room to the hallway. With less than one minute before the bell, I turned anxiously toward the hallway again. Instead of Ryan, Seth Winter sauntered toward me with his backpack dangling over his shoulder. My jaw hardened the instant my eyes landed on his icy grin.

His nose wrinkled. "Frrr-eed," he said, stretching out my name into two syllables. He stood so close that our noses were near enough to touch. I took a step back from his barrel of a pit bull chest but only backed into the wall. "Waiting for someone?"

"I—I—" I stammered. Of course, words failed me when I needed them most.

"If you're waiting for Ryan, I'll save you the trouble. He's not in school today."

I blinked. "Oh, okay." I turned for the door, desperate to be anywhere other than standing eyeball-level with Seth Winter.

But Seth pulled back on my arm.

I turned, startled, as Seth's icy smile faded. If ever I'd wanted Sam Tracy beside me, now was that time.

"You've really messed up his head, Pocahontas," he whispered. "Don't think I don't see what you're doing."

My eyes narrowed. "I'm not doing anything. And you're demented. I have no idea what you're talking about." I turned, but Seth yanked on my elbow. This time his fingers pinched.

"Sure you do," Seth said with an eye roll. "Don't play stupid."

My teeth clenched. "Leave me alone." I jerked my arm out of his hand and walked through the door.

The bell rang, and I hurried to my seat. Quickly, I sank into the safety of my plastic chair before I noticed a folded note on my desk. I opened it, and a tiny yellow flower dropped out—a wildflower, like the ones that grew at the end of Pecos Road.

Mrs. Weisz started to say something about *Macbeth* and an upcoming essay, but I only half listened. I leaned forward and carefully unfolded the note so that it lay flat on my notebook. I sucked in a breath and read:

Fred,
I need to see you. Can you meet me tonight at 8 o'clock at the end of Pecos Road? It's important. Please?
Ryan
P.S. You seriously need a cell phone.

I read it again.

And again.

The words made me smile. He wanted to see me, too.

My fingertips brushed across the black letters. The letters were angled funny, like they were written in a hurry. I brought the flower to my nose and inhaled. The petals were fresh, recently picked.

Carefully, I folded the flower back inside the note. I turned to Jon Romano, seated behind me. "Did you see who left this note on my desk?" I whispered, lifting the folded note.

Jon's pale brow furrowed. *No*, he mouthed before taking a hit from his asthma inhaler.

"Did you have a question, Miss Oday?" Mrs. Weisz said, pausing from her lecture. "A comment, perhaps?"

The room silenced.

I cleared my throat. "No, sorry. No question."

Mrs. Weisz returned to the whiteboard, and I slid Ryan's note into the pocket of my notebook.

Sneaking off to the end of Pecos Road again wasn't exactly how I planned to make things right with Ryan, but it was better than not talking at all. It was all I could do to keep from bursting before school ended.

During lunch period, I didn't bother scanning the cafeteria for Ryan.

All of his friends sat around his usual table by the window— Gwyneth, Henry, Seth, Zack, Troy. Only Gwyneth looked up at me curiously when I walked through the front entrance. For a rare moment, her mouth snapped shut and her eyes shot arrows at me. It didn't matter that we had never said more than a handful of words to each other, not since gym class freshman year when we'd been paired together for badminton. She hadn't seemed so bad back then. What had happened to her in the past two years to make her the nastiest girl in school?

I pretended to ignore the weight of Gwyneth's stare and hunted instead for an empty table where I could eat my lunch in peace. I found one just inside the door and slipped into a seat that faced away from the windows. Even though I had absolutely no appetite, I reached inside my backpack for my lunch bag and a book, mostly to keep my hands and eyes busy. Just as I took a bite of leftover fry bread smothered in honey, someone approached me from behind.

"Fred?" said a voice that I didn't recognize. It was too high for Kelly and definitely too sweet for Yolanda.

I turned my chin over my right shoulder a fraction. Then my eyes looked up.

A lanky girl with straight shoulder-length blondish-brown hair smiled down at me.

"Hi?" I said, wondering if the girl had me confused with someone else.

But the girl swallowed and took a step closer. Her books pressed against her chest like a shield. "I'm Riley Berenger. Ryan's sister?" She said it like it was a question, almost as if I wouldn't know anyone named Ryan Berenger.

I sucked back a breath at the sound of Ryan's name. "Oh," I said, as I began to take in the familiar shape and color of her eyes above a ribbon of dainty freckles. They shared the same exact eye color, blue as a morning sky. Definitely related.

"You mind if I eat with you?" Riley carried an armful of books but no lunch.

"Sure." I motioned to the table.

Riley smiled, relieved. She pulled back the seat right next to mine, bumping her knee against the chair in the process. "I wasn't sure if you'd know me, being that I'm a sophomore and all."

One corner of my mouth curled up. "I remember you from Ryan's party." Only, this time she wasn't hidden in the stairwell shadows.

Her eyes brightened. "Studying *Macbeth?*" Riley nodded at my unopened book.

"Trying." My nose wrinkled. "It's not my favorite."

Riley's nose wrinkled, too. "I'll have that next year."

"Yeah, I suppose so," I said. "Would you like some bread?"

Her eyes widened. "That looks so good. Did you make it yourself?"

"No. My mom did." *A rare treat.* I tore off a chunk.

"We only eat fry bread when we go to the fair."

I nodded, then took another bite, wondering why Riley Berenger had sought me out, of all people in the lunchroom.

"I wanted to tell you something," she said, as if she could read my mind. Her voice changed to a whisper. "About my brother."

I paused from chewing.

"He's a lot of things, but he's not like that."

I swallowed. "Like what?"

"He told me about the tournament. He would never have put his club in your bag. Not on purpose. I swear it."

I put the bread onto my napkin. Then I smiled at Riley. "I know."

Riley's bony shoulders caved forward underneath her pink tank top. "Good. I'm really glad you know that." She paused, dragging her tongue across her lips. They had become shiny with honey from Mom's bread. "He's a pretty good brother, actually. Once you get to know him."

"Why isn't he in school today?"

"He told my mom he wasn't feeling well." Riley frowned and rolled her eyes. "But he drove me to school and then left before Homeroom."

"So he came into the building?"

"Yeah. Just to drop off a term paper or something. But he left right after that."

"Too bad. I was hoping to talk to him."

Riley's head tilted to one side. "Maybe I can help?"

"Thanks, but that's okay. I already got his note."

"What note?"

"He left me a note for me in English class."

"Oh. So that's what he had to drop off," she said. "He probably wants to tell you the news."

"What news?"

Riley's small mouth twisted into a ball. "Well, he'll probably want to tell you himself...."

My eyes widened. I wondered if this had anything to do with golf. "Tell me, what?"

Riley sat back, clearly worried that she'd shared too much.

"Please," I begged.

Finally, she spilled it. "He's going to live with our uncle Mark for a while." Her whole expression crumpled.

"In Phoenix?" My eyes widened.

"No. In San Francisco."

My jaw dropped. Riley might as well have said the moon. "But why?"

Riley shrugged, but I suspected there was more she wasn't telling me. "Could you do me a huge favor?"

"Sure!" she gushed.

"Tell your brother I'll meet him tonight, exactly as he asked. Eight o'clock on Pecos Road."

"Okay." She seemed pleased to be the messenger. "I'll tell him as soon as I get home."

"Thanks, Riley," I said, as my appetite vanished. Now it was official. I would see Ryan tonight. "Want some more fry bread? I can't finish it."

Riley nodded at the bread hungrily.

"I'll bring you some next week, if my mom makes more." I pushed the last slice toward her.

Her face brightened all over again. "I'd like that. Thanks."

Riley stared at me, her gaze sweeping across my face but not in the usual way that I had grown accustomed to. If I didn't know any better, I'd say it was in admiration. "Now I know why Ryan has been acting so weird lately," she said suddenly.

I felt my cheeks tingle. "Why? What has he told you?"

"My brother?" Her lips sputtered. "Not a word."

"Nothing?" I replied, disappointed.

"He didn't need to. I may be a sophomore, but I'm not stupid."

I stared at my reflection in the small round mirror nailed to the back of my bedroom door.

I dragged my hands through my hair and then frowned in the dim light, wondering why I was getting all paranoid about my appearance. The sky would be marble-black when I met Ryan at the end of Pecos Road. It would be just as easy to show up covered in a hoodie.

My eyes darted again to the alarm clock. I'd already carved out a mile between the edge of my bed and my closet, trying to coax time to move faster. I hadn't stopped pacing since I got home from school. I'd practiced all the things I wanted to say to Ryan but then had berated myself when they sounded silly and childish. Just let Ryan talk, let him explain, I'd decided. That would be best.

I frowned at the clock again. Then I decided to start walking.

The trailer was mostly empty. Mom had left for work, and Trevor hadn't been home since Wednesday. I tiptoed past Dad. He was sleeping in the living room on his favorite chair, his legs propped up, snoring the night away.

I smiled at him. Sunday's newspaper lay in his lap, the same one with the tiny story about me in the sports section, the one where the reporter gushed about my winning streak. Dad had bought five copies and said that he was going to put one copy in a glass frame and hang it in the hallway with the rest of the family pictures. He hadn't been able to stop gloating about it. Because of the story in the *Arizona Republic,* I even had brief mentions in *Indian Country*

Today and the *Navajo Times,* to which Dad proudly proclaimed, "Even the Navajo are impressed, Fred!"

Holding back a breath, I walked the perimeter of the living room floor on the spots that groaned the least till I finally reached the front door. The screen door made the faintest pop when it opened but not enough to excite the dogs.

On the front step, I inhaled a deep breath of the cool evening air and pulled my sweater more tightly around my neck. Fall had finally arrived.

I pulled my shoulders back and walked straight into the desert toward answers and the end of Pecos Road.

I didn't use the flashlight until I reached the desert wash that ran perpendicular to Pecos Road. I knew the path by heart.

The edges of the wash were smooth and mostly flat, perfect for walking. The bottoms were still moist from heavy September monsoons and bounced with reflections from the moon and stars. Only my footsteps and breathing competed with the desert surrounding me: coyotes howling near the base of the Estrella Mountains, jackrabbits rustling underneath sage and the occasional hoot owl from the top of a saguaro. As familiar as my own hands. Nothing unusual.

The closer I got to Pecos Road, the easier it was to see the faint orange glow of the Phoenix streetlights. I began to hum and swing my arms forward, the flashlight making yellow half circles across the desert.

My heartbeat leaped when I spotted the bright white headlights of a single vehicle parked at the end of Pecos Road.

It's Ryan. And he's early.

I stopped, felt a smile fill my face and signaled my arrival with a couple of flicks from my flashlight.

Ryan waited just like last time, brightening the last stretch of my path with his headlights. He flashed his brights when I signaled with my flashlight.

I began to jog, jumping over a line of low sage bushes as if they were track hurdles. Anxious, I ran straight into the light beams, unable to bite back my smile.

Breathless from running, I stopped and waved one arm overhead. Ryan tooted the Jeep's horn and flashed the headlights one last time.

I beamed into the headlights.

But then the Jeep began to move down the pavement and cross over a broken piece of barbed wire.

My happiness froze. "Don't!" I yelled, lifting my palms and sprinting forward as fast as I could run. He had to stop. I had already warned him about the Tribal Police. Sure, our tribe might not have had a whole fleet, but if Ryan got caught driving on Rez land, he would get arrested for trespassing and my parents would finally have a reason to ground me for the first time in my entire life, especially when the police would inform them that I was meeting a boy they'd never met in the middle of the dark desert. Not cool.

Despite my warnings, the Jeep didn't stop. I thought maybe it was because I was too far away. Maybe he didn't see my flashlight. Or maybe he was more anxious to see me than I thought.

I halted at the end of the wash and watched helplessly as his tires squealed when they left the pavement. They ground into the soft dirt, lifting a smokelike dust cloud over the desert.

I lifted my hands to shield my eyes. I tasted his dust.

"Stop!" I screamed but the Jeep's engine drowned out my voice. "Stop!" I yelled again, squinting through my fingers, but the headlights raced straight for me.

The motor revved.

Instead of slowing, oddly, the Jeep charged faster through the desert. "What are you doing, Ryan?" I muttered.

My pulse began to pound at my temples as the headlights got closer. I took a step back, and then another, as the Jeep's tires ground harder and faster into the dirt. They pointed straight in my direction.

Somewhere deep inside me, my legs told me what to do before my brain took over.

My flashlight slipped from my hand and landed in the dirt. I didn't stop to pick it up. Instead, I began to run backward, my feet heavy as my heels dug into the ground.

But then I moved faster.

Every nerve, every muscle in my body sprang into survival. Nausea built deep in my throat, but I swallowed it back. Something felt very wrong.

I turned and raced back into the darkest part of the desert, away from the Phoenix streetlights and away from Pecos Road, as fast as my legs could carry me. Most of all, I ran away from the bright headlights. If I didn't, I was certain that the front tires would mow right over me like I didn't exist.

Way out here, no one but my ancestors would ever know.

RYAN

CHAPTER 42

WHEN RILEY RETURNED HOME after dinner, I was sprawled across the couch in the family room, my legs crossed at the ankles, parked in front of the television and chilling.

I watched the screen with my iPod blaring—anything to stop my brain from drifting to painful places.

At least things would be different once I got to Uncle Mark's.

Uncle Mark was Dad's younger brother but different in all the ways that counted. Sometimes I had a hard time believing they were related. Anyway, he always told me that I could visit whenever I wanted. He knew what Dad was like. "Your father is a great guy, but he expects everyone to be as driven as he is. Don't hold it against him," he had told me once.

When I'd called Uncle Mark last night to ask if I could finish my school year in San Francisco, he'd said yes without hesitation, almost as if he'd been expecting my call. Mom and Dad had barely put up a fight, which was rare for them. In fact, I'd sensed relief when I'd told them about it. Maybe a break would be good.

And now everybody was happy. Mostly.

In my periphery, I watched Riley tiptoe into the room, all cat-like. She tossed her pink gym bag at my feet. This was a little game we'd always played. Riley tried to scare me, and I let her think she succeeded.

"Hey!" I yelled, mostly for effect, but then I smirked when she stuck out her tongue. I pulled out my earbuds.

"How's your sore throat?" She pouted at me innocently and then faked a cough before plopping into the chair across from me. Gold-and-red pillows swished around her, and one fell to the floor as she drew her knees to her chest.

I bit back a grin. "Shut up and leave me alone."

"Can't," she said. "It's my mission in life to bug you."

"Well, you get a big star. Where've you been?"

"Dance practice." She chomped hard on a piece of gum. "I'm starved. Where's Mom?"

"Where do you think?"

Riley sighed. "You hungry?"

"Already ate," I said. "There's leftover lasagna from last night in the fridge. Mom left a note."

"Humph." Riley blinked at her wristwatch. "Hey." She leaned forward in her chair. "Aren't you going to be late?" She tapped her watch with a fingertip.

I chuckled. "For what?" Unless someone put a stick of dynamite underneath the couch, I had no plans to change positions until Dad got home.

But Riley's eyes narrowed at me, all irritated. "Please tell me you are *not* going to blow her off."

"Blow her off? Blow *who* off?"

"Your note."

"What note?" I sat up. "Riley, what are you talking about?" I reached for the remote and switched off the television.

"Didn't you leave a note for Fred this morning?"

"Noo," I said, stretching out the syllable.

Her voice rose an octave. "Seriously? You seriously didn't give Fred a note telling her to meet you tonight?"

"No," I said again, feeling my eyes widen. I stood up. "Where was I supposed to meet her?" Never mind that my little sister could carry on a normal conversation with Fred Oday while I messed it up every chance I got.

Riley stared across at me, her face turning paler. "She said something about..." Her brow furrowed.

"Where, Riley?" I stood over her. "*Think*. Where was I supposed to meet her?"

Her voice wavered. "I think she said something about...Pecos Road?" She winced like she wasn't entirely sure.

"What time?" My breathing quickened.

Riley glanced down at her wristwatch. "Five minutes ago."

Without another word, I sprinted into the kitchen for my car keys.

"I'm coming with you!" Riley followed me into the garage.

"No, you're not."

"Yes, I am. And you can't stop me."

Riley climbed into the passenger side of the Jeep, and I didn't stop her because there was no time to argue.

The garage door opened, and my foot was already on the accelerator. "Come on, come on!" I told the rearview mirror. "Open!"

"Your seat belt, Ryan," Riley instructed, strangely calm.

I latched the seat belt across my chest with one hand and steered with the other. As soon as the door opened, I floored the Jeep to the end of the driveway. The rear tires squealed the second they touched the street.

Then we flew out of our cul-de-sac and onto the main road. Riley didn't make a sound or threaten to tell Mom about my crazy driving. It wouldn't matter anyway. My foot cemented itself to the accelerator.

"What's wrong?" Riley broke the silence as soon as we turned onto Pecos Road. "Are you going to tell me?"

I didn't answer. I was too busy grinding my foot against the pedal and gripping the steering wheel as if I could rip it from the column.

Riley turned sideways, her voice wavering again. "Is this my fault? Did I do something wrong?"

I didn't answer. I was too busy picturing Seth Winter's face at the end of my fist. Or worse.

"Please, Ryan." Riley's voice began to crack. "Tell me. Tell me what I did wrong. Is Fred going to be okay?"

"You didn't do anything wrong," I said through gritted teeth. "But I did."

"What do you mean? How?"

I sighed inwardly. It would take all night to explain.

We sped the rest of the way down Pecos Road in silence, the plastic windows slapping in the wind. Thankfully the road was mostly deserted, but it still felt like we were going too slow. At last the Phoenix streetlights ended and the desert turned as black as ink, all except for two round, bright lights. They kept turning in circles.

"What's that?" Riley hissed, peering forward against the windshield.

The lights were well off the street on the other side of the barbed wire. As we got closer, the lights turned almost yellow from the dirt clouds swirling around them. It was like watching candles flicker in the middle of a tornado.

"That's a truck," I said, breathing hard.

"What's a truck doing so far off the road? And isn't that Indian land?"

I didn't answer. Instead, I yelled, "Hold on!"

Before Riley could grip the strap above her door, my foot slammed harder against the accelerator until all four tires left the smooth pavement.

The Jeep sailed headfirst into the dirt.

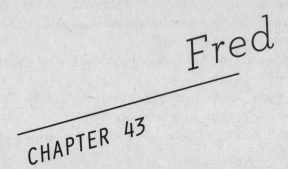

Fred

CHAPTER 43

COLD SWEAT TRICKLED BEHIND my ears, but that didn't stop me from running.

Panting till my ribs ached, I ran alongside the path next to the wash, the same way I'd come, but this time my shoes sank into the soft dirt. It was like running in slow motion.

The heaviness in my step didn't slow the truck, though. It only drove faster. A stereo blared from inside the cab, heavy metal with angry electric guitar. The closer it got, the louder it became, its engine grinding over the sound.

The headlights washed over me with blinding light.

And the lights only got brighter.

Finally the beams blanketed my body like a net, impossible to outrun. I looked for places to hide, but the desert was barren and as flat as cardboard. It would have been easier to outrun a sunrise.

When my heart threatened to leap out of my chest, I fell to my knees in the dirt. I could run no more. I gasped for air, shielding my head with both arms, heaving in bits of dirt with each breath. Dust covered the air, covered me. It filled my ears and nose. It stung my eyes.

But the truck and the music still barreled for me.

I screamed as the truck skidded alongside me, its front tires missing my body by inches before it started to circle me once, then twice, like I was an animal in a rodeo. Dirt swirled everywhere, turning the headlights hazy, choking me, hiding the moon.

Still shielding my face, I tucked low to the ground, dusted with dirt. I peered through my fingers at the settling dust as the truck made another turn. I finally got a good look. It was a silver pickup, the monster kind that looked like it could tow an elephant.

Then I saw the driver's face.

My body shivered with more fear than I'd ever known. His eyes glared at me through the open window, laughing.

"Seth," I exhaled, dragging the name out of my mouth. A sharp pain shot through my chest, a mixture of dread and too much adrenaline.

When the dust finally settled and we were able to lock eyes, Seth turned off the stereo, and the desert turned silent again, except for the grumble from his engine. "Freaked ya, didn't I?" He said it loudly. As if he liked it. "And you thought I was Ryan." His lips turned downward into a fake pout. "Sorry. He couldn't make it tonight. He's out with his girlfriend."

I didn't know whether to cry or scream, but neither would be helpful. No one would hear me in the middle of the desert. I tried to stand, but my knees shook from running and fear. I fell back onto one knee after my first try.

This pleased Seth.

He tossed his head back and laughed while I struggled to speak, struggled to breathe.

Finally, with all my strength I said, "What do you w-want?" My tongue dragged over my lips, tasting a layer of dust clinging to my lip gloss.

"What do I w-w-want?" Seth stuttered. His smile slowly morphed into something subhuman. His glare turned sharper beneath his backward baseball cap. All of his pale features glowed sickly green against the dashboard lights. He slapped the side of his truck with his hand. "Finally. Someone asks what *I* want." He paused to smack his lips, like he had to give my question serious thought. "I'll tell you what *I* want, you freaking Indian," he snapped.

I swallowed, hard.

"I want you to stop hanging around Ryan—and his sister, too!" he said. "Neither one can stand the sight of you. Can't you take a hint?"

I nodded, mostly so that he'd leave me alone.

"And tell your boy Tracy that this isn't over. Not by a long shot. He can't sucker punch Ryan and get away with it. Next time we'll be ready."

I nodded again. If I told Sam, Trevor, Peter and the others, I hated to think what they'd do to Seth Winter. Not that Seth wouldn't deserve it. "I'll tell Sam," I said, but the words stuck in my dry throat. I wasn't sure if he heard me.

With my pulse racing, I slowly moved my eyes to peer for the path alongside the wash. When Seth had chased me in circles, I'd gotten all turned around. I didn't know whether I faced north or south.

"Are you deaf, too?" he snarled, threatening me with another rev of the accelerator.

I jumped at the engine's growl. Then I nodded numbly, wishing that I could stop my legs from shaking.

"Good," he said. "And one other thing..." His hand dragged over his chin.

I watched him warily, waiting for the chase to begin all over again. "What?" I said, still breathing heavily. "Anything." My answer pleased him again, just like I thought it would.

Seth grinned. "I want you to quit the golf team. Or this isn't over." More rage filled his face. "You shouldn't be on the team. The coach should never have let you just walk on." He spat at my feet.

I didn't flinch from his spit. And my eyes couldn't leave his.

"I had to try out. Why not you? Where do you get off?"

Just as I was about to speak, another car approached behind me, its engine grinding across the desert just as Seth's had. I glanced quickly over my shoulder. Two tiny lights appeared in the distance.

They got closer.

The driver flashed his lights, and my heart started to race faster again. I looked back at Seth. His face turned even paler in the dashboard's glow, almost ghostlike, as the headlights approached. He squinted into the distance.

"What the...?" Seth muttered, sitting straighter.

As he studied the approaching car, I began to creep closer to the wash. First just an inch and then a handful more. I could see the path. The small bit of water at the wash's bottom sparkled in the glow of Seth's headlights.

I wondered if Seth noticed, but he was too fixated on the approaching car.

If I ran alongside the wash, it would take me straight home.

Home. How I wanted to be there.

"Hold up," Seth growled as I began to slip away. He revved the engine, warning me. "We're not done yet!"

But the other car came closer. It raced across the desert, its engine growing louder. The headlights bounced wildly against the darkness, and the driver never slowed.

Seth answered with a rev from his truck's engine. He swallowed, hard, his earlier bravado fading.

I chanced another small step in the direction of the wash. Then another. I didn't care who was driving the other car. I hoped it was the police. That would teach Seth Winter. The Tribal Police didn't look too kindly upon trespassers, especially at night. Especially ones chasing girls for sport.

The toe of my tennis shoe finally reached the top of the wash. I twisted it into the dirt, bracing my stance. Then I turned south.

And I started to run.

But Seth saw me.

I heard his truck shift into Drive. Within moments, his headlights outran me. Over the engine's roar, I could hear his laugh. It filled my ears and polluted the sky.

He's crazy, I thought. *Seth Winter is truly crazy.*

But his laughter was quickly drowned out by the engine from the other car. Instead of one set of headlights chasing behind me, there were two. Still running along the wash, I squinted over my shoulder through a new dust cloud. The other car was right behind Seth, flashing its brights and blasting its horn. The sky grew thicker with dirt and swirling sand, making breathing difficult. It was like being inside the center of a dust storm.

Seth moved slightly to one side, coaxed by the front end of the other car. That's when I realized that the other car wasn't hunting me. It was after Seth.

And it wasn't the Tribal Police. There weren't any red lights or sirens, but the second car wedged Seth away from me, forcing his truck into a ditch.

Both cars finally thudded to an abrupt stop, the rear wheels of Seth's truck wheezing in midair. The other car skidded alongside it.

Gasping, I stopped running and braced my hands against my knees, watching the cars through the settling dust. It was like watching a nightmare, the muted colors and sounds, the bright lights, the slow motion of the desert, the sound of my own breathing—all pushing against my temples. Chaos and confusion.

The second driver got out of his car. Without shutting his door, he stormed over to Seth's pickup. He kicked the driver's door with his boot, hard. "What the hell are you doing?" he screamed at Seth. "What is *wrong* with you?"

It was Ryan. But I was too numb to care.

"Berenger?" Seth's voice sounded suddenly small, his laughter gone. "You ran me into a ditch? Get me out of here," he yelled up at him. Ryan ignored him.

Instead, he turned to me as I cowered alongside the wash.

"Fred?" Ryan called out. He shielded his eyes in the corner of his elbow from the settling dust. "Fred? Are you all right?" He walked slowly at first, but then he started to jog when I didn't answer.

"Fred?" Another voice. A softer one. "Fred? It's me. Riley. Are you okay? I'm so sorry, Fred!" she said. "This is all my fault."

I swallowed back the tears that burned my throat. I couldn't speak, even if I wanted to.

All I wanted to do was go home.

I turned south and coaxed my legs to run again.

"Fred!" Ryan called behind me. "Wait!"

But I ran faster. Ryan couldn't catch me. I knew every part of this desert. Ryan only knew this side of Pecos Road from the window of his Jeep.

I kept running until my breathing drowned out Ryan's voice. Before long, the headlights and the voices grew so distant that it was as if they had never been chasing me at all.

RYAN

CHAPTER 44

I SQUINTED INTO THE DARKNESS until Fred's footsteps disappeared. I called after her anyway, my hands cupped around my mouth. "Fred!"

No answer.

Then I dragged both hands through my hair, gripping the sides of my head, as I waited for my heartbeat to slow. When I turned back to Seth, my rage returned. I stormed toward his truck, breathing so hard that I sucked in dirt that still floated in the air.

Seth grinned back at me, like everyone was out for a ripper. He'd played some dumb, crazy pranks before, even majorly stupid stuff, but nothing compared to this. I couldn't even put the right word on it, but it made my insides burn.

"Why'd you do that, Seth? What is wrong with you? Are you insane?"

Seth laughed.

I reached inside his window and grabbed his collar, wrapping it around my fist. "I could kill you!"

Riley jumped out of the Jeep. "Stop it! Ryan, stop!"

I didn't hear her until she wrapped her arms around my waist and pulled at my belt loops. I stepped back reluctantly, with Riley's arms twisting and pulling my body.

"What's your problem? Why are you going after *me?*" Seth yelled back. "I was only trying to help *you.*"

I shrugged off Riley's hands because I was seriously thinking about punching Seth again. My fists clenched. "*Help* me?" I stepped closer to the window, screaming. "I don't need your help. I never once asked for it. And this isn't even about me, Seth. You know it. It's all about you. It's always all about you."

"Me?" Seth glared at me. "Are you crazy? You were seriously going to take the hit for Pocahontas?" He paused. "You weren't supposed to get disqualified at the tournament. *She* was!"

"You're not listening to me."

"I hear every word," Seth says.

"You're an idiot."

"And don't tell me you were going to let Sam and his homeboys off the hook! If I hadn't come looking for you Saturday night, that Indian would have busted your head wide open. This is about revenge. Man up, Ryan."

"Shut up, Seth."

"You can thank me after you get me out of this ditch," Seth said, all bright smiles again, the innocent kind that I'd tolerated for too long.

"You have no idea what you've done."

"Sure I do," Seth said.

"What? So you were going to run her over?" I kicked Seth's door, frustrated. "Was that your brilliant plan?"

"Chill out, dude. I was just playing her."

I shook my head. "Playing? You're sick, Seth. You need help."

His face darkened again. "And you're a tool if you're hot for that Indian. Let them stick with their own."

I pulled back my right arm to punch him.

Riley shrieked. She dived for my arm and pulled it down like someone three times her size. This time she clung to me.

I backed away from Seth, my feet sinking into the soft dirt.

Seth spat.

"Come on, Ryan," Riley said, still pulling at me, but it was like I was walking in slow motion. I couldn't unlock my eyes from Seth, and I tasted bitterness and dirt. "Let's go home," she urged. "It's over. Fred's probably home by now. You can call her when we get home."

I stumbled backward. "I thought I knew you, Seth. I thought you were my best friend." Riley and I started back for the Jeep, me walking backward and Riley tugging my arm, but I couldn't peel my eyes away from Seth.

"Hey, I got your back! I always have," Seth yelled, frantic this time. "How come you don't have mine?" Seth pushed open his driver's door. Wedged against the ditch, it barely opened more than a few inches. "Wait a minute, Ryan. I'm stuck in here. You're going to help me out, aren't you?" He chuckled anxiously.

I finally turned around. "You're on your own. Get yourself out."

"Wait!" he shouted, but Riley and I were already inside the Jeep. I revved the engine to drown him out.

"Wait!" His voice strained over the engine.

But I put the Jeep in Reverse just as Seth crawled headfirst out the window. His body somersaulted into the dirt, but he was back on his feet in a heartbeat. Then he started to run after us, but we were already pointed toward Pecos Road.

In my rearview mirror, I watched Seth running in the dim glow of the Jeep's rear lights, waving his arms. "Wait!" he screamed, and for the first time in my life—at least since I could remember— I saw Seth scared.

I barely heard his voice over the engine.

He tried to catch up, running down the middle of a wake of dust, his arms waving, but I only pressed the accelerator.

I couldn't get away from my old life fast enough.

Fred

CHAPTER 45

WHEN MY EYES OPENED THE NEXT morning, sunlight was slanting through the sheer yellow curtain.

I pulled the sheet tighter around my neck and wished for the thousandth time that last night was a dream.

I brushed my fingers over my eyes, still raw from crying, my pillow damp from tears. Seems crying was all I did well lately. I squeezed my eyes shut against the morning sun in a futile attempt to erase the image of Seth Winter chasing me in his monster truck.

Finally, I pried open my eyes and lifted my head, listening for noises inside the house. But the trailer was silent.

Restless, I pulled on jeans and a gray sweatshirt and tied my hair back into a loose ponytail. I tiptoed to the bathroom and splashed water on my face. The water stung my bloodshot eyes.

I slipped on a pair of shoes and tiptoed into the kitchen for a glass of juice and biscuits for the dogs. Mom's empty wine bottle sat on the kitchen counter. My nose wrinkled from the sour smell. I tossed the bottle into the garbage. Quietly, I slipped a blanket over my shoulder and walked through the front door.

The morning air was still sharp enough to burn the inside of my nose. I inhaled greedy gulps of it anyway and forced a smile at the sun. It hung over the eastern horizon like an orange slice.

With my juice glass in one hand and dog treats in the other, I sat on a plastic chair near the front door and listened to the desert, considering what I should do. I had to tell somebody what had happened last night, but whom? Coach Lannon? Sam? Trevor? I shuddered when I thought about what Sam and Trevor would do. No, I had to think this through. People could get hurt—or worse.

Oddly, I noticed that Dad's van was still in the carport. He usually worked Saturdays and should have left by now.

A soft breeze blew through my hair, cooling my scalp.

As I sat with my eyes closed, concentrating on the cooing sounds from the mourning doves in the paloverde trees, I heard another noise in the distance. It was an engine, deep and grinding. Familiar.

It grew louder.

I pointed my chin toward the end of our driveway and waited for Trevor to coast down on his motorcycle. Without any prodding, the Labs charged down the driveway to welcome him home.

But when my eyes opened, my body froze. My stomach tightened with fear that had become too familiar. "This isn't happening," I murmured. "Not here." I closed my eyes, squeezing them, praying it was a dream, and then looked again.

He seriously wouldn't try it again. Would he?

I wouldn't have believed it if I hadn't seen it with my own eyes.

RYAN

CHAPTER 46

I DIDN'T SLEEP AT ALL.

I spent most of the night pacing back and forth in my bedroom or staring at the ceiling, begging for the darkness to end.

I had no idea of the street where Fred lived. Did the reservation even have street names? I didn't know.

I didn't have an address either, but I did have her phone number, not that it mattered. When I dialed the number, the operator said that it was disconnected.

As soon as a sliver of morning sun crept through the bay windows in my bedroom, I leaped out of bed, operating on pure adrenaline. Still dressed in the same jeans and jacket, I stuffed my keys in my front pocket so they wouldn't jingle. Careful not to creak the stairs, I took them two at a time and then glided through the kitchen.

I didn't expect to see Dad.

"You mind telling me where you're going at this hour?" Dad sat at the kitchen counter, a cup of coffee in one hand, the newspaper in the other. Although he was in his bathrobe, he looked like he hadn't slept all night. Or in several nights. I wondered, too late, if I was the cause.

"I need to go out," I said. It wasn't a request.

"Where?"

I swallowed. He wasn't making this easy. "Out."

"Let me take you."

My head spun. I wasn't expecting that. I shook my head no.

"Please, son. Tell me what's going on. What is so important to get you out of bed this early on a Saturday?"

I met his gaze. "I need to see Fred."

"Why?"

"Something crazy stupid happened last night."

Dad put down his cup. "Oh, no." He pinched the bridge of his nose. "Is she all right?"

"Yes." I paused. But then my chest caved forward with a sigh. "And no."

Dad rose from his chair, and his eyes widened. "Which is it?"

"I've been a jerk. I need to apologize. For a lot of stuff."

"Apologizing is good." Dad nodded.

I half laughed, half snorted. "Every time I try, I screw it up. I'm not very good at it."

His eyes narrowed at me. "You really like this girl, don't you?"

I nodded. "Yeah. I do."

He drew back a deep inhale. "Do you know where you're going? The reservation is a big place."

"Sort of."

Dad didn't look convinced, but after a few seconds that felt like centuries, he said, "Well, then, you better get going."

I spun around for the door. "Bye, Dad." But then I stopped and turned. "And thanks."

I turned back toward the door. This time, nothing could stop me.

"At least call me when you get there," Dad said, but I didn't answer.

When the garage door opened, I was seated behind the wheel of my Jeep, buckled and backing out. Before the door closed, I was already driving east to the freeway along a deserted Pecos Road. The only vehicle I passed was a newspaper delivery van.

The sun peeked over the Superstition Mountains and not even the visor could stop the glare from burning my bloodshot eyes. I turned slightly to the right, scanning miles of uninterrupted desert and saguaro. A mist hovered inches from the ground like silver moss. I opened the windows, letting the cool air fill the Jeep.

Before the engine got warm, I reached the freeway exit and traveled south along the four-lane highway with only a handful of other cars and trucks. I took the first exit after Chandler Boulevard and headed west onto the Gila River Indian Reservation with the sunrise in my rearview mirror.

Silence replaced the rush from the freeway as soon as I drove onto the main road. It was the only one I knew on the reservation. Along each side of the two-lane road, modest stucco houses and trailers dotted the open desert, not in crowded cookie-cutter lines but haphazard-like, as if each house was an afterthought. Most were hidden by overgrown mesquite and paloverde trees, along with the occasional rusted car on blocks. A few stray dogs sauntered between the houses and across the deserted road.

I slowed as I passed each house, looking for something familiar, peering through overgrown foliage. I felt like a trespasser, and I supposed I was.

No one was outside. I squinted through leafy tree branches, carefully scanning each house for any sign of the Odays' van. If I could find the van, I'd find the house.

Anxious, I pressed the accelerator and drove deeper into the reservation. The two-lane road narrowed into one paved lane. I assumed that the single lane reached all the way to the foot of the Estrella Mountains. But, from a distance, the lonely road looked like a vein that wrapped around the mountain and stretched forever. Finding Fred's house somewhere along this endless loop seemed impossible.

My foot lifted from the accelerator when I spotted the outline of someone walking alongside the road in the mountain's shadow. Curious, I sped up for a better look, afraid that the shape would disappear like an optical illusion, water in the middle of a scorching desert that wasn't really water at all. It was the only human being I'd seen on the reservation all morning.

I approached from behind, careful but not slowing too much.

It was a man, tall and slender. A braid curved down the middle of his back. When I got about a half-dozen car lengths from him, I slowed and veered left, but the man didn't turn. He kept walking, his chin held high.

As the front of my Jeep passed him, the man finally turned, nodded his chin and lifted his left hand in greeting. The brown fringe from his jacket flapped in the breeze.

I blinked in disbelief.

It was the man from the golf tournament, the one who'd given the blessing, the same man who'd told stories to my fourth-grade class. I was sure of it.

George Trueblood.

I slowed the Jeep to the side of the road. He was my only chance.

I watched my rearview and waited for him to approach. When he finally got closer, I leaned out my window, drumming my fingers against the steering wheel.

"Hi," I said when he stopped at my passenger window. "You're Mr. Trueblood, aren't you?"

Silent, he bent over, as if he had all the time in the world, and peered inside my Jeep. Then his arms straddled the passenger window. He nodded back at me, once. And waited.

His expression wasn't really a smile or a frown. It wasn't curious or suspicious either. It was probably the calmest face I had ever seen.

"I was hoping you could help me," I said, dragging my tongue across my dry lips.

George Trueblood's dark brown eyes narrowed and crinkled in both corners. His face was as weathered as a saddle, soft in some parts and worn in others. A turquoise earring dangled at the end of a silver chain from one ear and almost reached his shoulder. He said nothing, and my thumbs, nervous, began to thump against the steering wheel, the only noise in the whole car, the whole desert. He waited for me to speak, prodding conversation with his eyes.

I cleared my throat. "I'm trying to find a friend of mine from school. Her name is Fred Oday. I think you know her?" I said it like a question and felt stupid, especially since I already knew his answer.

He nodded again, once, with his granitelike face.

"Could you tell me where she lives?"

He turned his head sideways and buried his chin in his shoulder. For a moment, I believed that he was going to push away from the Jeep and continue walking. I wouldn't have blamed him.

But I persisted. "It's kind of important that I see her," I added. "It's important that I talk to her." I paused to inhale. "Please," I said, not hiding my desperation. I was ready to beg if I had to.

He turned back to me. "I know Fred Oday, Daughter of the River People."

My chest lifted with encouragement.

He leaned closer in the window. "I've known her all her life. Are you sure you know her?"

I nodded, but his eyes narrowed even more, and I feared he was assessing me as some kind of serial killer. At least he didn't back away from the Jeep.

I took a chance. "Will you tell me where she lives?"

His hand dragged across his chin, revealing silver bands on each of his thick fingers.

"Please?" I begged again.

"Only if you answer three questions."

"Anything."

George Trueblood leaned back from the door, and his wide, weathered hands curled over the door frame. His chin lifted as he took a deep breath and stared sideways at the sun with closed eyes. The sunlight reddened the tips of his eyelashes. Finally, he opened his eyes and stared at me straight on, his eyes locking onto mine.

"Anything." My reflection froze in his shiny marble eyes.

"How do you know the Daughter of the River People?"

I opened my mouth to answer but then shut it quickly, considering the question. Was it a trick? And who were the River People? Fred had never mentioned them, and I felt like a tool for never asking, even lamer for not knowing.

"I met Fred for the first time when we were in the fourth grade. I visited her school on the reservation. You were there, too. You told us stories."

His eyelids flickered.

"But I never talked to her till this year."

He nodded.

"Now we're on the golf team together." I paused. "I want to know her better. I want to be a better friend. If she'll let me." But that wasn't the whole truth.

His chin lifted a fraction, and I continued to watch him anxiously, wondering if I'd said too much. Or not enough.

"Why do you need to find her today?"

"I need to apologize." My hand gripped the steering wheel tighter. "I said some really stupid things, some things I shouldn't have." I paused to steady myself. "And didn't say things I should."

The corners of his mouth turned up, the closest thing he probably got to a smile. "And who might you be?"

"I'm the biggest idiot in the world." My voice cracked with relief. "But most people call me Ryan. Ryan Berenger."

George Trueblood nodded, and my breath hitched, waiting

for what I needed most of all. Without directions to the Odays', I could drive for days across the reservation. It stretched for miles in a hundred different desolate directions.

"Turn around and go back down this road," he said slowly. "Take your first left. Then take that road all the way to the end and look for a paloverde tree filled with mourning doves. Two black dogs will guide you the rest of the way."

For real? I blinked at the unusual directions. I couldn't exactly plug them into the GPS. But then I repeated them to myself, slowly. "I take the first left and take it to the end. Dogs guide me the rest of the way. Got it." His directions would have to do. I had to find her. "Thanks."

But he didn't answer. Instead, he patted the window frame and backed away from the Jeep.

I called out before turning the Jeep around. "Do you need a ride somewhere?"

George Trueblood smiled, another small grin where his cheekbones barely moved. He shook his head. "I've already got everything I need."

Without another word, he turned down the road and walked toward the base of the mountains like it was the last thing he'd ever do.

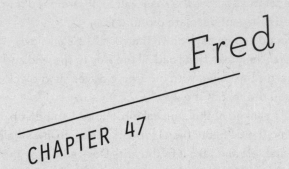

Fred

CHAPTER 47

AN ENGINE REVVED AS A VEHICLE turned into the dirt road that led to our trailer.

My glass of orange juice slipped through my fingers.

When I stood, the glass dropped to the dirt and landed with a *thud*. Every muscle in my arm and fingers froze. Without warning, the quiet morning turned sideways.

"Seth," I murmured darkly. The roar from his monster truck haunted my thoughts whether I was awake or asleep.

The vehicle wound its way among the leafy paloverde branches that hid our trailer from the road, its tires creeping along the dirt like snakes. The Labs barked and circled, but even the echo of their anxious yelps didn't drown out the pounding at my temples. My eyes clouded with fear.

When my knees threatened to buckle, I gripped the back of the chair. I should have bolted, but my legs wouldn't budge.

The car stopped at the edge of the front yard. The driver turned off the ignition and climbed out of the vehicle, slowly. The sky went silent, and for some reason my eyes could focus only on the ground.

I watched as a pair of black Converse shoes hit the ground, both at the same time. The door closed quietly. My eyes traveled from the rubber soles to the top button of a faded pair of jeans. I couldn't meet his face, not yet.

I swallowed. "Seth." I braced for the worse.

The voice said, "No. It's me."

I blinked, my vision clearing. "Ryan?" My jaw loosened with the sound of his name.

Ryan walked toward me with his palms raised as if I were getting ready to jump off a twenty-story ledge and he was trying to talk me down. His hair looked like he'd dragged his hands through it a hundred times and hadn't bothered with a comb in a week.

"Fred," he said. "Just hear me out. Please." He looked as shocked to see me as I was him.

The dogs trailed alongside his legs, their tails wagging. He lowered his hands, but he didn't unlock his gaze from mine. He took a few more cautious steps, closing the distance between us.

"Ryan?" I said again, tilting my head in disbelief. I couldn't believe that I was watching Ryan Berenger move toward me like an apparition in my own front yard. Was this a dream, too? I was too numb to be embarrassed. "I thought you were Seth—"

"I'm definitely not Seth," he added quickly.

I nodded, though still not completely convinced. I didn't know what to believe at this point.

"I tried calling you. Last night. After..." His voice trailed off, and then he swallowed. As if he needed to remind me. "I guess your phone doesn't work."

He bent down and picked up my fallen blanket. I watched the top of his head shimmer in the morning light.

"Sorry about the juice," he said, dumping the rest of it in the dirt. He put the glass on the chair and cleared his throat. If he noticed the crushed beer cans littering the front yard, his eyes didn't say.

"What," I said, summoning each word. "Are. You. Doing. Here?"

"I had to see you." He laid the blanket on the chair.

"But—"

"And I know you just want me to leave you alone, and I will, I promise, but I needed to apologize. In person. This couldn't wait."

I finally remembered to breathe.

"I didn't know about the note till Riley told me."

"Riley..." I said.

"It wasn't from me." He stuffed his hands in his front pockets. "It was Seth." He paused and inhaled loudly. "He's an idiot. And so am I. I am so sorry, Fred. I never meant to hurt you." He extended one hand but then pulled it back when I didn't reach for it.

"But..." I said, my body still reeling from seeing Ryan. "How did you find me?"

One corner of his mouth turned up in a sheepish smile. "I saw George Trueblood. He was out walking next to the road. I asked him. He told me."

"And you drove all the way out here to tell me that the note wasn't yours, that Seth wrote it?" Still not computing.

Ryan nodded again, slowly, like he was waiting for me to catch up. "But there's more I'd like to say."

My hands began to shake. "I have to sit down."

Ryan continued to stand while I sat. Finally, he said, "Can I sit with you?"

I waved absently to the other plastic chair and then buried my shaking hands between my legs.

"It's so quiet out here," Ryan said, looking all around the yard as he carried the other plastic chair from next to the house and placed it across from me.

"Uh-huh," I said vaguely. "Well, it is kind of early."

"I can see why you'd like living out here," he added. "All of this space." His eyes scanned the carport and along the front of the house before finally landing on the putting green. My putter leaned against the house. "Seriously?" he looked at me, wide-eyed.

I knew what he was referring to. It wasn't every day you saw a putting green made up of multicolored carpet samples. "Ryan."

I grew a little impatient. "What else do you have to tell me? This could have waited till Monday."

"No, it couldn't. What Seth did was too—" he paused, shook his head and sighed "—whacked. I mean, he should be arrested for what he did."

"He's nothing but a bully, Ryan. And if he's your best friend, then you're just as bad."

Ryan winced. "I am not a bully, Fred."

I didn't answer. I wasn't sure whether to believe him, not after last night. Not after everything that had happened.

"And I know this is going to sound crazy, but Seth used to be a pretty good guy. I know that he's changed recently and what he did last night was horrible. But if you got to know each other..." His voice trailed off.

My eyes widened. "Yeah, well, I don't see that happening."

"He was picked on pretty badly when we were kids. His real dad got killed by a drunk driver when he was just a baby and his step-dad is pretty tough on him."

"So that makes it okay?" I snorted.

"I'm just asking you to try to understand—"

I lifted my palm, stopping him. "You think Seth Winter is the only one who hasn't had it easy? Look around, Ryan. You've got to wake up."

"I know." He dragged his fingers over the front of his head. "I'm trying."

Another wave of reality washed over me, enough for my entire body to shudder. My gaze darted back to the road leading to our trailer. Trevor could arrive any minute. "You better leave before my brother gets home."

"You have a brother?"

"Yeah. The one you and Seth ran off the freeway a while back."

Ryan looked at me, stunned. "That was your brother?"

I shot up, knocking back my chair, glaring down at him. My

chest ached from breathing so hard. "So that *was* you! How could you? You ran my brother off the road? You could have killed him! How could you be so cruel?"

Ryan's head dropped into his hands. He faced the dirt. His fingers wound through his hair. "I wasn't driving, Fred. It was Seth."

"So that makes it okay?" I yelled.

His face turned up to me, paler than before. "Of course not." In a softer voice, he said, "I am so sorry. I didn't mean for it to happen. You've got to believe me. Please..."

"Did you even try to stop Seth before he ran Trevor off the road?"

"Yes."

I shook my head, my voice hoarse. "Well, you didn't try hard enough."

He nodded, his gaze locked onto mine. "You're right. I should have tried harder. I should have forced him to stop. And I am so sorry, Fred."

My breathing slowed, watching his head drop again, his fingers thread through his hair. I sank back into my chair, thoroughly and utterly exhausted. I wanted Ryan Berenger away from me, away from our home, and yet I couldn't say the words that would make him leave. "You've got to wake up, Ryan," I said again.

Ryan inhaled and then said, "But that's not everything I wanted to say." He leaned his elbows onto his knees. "There's more—"

I interrupted him. "Riley already told me."

His eyebrows pulled together. "Told you what?"

"That you're leaving. You're going to live with your uncle." The words tasted bitter in my mouth. I hated myself for caring that Ryan was leaving. I hated that, despite everything, the news pulled on my heart.

"Yes, I am. And—"

A high-pitched scream filled the inside of the trailer, shattering the silent desert.

"Oh, my god." I sat up and turned toward the front door. But it was closed.

"Who was that?" Ryan sat straighter.

I leaped up. "My mom." I ran for the front door. I could feel Ryan running behind me. I didn't even think about telling him to wait outside.

"Mom!" I yelled as I burst through the door and ran through the house. "What's wrong? What happened?" A sick feeling rose to the top of my throat, fearful that she'd picked today of all days to start drinking early. What would I tell Ryan? A hundred ugly thoughts filled my head.

Mom wailed again from her bedroom, long and loud. Wounded.

"What is it? What's happened?" I raced into my parents' bedroom, Ryan at my heels.

The window shade was still drawn, and I squinted against the dim gray light. All I saw was Mom in her white nightgown. She floated around the dark room like a ghost, wringing her hands over her head, screaming.

"It's your father!" she yelled, leaping back onto the bed. "Oh, my god. He's not breathing!"

"Oh my god oh my god oh my god," I said, my whole body shaking as I felt my way to the right side of the bed. "Dad!" I dropped alongside him to the floor and reached for his hand. His skin was clammy and cold. "Dad!" I screamed, patting his hand to wake him.

"Call 911," Ryan said, his voice the only calm tone in the room. "Now."

"But the phone," I cried. Had he forgotten already that our number was disconnected? Again?

Ryan tossed a cell phone from his pocket and wedged himself next to Dad. I shifted so that I sat closer to Dad's head. "Let me through, Fred," Ryan said, sounding strangely steady, as if he did this kind of thing all the time. "I can help."

Maybe it was the tone of his voice, or maybe it was the effortless way his body moved, but I obeyed Ryan without question. I leaned against the headboard and watched him like we were all characters in some kind of hazy dream.

Oddly, Mom didn't ask about Ryan or wonder why a strange white boy was inside our trailer giving orders. She was too busy wailing into her hands.

"Hank." Mom choked back a sob. "Please, don't leave me. Please." She stroked the hair off his forehead.

Mom's pleas tore at my heart. It was rare to hear her speak so tenderly to Dad, to anyone. My hands shook as I pressed the buttons on Ryan's cell phone, coaxing myself to concentrate.

The keys glowed green in the muted darkness. With my left hand, I dialed the phone with my thumb. My right hand stayed wrapped around Dad's hand. Not a muscle stirred inside mine, but I continued to squeeze his hand anyway.

"Mr. Oday?" Ryan said loudly. "Can you hear me?" He pressed his fingers to Dad's neck. "Fred, Mrs. Oday, I need you both to sit back and give me some room. Please."

I inched deeper into the headboard, waiting for an operator to answer, my left hand shaking as I clutched the phone to my ear.

Mom knelt higher in the middle of the bed. "Hank." Her moans sank along with her body. "Hank..."

Ryan pressed both palms against Dad's chest. "One, two, three, four..." he said, pumping his chest.

The operator said, "Nine-one-one, what is your emergency?"

"My father isn't breathing," I cried into the phone.

"What is your location?" the operator asked, blessedly calm, and I told her. "Please, hurry," I said, but the operator instructed me to stay on the line. I kept the phone pressed against my ear, watching Ryan, tears streaming down my face.

Ryan continued to count, unruffled. Hovering above Dad's chest, he inhaled and exhaled in clipped, ragged breaths, like he was getting ready to dive into a pool. His palms continued to press against Dad's chest, and, for a moment, I thought I felt Dad squeeze my hand.

My heart fluttered its own anxious response.

"He squeezed my hand!" I said, my voice cracking, but Ryan ignored me. His hands still pumped against Dad's chest.

Then Ryan pressed his mouth over Dad's, blowing hard. After three quick blows, he sat up, still pumping Dad's chest. "Come on, Mr. Oday. Come on!" he yelled over Mom's cries.

"Please, Dad," I sobbed. "Please, wake up. Please!" The room continued to spin with the weight of all of the sounds, Mom's wails, Ryan's steady chants, my own heavy breathing, even the growing thickness of the air.

The operator returned to the line and said, "The paramedics are almost there. Stay strong, young lady."

"I will," I muttered breathlessly. "I am."

"One, two, three, four..." Ryan continued to chant, pressing all his weight against Dad's chest. He bent over him for more mouth-to-mouth in steady, even breaths. He leaned back on his knees and sucked in a breath

My own breathing stopped. I thought Ryan was giving up.

But then without another word or even a glance at me, Ryan balled his fist, lifted it high above his head and let it crash against the middle of Dad's chest.

Somewhere between Mom's screams and the three paramedics who flooded the trailer, I watched, paralyzed, as Dad was connected to a hundred different clear tubes and then lifted onto a stretcher.

Strange smells filled the room, sharp ones that you'd prefer to forget. Someone turned on the overhead light and raised the window shade, drenching the bedroom in morning light, making it bright and cheery when it was anything but. Ugly words like *faint pulse, barely breathing, cold skin,* and *heart attack* invaded the bedroom like stains.

When the paramedics hauled in the stretcher, Ryan gently pried my fingers from Dad's hands, one finger at a time. "He started to squeeze," I insisted, daring anyone to doubt me. "I know he did. I felt it. Twice, I think."

"Yes, you did," Ryan said quietly. "Come on, Fred. I'll drive you to the hospital."

"What about Mom?" I said, my voice cracking. "Where is she?" I suddenly realized that the wailing and moaning had stopped. She was gone.

"She'll ride in the ambulance with your dad." Carefully, he took both my hands in his and coaxed me to my feet. He held me till my knees stopped shaking. My legs tingled from being wedged into a single position for so long. How long, though? I wasn't certain.

Ryan dropped one of my hands but held the other.

"Where are they taking him?" I dragged my free hand down one cheek. It was damp from tears.

"Phoenix General," Ryan said. "I know the way."

We followed the paramedics, but I stopped at the front door, staring at all the red-and-white flashing lights outside the window. The ambulance and fire truck dwarfed the front yard. "Will he be all right?" I whispered to Ryan, tugging back on his arm. Pleading. Begging. "Will he?"

When Ryan didn't answer right away, my chest tightened.

But then he said, "Yes. He'll be okay."

"You're sure?"

"The paramedics are doing everything they can."

I drew back a breath, mostly to steady another wave of nausea. My body began to sway. Ryan swept his arm around my shoulder. My vision turned cloudy again.

"Come on," Ryan said. He pulled me forward, gently. "Let's go."

As I climbed into the passenger seat of Ryan's Jeep, the ambulance had already vanished down the driveway with its sirens wailing and lights flashing. "Hurry, Ryan. Please."

Ryan turned the ignition, and within seconds, we were behind the ambulance. "Seat belt, Fred," he said, buckling his own.

I pulled the strap across my chest and then placed my hands in my lap. I stared ahead, anxious, until Ryan placed his warm hand over mine. My eyes dipped briefly to study our hands. Then, slowly, I studied Ryan's profile. His brow was furrowed; his jaw, set. He concentrated on the ambulance like he expected it to disappear. Finally, I said, "How did you know what to do?"

Ryan swallowed, pressing hard on the accelerator to keep up with the ambulance as it approached the freeway. "My mom's a doctor." His shoulders shrugged. "Some parents take their kids to the zoo when they're little. My mom took me to medical seminars. I just kind of learned." He sniffed, embarrassed-like. "From watching people."

I looked back down at his right hand like I was seeing it, touching it, for the first time. It was smooth and slightly tanned with a smattering of freckles, brownish-orange like his sister's skin. A blue vein bulged above the middle knuckle. Suddenly I felt compelled to press my cheek against it. And then I kissed the back of his hand before brushing it against my cheek. A few stray tears landed on his knuckles, but I quickly wiped them away with my thumb. "Thank you," I whispered, my voice catching again, just as Ryan's Adam's apple rose very slowly. When it finally returned to the base of his neck, I threaded my fingers through his hand and concentrated on the windshield.

I watched the ambulance's silver bumper all the way down the freeway, each shiny red letter searing itself permanently into my brain. I was afraid to blink, afraid that if I did, Dad would disappear forever.

We didn't speak again until we reached the hospital.

RYAN

CHAPTER 48

THE SLIDING GLASS DOORS to the Phoenix General emergency room burst open when Fred and I raced through, making that sharp, *swishing* airport sound the moment our feet met the mat.

I knew hospitals well. The incessant buzzing and bells and antiseptic smells were familiar. I'd seen this one's pale yellow walls and linoleum floors plenty of times and plenty of places like them. Cold, impersonal, detached. Oddly, I felt right at home.

"Where's my father? Where'd they take him?" Fred whispered behind her hand as her gaze darted about the room.

"Sit here." I motioned to a set of yellow padded chairs off to the side of the door. Four other people were already seated in the mostly colorless waiting room, numbly turning magazine pages in their laps, awaiting their fates. Saturday-morning cartoons blared across a television mounted in the corner.

Fred nodded at me and then walked to a chair, but she didn't sit. Instead, she paced in front of it while I walked to the admittance window.

A gray-haired woman with a pinched face behind wire-rimmed bifocals peered up at me through a round hole in the glass window. Her name tag said Rita. "May I help you?"

I gripped the end of the counter and leaned forward. "A man

was just transported here from the Gila River Indian Reservation."
I lowered my voice. "He had a heart attack."

"Name?"

"Hank Oday."

Rita checked her clipboard. The tip of her pen brushed down
the page before her wrinkled eyes rested on a name in the middle.
She looked up, and her mouth twisted. "Are you family?"

I swallowed and glanced over my shoulder at Fred, chewing on
her thumbnail. "No. Not exactly."

"Your name?"

"Ryan Berenger. I'm here with Mr. Oday's daughter, Fredricka
Oday." I nodded over my shoulder at Fred.

The tightness around her eyes softened. "Berenger? You're
Doctor Berenger's son?"

I nodded.

A smile lifted her lips before she examined the clipboard again.
"Well, I can tell you that they've currently got him sedated in the
Coronary Care Unit. They're locating a doctor now. He'll need
surgery."

"Will he be...okay?" I whispered into the glass hole.

Rita's smile faded. Her head tilted slightly as I waited. I'd seen
that look before.

Then Mrs. Oday burst through the windowless metal door next
to Admittance wearing an oversize green parka over her white
nightgown. The door crashed against the rubber stopper at the
bottom.

"Fred!" Her gaze bounced frantically about the room.

Fred ran into her mother's arms.

I left Rita and followed behind Mrs. Oday.

"Your father," she said, each word catching as the words struggled to leave her lips. "It's not good. He needs some type of surgery."

Fred grabbed her mother's elbows. "Will he be all right?"

Mrs. Oday's nostrils flared, and my stomach tightened. Her mouth pulled back in a kind of brave smile.

"Mother. Tell me," Fred said as her shoulders began to shake. I wanted to wrap my arms around her, around both of them.

"He's had a heart attack, Fred. A serious one." She paused. "They're trying to find a doctor now. Some kind of specialist..." Her voice trailed off as her whole body shook. What little composure she had from earlier vanished in an instant. "I don't know, Fred. I don't know." She fell against Fred's shoulder and buried her face, trying to muffle her sobs.

Fred hugged her. With her face peering over her shoulder, she looked up at me, and her eyes overflowed with more tears. The way her lower lip quivered made my chest ache in a way that it had never done before.

I swallowed back a lump building in my throat as I pulled out my cell phone from my front pocket. My thumb punched 1 on the speed dial. A few moments later, a woman answered. I turned away from Fred and her mother.

"Mom?" I said into the phone. I cleared my throat and lowered my voice. Then I said, "It's me. I really need your help."

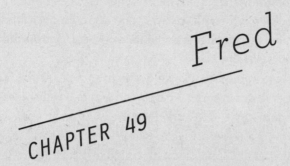

Fred

CHAPTER 49

"SOMETIMES IT TAKES BAD things to see the good," Trevor said to me as we sat in the hospital waiting room.

I nodded numbly at my brother, unsure who he was trying to convince. Me? Or himself?

That bit of wisdom might make more sense tomorrow. Today, it was just a string of meaningless words when all I wanted was to see Dad again, alive.

I craved Dad's reassuring hand squeezing mine. I wanted another afternoon with him as he worked under our perpetually creaky van with a couple of warm sodas beside us. I wanted him to tell me all over again how the Gila River once flowed free like its people. I wanted to hear his stories about how the Indian woman with hair as long as a river captured the moon and became the mother to the stars. I wanted, I wanted...

Most of all, I wanted Dad.

Trevor nodded back at me when he thought I was listening. He'd arrived at the E.R. soon after I'd reached him at Ruth's on Ryan's cell phone. He leaned forward, his elbows resting on his knees, rocking to hold himself together. If he recognized Ryan as the one who'd run him off the road, his face didn't show it. Funny how none of that seemed important now.

Ryan sat on my other side, silent and watching the windowless door next to Admittance. Every time someone walked through the door, his back straightened like everyone else's, anxious for news. I'd already told him to go home, but he'd refused, even as half the Rez filled the waiting room.

One of the paramedics was Kelly Oliver's uncle. After we'd arrived at the emergency room, he'd placed a phone call home. That had led to another phone call, then another. Within an hour, someone had brought a cooler with sandwiches; another had brought a change of clothes for Mom. And in the middle of the fray sat George Trueblood, his eyes closed, mumbling to himself. Another blessing? If the hospital was bothered by the crowd, they didn't say. All my family's friends were here, even all my friends from school— Kelly, Yolanda, Sam, Peter, Martin and Vernon.

"I wish someone would tell us what's happening," I whispered to Ryan for the tenth time.

"Your mom said that they'd give us an update after the surgery," he reminded me.

I looked up at the clock above the Admittance window. "But that was three hours ago."

"It's a delicate surgery."

"How do you know so much?"

"I told you." He lowered his voice. "My mom's a doctor."

"Where's Mom?" Trevor said, lifting his head from his hands. He'd been drifting in and out of conversations with me since he'd arrived.

"She's talking with one of the surgery nurses," I said. "Back there." Wherever *back there* was. There apparently was another waiting room outside of Surgery, but that room only allowed immediate family. For now, I needed to be surrounded by my friends.

I returned to watching the door next to the glass window. Every few minutes, the metal door clicked open as if it led to some kind of bank vault. Everyone in the waiting room swiveled toward the sound, tracking nurses and doctors dressed in green scrubs and hairnets who raced along the edges to another windowless door, their rubber soles squeaking on the linoleum. They rarely made eye contact with anyone in the waiting room either, not that it mattered. No one would dare stop them. It would be easier to halt a moving train.

But then, finally, one of them stopped, and my throat tightened.

A woman in green scrubs approached the edge of the waiting room. Short blond hair peeked from underneath her cap. Her eyes scanned the room as she pulled the white elastic mask away from her mouth with her right hand. It dangled loose around neck. She cleared her throat. "Oday family?" Her unwavering voice announced to everyone in the room that she had delivered news before, the kind that you were never totally prepared to hear.

The crowded room quieted. I felt everyone's eyes resting on Trevor and me.

After hours of waiting for news, I wasn't sure that I was ready for it.

The muscles in the woman's cheeks barely moved in her unreadable face.

Tentatively, Trevor and I stood and stepped forward. I felt Ryan standing behind me, along with the weight of the crowd at our backs.

"That's us," I said to the woman, my voice straining to keep the cracks together. I folded my arms across my chest, bracing for the worst.

The woman lowered her voice. "Your mother asked me to talk to you." Her eyes, blue as turquoise, flickered between Trevor and me. "We were unable to perform an angioplasty on your father. There was too much blockage."

I listened numbly, waiting for the only words that mattered.

"So," the woman continued, "I had to perform a coronary bypass—"

"Is he all right?" Trevor interrupted.

The woman's thin lips pressed together. "He's resting now. He's heavily medicated."

My temples began to pound harder. "Will my father get better?" My voice caught on the last word. "When can we take him home?"

The woman blinked. Then the corners of her lips turned up into a small, tired smile. "Yes, I think your father will be fine. With enough time and some bed rest—"

I gasped. Then I threw my arms around her neck. "Oh, thank you. Thank you!" I sobbed. I didn't care that an ice-cold stethoscope jabbed my ribs. I felt a dozen warm hands on my head and back. Relieved sighs and nervous chuckles filled the air. The room felt suddenly lighter, the smells not as sharp. Laughter and voices sounded familiar and comforting again.

And I couldn't stop crying. I cried against the woman's neck, sinking against her. My tears soaked her shoulder.

"It's going to be all right," the woman said, stroking my head. "It's all right," she whispered.

"Thank you." The words choked in the back of my throat and competed with my sobs. "Thank you."

"You're welcome," she said, still stroking her hair. "You're very welcome, Fred."

For an instant, my crying stopped. I sniffed.

Fred?

I unlocked my arms from around the woman and pulled back. I wiped my face, still soggy wet from tears, with the back of my hand. "Wait," I said, blinking the cloudiness from my eyes. "You know me?"

The woman smiled, wider this time, revealing perfectly white teeth. Then she nodded over my shoulder. "Ryan?" she said. "Isn't it about time you introduced us?"

Still blinking back tears, I turned to Ryan.

Ryan's face flushed the deepest shade of red I'd ever seen when everyone in the waiting room stared back at him, even me. But then he swallowed and said, "Fred, I'd like you to meet my mom." His voice was clear. "Doctor Meredith Berenger."

RYAN

CHAPTER 50

MOM GUIDED FRED AND TREVOR to their father's recovery room, leaving me alone with half the Gila Indian Reservation in the Phoenix General Hospital waiting room. As soon as the heavy door shut behind them, the waiting room grew silent. Someone had turned off the television. Even the two babies had stopped crying in their mothers' laps.

My throat turned dry almost immediately as I turned to face them. I could feel every black-eyed gaze sweeping over every inch of me. They probably didn't think very much of me, especially after last Saturday night, and who could blame them?

I thought about walking to the safety of the cafeteria, making an excuse about needing another soda, another bag of potato chips—anything! Instead, I turned around and walked straight into the middle of the waiting room and found an empty chair. It felt like walking into the middle of a shooting range without a vest.

But before I sat down, Sam Tracy met me at the chair.

"Hey. Dude," he said gruffly. He peered down his nose at me. Jeez, the guy was scary-looking, especially with his low-slung jeans and barrel chest as wide as a flat-screen TV.

My forehead began to pound. "Hey," I said, wondering if I needed to ready myself for a punch to the gut. Or worse. Sam was flanked on one side by Peter. On the other, Kelly and Yolanda. I stuffed my clenched hands in my front pockets, expecting the worst.

But Sam's tone softened. "I want to thank you for what you did for Mr. Oday."

My chin pulled back. "Um. You do?"

"Yeah." He nodded. "That was pretty cool."

I swallowed, speechless. So not what I expected.

The people crowded behind him began to nod and smile silently in my direction before returning to their seats and the cooler in the corner of the room. Someone reached up and turned the television back on.

"We heard about what you did. Everybody did," Peter added. "Kelly's cousin said you saved Mr. Oday's life."

I certainly wasn't going to take credit for anything. It didn't seem right. Instead of saying anything, I just shrugged my shoulders, my eyes darting between them. It was like they had more to share.

Then Sam extended his beefy hand. "Thanks, man."

For a moment, I looked at Sam's hand. I clasped it with mine. It felt good. "No problem."

"Sorry about throwing you across the parking lot the other night," he added.

I smirked at him. "Sorry about the punch to your jaw."

"What punch?" Sam's eyes widened with mock innocence. He chuckled. "Seriously, you clocked me good. Surprised me, even." He rubbed his cheek, the tiniest glint of respect in his eyes.

Then Peter extended his hand. I shook his, too. Until today, apart from the fight with Sam, I'd probably never said more than two words to either of them.

Too soon, they turned around and left me with Yolanda and Kelly. From the pinched looks on their faces, I gathered we wouldn't be shaking hands and making up anytime soon.

Kelly spoke. "First thing you should know is this—Fred is like a sister to us."

"A little sister," Yolanda added, nodding.

"We're grateful for what you did, Ryan, but we're still mad at you. You broke her heart, you know."

"Mean fuck," Yolanda said underneath her breath.

Kelly's eyes rolled. "Watch your language, Yo."

"I deserved that," I said.

"Damn right you do," Yolanda said to me.

Kelly sighed and rolled her eyes at Yolanda. She lowered her voice so that no one except me would hear. Then her eyes locked onto mine. "Anyway, we're watching you. And if you hurt her again, we *will* hurt you." Her eyes widened. "Clear?" Then she smiled sweetly, the dimple in her cheek belying her threat.

"Totally." Not a single part of me doubted these girls. In truth, I probably feared them more than a hundred Sam Tracys. And I had no intention of ever hurting Fred Oday again.

But I wasn't certain I had any chances left with her. I wasn't sure I deserved her either.

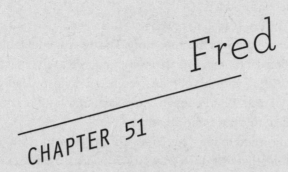

Fred

CHAPTER 51

"I CAN TAKE HER HOME," Ryan said, his gaze bouncing between me and my brother with a new surge of energy. "I don't mind."

"*I* mind." Trevor's eyes narrowed at Ryan. "I'll take her on my *bike*," he said.

From the nervous flicker in Ryan's eyes, the double meaning was not lost on him.

Ryan and Trevor stood chest to chest in the hospital waiting room. All of a sudden, the room lacked oxygen.

"Trevor," I said, pulling back on his elbow. "Not now. It's been a long day. Everyone's tired."

Trevor didn't brush away my hand, but he still ignored me.

"You're the dude from the freeway," Trevor said. It wasn't a question. "You and your genius buddy tried to run me off the road."

Ryan's jaw hardened, but he nodded, surprising me a little. "Yeah. That was me."

"I recognized you earlier. Just couldn't find the words at the time."

"Whatever your words, I'm sure I deserve them," Ryan said, but he didn't back away. If anything, his body held steady, as if he was expecting punishment.

"Damn right."

"I'm really sorry," Ryan added. "It was stupid. I hope you can give me a second chance."

"Trevor," I blurted, feeling my cheeks flush. I looked around the room. Fortunately, it was mostly empty. The evening news blared on a television set that no one was watching. "Please," I hissed at my brother. After everything Ryan's mom had done for Dad, I felt bad that my brother had chosen this moment to make a scene. "Can't we hash this out some other time?"

But Ryan turned to me. "No, Fred. Your brother is right. I deserve anything that he's got to say. Now's as good a time as any."

Trevor's nostrils flared. "I just wanted you to know that I recognized you. I'd recognize you anywhere. I'd recognize your crazy friend, too."

Ryan nodded. I held my breath. "I should have stopped Seth and I didn't," he said. "I'm sorry. I'm sorry for what we did. Even though I wasn't driving, I'm just as guilty."

Trevor's expression softened a fraction. "Look, I'm grateful for what your mom did for us, Berenger. But I'm still not happy with you."

"I wouldn't be either."

"I'm not sure I want you hanging around my sister."

"Trevor!" I blurted, more heat rushing up my neck.

Once again, Trevor ignored me. "And I'm still taking her home."

Ryan looked from me to my brother again. I didn't know what to say. It was like my brain froze, along with my mouth, from exhaustion and frustration. From surviving the longest day of my life. From being grateful for such a wonderful brother and at the same time wanting to scream at him for treating me like a child.

Finally, Ryan exhaled and said, "Okay," and for that I was relieved.

When Trevor drove me home on the back of his motorcycle, the sky was moonless and still again. The air felt soft and welcoming after sitting inside the sterile waiting room all day.

I rested my head against his shoulder and closed my heavy
eyelids as we raced down the freeway and back toward the Rez.
It felt like weeks had passed since Dad's heart attack, instead of
twenty-four hours. Maybe that's why breathing had become difficult. It was as if time had fast-forwarded and I was struggling
to catch up.

Mom had stayed at the hospital, and Trevor and I had promised
to return the next morning.

As I climbed off the back of Trevor's motorcycle in front of the
trailer, my legs felt like tree trunks, every muscle weighted by a
list of things I needed to do:

Feed the dogs.

Clean the house.

Make something to eat.

*Call the restaurant and the golf course and tell them that Mom
and Dad won't be at work for a while.*

Call the high school.

Call Coach Lannon.

Calling the coach was the thing I dreaded most, only because
of what I needed to tell him.

I fingered Ryan's cell phone, just to make sure it was still safely
tucked inside my pocket. I would have hated to lose it, especially
after he'd insisted that I keep it, at least until our phone got recon-
nected. "I just charged it, so it'll be good for a while," he'd told me.
"Use it whenever you need to."

I smiled, but then the warm feeling faded when I remembered
he was leaving for San Francisco. How could his parents let him
leave? Dad barely liked that I left the house to attend Lone Butte
High School. I couldn't imagine that parents like the Berengers
would let their son leave for another state. They loved him too
much. Even I could see that.

Ryan had asked me to call him later, if it wasn't too late. "Just
press 1 on the speed dial," he'd told me. "That's my home number."

With my eyes half-closed, I stumbled onto the front step with Trevor right behind me. I flipped on the light switch just inside the front door.

"Oh. My. Gosh." My eyes burned from the bright light.

"Jeez..." Trevor mumbled.

Someone had already been to the house. The trailer had been cleaned, top to bottom. Chairs that had been knocked over by the paramedics had all been straightened. All blankets, folded. The bookcases were shiny and dusted. Even the rugs had been vacuumed. The sharp, ammonia-like medicinal smell was gone, replaced by something lemony. The windows were all open, and a sweet desert breeze wafted through the house. Everything felt almost, well, normal.

Or like normal had a chance inside our trailer.

"Check this out," Trevor said, stepping around me.

A platter of cheeses and fresh fruits covered in plastic, left-overs from the impromptu hospital-waiting-room picnic, sat on the kitchen counter next to a clear juice glass overflowing with yellow wildflowers, round silky petals and green skinny stems. A handwritten note balanced against it. It said:

Come find me if you need anything. You know where I'll be.

"Who did all this?" I said, my eyes sweeping across the front room and the kitchen. No one had ever cleaned our trailer before, no one except us. I wasn't sure if it had ever looked so tidy. Even the picture frames and family photos on the wall had all been dusted and straightened where before there had always been one or two that hung crookedly.

"Doesn't say," Trevor said. He lifted something small from the kitchen counter. "It was folded inside the note." He turned to show me. It twirled between his thumb and forefinger.

A feather, white and as delicate as silk.

Trevor and I stared at each and grinned tired smiles. "George Trueblood," we said together.

RYAN

CHAPTER 52

I LAY IN BED IN THE DARK, my legs crossed at the ankles. I was still dressed, the house phone resting on the pillow next to me. I didn't know how long I'd been without sleep—two days? Three? Despite the sleepless nights, my head buzzed like an airplane during takeoff.

I kept playing the day over in my mind. It was as if someone else had pulled the strings, making my arms and legs move. I wanted to talk about it, which was crazy weird for me because I wasn't like that. I never talked about my feelings. Until recently, I wasn't sure I had any. Normally, I held everything inside like a deep breath. But the day pressed against my chest, begging for release. Unfortunately, the only person who mattered barely knew how to use my cell phone.

"Ryan?" Mom knocked on my door. "Mind if I come in?"

I rubbed the burn in my eyes with the back of my hands. "Sure, Mom." My voice was raspy from exhaustion.

Mom opened the door, just a crack at first and then wider. The glow from the hallway dome light shone over the bottom half of my bed. Quietly, she approached the edge of my bed and sat on the right side, adjusting the belt on her robe. "Can't sleep?"

I shook my head.

Mom placed a cool hand on my forehead. With her fingertips, she swept my bangs to the side. It felt so good.

"I wanted to talk to you..." she started in her mom voice, not so different from her Doctor Berenger hospital voice.

My body tensed, and her hand snapped back. As usual, I wondered what I'd done wrong.

"Easy, Ryan."

I said nothing.

"I just want to talk."

But then she surprised me. Her voice lost some of its edge. "I wanted to tell you how proud I am of you." She paused, unable to hide a small crack in her voice. "How very proud your father and I are of you today."

My breathing stopped. "What?"

"You heard me." There was the hint of something else in her voice. Pride?

"But I didn't do anything. You're the one who saved Mr. Oday's life. Remember?"

Mom chuckled. "No. That's where you're very wrong. I wouldn't have had anyone to save if you hadn't done CPR." She paused. "When did my baby boy grow up? How did I miss it?"

"Mom. Stop. Please." My cheeks flushed.

Her voice cracked again, and in the dim light, I could see that her face was shiny with tears. She didn't bother to hide them. Totally unlike her.

"Really, Mom." My feet began to cross and uncross at the ankles. "It was nothing."

"It was certainly something," she insisted. Then she began to stroke my forehead again with her fingertips, and I closed my eyes. "Who knows? Maybe you'll be a doctor someday."

Instead of tensing up like I normally did whenever they tried to predict my future, I just said, "Maybe." Seriously, it had felt good helping someone else for a change.

"I do wish you'd reconsider staying with your uncle, though. I'll miss you terribly. We all will."

My throat thickened. She'd never said that before either. "I don't know, Mom. I think it might be a good thing. All I ever seem to do is get on your nerves."

"Not true."

"So true."

Instead of arguing, she bent down and kissed my forehead. "You need sleep. We all do. We'll talk more in the morning. But promise me you'll reconsider?"

I couldn't promise.

Sighing, Mom lifted from the bed. She shuffled to the door in her slippers. Then she turned one last time and looked at me over her shoulder in the dim glow of the hallway light. I saw the whites of her teeth. She was smiling.

I smiled back.

Her voice cracked. "I love you, Ryan." Then, very quietly, she shut the door.

"I love you, too, Mom," I said to the closed door, but loud enough that I was certain she could hear me. I think my eyes finally shut about the time Mom's last footstep reached the end of the hallway.

But I was pretty sure that I fell asleep happy, and maybe even a little proud. And it felt good.

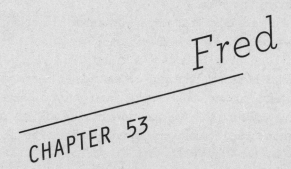

Fred

CHAPTER 53

"MR. LANNON? HI. It's Fred Oday."

"Fred? What can I do for you?"

It was Monday morning. I pictured Coach Lannon sitting in his office, his sunburned eyelids narrowed as he stared at the golf bags stacked against his back wall, probably wondering why he didn't see the plaid eyesore.

"We had an emergency this weekend. At home." I paused, wondering if I was talking too loudly into Ryan's cell phone. My voice echoed in my ear. "I won't be at school for a few days."

"What happened?"

I swallowed. It wasn't easy to say the words, even though the doctors said that Dad would be fine. He didn't look fine, especially lying in a hospital bed hooked up to a million clear tubes and silver machines that never stopped buzzing. "It's my father. He had a heart attack on Saturday."

"Hank? Oh, my god." Coach Lannon exhaled. His chair creaked in the background. "I am so sorry, Fred. Is he all right?"

"Yes. He's better."

"Good, good. So glad to hear that." He paused. "What can I do?"

"Nothing. But thank you."

"When do you think you'll be back?"

"I'm not sure, exactly. I need to help my mom. Wednesday? Thursday, maybe. I don't know."

"So you'll have to miss Thursday's tournament." He said it like it was already decided.

"Maybe."

"No worries, Fred. You take care of your father. That's what's most important. You can't replace family, and golf you'll have forever. I'd give anything to have one more minute with my dad." Coach Lannon's voice actually cracked a little before he cleared his throat. "Golf can wait, Fred."

I took a deep breath. I had practiced this last night a thousand times, but it didn't make me any less nervous. And it just felt strange asking for something, especially from a teacher. I pulled my shoulders back and did it anyway. "I do need a favor."

"Anything," he said, his voice back to normal. "Name it."

"It's about Ryan Berenger...."

"Ryan?" His voice got louder. "What about him?" I heard the wheels of his chair shift and shuffle.

"I'd like you to put him back on the team."

Coach Lannon laughed nervously. "But I can't—"

"Yes, you can, Coach. You have to. Ryan didn't put that club in my bag." I paused.

"Who did?"

"Someone else" was all that I'd say.

Silence.

Coach Lannon breathed heavily into the phone. Finally, he said, "But I've already told Ryan—"

I gripped the edge of the kitchen counter to steady myself and squeezed my eyes shut. The coach wasn't making this easy. But it was the only thing that made sense in a sea of so many things that didn't.

Finally, I said, "If you don't put Ryan back on the team, I'll have to quit."

RYAN

CHAPTER 54

RILEY AND I DROVE INTO the school parking lot on Monday morning with time to spare before Homeroom. I even stopped to talk with Peter and Sam after Peter's dad dropped them off at the curb. We talked about meeting up for lunch in the cafeteria.

Then, instead of walking straight to the courtyard to hang with Seth and Gwyneth, I went to the library to study. It felt totally weird, but it didn't feel wrong. More like I needed to practice it.

As I opened my backpack inside a library cubicle, I heard the front doors open followed by heavy footsteps across the carpet. They came straight toward me. I lifted my head, curious.

"Coach?" I said, surprised. I rarely saw Coach Lannon away from the locker room or the football fields.

"Berenger," the coach said with one of his trademark tightly wound smiles that really wasn't a smile at all. It was usually a prelude to bad news, and I wasn't sure how much worse the news could get. I guess I was about to find out. Was I getting expelled? The idea should have bothered me more than it did.

"How'd you know I was here?"

"Just talked to your sister. She said you'd be here," he said, as he dragged a chair across the carpet from the adjoining cubicle. "Mind if I sit?"

Like I had a choice.

"Um, sure." I leaned back in my chair, my chemistry and English books unopened on the desk. So much for the extra studying time.

Coach Lannon cleared his throat. "Anyway..." He scratched the side of his head. "I've been doing some thinking." He cleared his throat again.

I sank lower in my seat. This sounded bad.

"And I think I may have reacted a little too harshly last week." *Huh?*

"I've recently been handed some new information about last week's tournament." He paused. "What I'm trying to say is that maybe I shouldn't have taken you off the team without asking a few more questions. Dropping you was probably a little extreme, considering."

Considering what? I blinked slowly. "But I told you that I was the one who put the club in Fred's bag. Isn't that grounds enough?"

The coach leaned closer, close enough so that I could smell the morning coffee on his breath. "But did you? Really?" His eyes leveled with mine.

My throat turned dry. I said nothing.

The coach lowered his voice and leaned even closer. "Will you tell me who did?"

I shook my head slowly. *No. Way.*

"That's what I thought." Coach Lannon exhaled and leaned back, his eyes still locked on mine with his chin lowered, assessing me. "So," he said after a pause that lasted an eternity. "What d'you say?"

This was completely unexpected. I had accepted that I was off the team. "I'm not real sure," I said finally. "I'm going to be moving to my uncle's house in a couple of weeks."

"Moving?"

"Just for the rest of the school year." *Just till I get my head screwed on right.* "Then I'll be back."

"But what about golf?"

"They have a golf team at the school in San Francisco. A pretty good one, too," I added, although I really didn't know for sure. My uncle said they did.

"But…" the coach stammered. "You're needed here."

"Thanks," I said. "But my mind's made up."

"You're sure? You're completely sure?"

I nodded.

Coach Lannon dragged his hand through what was left of his hair. "Well, someone's going to be real disappointed if you don't return to the team."

"My parents?" I shrugged. "Yeah, I know that already."

The coach's hand moved to his chin. "Well, not exactly."

I shook my head, confused. "Who, then?"

The coach sighed heavily as his hands dropped to his knees like gavels. "Fred Oday. She insisted that I reinstate you. Starting immediately."

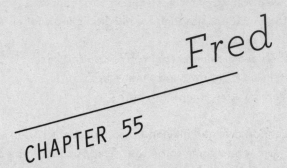

Fred

CHAPTER 55

"WHAT IS SO FASCINATING about that damn phone?"

Mom sat alongside me in a mostly stuffed vinyl chair at the foot of Dad's bed in the hospital. She continued to watch me press buttons on a cell phone no bigger than a candy bar. It became impossible to pretend I didn't notice.

Then she purposely dropped her *People* magazine to the linoleum floor when I didn't answer. The magazine opened to a page of a bare-chested Liam Hemsworth. "And where'd you get it anyway?" she added.

I turned to her and smiled sheepishly. Mom made a playful face, too, despite her snippy tone. For once, her expression wasn't pinched around the eyes and mouth. She'd been a lot happier—a lot calmer—since Dad had improved. "It's Ryan's. He lent it to me."

Her eyebrow arched. "The white boy?"

I sighed. We'd been doing so well. "Please don't call him that. It sounds awful. And I hate it."

Mom's eyes dipped briefly. "Sorry, Freddy."

I looked across the hospital bed at Dad. Still pumped up with heavy medication, he lay motionless, wheezing loudly, a clear tube jammed up his nose. Even so, I would swear that he heard every word we said. Whenever Mom and I started to talk, his purple eyelids flickered.

"So, this Ryan—what's his last name again?"

"Berenger," I said, turning toward her. Then I lowered my voice. "His mom is Dad's surgeon. Remember?"

Mom nodded. "I know that, Freddy. I may be exhausted, but I'm not a moron." She swallowed back her sarcasm and then looked across the bed at Dad. A wistful smile spread across her face. Still watching Dad, she said, "So, is this Ryan Berenger someone... special to you?"

My hands began to fidget. *Special?* He could be.

Currently our relationship felt pleasantly mushy again, its lines fuzzy and undefined. But then I remembered that he'd be leaving soon. "He's just a friend," I said finally, palming the cell phone in my hand. "A good friend."

"Is that what they call it these days?" Mom chuckled. "Okay, Freddy. If you say so. But then, why do you stare at his phone all day?" Her head tilted as though she already had her answer.

I bit down to suppress a nervous grin. "Well, for one thing, he's popular. He gets a ton of calls. I just want to keep track of who's calling him, you know, in case he wants to know. It's the least I can do, after everything he's done for us."

Mom rolled her eyes predictably, but at least part of my lame explanation was true. I'd already had to tell him that Gwyneth had called him six times and Seth once. Ryan had said not to worry about it and to let the calls go to voice mail, not that I had any intention of taking phone messages for either of them. Mostly, I just waited for Ryan to call.

"Well, he does sound kind of special," Mom said. "Just like my daughter." She reached for my hand and put it between hers like a sandwich. Her skin was so smooth and cool. I couldn't remember the last time Mom had reached for my hand, except to slap it.

When she looked at me, her eyes brimmed with shiny tears. It was a wonder she had any left.

"It's okay, Mom," I said, swallowing back a lump in my throat. "Everything is going to be okay." I suddenly remembered an old Indian legend that Dad once told me. He'd said that stars in the night sky were made from the tears of Indian mothers.

Mom choked back a sob. "I know," she whispered. "I know it will." She brought my hand to her face and brushed it against her cheek. "But I've been such a lousy mother, a lousy wife. A lousy everything." Her voice cracked. It was difficult not to start crying with her. "Look what I've done to your father."

"You didn't cause his heart attack, Mom," I said quickly as my throat thickened. "Dr. Berenger says the buildup in his arteries had been going on for years."

Mom chuckled. "Yes, but living with me didn't help any."

I said nothing. I knew that I should have said something reassuring like *No, Mom, that's not true,* but I'd have been lying, not that there hadn't been better times at home. I remembered when I used to sit at Mom's feet while she wove straw baskets with bright patterns, telling endless stories about the Children of the Clouds and the Fox Woman. Or how Dad used to compete at the all-Indian rodeo every year at Mul-Chu-Tha, the place where they first fell in love. I'd begged her to tell that story a zillion times, scolding her if she tried to gloss over the slightest detail, like how her hair was braided or the color of Dad's cowboy hat.

But then one day, just like that, the stories had stopped. Like they'd never happened at all.

Mom wiped away a line of tears streaming down her cheek with the back of her hand. "I can't promise I'll be perfect." She sat straighter, her nostrils flaring. "But I can promise that I will be better."

I smiled, my chest filling with love for her, for my parents, my heart bursting with hope. Then I squeezed her hand. "It's a start, Mom. That's really all anybody can ask."

Out of the corner of my eye, I watched as Dad's eyelids flickered again.

And I'd have sworn I saw him smile, too.

RYAN

CHAPTER 56

AFTER GOLF PRACTICE ON Wednesday, I raced home to call Fred.

She had told me yesterday that there was a chance her dad would be released from the hospital today. Even Mom was pleased with Mr. Oday's progress, and Fred's voice had sounded so happy and light that it had lifted my spirits, too. That's why I figured tonight would be the best night to talk.

I sat on the edge of my bed with the cordless phone in one hand. I was alone in the house, but I closed the bedroom door anyway. I drew in several steadying breaths before I dialed the phone. This was turning out to be harder than I'd thought. My stomach kept churning and making noises like I hadn't eaten in a week.

"Hi, Ryan," Fred answered on the second ring, surprising me. Then I remembered my cell phone had caller ID.

"Hey, F-Fred," I said, trying so hard to sound casual that I started to stutter. Unfortunately, Fred's voice had a way of making me do that. Around her, I always talked a little faster than normal. It usually took a few sentences before I found my rhythm. I couldn't be any less cool around her. "How's your dad?"

"Better. We brought him home this afternoon. He's sleeping."

"I'm glad. Your mom must be pretty happy."

"She is."

"So you're home now?"

"Yep."

"Good." No wonder we had such a clear phone connection. The cell-phone reception from the hospital was either bad or terrible, depending on where Fred was when I called.

"How was practice?" A door closed in the background. A screen squeaked.

"Good," I said again, "but the coach is working us like we're at boot camp or something. You've gotta get back to practice. Soon, Fred. Or he's going to kill us, for sure." And it was true. Coach Lannon had extended practice by thirty minutes and required everybody to blow through an extra bucket of practice balls, probably to make up for the huge void left by Fred. "Um, when do you think you'll be back?" I tried for casual again.

"Tomorrow, maybe. Or Friday."

"Will you be at the tournament tomorrow? It's at Ahwatukee again."

"Maybe. I mean, I hope so. But I won't if my mom has to be back at work. Someone has to be here to watch my dad." She paused. "Will you be there?"

My chest tightened. "Not sure."

"Why?"

"I really should start packing. I'm supposed to leave for my uncle's house this weekend."

"Oh," Fred said, her voice sounding smaller. "So, you're really going through with it?" It came out more like a question.

"Yeah. I think it'll be good."

"For you?" Her tone was doubtful. "What about your parents?"

"I don't think they're crazy about it. My sister is kind of bummed. But it's not forever."

"How long?"

"Six months. Eight at the most."

The line turned quiet.

"Fred?" I said. "Are you still there?"

"Why'd you really call me tonight, Ryan?" One of the dogs barked in the distance, and I figured she must be sitting outside.

"Where are you, exactly?" I stalled.

"Outside. Putting."

"You're practicing?"

"Have to. I haven't touched a club in a week."

The line went quiet again. I moved the phone away from my mouth so I could take a breath and gather up some nerve. Finally, I said, "There is something I wanted to tell you..."

"Yeah?" she prodded.

I heard a golf ball drop into a cup.

"Oh, no..." Fred said.

"Oh, no, what?"

"The phone is starting to beep in my ear. What do two beeps mean?"

"Ugh," I muttered. "It means the phone is going dead." *Freakin' phone battery!*

"Humph."

The phone started to beep again. This time I heard it on my end.

"I think the phone is about to die." Fred's voice faded in and out between beeps. "We'll have to talk about this lat—" She didn't finish.

The line bugged out.

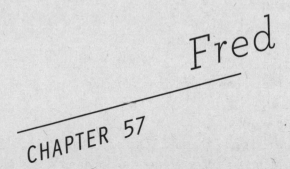

Fred

CHAPTER 57

I TOSSED RYAN'S DEAD CELL phone into my backpack.

"Great timing," I muttered to the opened backpack like I expected it to answer back. I dropped to my bed and frowned at the ceiling. Sighing, I turned to look at the clock on my nightstand.

Seven o'clock.

"It's not too late," I reasoned. "If I hurry, I could be there by 7:30. Eight, at the latest." That didn't sound too bad. In fact, it sounded like a reasonable plan.

I popped off the bed.

I raced to the kitchen to find Mom. She was standing at the stove, stirring a copper pot of soup. Tomato, from the smell of it. The ladle clinked against the sides.

"Mom," I said, out of breath. "Mind if I drive to Ryan's?"

"Why? Isn't it getting kind of late?" Mom looked at the stove clock.

"I won't be gone long. I promise."

"Can't it wait till tomorrow?"

I shook my head. "I need to return Ryan's cell phone."

"Why tonight?"

Because tomorrow might be too late. "He's leaving for San Francisco and needs it before he goes." Kind of true.

"Oh," Mom said, pulling her chin back. "But it is late, Fred. And that's a long drive."

"I'll be careful," I said quickly.

Mom inhaled, considering this.

I sucked in a breath, waiting. My whole life hinged on one simple answer. I could barely hold myself together.

"Okay, then…"

Breathing returned.

"But there and back," she said. "That's all. Don't stay too long."

"I won't, Mom." I skipped across the floor and kissed Mom's soft cheek.

I parked the van alongside the curb in front of the Berengers' house. This time I didn't worry about parking halfway down the block where the streetlights ended.

Every light was on inside Ryan's house, and it had to be the cheeriest looking one I'd ever seen.

With his cell phone clutched in my hand, I climbed out of the van and practically floated up the circular flagstone path to the front door. I pushed my hair behind my ears and adjusted my favorite blue sweater over my jeans. My heart raced faster than it should have, and I drew back a steadying breath. Then I rang the bell.

"I'll get it!" said a muffled voice on the other side of the enormous door.

I smiled. *Riley.*

The door opened to the brightness of the chandelier hanging in the foyer. I squinted into the light.

"Oh," said a surprised voice.

Wrong on all counts. Definitely not Riley.

"It's you," said the voice.

I blinked a couple of times. "Gwyneth?"

"Yes?" Gwyneth said it like she had every right to be inside

Ryan's house beneath the birthday chandelier, and I most certainly did not.

My heart thudded to a complete stop. Gwyneth was still wearing her pom outfit, a short purple pleated wool skirt number with a cream sweater. The curlicue letters *LB* covered her chest. I looked past the waves of her blond hair. "Is Ryan here?"

Gwyneth leaned against the door. "Yes," she said. "This *is* his house." She blinked wide. "But he's taking a shower." Her lips pursed.

"Oh," I said, suddenly nauseated. There was something about Gwyneth Riordan that always made me feel less than a lump of dirt.

She adjusted her weight so that she balanced on the ball of her perfectly small right foot. And she stared back at me like I was insane. "Is that it? *Oh?*"

I exhaled and fought the urge not to run. "Could you just tell him I stopped by to deliver his phone?" I held it out to her in my now-clammy hand. Five minutes ago I couldn't wait to see him. Now I wanted nothing more to do with Ryan's phone or his plastic girlfriend.

One of Gwyneth's thin blond eyebrows arched. "Of course." She stared at the cell phone like it carried a disease. Finally, she plucked it from my hand with two fingers.

"Thanks," I said, turning. I couldn't wait to be out of this neighborhood with its stale, thick air. I should have never come. For once, I should have listened to Mom. She had been one thousand percent right.

"Wait," Gwyneth said.

I stopped, midstep.

"Just some 411." She paused for a deep inhale, like she was about to reveal something ridiculously obvious and important. "Look, we're all real sorry about your father—"

"Don't mention my father," I interrupted her. I didn't want Gwyneth to have the slightest thought about Dad in her blond brain. I certainly didn't need her phony pity.

But Gwyneth was hardly concerned with what I wanted. "You know, this little infatuation you have with my boyfriend needs to stop. It's become quite annoying. For everybody. I'm surprised Ryan hasn't said something already." Her head nodded behind her. "Am I getting through?"

I licked my now-dry lips and tasted the last of my lip gloss. "Totally," I said, careful to keep my voice from cracking.

And then I turned toward the van, not even flinching when the front door rocked shut behind me.

RYAN

CHAPTER 58

"HOW'D YOU GET IN HERE?"

I trotted down the staircase in bare feet, a bath towel draped across my bare shoulders and a shoe box underneath my arm.

The sight of Gwyneth made me groan inside, but she smiled anyway. "The usual way," she said, blinking innocently. Too innocently. "The side gate was open."

"Yeah, but what are you *doing* here?" I'd told her last week that I didn't want to go out anymore. It had felt good to finally make it official.

"Why do you think?" Her smile faded. "I came to see you. To talk." Then her smile returned and I felt uneasy all over again. "Your parents are out back. Your dad's even cooking barbecue. What drugs are you feeding them?" She snorted quietly. "They even invited me to dinner."

I doubted that.

I wasn't about to tell Gwyneth that my parents were doing better lately. We all were. My eyes dropped to her hands. "How'd you get my cell phone?"

Her eyes narrowed at the box under my arm. "What are you doing carrying women's golf shoes?"

I ignored her. "My phone?"

Gwyneth's eyes fluttered. "Oh," she said, as if she just remembered something. "That Indian girl just dropped it by. What's her name?" She snapped her fingers, trying to recall.

"Fred?" I said through clenched teeth.

"She asked me to give you this." She extended her hand. "I invited her in, but she couldn't stay."

"Fred was here?" My voice turned louder. I didn't reach for the phone. "When?"

She shrugged like it was no big deal. "A little while ago."

I stepped around her and reached for the door. I pulled it open and walked outside. In the distance, I heard an engine chugging down the end of the street. "Shit!" I slapped the door.

"You can say that again," Gwyneth said, hanging on my arm. Her touch felt oppressive. "At least I know why you haven't been returning my calls."

I shrugged off her arm and closed the door. Then I snatched my cell phone out of her hand.

She stepped back, her mouth open.

"Jeez, Gwyneth." I could barely look at her. I could barely stand to breathe the same air. "I can't believe you." Like Seth, it was as if she had turned into a different person, someone unrecognizable. Had she always been so cruel, and I'd only just started to recognize it?

"Believe what?"

"What'd you tell her?"

"Who?"

"Fred!" I yelled.

She lifted her palms. Her eyes hardened. "Nothing."

"Sure," I said as I brushed toward her to the kitchen. "That's what I thought."

Fred

CHAPTER 59

I LEFT RYAN'S NEIGHBORHOOD and began the long, desolate stretch down Pecos Road toward the freeway.

A few cars passed me, so I accelerated, thinking that going faster could stamp out the image of Gwyneth's perfect face and her perfect white pom shoes—her perfect white everything—at Ryan's front door. I felt like an idiot for caring.

I rolled down the window, grateful for fresh air. I inhaled greedy gulps of it as the wind whipped my hair around my face.

But then I smelled something sharp. Really putrid.

Smoke.

"Oh, no," I moaned. I pulled myself closer to the steering wheel, batting the hair from my eyes. Silvery wisps floated into the sky from somewhere near the front of the hood.

"I do not believe this," I said, just as the thin wisps morphed into billowy clouds.

Not good.

The engine began to cough and sputter. My eyes dropped to the dashboard. An angry orange light blinked back at me. I had no choice but to pull over.

I coasted on fumes to the side of the road, my foot pumping the brake pedal, till the pavement ended and the dirt began. Finally, the van bounced its way to a stop, coughing and sputtering.

I shut off the engine, but the van continued to sputter and hiss, loud at first and then softer, till all that was left were wispy circles of silvery smoke that floated into the night sky.

My nose wrinkled from the smell as I tried to remember what Dad had told me about smoke. Did blue smoke mean motor oil? Or gas? Either way, smoke couldn't be good.

I slapped the steering wheel, cursing my bad luck and going over my options.

I was stranded on the darkest stretch of Pecos Road without a phone. Mom would be frantic. *So* not good.

I'd have to wait till the engine cooled to try driving the van again, and even then it might not start. And there was absolutely no way I was walking back to Ryan's house to beg for help. I'd rather walk through a rattlesnake pit in my bare feet.

I threaded my car keys through my fingers and opened the door. I locked it, not that it mattered. Who'd be desperate enough to steal the thing?

Then I spotted the headlights of an oncoming vehicle.

I held a breath, wondering whether to pull out my thumb and flag it down. If I were on the Rez, I wouldn't hesitate. But this wasn't home.

I stood off to the side of the road, in front of the van, waiting.

Except the car didn't pass.

It flashed its lights and began to slow.

Instantly, my heart started to race as I squinted into the yellow beams. The air suddenly turned colder. I wrapped my arms across my chest.

The car pulled over behind my van, its headlights stinging my eyes. I pressed one hand above my forehead to cut the glare, but it didn't help much. I heard a door slam and then the approach of footsteps in the gravelly dirt.

"Fred?" said a voice.

"Oh, god," I said as my head began to spin.

It was my worst nightmare on replay.

"I thought I heard your ride drive through the neighborhood again."

My throat thickened. It felt impossible to speak. *This can't be happening.*

"Lost?" Seth said when I couldn't answer.

My fingers tightened around my keys. Sharp tips pressed against my palm.

Seth walked closer to where I could see him. He wore his baseball cap backward. His face was even paler in the glow of his headlights. "Car trouble?" His eyes widened with mock innocence.

What is his problem?

My eyes darted across the road, wondering where I should take my chances. I figured it was about twenty-five yards down the embankment to the barbed wire. If I concentrated, I could probably beat him to the wire, but then I'd have to leap over it and hope I could make it. And I could, if I had had a running start.

"Still having trouble answering simple questions, Fred?" His car keys jingled. He spun the key ring around his finger until he stood only an arm's length away.

I stepped back deeper into the gravel. "Look, Seth," I said, irritated that my voice had already begun to shake. "I know I've made you angry, and I'm sorry. I really am. But this is getting out of control." I took another careful step back. My foot crunched over more loose gravel.

But he matched my step. His throaty laughter crackled in the darkness. "You have no idea."

"Do you really want my spot on the golf team? Is that it?"

He didn't answer, but the sky turned eerily silent as I waited for his answer.

"Because I'll tell Coach Lannon tomorrow that I'm off the team and you should have your old spot back. Will that make you happy? Then will you leave me alone?"

Seth smacked his lips together. "Too late for that."

He reached for my shoulder, each of his five fingers pressing down, but I shrugged off his hand.

Then the engine of another car revved down the road.

Seth turned toward the headlights, shielding his eyes against the glare with his arm, and I found my chance.

I darted down the embankment toward the barbed wire.

"Hey!" Seth snarled, spinning around. "Where do you think you're g-going?" He started to stutter. "We aren't f-f-finished!"

The car flashed its brights, lighting up the desert. Its horn beeped, but I had already skidded down the hill toward the Rez. Half walking, half gliding through the soft earth, I finally reached the fence. Dirt rose up in my tennis shoes like water.

When I reached the barbed wire, it met my chest. Too high to hurdle. Frantically, I searched for an opening.

I had to get as far away from Seth Winter as I could.

But then there was a new voice. "Fred?" someone yelled. Quickly, he said, "Seth? What the hell are you doing here?" His voice echoed all around me.

It was Ryan. And this time there was no question that he was out-of-his-mind furious.

RYAN

CHAPTER 60

I PULLED MY JEEP OFF THE SIDE of Pecos Road like the wheels had caught fire.

I recognized Seth's oversize tires immediately. He'd parked right behind Fred's van, dwarfing it.

My breathing quickened.

I opened the door before jamming the gear in Park. I left the keys in the ignition, the engine running.

"Where is she?" I said, running toward Seth. His arms lifted against the glare of my headlights.

"Her v-van went all ape-shit," Seth said, stuttering a little. He motioned to it. Smoke drifted from beneath the hood in grayish-white wisps.

"Just thought I'd stop and give her a ride, but she bailed on me." He nodded toward the open desert like Fred was the one who was crazy.

"Fred!" I yelled, my eyes squinting against the darkness. All I saw was black. It was like trying to focus on a single stone at the bottom of a murky river.

Seth yelled with me. "Fred!"

I cringed at his lame attempt at helpfulness. Then I turned to him. "What are you doing here?"

"Like I told you, just cruising down the road, saw her van and stopped to help. End of story."

"Liar," I said.

"Why so paranoid?" He laughed.

"Then why isn't she here?" My hands felt like they were on fire, the weight of all my bad decisions electrifying each finger. Before I could think, I turned to Seth and smashed my fist across his chin before he could answer. It felt better than good. Seth's bone cracked beneath my knuckles.

Seth fell backward, cupping his jaw. "What was that for? I think you broke my tooth!" he yelled, flexing his jaw. But then he leaped to his feet and lunged at me before I could catch my next breath. He plowed right into my chest.

I fell back with Seth crashing on top of me.

In the beams from the headlights, we spun around in the dirt and gravel, arms flailing and fists flying. I tasted blood and dust. And rage. Palpable, bitter, explosive rage. Our bodies rolled over each other, sharp rocks piercing through my clothing. Seth's hot breath blanketed my face each time we spun.

I pummeled Seth till my knuckles ached. He punched me good in the ribs and the sides, but I was too enraged to feel pain.

I almost didn't hear Fred. "Stop it!" she yelled over us.

I saw her legs sidestepping our bodies as Seth and I thrashed in the dirt, back and forth.

"Stop it!" she yelled again, but we punched harder.

"Move away!" I grunted through my teeth as Seth met my side punch with one of his. He nailed me again in the ribs.

Standing above us, Fred didn't listen. Instead, she followed us as we flailed and kicked and punched, begging us to stop, zigging then zagging around us.

Then our bodies reached the edge of the road, oblivious to the embankment. We began to roll, slowly at first, and then faster as the incline dropped. I tasted more dirt with each roll.

One.

Two.

Three.

Four rolls in the rocky dirt?

I lost count.

Finally, we crashed in a heap against the barbed wire where Phoenix stopped and the Gila Indian Reservation began. Seth caught the brunt of it. His chest pushed into mine on impact.

He moaned.

"Stop it!" Fred yelled again and again, her voice frantic as she skidded down the hill with us. It sounded like she was crying through her screams.

The beams from the headlights barely provided any light so far off the road. "Please. Just. Stop." She fell to her knees alongside us as our punches grew weaker with our exhaustion.

My whole body felt like it'd been in a grinder. Slowly, I pulled myself away from Seth and sat back on my knees. My chest ached. My knuckles throbbed. Every muscle in my body burned like it was on fire. I wiped my hand across my mouth and tasted more dirt, more blood. One of my front teeth wiggled against my tongue. I swallowed and then spat.

Seth lay pinned to the fence, breathing just as heavily, the fabric from his jacket stuck to the wire like Velcro. His arms extended against the barbed wire like a scarecrow.

I finally stood, unsteady at first, and then considered whether to punch Seth again, a defining one to the gut.

"No," Fred said, taking my hand between hers. She pulled back on my arm. "That's enough." In the dark, her hand moved down to mine. My hand was wet from sweat and blood, but she threaded her fingers through mine anyway. Her voice cut through our panting. "Please. Stop this. Enough."

When she squeezed my hand, I blinked back sweat trickling down from my forehead. I took one last long look at Seth. I didn't know what to say to him. It was like being inside an endless nightmare loop.

"Come on," Seth said, still pinned. "Hit me. You know you want to." The whites of his eyes gleamed against the darkness. He laughed, but his voice was as tired as mine, his chest writhing as he wriggled to escape the wire.

I waited for him to break free and charge me again. I wanted it. Bad. But he didn't. Couldn't.

Finally, Fred pulled at me. Together, we turned toward the embankment. Seth's jacket tore as he pulled away from the barbs.

"You were supposed to be my best friend," Seth yelled into the night, his voice echoing all around us.

My chest tightened again. Then I stopped. I turned. "I was. Just not anymore. I'm done."

Fred and I began to climb in the soft dirt toward the road, our feet sinking with each step. It was like walking up a mud bank. We leaned against each other for support, saying nothing. I just wanted to get away. And I wanted to get Fred away from Seth, as far from his hatred as possible.

But then Seth's laughter grew softer, almost like a whimper.

My chest tightened again, but for a different reason.

Seth did something that he hadn't done since we were nine years old when his stepdad belted him, right in front of me, for forgetting to lock his bike at school the same day it turned up stolen.

Seth started to cry.

My traitorous throat thickened, listening to each sob.

He tried to choke them back.

"Wait," he said, more like an exhale.

We didn't answer.

"I'm so sorry for what I did. I'm sorry, Fred." His sobs filled the sky. "Help me," he begged.

I stood frozen and silent, holding on to Fred, not knowing whether to walk backward or forward.

"Please, dude," Seth said. "Please don't leave. Help me."

"How can we trust you?" I called down to him.

Seth didn't answer. His cries turned muffled. The ripping noises from his jacket stopped as he continued to hang, trapped, against the fence.

I sighed, listening to him moan. Then I knew.

Fred tugged on my hand, pulling me back, like she could read my mind. There was just enough of a muted glow from the road to see tears in her eyes.

Without another word, we turned around and skidded back down the embankment.

Seth's legs were outstretched on the ground but his back and arms were pinned to the wire. His hands hung limply at the wrists.

"I'll pull his right arm. You pull his left," I told Fred as we stood on either side.

Seth didn't protest.

Silently, we tugged forward on both shoulders, ripping his jacket even more as the wire twisted and pinched the fabric like sharp fingers. If it hurt, Seth didn't complain.

We finally freed him. He collapsed forward and gasped. Then he drew his knees together and buried his head between them like he was too ashamed to look at us.

I sighed tiredly, looking down at him, seeing only his dark, cowering outline. Then I extended my hand. "Come on, Seth. Let's go."

He looked up, swallowed back a sob and reached for my hand. His was slippery like mine with sweat and blood. He rose to his feet, almost falling backward again on the first try.

Without another word, the three of us climbed up to the road. I took Fred's hand again, threading my fingers through hers. Seth trailed behind us, silent, one heavy step forward at a time.

All of a sudden, two red flashing beacons lit up the sky.

We stopped and stared up at the road. A flashlight's beam washed over us, and I had to squint from the burn of the glare.

"This is the police!" a man bellowed down at us from a megaphone. His deep voice boomed across the desert. "Is everyone all right?"

It was hard not to laugh.

EPILOGUE

WITH A SHRILL BLOW ON HIS silver whistle, Coach Lannon started the tournament between Lone Butte and Anthem High at the Ahwatukee Golf Club. If we won, our next meet would be the state championship.

The coach stood on the first tee with most of the Lone Butte players waiting behind him. He began to bark out names and pairings beneath a cloudless sky. For a moment, the low hush from the swelling crowd turned silent.

I stood alongside Ryan at the bottom of the first tee box with our golf bags, oblivious to the commotion. We were hidden behind a crowd that that had begun to line the cart path. It was the first time we'd been alone all day.

"Does it hurt?" I pressed my fingertips below Ryan's temple. Though his sunglasses hid most of the bruises, a red blotch above his right eyebrow still peeked out. The fight with Seth seemed aeons ago, but the fresh marks on his face and knuckles said otherwise.

Ryan winced. "Only when you touch it."

"Sorry." I cringed.

But then Ryan smiled at me. "This is better." He took my hand in his, and a new line of goose bumps flew all the way up my arm.

"You sure you can play?"

"Wouldn't miss it."

More goose bumps.

"How do the shoes feel?" Ryan asked me.

I looked down at my brand-new golf shoes, the white ones with the pink piping that matched my golf glove. A present from Ryan. He'd insisted, no matter how much I'd protested. "They feel great." But that was an understatement. Next to my golf glove, the shoes might have been the nicest present I'd ever received. "How'd you know my size?"

"Your mom told me." He smiled. "I think she's starting to dig me."

"Yes, but how did you know these were the ones I wanted?"

Ryan just looked at me with a crooked grin, like he preferred to keep that a secret.

I smiled back at him, shaking my head, even as Coach Lannon's voice boomed in the background with names and instructions that didn't feel so strange anymore. I wondered if that had to do with me or whether that had everything to do with Ryan.

"I've missed you," Ryan said, and I thought my chest would burst from wanting him.

"I've missed you, too," I said, even though we'd only been apart a day. It might as well have been a year. A thousand years. After golf, Ryan Berenger was all that I could think about, wanted to think about. I had it bad.

The coach waved at us from the top of the tee box, his arm moving back and forth like a windmill. It became impossible to ignore him.

"Oday! Berenger! Get up here!" he yelled. "You're up!"

"Oh, no," I said.

"What?" Ryan chuckled. "Is the coach trippin'?"

"Do you hear that?" I tilted my head. A steady beat hovered above the crowd from somewhere on the fairway. But it came from the direction of the tee box, just below Coach Lannon. I squinted through the crowd for a better look.

"Is that a drum?" Ryan said.

"I think so."

"Well, that's a new one."

We moved closer to the cart path to peer above shoulders and heads. I stood on tiptoe, as tall as I could go without falling forward.

The drumbeat drowned out Coach Lannon until even he had no choice but to turn silent. Slow and steady, the drumbeat replaced the voices on the golf course.

Thump-thump-thump.

Then the drumbeat grew frenzied, louder and faster, until it stopped abruptly, quieting the sky.

The crowd froze, even me.

George Trueblood began to chant as steadily and deeply as his drum. With his face lifted toward the sun, he extended his arms like he was trying to greet the entire sky and everything in it. His feet shuffled and stomped in small, deliberate movements as the fringe from his jacket fluttered all around him.

"Oh, no," I whispered.

"A lot of people from the reservation are here today," Ryan said, unfazed. "I saw Sam and Pete. And Kelly and Yolanda. Your brother even nodded at me. I'll take that as a good sign."

"Just be patient, Ryan. My brother needs time."

"I got time." He squeezed my hand.

"He's stubborn. And annoying."

"He's being a good brother. Can't blame him. Anyway, I saw a bunch of other people from the hospital here, too. Seems you've got a real fan club. Guess this isn't just about you anymore, is it?"

I bit back a smile when I remembered the banner hanging across the front of the community center on the Rez. I'd seen it on the drive to the freeway and it made me feel as tall as the Estrella Mountains. It said, *Good luck, Fred Oday. You make us proud!*

It wasn't professionally done or anything, just a long white sheet with blue-and-black loopy painted letters made by Rez kids at the elementary school. I would never forget it as long as I lived.

"That's what George Trueblood told me," I said.

"Smart dude."

"More than you know."

Scanning the crowd for George Trueblood and his drum, I found Mom. She stepped out of the crowd and began to dance alongside him on the fairway, her feet pivoting in small steps from underneath her long denim skirt. The crowd parted to make room for her. She wore Grandmother's silver-and-turquoise necklaces, blue flat stones the size of my fist. I hadn't seen Mom wear the jewelry since I was in grade school.

She danced next to George Trueblood with her eyes closed. A few weeks ago, I would have been mortified. Today, only pride filled my heart.

Then George Trueblood began to speak:

Hold on to what is good, even if it is a handful of earth.
Hold on to what you believe, even if it is a tree which stands by itself.
Hold on to what you must do, even if it is a long way from here.
Hold on to life, even when it is easier letting go.
Hold on to my hand, even when I have gone away from you.[5]

"Oh, no," I whispered again to Ryan behind my hand. My eyes shifted to the right of George Trueblood.

"What?"

"Your parents. Next to my mom." I said.

The Berengers stood behind Mom. Dr. Berenger was smiling, but in a tight-lipped kind of way as if she wasn't completely sure of protocol. Clearly she hadn't seen a chanting Indian at a golf tour-

---

5 Pueblo Blessing.

nament before. Mr. Berenger looked every bit as uncomfortable with his arm around his wife's shoulders. But I could tell that they were trying. That was something.

Instead of looking at his parents, Ryan's eyes stayed locked on mine. "Is my mom cringing yet?"

I looked over his shoulder at his parents. "A little." I smiled. "Can you blame her?"

Ryan chuckled. "It's the first time my parents have come to one of my tournaments in two years. You're probably just seeing them in a little bit of shock. Don't worry about it. They'll be okay."

"You're sure?"

"Definitely," he said. "It's getting better."

"For you, too?"

Ryan nodded. "They grounded me for a week this time, but I deserved it."

"Sorry," I said.

"Don't be." He squeezed my hand. "It's all good, Fred Oday, Daughter of the River People."

My breath caught in my throat. Ryan looked down at me with that smile that reached deep inside my soul and lifted my spirits into the clouds. "How'd you—"

"I'm learning. And you have a lot to teach me."

And then, as George Trueblood continued the blessing in his deep, clear voice, Ryan kissed me. He placed his hand behind my neck and pulled me closer, pressing his lips against mine. He tasted sweet, just like on Pecos Road all those weeks ago. I wanted more of Ryan Berenger, more than just his lips.

Too soon, we pulled apart, and I'd swear I saw stars when my eyes managed to open, and it had nothing to do with the sun.

"You're absolutely right." My voice cracked. "I have a lot to teach you."

His chin pulled back.

"About the River People, I mean," I added, a little breathless, still focused on the perfect curve of his mouth.

"Can't wait."

I could tell he meant it.

"Does this mean you're not leaving Phoenix?" I'd been dreading his answer all day.

He shook his head and smiled. "I'm not going anywhere unless it's with you."

I leaned against him, relieved. "I am so glad." It felt like my cheeks would break from smiling, even as my eyes turned a little blurry.

"Me, too."

George Trueblood finished his chant and the crowd clapped. The coach blew his whistle and began waving like a windmill again.

I wished that Ryan and I could have a few more minutes, just us. Alone.

Then Ryan took my hand again. This time he didn't let it go. "Good luck today, Fred."

"Same to you, Ryan."

"Don't forget to crank the ball." He squeezed my hand.

"I intend to." It was impossible not to smile. It was also impossible not to love Ryan Berenger.

With my hand in his, we walked through the crowd toward the first tee with our golf bags threaded over our shoulders, two puzzle pieces that found a reason to fit.

* * * * *

GOLF GIRL GAB

⚑	*BACK NINE*	The last nine holes of an eighteen-hole golf course.
⚑	*BIRDIE*	One under par.
⚑	*BOGEY*	One over par.
⚑	*CLEATS*	The pointy metal prongs on the bottom of golf shoes. They help the golfer grip her stance.
⚑	*DIVOT*	The round mark left on the grass in the tee box or the fairway after a golfer has swung at her ball. All golfers are expected to return the clump of grass to its rightful place after hitting the ball.
⚑	*DOGLEG RIGHT/LEFT*	When a hole on a golf course is said to be dogleg left or right, it is just that: it veers to the left or right along the fairway, just like the shape of a dog's hind leg.
⚑	*DRIVER*	Usually a golfer carries two to four drivers in her golf bag. They are the clubs with the wider face, usually used for long distances. Sometimes called woods.
⚑	*DRIVING RANGE*	The wide-open spaces where golfers go to practice their swings without fear of hitting anybody. They're usually adjacent to a golf course.
⚑	*EAGLE*	Two under par.

GOLF GIRL GAB

FAIRWAYS	The space between the tee box and the putting green, usually the longest part of a hole.
FRONT NINE	The first nine holes of an eighteen-hole golf course.
GOLF GLOVE	Some golfers wear gloves on both hands; most just wear one. If you're right-handed, you wear a glove on your left hand. If you're left-handed, you wear the glove on your right. The glove helps the golfer grip the club.
GREEN	The place where a golfer putts. The grass on the green is usually cut with a special lawn mower so that the grass is very low.
GREEN FEES	The amount a golf course charges to play nine holes and/or eighteen holes.
HANDICAP	The number of strokes a golfer is allowed in order to compete with golfers of all levels.
IRONS	Usually a golfer carries around eleven irons in her golf bag. They have smaller faces than woods.
MARKER	A flat plastic or metal piece the size of a penny with a small prong on the underside that's used to mark balls on the putting green. Some golfers use coins like pennies or dimes.

GOLF GIRL GAB

⚑	*PAR*	The number of strokes it takes to reach a hole on a golf course. For example, if a hole is a par 5, a golfer will need to reach the hole and sink the putt in no more than five strokes in order to "par" the hole.
⚑	*PUTTER*	This is the club you use when you reach the green.
⚑	*SAND TRAPS*	These are also considered "hazards." Oftentimes you'll find sand traps near putting greens.
⚑	*SAND WEDGE*	The club you use when your ball has dropped or rolled into a sand trap.
⚑	*SCORECARD*	The card that a golfer uses to record her strokes for each hole. The fewer the strokes, the better the score.
⚑	*SCRATCH GOLFER*	A golfer (e.g., a professional golfer) who doesn't have a golf handicap.
⚑	*TEE BOX*	The starting place, usually a flat, grassy area, on a golf course where a golfer uses her drivers or irons to launch her golf ball onto a fairway or green.

ACKNOWLEDGMENTS

AS I WAITED FOR THIS BOOK to be published, the impossible happened: my parents died. They died within six months of each other and my world got rocked in ways that I never imagined. Regardless of age, a child always believes her parents are indestructible, even immortal, and I was no different. I was blessed to have a wonderful mother and father, and that is why I'm proud to dedicate this book to them. You'll find their smiles, quiet wisdom, love and laughter within its pages. I miss you, Mom and Dad, each and every day.

It takes a village to publish a book, and I am honored to share mine with many talented and wonderful people:

Superwoman Literary Agent Holly Root for being the first person besides my parents to believe in me and love my stories. Thanks, Holly, for sticking with me through thick and thin.

Tashya Wilson and the entire Harlequin TEEN Dream Team. Thank you for loving Fred and Ryan and helping their story to shine brighter. Every author should be so fortunate to have such a supportive publishing house.

Dana Kaye with Kaye Publicity. I am so grateful our paths crossed.

My early readers for their invaluable input and willingness to eat out: Mary Fichera Zienty, Olivia Zienty, Susanna Ives, Tamera Begay and Jessica Bradley.

The Native American communities throughout Arizona and the American Southwest. Thank you for sharing your enduring spirit, beautiful cultures and lands.

All of the book lovers, librarians, teens, bloggers and online writing community members that I've met these past couple of years. Because of your love of stories, being an author is the best job in the world.

My crazy family, Mary, Joe, Joe Z, Kaz, Olivia and Andrew. Thanks for your infinite supply of love, unwavering support and tolerance for my constant *Seinfeld* references.

My sister, Mary, especially, for being the one I've always been able to count on.

And, finally, my husband, Craig. My light and my rock. Thanks for putting up with my nocturnal ways. Life wouldn't be any fun without you.

Ryan and Fred have found each other, but is there
someone out there for Ryan's little sis, *Riley?*
Perhaps...**SAM TRACY?**

Read on for an exclusive excerpt from Liz Fichera's
next Harlequin TEEN novel,

PLAYED

Coming soon!

Riley

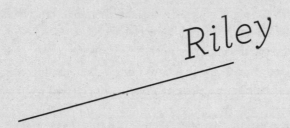

OH. MY. GOD. OUTRAGE STUCK like gum inside my head as Sam shifted beside me. *What a jerk.* Drew was never going to believe this. I pulled out my cell phone and began to text her.

I should have taken that seat way in the back of the bus after all, despite the sea of juniors and seniors. I'd had no idea that Sam Tracy was so in love with himself. *I know who you are?!* Seriously? I mean, get some manners.

I had seen him talking with Fred a couple of times in the cafeteria, and he'd seemed nice enough on school territory, but what was the deal with off-hours? Total loser.

My nose wrinkled. *Great!* And he reeked, too. Eau de Charcoal Grill.

I wanted to scream, *Just because you're a junior doesn't make you smarter than everyone else.* Because he was so tall, I supposed he'd want to claim most of the legroom underneath the bench in front of us, too. Not gonna happen.

Once I got my internal hyperventilation under control, I curled my legs underneath me, finished a quick text that Drew wouldn't see until at least noon and then pressed the volume button on my *Friends* episode. I'd rather listen to Chandler and Joey any day and sketch in my notebook. But no such luck.

Mr. Romero turned around. He looked at Sam and me over the tops of his wire-rimmed glasses. "Could you pass these back?" he said, handing us a stack of papers. "It's the agenda for the weekend."

I removed one earbud, one eye trained on my iPod screen as I grabbed the papers with my right hand. And it was my favorite *Friends* episode, too, the one where Ross gets his teeth whitened so pearly-white that they glow in a black light. Hilarious. Enough to forget about Sam Tracy and his smug attitude. Almost.

Mr. Romero stood. "Can I have your attention?" His chin lifted while his gaze swept over the rows. "Pause the texting for a moment, people. I promise your brains won't self-destruct."

A few people chuckled anxiously, as if they didn't quite believe him, and the bus grew quiet.

Mr. Romero moved to the center of the aisle, still hanging on to the back of the seat with his free hand as the bus headed down the freeway toward the rising sun. "Since we've got two hours to kill till we reach the campground, we might as well go over a few details. As many of you know, we've reserved two large cabins—one for the girls, one for the boys."

"Damn," someone behind me said. People around him laughed.

Mr. Romero smirked. "Watch the language, Mr. Wolkiewski."

"Sorry, Mr. Romero," Peter said, but he didn't sound the least bit sorry.

Mr. Romero continued, "Anyway, we've got a busy weekend planned, and you can read all about it on the agenda that's being distributed as I speak. There will be competitions and contests, and tonight we will have a barbecue. Keeping up so far?"

No one spoke. Most of us were too busy looking over the agenda. It seemed that at any given minute there was an activity—from rope climbing to scavenger hunts to leadership tests that were supposed to reveal our leadership styles. I had a style? It kind of looked as if it might have the potential for fun, in a weird, dorky way. I always preferred variety.

"As soon as we arrive at the campsite, we'll unpack the buses, get you settled and then get started on a scavenger hunt so that you can become familiar with the campground. Everyone has been organized into teams. They're listed on the back of the agenda."

I flipped over the page and scanned for my name. There were six groups of ten. I was on the Green Team. I only recognized one other person on my team: Sam Tracy.

It was impossible not to groan.

I swallowed back a sigh and stole a sideways glance. Sam and I locked eyes for a millisecond. He had these impossibly dark eyes, the intense kind that looked as if they knew what you were thinking, even before you did. And it happened so fast that I had to wonder if we'd eye-locked at all.

I guessed he was as excited about seeing our names together as I was. I just wish I knew what I'd done for him to hate me so much. But I was probably making something out of nothing. I did that a lot. It was a sickness.

To stop stressing, I sneaked a glance in my periphery and began to sketch his profile, starting with his long, flat forehead.

SAM

I FOLDED MR. ROMERO'S FANCY agenda and stuffed it in the back pocket of my jeans. Then I sank lower in the chair until my feet practically popped out from underneath the bench in front of me. I leaned my head back, closed my eyes and begged for sleep.

The next thing I knew, my head was bouncing off Riley's pink shoulder and onto the back of my seat. It was like pounding against a two-by-four.

"You mind?" She glared at me, her blue-green eyes open wide below the brim of her baseball cap as she held a thick pencil in midair. Jeez, she looked exactly like her brother, that same know-it-all, confident face that always stomped on my last nerve.

"Sorry," I mumbled, sitting upright, facing forward, hoping that drool hadn't made an appearance.

Just then, the bus exited the freeway. My ears began to pop. I was beyond pleased to see that we had already reached the top of the Mogollon Rim. A brown sign with white letters welcomed us to the Woods Canyon Lake campsite. The bus shook from side to side as it made its way deeper into the campground on a stretch of narrow two-lane road that alternated between pavement and dirt. Exactly as I remembered.

I hadn't been to Woods Canyon since I was a kid. One August

weekend, my parents and Martin's parents had lugged all the kids, including his older brother and sister and my older sister, Cecilia, to the campground. Martin and I had probably been around twelve years old. We'd thought it was killer to be camping in tents and fishing for trout. Our parents had been thrilled to escape the desert heat and probably a weekend of night shifts at the casino. Who knew then that I'd be back five years later with two busloads of students that I barely knew?

Mr. Romero stood, stretched his arms overhead and then turned to face us. He had a look on his face that demanded our attention. "Look, I know you're all probably pretty anxious to get off this bus and have some fun. I am, too. So that's why I'm going to ask you to dump your stuff quickly once we reach the cabins. Don't worry. Nothing will happen to it." He rubbed his hands together. His eyes squinted. "And I hate to be the bearer of bad news, but your cell phones probably won't work way out here." He air-chuckled darkly.

A few people gasped, and I rolled my eyes.

I was probably the only person on the whole bus without one— not like I didn't *want* one. But it was the kind of luxury that I couldn't really afford. Maybe when I started college. That had to be a given, especially since I'd be able to work full-time during the summer before the first semester. Vernon Parker was the only one of our friends back on the Rez who had one, although I wasn't sure why. Who was he calling, if not us?

"I want you to find someone within your group and pair up." Mr. Romero looked at Riley and me and smiled.

I sank lower.

"If it happens to be the person sitting right next to you, all the better," he said. "If not, start to get to know those around you. You're some of the smartest kids—the leaders—from your respective schools. I'm sure you can figure out how to meet those around you and find a partner without bursting a blood vessel."

Students began calling out. "Who's on Blue Team?"

"I'm on Red Team. Anyone else on Red?"

"What about Yellow?" said another.

Through the moans, laughter and general commotion, Mr. Romero said, "Let's get started!"

And with that, the bus pulled up in front of two cabins that looked as if they'd been built with red LEGO. I didn't remember them from five years ago. Each one was as big as a two-car garage. Like one huge room. I would have preferred to sleep outside under the stars like Martin, Peter and I did a lot during the weekends on the Rez.

A flash of pink stung the corner of my eye. "So I guess we get to do this first activity together?" It was the third time Riley had spoken the entire trip.

"Yeah. Guess so," I said, matching the disinterested tone in her voice. I turned to the others at the back of the bus, wondering if it would be too terrible to partner with someone else. Maybe Riley would prefer to be with a girl, maybe even a sophomore.

"Looks like we have to find stuff around the forest." Her nose wrinkled, and I guessed she wasn't much for nature hikes. "Pinecones, bark, berries and...stuff."

"Yeah," I said again, although I hadn't really read through the pages that were attached to the weekend agenda. I mean, how hard would it be to find stuff that littered every foot of the forest?

"Even petroglyphs," Riley added.

I looked at her. *Okay.* That could be a challenge.

"How do we take a petroglyph from a rock?" She paused from reading her agenda, which, I noted, was already highlighted in places with a pink highlighter, along with some pretty intricate curlicue doodling and fancy arrows around the margins.

My shoulders shrugged. "I suppose we have to figure that out. You got a camera?" I nodded at the killer stash of electronics on her lap—an iPod, a cell phone and no doubt she'd brought an iPad somewhere in the pink blob that peeked out from below our seat.

She nodded.

"Then we'll take a picture. Problem solved." I reached for my backpack, but I couldn't help noticing that Riley looked mildly impressed, even if she tugged her cap lower on her forehead.

The bus came to a stop. Riley and I were the first to get off after Steve and Mr. Romero, thank god. My legs ached from being in the same position for two hours.

When I got up, all the bones in my neck and shoulders cracked. I stood behind our chair and waited for Riley to go first as my arms stretched overhead. "Let's get this over with." I yawned.

Riley hitched a pink bag over her shoulder, not bothering to hide the eye roll from beneath her matching hat. "Absolutely. The sooner, the better."

THE GODDESS TEST NOVELS

Coming March 2013!

Available wherever books are sold!

A modern saga inspired by the Persephone myth.

Kate Winters's life hasn't been easy. She's battling with the upcoming death of her mother, and only a mysterious stranger called Henry is giving her hope. But he must be crazy, right? Because there is no way the god of the Underworld—Hades himself—is going to choose Kate to take the seven tests that might make her an immortal...and his wife. And even if she passes the tests, is there any hope for happiness with a war brewing between the gods?

Also available:
THE GODDESS HUNT, a digital-only novella.

THE LEGACY TRILOGY

"I recommend you get this book in your
hands as soon as possible."
—*Teen Trend* magazine on *Legacy*

On the eve of her seventeenth birthday, Princess
Alera of Hytanica faces an engagement to a man she
cannot love. But she could never have imagined falling
for her kingdom's sworn enemy. Amid court intrigue
and looming war, Alera must fight the longings of
her heart and take the crown she is destined to wear.
But as magic, prophecy and danger swirl together, it
will take more than courage to lead a kingdom.

AVAILABLE WHEREVER BOOKS ARE SOLD!